MICHAEL HOME

Grain
OF THE
Wood

THE MACMILLAN COMPANY
NEW YORK 1951

CONTENTS

The characters in this story, except the prototype of Ted Burling himself, are wholly imaginary. Whatever the chance similarity of a name, no reference is made or intended to any living person.

TO THE READER

Only a brief explanation seems needed for the use of whatever dialect appears in this novel, since in the opinion of the author such dialect can without any difficulty be understood. The use of footnotes or a glossary might have proved cumbersome and distracting, and these seem unnecessary too.

A participial *ing*, rarely heard in the rural Norfolk of fifty years ago, has been printed as *in*. As for the apparent discrepancies, these are intentional and actual, since a man might use in almost the same sentence *allust* and *always*, *bin* and *been*, *get* and *git*, *afore* and *before*, and so on, according to his mood, his degree of education, and the particular circumstances.

The use of the final *s* in third person singular verbs was less fluctuating, and it would almost always be, "It fare to me," or, "Here he come," rather than *fares* or *comes*.

With regard to the story itself, it might be added with reference to the commodes and their description that a similar pair was sold at Christie's in 1923 for 8,000 guineas. Stanford Watering and the neighbouring heaths were taken over in the late war and still remain a training ground for combat troops.

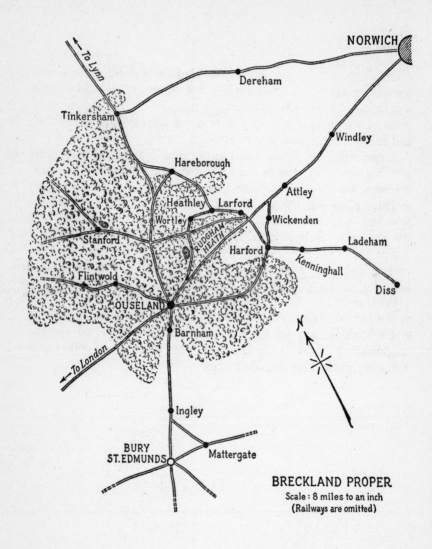

NORWICH

→ To Lynn

Dereham

Tinkersham

Windley

Hareborough

Heathley   Larford

Wortley   Attley

Stanford   RUDGHAM HEATH   Wickenden

Ladeham

Flintwold   Harford

Kenninghall

OUSELAND   Diss

Barnham

N

← To London

Ingley

BURY
ST. EDMUNDS   Mattergate

BRECKLAND PROPER
Scale : 8 miles to an inch
(Railways are omitted)

PART I

Country Lane

CHAPTER I

July, 1896

THERE was no special reason why in afteryears he should so often have thought about that July day. It was not a day on which he had done particularly well; in fact, though he could recall almost every minute from the time he had left Ouseland, and each individual article that he had bought, the strange glow that always came with the recalling was not for the profit he had chanced to make, vital though that profit was at the time. Indeed, it would have been hard for him to assess wherein lay the pleasure of that day. It should not even have been a day of pleasure, for throughout its length he had kept remembering Jenny, with his conscience telling him that, though she had laughed at his fears, he should not have left her alone in the shop. And then, of course, his thoughts had left the particular moment and place and were already at the evening and the anxious moment of return.

Perhaps some of the pleasure had been in the beauty of the day itself. He had been up at five and had seen to the cob; and though he had intended to be away and gone, as they say, by eight o'clock, it was after nine when he had finished his jobs in shop and house, and the morning was halfway through by the time he had reached the four crossways at Smoker's Hole and taken the narrow road through the open heath towards Stanford Cock.

It was new country, one that he had been chary of exploring, for between the sparse hamlets were great stretches of heath and breck with never a cottage or farm, and that meant an unprofitable deal of travelling. Then there were the marled roads which, still scattered with their winter flints, were treacherous for a horse's feet. Badly filled potholes that the rain had loosened again were liable now to break a spring of the cart if one's eyes were off the track. But that had been all the more reason, as Jenny had convinced him, that he should try those villages like Stanford and the Tofts, for their very isolation must have kept travelling dealers away; and as she had talked about it her eyes had lighted up as if she saw herself entering this room and that and spying things at which no dealer's eye had ever looked.

In that stretch of country towards Stanford, his worries about Jenny soon lost themselves in the loveliness of that July morning. Most of his young life had been spent in the open, but here was a country more airy and spacious than any he had ever seen. In the years to come he was to know each dip and fold as one knows the palm of a hand, but on that perfect summer morning each turn of the road brought a new revelation. The land was flat and yet undulating, with the horizons curiously low; and as the cob slackened its pace up a rise of ground, his eyes would be away in the colourful distances. Where the bracken brushed the very wheels of the cart it was already a sombre green and dusty from the blown soil, but farther away the sun lighted it to gold; and when a scant cloud went across the sun, the colours would miraculously soften and change. At one moment the young heather would be lilac and then as suddenly a flaring red or purple. There would be a streak of dull and distant amber where canker-weed lay across a breck, and then, as the full sun caught it, it would be a gaudy yellow, harmonious against its background of green. Then there might be clumps of gnarled and twisted pines, their trunks a vivid orange in the sun, or a dazzling emerald of moss in the now dry bed of a pool; and there was always the silver of the sand from innumerable rabbit burrows. On the brecks where the bracken ceased would be the blues and yellows of the squat, flowering weeds, and even the drab of the arid, sandy soil took on colour from the sun.

"Jenny'd like this," he told himself, and nodded at the thought of it. "I'll hatta bring her one o' these times, as soon as she can."

And it might be a good idea to bring some victuals and drink and have what they called a picnic. There, for instance, would be a rare nice place, sitting on the dry needles under those pines, with all the spread of sunny country away to the south. As he jogged the cob on, a curious flash caught his eye, and there, in the hollow to his right, lay the stretch of Stanford Watering. The water lay placid in the morning sun, and below the far bank the trees and the red roofs of the buildings of a farm were clearly mirrored. The picture held his eye till a flint wall obscured it, but he was seeing it still in the eye of his mind.

His thoughts had almost taken him past the Cock, but he pulled up just in time and turned the horse into the inn yard. He saw the landlord and arranged about feed; later there would be bread and cheese and a cup of tea for himself. In a few minutes he was beginning his village rounds. July was a good time, he had told himself. Money would be scarcer than after harvest. Children would be at school and men in the fields, and it would be the women he would see. Somehow, in the few days of searching he had already spent elsewhere, he had found it easy to get on with women, though he would have been hard put to it to find a reason why.

But though he was wholly unaware of it, the reasons lay solely in himself. There was no carefully reasoned technique of approach and none of that blustering geniality that was part of the stock in trade of the travelling dealer. His manner was quiet and almost diffident, giving him, in women's eyes at least, something of a forlornness and winning him a response of sympathy. And since his manner had no source of artifice but was the natural man, there was about him a curiously appealing dignity. The dark brown eyes looked straight at one, and there was in them nothing of the furtive or shifty.

"A rare nice-lookin young chap," was how women would often sum him up to their husbands, though that was more of a summary of the man himself than what the mere face had told. The eyes were the best part of it, though the mouth had about it something gently humorous, as if he were always on the edge of a smile. The teeth were neat and white, and he took something of a pride in them; but the nose had a kind of upward quirk and the black hair an unruliness that defied Jenny's attempts to keep it in place and flat. In height he was just short of six foot, thinnish but wiry; and his speech was the dialect of Breckland, but softer and without the jerkiness.

It was the back door, as propriety demanded, to which he would always go. A woman would be in the kitchen there, or the back garden, or would come at his knock.

"Mornin, ma'am," he would say quietly, and a finger would flick to his hat. "I'm buyin what they call antiques. If you have any old chairs or china or suchlike you'd like to part with, I'll be pleased to give you a good price."

He would never force himself into a house nor let talk become a nuisance, and yet more often than not he would be asked inside. Sometimes he even managed to see the upstair rooms. Upstairs was the place to get, as Mark Shadd had once told him. That was where most dealers rarely managed to get, the place where you found a fine old chair or chest of drawers; and there was fifty times more profit in things like that than in buying trumpery knickknacks with their profit of a shilling, perhaps, or half a crown. But whether he bought anything or not, he would always hand the woman one of the cards that Jenny had had printed.

"I'm much obliged to you, ma'am," he would say, "and here's my name and where I live. If you should happen to run across any o' them things I've been tellin you about, perhaps you'll drop me a postcard. I'll see you get the postage back, and I'll be beholden to you into the bargain."

If there was something she would like to sell but about which the husband would have to be asked, then he would give her an addressed envelope already stamped, and it would somehow seem as if it were she who was doing the favour. And so a day would go on, with oddments picked up here and there and now and again a larger piece or even a fortunate find in the most unlikely place. And there was always the friendliness and courtesy to stand him in good stead when he came that way again.

It was nearing five o'clock when he came to a smallish but somewhat superior sort of cottage that stood back from the road not far from Flintwold Village on the homeward way. The front garden was well tended, and though he had been minded to make no further calls some instinct told him that there was a last likely house. A pond, guarded by railings, lay on the opposite side of the lane, and he tied the cob to one of the posts and made his way to the back door. In the large kitchen a woman was ironing.

"Excuse me, ma'am, but do you think I could have a pail o' water for my hoss?"

She was a woman of well over sixty, ample-bosomed and buxom almost to fatness. Her snow-white hair, wet and wispy from the ironing, showed streaks of yellow, and she blew the wisps back as she turned. Even the sudden voice had not startled her, and her self-possession and the slow way her eyes went over him gave him for a moment a quick inferiority. Her starched apron rustled as she moved.

"I reckon so," she said. "If I find ye a pail you can draw yourself a bucket from the well. Better have this here scrubbin-up bucket o' mine."

There was a brisk importance about her, and she watched from the front while he watered the horse. He was wiping the sweat from forehead and neck as he came back with the empty bucket.

"Look as though you could do with a drink yourself. Been a master hot day. Enough to fry you in this here kitchen when the sun was on it."

"Thankee, ma'am," he said. "Reckon a glass o' that well water wouldn't do me no harm."

"Sit you down there," she told him briskly. "You'd better have a cup o' tea. My husband he won't be home till after six, and I allust have one about this time. You rest yourself there till the kittle boil."

"That's kind of you, ma'am. Only you'll hatta let me pay you for it."

"I hain't got yet so's I want to take money for a cup o' tea," she told him, and began putting the ironing things away. His eyes roved round the room and took in the Staffordshire Dick Turpin on the mantelpiece, the early candlesticks with their snuffers, the crockery on the dresser, and the dresser itself. There was an engraved glass with a spiral stem that looked as if it might be good and a resist-lustre jug— if it was undamaged.

"You're a stranger round here?" she was asking him.

"My name's Burling—Edward Burling, though most people call me Ted. I'm buyin antiques. I've got a shop at Ouseland."

She was putting question after question, and he was telling her more about himself. That was never his way, and yet he found himself saying this and that almost before he was aware of it. A brisk, comfortable sort of woman she seemed, and a rare one for gossip. Good-hearted too, for it was the first time on his travels that any-one had thought to offer him a cup of tea. And it was restful and cool in the kitchen after the scorching heat of the afternoon.

"Well, there's the tea made," she said at last. "Better give it time to draw. Reckon you'd better have one o' these shortcakes to keep it down. It'll be a goodish time afore you get another bite to eat if you're goin all the way to Ouseland."

She began telling him about herself. Her husband was steward at the Hall Farm and one of her sons was in the gardens.

"You've had a family then, ma'am?"

"Seven," she said, "and never a doctor to one on 'em, not after they was born, and some of 'em not then."

She began telling him about them, and again, before he knew it, he was venturing a something himself.

"Reckon I shall be a father myself in about another fortnight."

"You don't say!" she said. "And I never even thowt you was married! You don't look that old."

"I'm twenty-two."

"I had my first when I was eighteen," she told him. "That was my Maud, the one that now live in the sheers. And this one'll be your first, then."

On some men's faces there might have been something sheepish, or even a bravado, but his face had a grim earnestness.

"Your first," she said, and her ample bosom shook as she laughed. "You sound as if you wish it was the last."

Then she was shaking her head at the solemness of his face.

"You're just like my George when his first was comin. Almost fretted hisself to dead. Anyone'd a-thought, as I telled him, he was havin the baby stead o' her. He got over that, though. He've three now and another on the way."

"But you, Mrs. Chapman. Weren't you nervous yourself? I mean when your first was comin?"

"Me?" she said, and frowned as she thought back. "Reckon I was —just a mite. But then I hadn't no mother to tell me different. I often laughed since at what a silly grut gawk I was." She let out a sigh. "Still, I reckon your wife ain't like that."

She was filling his cup again, and he made no protest, although he knew he should have been on his way.

"I reckon she ain't," he said, and knew in his heart of hearts that it wasn't true.

"A good wife to ye, is she?"

He smiled to himself, the teacup held in air. He slowly put it down again.

"There ain't anyone better. I reckon most men what haven't been long married speak well of their wives, but my wife's different, Mrs. Chapman. She was too good for me, if you know what I mean. I never went to a good school like she did. I had to leave when I was twelve and had to start fendin for myself when I was eighteen."

"Schoolin ain't everything," she told him. "Soon as I saw you I thowt how like you was to my Harry. He never had mor'n village schoolin, but he've got on. You're goin to get on too. Only you've got to stand up for yourself. Don't let people stomp on your toes."

"I've had to stand up for myself more'n once," he told her, and there was a dry smile as he said it. "You have to when you've only yourself."

"That's only too true," she said. "But this here antique business, as you call it. How did you start in on it? Did you have to serve an apprenticeship like my Fred?"

"I don't hardly know," he said. "Reckon I sort o' slipped into it gradual-like. You know how it is. You get interested in somethin and then a bit more interested and afore you know where you are you think you'd like to make a livin at it."

"A good livin, is it?"

"We manage," he said. " 'Tain't much more'n a livin, not at present. But we're goin to get on, though, even if it do take time."

He refused a second shortcake and was getting to his feet.

"Reckon I'll hatta be on the move. It's a tidyish way back to Ouseland."

"Well, mind you come and see us again if you're ever this way."

"That's real kind of you. Reckon I'll be glad to. But somethin I was meanin to ask you. Have you had many antique dealers round this way?"

"Only one as I actually know on," she said. "I didn't see him myself. Last summer it was, and a rare lot o' old rubbidge he bowt, so they tell me. Norwich was where he come from."

He was frowning as he gave her one of those trade cards of his.

"Perhaps you wouldn't mind havin this, Mrs. Chapman. I'm not like them Norwich dealers. They can come round here and glean what they want and give what they like and you never clap eyes on 'em again. That ain't like me, though. I'm at Ouseland and I'm allust there. I hatta deal straight with people so's they don't come into my shop and reckon they've been swindled. Same as when I come this way again. I hain't got to be ashamed to look people in the face."

There had been a startling vehemence in that declaration of faith, and for a moment it left her tongue-tied.

"Now about the tea, Mrs. Chapman," he was saying with his old quietness. "Sure you won't let me pay you for it?"

"Not a farden," she told him. " 'Tain't often I get the chance to talk to anyone sort o' sensible. It do you good to have a bit of a rest."

"Then perhaps there's somethin you'll let me buy, and pay you that way."

She frowned.

"Don't know as there's nothin I'd want to part with. Nothin as'd suit you."

"What about this glass? It look pretty. I could give you half a crown for it."

"Fare a lot for that old thing," she told him. "There used to be two on 'em, only one got broke."

He gave her the half-crown. The jug he left because it was chipped at the spout. Then he held out his hand and thanked her again.

"Next time you come, bring your wife and that baby o' yours," she called from the gate. "Come about five, together, so's you can have a cup o' tea."

He was late and at first he pushed the cob along. Then slowly his thoughts and the warm beauty of that early evening made an ease in his mind, and he seemed unaware when the horse slackened its pace. In that restful half-hour things had been said that took him back among the years, and forward, into others that thrust inevitably towards a wished-for future. But at the back of everything was the first real and utter confidence as he told himself that Jenny would be all right. That Mrs. Chapman knew—and who else should know better? Not even Dr. Soffe. There was a sheepish smile at the way the old doctor had rounded on him when he had asked about the risk.

"Is yours the first baby that's ever been born?" Soffe had said in that gruff, almost blurting way of his. "You stick to your business, young man, and allow me to know mine."

Then he had glared and wagged a monitory finger.

"And don't go about with a face like a fiddle. Keep your wife cheerful; that's what you've got to do."

He had gone on muttering about having brought hundreds of

babies into the world and never having lost a mother except one, and that was not his fault. But that was the very last thing he should have said, for it was that one lost mother that kept coming back to the mind. For if one mother, then why not two? But now he could tell himself that the doctor had been right, and the knowledge brought a realization. Whether it were a girl, as he wanted, or a boy, as Jenny wanted, there'd be another someone for whom to work and plan. A kind of glow came over him then, as of some new vitality, and his shoulders straightened and he drew himself up on the hard seat. Some day he would make good what he had told Clemming. He'd have a finer shop than Clemming's, and that would take the sneer from his face. Maybe one day he might even buy Clemming up and see his own name across the front of that Norwich shop.

The first cottages of Stanford were once more in sight, and he shook the reins to quicken the pace of the horse. At the Cock he turned into the narrow road by which he had come, but when he came to the crossroads again and the turnpike there was no need to crack the whip, for the animal was pricking its ears as if it snuffed the very scent of home. But it was well after the promised time when Ted turned at last into the yard.

He had the traces unhooked in a flash, coiled them, and let the horse into the stable. He almost ran to the house, but Jenny had heard him and was at the back door. It was always dark in the kitchen, even of a summer evening, but a lamp was lighted and there was the savoury smell of food.

"You all right, Jenny?"

His arms had gone about her and his cheek touched her hair.

"I'm all right, Ted. And you? Did you have a good day?"

"Not too bad. Got a pretty fair load, as you see."

With arm still about her he drew her back into the kitchen.

"Did the doctor look in as he said?"

"This afternoon," she told him. "Everything's just as it should be, so he said. And it's going to be a lovely baby."

Suddenly there was a something in his throat, and his arm tightened about her. Maybe she knew, for she smiled up at him and her hands went up to draw his head down to hers.

"Now you go and see to the horse. Supper'll be ready by the time you're back."

He racked the cob down for the night, for it was too late now to take it to the meadow. Then he carried into the house the things he had bought and put them in the room at the back. Over the meal she told him what the day had been like in the shop. It had been quiet, but a good day; as good a day as they'd had. The vicar of Frenham had been in with a niece who was getting married and had bought the Chippendale chest and the pair of hall chairs. A London gentle-man had called and had bought that piece which they'd thought was Lowestoft, though he was really interested only in Chelsea and Bow figures, and he'd left his address. After his call the doctor had had yet another look at the walnut table, and she was sure he'd buy it yet. Also, a woman had brought in two needlework pictures in early frames and had seemed pleased at the offer of ten shillings.

He told her about his day: the things he had bought and even the things he might perhaps have bought if he could have trusted his judgment sufficiently to take a risk. He told her about the kindness of the woman of the pond cottage, but with never a word about children. After the meal he washed up the supper dishes, and then the two of them priced the things he'd bought. That was always the excitement and recompense of a day, and that day had been better than he had thought.

When they had finished, Jenny was looking tired; and though it was short of nine o'clock, he made her go up to bed. He would just make the entries in the stock book, he said, and then be up himself. As soon as she had gone, he put on his slippers and lighted his pipe. It was an extravagance, that pipe, as conscience still would tell him, and yet he had come to look forward to it after a meal, perhaps, or at the end of the day. It was Jenny who had laughed away his qualms. A man ought to have some small pleasure of his own, and there was something homely about the smell of tobacco in a house. Those had been her arguments, and she had bought the pipe and the tobacco jar out of her own money. But perhaps Jenny was some-times a bit homesick for the scent of old Mark's cigars and pipe.

That night the stock book failed to hold him, and soon he pushed it aside and leaned back in his chair. At first he thought of what the morning would bring: he must take the chest and chairs to Fren-ham; and that somehow brought his thoughts to the day that had gone. It was in the kitchen of a cottage that his thoughts lingered, and his mind began rehearsing each comforting word that had been said. Then he recalled that question, the one he had been asked for the first time in his life: what it had been that had made him an antique dealer. He saw himself as he had tried to answer, and wondered if what he had said had been true. In a way it was, for Jenny had once told him that almost every dealer began that way: knowing little and learning as he went along. And then he was telling himself, and there was a momentary pride as he knew it, that whatever Jenny might say, no dealer in all the county had begun so strangely as he.

Soon the pipe was cold as he sat there in a young past that had so magically gone. On his face, shadowed by the lamp, was a curious maturity as he saw again those years that had made him a man. Sometimes the brows would knit and the teeth bite hard on the cold pipe, and the lips would purse or perhaps smile as his thoughts had their sway. They would always centre about one distant day, and then the day would become one place and a mere minute or two of time. Then he would be in the bitter coldness of the woodshed, staring at the bureau while his fingers grasped the handle of an ax. Then his brows would knit in the incredible nearness and the drama of those frenzied minutes. He could feel again the smooth shaft in his hands and hear once more the very splintering of the wood.

CHAPTER 2

Beginnings

THE Burlings came of good farming stock even if in their latest generations there was a strain of eccentricity. Take the matter of names, for instance. Whereas the sound old Tom, Dick, and Harry names, with a good mixture of biblical worthies, were almost obligatory in Breckland and on its fringes, the last two Burlings were given the names of Mortimer and Frankland; and their father was old Anselm Burling, who had once owned his own large farm near Wickenden. He had lost it because, at the age of forty, though hale in body, he had taken to his bed on the death of his wife; and there he stayed until he died at just over seventy.

Mortimer, eccentric in most eyes because he had never married, had a hired farm near Attley. Frankland, the elder brother, had quarrelled with his father and found work at Norwich. There he had married a schoolmistress, much older than himself, and she had died at the age of forty-two, soon after the birth of a son who was named Edward. Frankland, then working in the office of a firm of timber merchants, managed with an old housekeeper; but she fell into drinking ways and neglected the child, and finally he decided to emigrate. So he went to see his brother, who took at once to the boy and was willing enough to keep him till Frankland should have settled down in Canada. Edward was then of school age, and one letter reached Mortimer from his father. Mortimer answered it but there was never a reply, and as the years went by he could only assume that his brother was dead.

Meanwhile Mortimer—Mort as he was always known—had ceased to be a farmer. A crushed leg had had to be amputated, and, as he said, whoever heard of a wooden-legged farmer?

"Would a-bin a master rum job stompin along behind a plough, wouldn't it?" he would often say. "Bin rare handy for tater-settin, though, sorta dibbin 'em in as you went along."

So he became a somewhat better kind of dickey-dealer; better because his wasn't a donkey cart but a heavy cart and a strong nag that could move at a fair pace and also pull a plough, even if a neighbour now did his small amount of ploughing. And he went back to the family home at Wickenden, which is just to the east of Harford, and there he hired a little holding from Squire Trench: a cottage, a few outbuildings, and six acres of land, including a two-acre meadow. Old Dolly Carter, a widow of sixty, kept the cottage reasonably clean, did the washing and, if Mort were on his rounds, had a hot meal ready when he came home at night.

That was the home to which young Ted Burling came, and he liked it from the first. Mort was a big, jovial, red-faced man with an enormous kindness of heart; and though there were some, like Harriet Harefield at the vicarage, who thought he was neglecting the boy, Mort would have been indignant if such a charge had been made to his face. So, perhaps, would have been Ted, who had no sense whatever of neglect. On Saturdays and Sundays, when he was home from school, his uncle would almost always be at the holding; and in the holidays he would be away in the cart with his uncle, calling at cottages and farms, or going to market, and on rarer occasions, even to Norwich itself. He loved those days in the country, even in winter, for Mort would see that he was wrapped in voluminous if outlandish garments, with a sack round his legs and a scarf round his ears. Mort knew everyone and would buy anything. When the cart drew home, there might be a couple of calves and a sow and litter under the pig net across the back of the cart, and a crate or two of hens and ducks or geese lashed somewhere behind.

But it was the adventure and the friendliness of those days that Ted loved—the hearty hail that his uncle would give to all, sometimes even stopping the cart for a few moments of wayside chat. Mort would be asked what pigs had fetched at So-and-So, or what the price had been like at such-and-such a sale; and in time, when people got to know him, Ted would get a word of greeting too. The women at farms always seemed to take to the boy.

"Boy, you must be half-frooz," a farmer's wife would say. "Come you on into the house while they go traipsin about."

So while his uncle and the farmer talked business and argued out-side, Ted would be given something warm to drink and a bun or a slice of cake. Purely in the way of friendliness, he would be asked all sorts of questions about school and himself and what he wanted to be when he grew up. Then at midday there would be a halt at a pub for bread and cheese, with Mort having his usual pint and the boy a small lemonade or a bottle of ginger pop. But Mort allowed no loose or bawdy language in the boy's hearing, for though he was pretty free himself, he would more than once surprise a man by pulling him up short at that kind of talk.

But most of all Ted grew to love auctions with their life and colour. To him there would seem to be innumerable traps and carts and innumerable people: dealers like his uncle, gypsies even, coun-try women making the event a holiday, and sometimes some of the gentry. Solemn-eyed and attentive, he would make his way round with the auctioneer when the cheaper lots were sold; and when the auctioneer came to his rostrum, he would wriggle a way through and contrive somehow to be in the very front. What he loved most was when his uncle bid and bought.

"Another two bob," Mort would say, or, "Make it ten," and the boy would hold his breath and long for the fall of the hammer. There would be a surge of joy at the auctioneer's "Sold, to Mr. Burling," and a corresponding depression when his uncle lost the lot. But, as Mort was to explain, there was only one way to buy, and that was at the right price. He had his price beforehand, and those who chose to bid higher were welcome enough. But sometimes Mort would be a seller.

"What do you think they'll fetch, Uncle?" Ted would always want to know, and Mort would quote a margin price. Then when whatever it was came under the hammer, Ted would have moments of anguished anxiety; and when the bids hovered short of the ex-pected, he would be in an agony of apprehension. Mort would be unperturbed when a lot had to be bought in, but to the boy it was a small tragedy; and though Mort would tell him they'd make more money at So-and-So, Ted felt in his small heart a misery and a frus-tration—but not for the things themselves or for the mere matter of money. Ted worshipped his uncle, and it was for him that he had those young agonies and for him that he had his triumphs. And even when Mort bought in a lot and then sold privately at a profit before a sale was over, there was never any real triumph in that or wiping out of what had seemed a public defeat.

"Why'd you let them best you, Uncle?" he once asked.

Mort looked astounded, then chuckled.

"They didn't best me, boy." (It was almost always *boy* and hardly ever the name.) "They'll hatta git up early to best me."

Then he explained the intricacies of dealing and though much of it was over the boy's head, he gradually learned. Meanwhile he was doing well enough at school. Henry Clare, the master, spoke well of him to Mort. Harriet Harefield liked the boy too, and contrived—though Mort didn't think there was much to it—to get him into the church choir, even if it was only in the evenings that Ted was regular, for there was often a Sunday morning job that kept him away.

But it was a curious kind of life when Mort was on his rounds. Old Dolly would leave the boy bread and butter or dripping or jam for his midday meal, and perhaps there would be some stock to water or feed. When he came home in the afternoons Dolly would be there, and he would have what was known as a bite to eat and a cup of tea, and then see to the stock again. After that, if it were winter, he would curl himself up with a book that the master or Miss Hattie had lent him, or it might be a book from some job lot that his uncle had picked up for next to nothing at a sale.

"Boy, you'll ban your eyes out," Dolly would often say when he was curled up on the rag rug and reading in the dim light of the shaded lamp. "What good it do you, readin all that rubbidge, I don't know."

But Ted learned that Dolly's bark was worse than her bite, and he never stirred. But as soon as the wheels of the cart were heard in the lane, he would be up and out. While he helped to unharness the horse, he would pester Mort for the news of the day. After the hot meal on winter nights, Mort would go out to give a final look to any stock there might be; when he came back, he would find the table cleared and the boy at a book again. Mort would read the local paper, but rarely for more than a few minutes, for then he would drop asleep. Ted would be careful to make never a sound and often he was lucky, for his uncle would sleep and snore till well after time for bed. When he did wake up, Mort's eyes would always bulge in the most comical way, as if it were preposterous that he should have been sleeping at all. Then his eyes would fall on the round-faced kitchen clock that hung over the mantelpiece.

"Boy, slip you up them stairs! Owt to've bin in bed hours ago."

Then there would be the nightly ritual. Ted would kiss his uncle's cheek and Mort would always pat him on the shoulder. The candle would be lighted and up Ted would go to bed. If it were as late as nine o'clock, he would hardly be ready for sleep before there would be the shuffle of the grandfather chair as Mort pushed it back, and the dropping of the heavy boots on the brick floor. The key would turn in the door, there would be a pause and a grunt or two while Mort lighted his own candle, and then the sound of one stockinged foot and the clump of a wooden leg on the stairs.

When Ted was twelve, Mort had pneumonia and lay for some weeks in the upstair room. Dr. Soffe of Harford said that it was only his amazing constitution that pulled him through; but Ted had to leave school, and when his uncle got about again he didn't go back. Thereafter he slowly became an integral part of things. By the time he was sixteen he had a pretty good knowledge of the dealing business, and, in a rather curious way, he had begun a little side line of his own.

It began on a summer day when his uncle was out. Ted was hoeing mangolds on the half-acre or so that was grown for the horse when he saw a smart horse and trap draw up outside the entrance to the yard. A well dressed stranger got down and came through the yard to the back door. Ted met him there.

"Mornin," he said. "Got any old chairs or china you'd like to part with? I'll give you a good price."

He appeared to be a man of little over thirty; tallish, beefy, and red-faced, he seemed more like a farmer or the landlord of a pub than a dealer.

"Don't know as we have," Ted told him.

"Is the woman of the house in?"

"There ain't one," Ted told him. "I'm the only one here."

"Won't be no harm in havin a look round?" the man said, and was somehow through the open door and in the kitchen. He stood just inside, with his eyes roving this way and that.

"What about that dresser?" he said. " 'Tain't much good, but I could give you fifteen bob for it."

Dr. Soffe had offered Mort £2 for that dresser and Mort had said he wasn't selling. Ted merely said that the dresser wasn't for sale.

"Anything in here?" the man said, opening the door of the tiny parlour and stepping inside. It was a room that was rarely used, and a musty smell came through the opened door. The man's eyes were everywhere.

"What about them two chairs? Ten bob each. Here y'are—look! Here's the pound."

Ted refused the offered sovereign. He didn't think his uncle would sell. Then he explained about Mort. The name conveyed nothing to the dealer.

"Here's my card," he said. "Do you ask him and let me know." He gave a quick wink. "Might be half a crown in it for yourself."

That was that, except that his eye caught an old ornament on the mantelpiece. He fingered it, then took it to the window and had a nearer look.

" 'Tain't what I thowt it was," he said. "Still, it's pretty, though. Sort o' thing my missus like. 'Tain't much good to you, I reckon."

"Don't know as it is," Ted told him.

"Give you half a crown," he said, and the money was in Ted's hand before he knew it. "And don't forget there'll be another half-crown if I buy them chairs."

He gave Ted a card that showed where to write, and then asked if there wasn't anything upstairs. Ted said there was nothing, but the dealer pestered him with a list of the things that might be there. But some vague dislike or uneasiness kept him from opening the door to the stairs, and at last the dealer went away.

That night Mort seemed perfectly satisfied with the price for the ornament. He had a look at the dealer's card. Percy Clemming was the name: Dealer in Antiques, of 71 Castle Street, Norwich.

"Never heard on him," Mort said. "What ornament was it you sold? Not one o' them vases?"

It was a figure of a woman sitting under a tree, and the tree was full of little flowers, Ted said. Mort just remembered it and no more. As for those chairs the dealer wanted, he said he'd see.

On the following Saturday the two went to Norwich. Mort was looking for a pony for a customer, and Ted left him with some other dealers on Castle Hill and had a look at the shops. It was by chance that he saw the name *Percy Clemming* across a shop on the other side of the street.

It was a big shop with twin windows crowded with furniture and china and silver. There were mirrors and pictures hanging above, and the tops of grandfather clocks could be seen in the comparative dimness of the shop itself. Then something held his eye: the ornament that had stood on his own mantelpiece. Now it stood with two other figures somewhat like it on a mahogany table with a piecrust edge. It had a little label on it, but he couldn't see what the label said.

At the shop door he turned away, for the moral courage was suddenly lacking. A minute or two and he was back. A youngish man was standing near the window, but had that man been Clemming he would never have turned the door knob and gone in. Before the man could speak he was asking the price of that little ornament, on that table there in the window—the one in the middle.

The man ran a dubious eye over him, then had a look at the label.

"This one? . . . Seven pounds ten. It's Chelsea. Absolutely perfect condition."

Ted could never remember what he said or did. But what he did was to mumble a something about a lot of money and make his way out of the shop.

No word was ever said to Mort about that ornament; but that autumn, when the usual mass of farm sales were on, and they happened to include the furnishings of a house, he began buying on his own account the trays or boxes of oddments and knickknacks that could often be bought for a shilling or half-crown. When he brought his first purchase to the cart, Mort stared.

"What have ye got there, boy? Lot of old trinkums, aren't they?"

"Somethin I thought I'd buy," Ted told him, and Mort didn't press the matter. Ted was like that, as he knew, now that he was turning from boy to youth. Not secretive but reserved, and just a bit obstinate at times, with queer silences that Mort could neither understand nor explain. But he was a good boy, a rare one to work, as Mort would put it. Always willing too, and never a one to grumble.

Ted had money now: not much but enough. Mort was openhanded and would often hand out a half-sovereign when he had had a good deal. Ted now had a sow of his own and had sold two litters, and Mort had promised to buy him a strong bud that he could bring on into a good fat bullock by spring. It was with his own money, then, that the tray of oddments had been bought; but Mort could see no sense in it for all that, especially when Ted didn't bring them into the house but made a shelf for them in the wood-shed. Then other lots were bought and a second shelf was built. Though Mort still asked no questions, he found the whole business mightily perplexing; but he was to do Ted a good turn.

He was off one morning in the cart when Harriet Harefield hailed him. Ted had not been at church at all on the previous Sunday and she wondered if he were unwell. Mort said he was well but he hap-pened to mention Ted's new activity. Harriet came to the cottage on the very same morning.

"Why, Edward!" she said, when he had brought out the contents of the shelves for inspection. "These are dreadful rubbish. What-ever made you buy them?"

He liked Harriet Harefield, and perhaps there was no one else to whom he would have told the truth, though even to her he kept something back. He knew a dealer, he said, who had bought an old ornament for half a crown and had it marked in his shop window at £7 and more. That was why he'd invested money himself, hoping that a dealer would come that way and find something valuable.

"But dealers know and you don't know," she said. His look was so downcast that she gave a little click of the tongue.

"If I lend you a book," she said, "will you read it? It tells you all about china and what's valuable and what isn't."

"Thank you, miss; I'll be glad to," he told her, and she smiled at the way his face had lighted.

She lent him two books, one on earthenware and one on china. Each was highly didactic in style and somewhat old-fashioned. When he had read them—more than once—from cover to cover, his brain was a turgid bewilderment of factories and marks, glazes and pastes, and this ware and that. But the books did teach him one thing. The stuff that they called porcelain or earthenware was not something abstract or remote that existed only in books, for among the old-fashioned illustrations he recognized jugs and figures that he had seen on farmhouse mantelpieces; and there was even a figure the very image of the one that Clemming had bought.

When he took the books back, Harriet noticed a change in him.

"You're not thinking of going in for buying things, are you, Edward?"

"I don't reckon so, miss," he told her, and then unconsciously modified the assertion with a queer sideways nod of the head. "Not that I don't like all them old things."

She lent him the two volumes of Stevenson's *History of English Furniture*, and there was something into which he could really get his teeth. In those books there were again things that he had seen, but infinitely more of them. He could show Mort a drawing of a chair the perfect likeness of the two in the parlour. He even went into the parlour and brought one out for Mort's inspection. Mort's eyes opened a bit wide. Maybe there was something in that antique business after all.

Ted was then in his eighteenth year. He was now handling the small arable holding himself and it was less often that he went with Mort on the rounds. Deep within him were vague stirrings that had taken all edge of pleasure from a profitable deal in stock. He was like a man afloat, with the voyage end already in his mind, and yet without chart or compass or even a rudder by which to steer. Though he gave never a vague hint in the house, Mort knew there was a restless something on Ted's mind; and it wasn't a girl, for Ted had no eye for women. That it might be all that business about antiques he was beginning to have a shrewd idea.

But he didn't live to know the truth. Perhaps the wooden leg had something to do with his death, though he had perfected a method of his own for getting in and out of the cart spryly enough; but when the horse fell that February night on the glassy road about a mile from the village on the Norwich turnpike, Mort was pitched headlong out. The horse got to its feet again and contrived to make its way home with the reins dangling and a snapped trace. Ted went out to find the cart empty.

Mort was dead when they found him, and Soffe said he had felt nothing. But there was a disaster almost as great as the death. Mort's hessian bag was missing. He had distrusted banking accounts and his capital of roughly a hundred sovereigns was always carried on him. The Harford police were busy for weeks but unearthed nothing. There was always traffic on the turnpike, and some traveller must have discovered Mort, robbed the body, and then driven on.

When the funeral expenses were paid, Ted found himself the owner of a couple of bullocks, two sows—one with litter—the horse and cart and a certain amount of implements and oddments. In a drawer of the oak bureau he found fifteen sovereigns that had been put there for some special reason and forgotten, and that, with the few pounds he had himself, was his working capital. Expenses were eleven pounds for rent and rates and the half-crown a week for Dolly Carter, and there would be food and clothes as well. Those were the days when a labouring man had twelve shillings a week, or thirteen if he was a teamman and saw to his nags on a Sunday. Ted worked it out that he needed twenty-five shillings a week to pay his way and leave a little for eventualities, for, like Mort, he had a hatred of debt.

It was time that he was out and about, and yet it was weeks before he made a move. By then his capital was shrinking. Mort's death had been a tremendous shock that had caused him to withdraw still more within himself, so that when at last, after the oats and mangolds were in, he set out one morning on a round his heart was not in it. But the day cheered him, for old friends of Mort—and, to be truthful, of his—showed sympathy and friendliness. Slowly he settled down to dealing. But the savour had gone; now that he had come to the test, he knew he lacked Mort's instinct. Even the patience was somehow not there.

One day he went to a sale. It was a day of drenching rain, and only Sam Wrightson, the Ouseland dealer, was there. Ted bought two Windsor chairs of the better class which he seemed to remember as having been illustrated in Harriet Harefield's books; he also bought a gate-leg table. His total expenditure was under two pounds. What he would do with them he had no idea, and then it was decided for him. A village man—a young gamekeeper—came to the cottage a few nights later. He had heard that Ted had some chairs and a table and he wondered if he'd sell. He was getting married and would be glad to buy if the price was right. Ted sold him the chairs and the table and made a pound profit, even if he didn't get his money till after harvest.

It was the stimulus he needed. Now whenever there was a sale within driving distance, he would be there, speculating on this and that, though rarely going beyond a pound or two. Some of the things he sold to couples setting up house, and he had a stroke of luck with a Bible box that had taken his fancy and which Soffe saw and bought. But in one of the sheds there was a small accumulation; and though his capital hadn't shrunk, it hadn't increased.

Gradually he began to learn the names of the dealers. Sam Wrightson of Ouseland he knew, and there would be Walter Rape of Bury and Ben Harris of Dereham. Clemming was always at the larger sales, but the first time Ted saw him at one he gave no sign of recognition. Other Norwich dealers would be at important sales, and once there was a man from Lynn. Dealers like Rape and Harris would give him a nod, and Sam Wrightson would always come up and pass the time of day.

The months went by till that day of the sale at Larford Vicarage. It was a fairly important sale; all the dealers were there, and things brought such prices that Ted never opened his mouth to make a bid. A marquetry clock was the sensation. One man—a short, bearded man of about fifty—seemed to be bidding against the rest of the room, and the clock was knocked down to him at what to Ted seemed the stupendous figure of forty-five guineas. The same dealer bought other items, and throughout the sale Ted felt a curious tension in the room.

"Who was the dealer who bought that clock?" he asked Sam Wrightson.

"Mark Shadd o' Yarmouth," Sam said. "If it hadn't been for him, we'd a-had it for a ten-pun note."

The next day Ted went to the vicarage. He told Harriet Harefield about the clock and said that he thought he remembered a drawing of one like it in one of her books. They looked it up and there was the drawing—an inlaid walnut grandfather clock described as Queen Anne.

That autumn there was a sale at Barngate Hall. It had been too far for Ted to have a preview; but when he had a look around just before the sale started, he saw a clock that seemed to him the very image of the one for which that Yarmouth dealer had given nearly fifty pounds. Though the Yarmouth dealer was not there that day, Clemming was there and all the other dealers that he knew. Ultimately the clock came up. Who was bidding he couldn't see, but the dealers, for some queer reason, didn't seem interested. The bidding went to seven pounds ten and halted.

"Seven fifteen!"

Ted hardly recognized his own voice. Within him was some instinct of which he was unaware, for he went on bidding like a man in a maze. And it wasn't the fever that takes one sometimes at sales.

"Ten guineas!" came the unknown voice. With that Ted came partly to himself.

"Ten guineas. Ten guineas only I'm bid. Any more for you, sir? Going at ten guineas."

Ted shook his head and the hammer fell.

There was a break for lunch. Ted made for the inn where he had stabled the horse.

"Hi! young feller. I want a word wi' you."

It was Clemming. He had grown stouter with the years and his fat face had purpled. There was a floridness about his clothes, and a handsome chain with dangling seals was stretched across his waist-coat.

"Me?"

"Yes, you," Clemming said. "What'd you mean biddin for that clock? Didn't you know it was bein knocked down to us at seven pun ten till you started puttin your spoke in?"

"Why shouldn't I?" Ted told him. Memory was bringing a quick hostility. "It's a free country, ain't it?"

"Is it? What about all the things you've bowt at sales? What we've let you have."

"And who's we?"

"You know who we are," Clemming told him. "The dealers—that's who we are. We can make you or break you. Next time we're biddin, you keep that mouth o' yours shut and maybe we'll put a bargain or two in your way from time to time."

"When I want to bid, I'll bid, and it'll take more'n you to keep my mouth shut."

"Oh?" said Clemming, and gave a bit of a laugh. "So that's the way you talk, is it? You see where it get you to."

He gave another little laugh and a wave of the hand and moved away. Ted felt himself shaking, but it wasn't entirely with anger. That night, as he drove home, he was once more like a man with neither chart nor compass, and in some strange way he felt incredibly alone. Puzzle as he might, he could make no real sense of the things that Clemming had said. And though neither the threats nor the sneering laugh had frightened him, he felt a great disquiet.

Sam Wrightson turned up the next day.

"Happed to be this way," he said, "and I kinda wondered if you'd got anything you'd like to part with."

In the reaction to the previous day, Ted felt an enormous friend-liness towards the man. The two went into the shed. Sam cast a dubious eye on the accumulation but he did make a deal or two.

"Mr. Wrightson," said Ted, and then stopped.

"Yes?" Wrightson said, looking at him.

Ted stammered a bit more, then told him what had happened at the sale.

"Yes," Wrightson said. "I was meanin to have a word with you about that. Why don't you come into the ring and do things proper-like?"

It was a moment of decision, and in after years he would blush for himself and the greenhorn he had been.

"The ring? What's the ring?"

Wrightson took the naïveté for craftiness, but he carefully ex-plained. The ring were the dealers. Most dealers were in the ring. One or two of the big dealers weren't. Take Mark Shadd, for in-stance. He'd fallen out with the ring years ago and now dealt on his own. That was why that clock he'd bought cost him what it had.

Ted still didn't understand. Wrightson went patiently on.

"Only one of us bid," he said, "and soon as any private bidders drop out, then he have it, and the same with anything else what we want. Then after the sale we have an auction of our own and the man what really want it, get it, only he have to pay the difference into the pool. Then the pool's divided up and all on us what're in the ring get a share." He chuckled. "Many a time I've bin to a sale and haven't opened my mouth either there or arterwards, and I've gone home with a fi'-pun note."

"And what about them that the things belong to?" Ted said. "Ain't that sorta robbin them if they don't get a fair price?"

"Them?" Sam said. "They can be there, can't they? They can put a reserve on, can't they, and have 'em bowt in?"

It was complicated. Ted licked his lips and shook his head. "Reckon I'll hatta think it over."

"You do as I say," Wrightson told him. "The best day's work you'll ever do in your life. Mind ye," he had to add, "you won't be what you might call a real member. Can't expect it, seein you're not a regular dealer; but I'll see as how you get plenty put in your way."

That was how it was left. The days went by and he was still

thinking it over. Sometimes he knew that Wrightson's arguments had been a bit too smooth; and even when he did see something of his point of view, the figure of Clemming would loom up again and he would hear the threats and the chuckling laugh. For the first time in his life Ted Burling had a deadly hate, and in the long hours by himself there would be a reproach for the things he had left unsaid.

"I know you, Clemming," was what he should have said. "You're a liar and you're a thief. I'm the one you bought a china ornament of when he was little more'n a boy. Half a crown you gave him for it, pretendin it was for your wife, and then got over seven pound for it yourself."

No man was going to threaten Ted Burling, he would tell himself. Neither Clemming nor any other dealer was stopping him from bidding if he wanted to bid. And that was how things stood on that momentous morning when Harriet Harefield came to speak to him about a bureau.

CHAPTER 3

The Bureau

"I HEAR you've begun buying furniture, Edward," Harriet Harefield said, "and I'd like you to buy a bureau for me."

"A bureau, miss? What sort of bureau?"

"Well, a nice bureau," she said. "I want it for myself."

"Anything like mine, miss?" He was referring to the one he had inherited from Mort.

She looked at it and it didn't please her at all. It was oak, for one thing, and she wanted mahogany. And something neat and nice to suit her room, with far less clumsy inside fitments. But Edward would know what she meant.

"I think I can manage that for you, miss," Ted told her. "But what about price?"

"You might be lucky and get one for three or four pounds," she said. "Of course if it was something special, like Chippendale, you might have to pay as much as ten."

"Ten's your limit then, miss."

"I think so," she said, and that was how it was left. Ted, to tell the truth, had been flattered by her approach. The confidence which he had somehow felt bound to show had fed upon itself, and when she had gone he felt a young importance. Bureaus were always being sold, and in the flush of that new pride it seemed the easiest thing to buy one. That the objects he had picked up at sales had been by the favour of the ring was something he had never believed, and in any case he had no mind to be deterred by the threats of a man like Clemming. As for that mention of Chippendale, he was cocksure even in that. Something told him that he should have had the courage to admit an ignorance or forgetfulness and to have asked for another look at those furniture books. But Chippendale, as he did remember, was good-class mahogany, and that knowledge seemed enough.

It was not till late in November that an opportunity occurred. It was a fairly important sale at Diss, and as soon as he arrived he saw the very thing he wanted—a mahogany bureau in quite good order and remarkably well fitted inside. He spent a good time examining it. It seemed to be a handsome piece: it had a fine polish, the inner drawers were neat, and, instead of the usual green baize on the flap, there was red velvet that seemed to him to go well with the colour of the stout mahogany.

There was a good muster of dealers at the sale. Clemming was there, and it was the first time he had seen him since the day of the threats. Now that Wrightson had enlightened him about the ring, he had questioned people elsewhere, and that morning he kept his eyes and ears open and he could see that what he had been told was true. Rape of Bury seemed to be the principal bidder, the other dealers showing a lack of interest that was only too revealing. He became apprehensive about the bureau and wondered if he would have to go up to his limit of ten pounds. There was even the fear that the bureau might be more valuable than he had thought and that the ring would outbid him after all.

Late in the afternoon the bureau came up. The bidding stayed at fifty shillings, and then he spoke. At three pounds ten there was an advance of five shillings, and he saw that the bid had come from Clemming. He bid again. At five pounds the bidding advanced by ten shillings. Only he and Clemming were in, and the bids came at a quick-fire rate. Whenever he looked at Clemming, he saw that Clemming and the dealers were watching him too.

"Nine pound!"

"Nine pound ten!"

Ted moistened his lips, then bid his limit.

There was a silence.

"Ten pounds," said the auctioneer. "Ten pounds I'm bid. Any more from you, Mr. Clemming?"

"He've bowt it. Let him have it," Clemming said, and laughed. There was a chuckling from where the dealers stood, but Ted heard it and no more. His was a sense of triumph. He had beaten Clemming at his own game; but when he looked round to catch his eye,

Clemming was looking at his catalogue and the droop of his own lip was wasted.

The very next morning he sent word to the vicarage that he had what Miss Hattie wanted, and that afternoon she came round. He had given it a polish, and it stood outside on a sack in full view.

"But, Edward, this isn't what I wanted at all!"

His mouth gaped.

"What's wrong with it, miss?"

"It isn't old," she said. "It's almost a modern one. And look how clumsy it is. Why, you could buy one like this in a furniture shop for four pounds!"

"I don't think you're right, miss," he told her. "All the ring was biddin for that bureau at yesterday's sale. A dealer bid nine pound ten for it, only I bested him at ten."

It was an incredulous look that she gave. Then she shook her head.

"Well, I'm sorry, Edward, but really it's no good to me. Perhaps you can sell it to someone else."

"You needn't worry about that, miss," he told her. "Reckon I can sell it all right."

But he soon felt uneasy. Ten pounds was a lot of capital to have tied up, and he already had quite an accumulation in the shed. But when he'd made a place for it in the woodshed by the far wall where the light fell on it, he had an idea, and a day or two later Dr. Soffe came for a look.

"No use to me," he said. "What'd you give for it?"

Ted hesitated, then owned up to ten pounds.

Soffe made a wry face.

"Looks to me, young man, as if you'd better stick to four-legged bureaus that you know something about. That sort of stuff can be picked up anywhere for two or three pounds."

His uneasiness grew, and yet one argument seemed unchallengeable. That bureau had been worth almost ten pounds to Clemming, and Clemming would have had to sell it at a profit. Some of his depression left him; he told himself that sooner or later he'd find a purchaser, even if he made no profit himself.

He mentioned the bureau to one or two likely people on his rounds, but the price was always far too much. December was well on the way, and he began to feel a new alarm; but then he had another idea. Wrightson would take it off his hands. If it had been worth nine pounds ten to Clemming, Wrightson ought to jump at it at nine pounds.

He took the Harford train to Ouseland one afternoon and found Wrightson in his shop.

"Hallo, Ted. What bring you this way? Somethin you want?"

"Not today," Ted told him. "To tell you the truth, Mr. Wrightson, I want to sell you somethin. A bureau I bowt."

"Oh?" said Sam, and then his mouth gaped. "Not that one you bowt at Diss?"

A minute and Ted was hearing the truth.

"What the davvul come over you, beat me," Sam said. "I tried to catch your eye but you didn't give me no chance. But I'd warned you, hadn't I? So'd Clemming. He told you what'd happen. And there you went and stepped right into it as though you was the biggest fool alive."

It almost angered Sam that anyone should show such ignorance. There Ted had been, fussily examining that bureau and as good as telling everyone he wanted it. As soon as he bid, all Clemming had to do was to step in at the right time.

"Look," said Sam, with an enormous patience. "I'm tryin to tell ye, and larn ye. Clemming know. That's why he've got the business he have. Compared with him you haven't got the cradle marks off your bottom. He guessed you'd go to ten pound, and so did everyone else. A nice round figure, ain't it? He knew where to stop and you didn't."

Sam refused the bureau even at three pounds, and that was the final collapse of Ted's pride and assurance. All that was left was a fierce resentment.

"I don't say Clemming was altogether right," Sam admitted, "but that's how it go in business. You needn't have bid, you know."

His hand went to the young fellow's arm.

"Why don't you change your mind and come in? Clemming ain't so bad when you get to know him. It'll be the makin of you, same as I told you afore."

His hand fell away at Ted's scowl.

"I can't do more'n advise ye. And warn ye too. What happened with that bureau is likely to happen with anything else what you try to buy from now on when the ring's there. They can afford to outbid ye because all on 'em will share any loss. Either you come in or your goose is cooked—far as antiques is concerned. And them's my last words. I don't wish ye no harm—you know that. I'm just tellin you."

It was a bitter pill to swallow, yet the strain of obstinacy, buttressed by that bitter hatred of Clemming, still held. But there was worse to follow.

Just after Christmas he went to a sale. At the sound of the auctioneer's bell he made his way to the sale room, wedging his way in at the back. He found himself quite near the dealers.

"Anyone want to buy a bureau?"

A laugh went round the ring. The voice, he was almost sure, had been Clemming's, and his face went a fiery red. His fists clenched, and if it had not been for the people between him and Clemming he would have smashed a fist in the dealer's face.

"Not at ten pound a time."

That was a strange voice, and there was another laugh. Suddenly Ted turned like a man in a panic and forced a way through, and out at the door. Then he knew the cowardly fool he had been, and turned back. A moment of indecision and he found himself making for his trap; in a few minutes he was driving away.

A fortnight later he went to another sale at Attley, and his mind was made up. He went deliberately late into the auction room, and a lot or two had been sold when he edged his way towards the dealers. Clemming caught sight of him and turned to Harris, the Dereham dealer.

"Didn't see no bureau in the catalogue, did you, Ben?"

Ted's left arm pushed aside an intervening man and he made for Clemming. Someone held the drawn-back arm and the small commotion grew and spread. Clemming's fist was raised too, but someone else was holding him back.

"You keep your tongue off me, you dirty thief," was what Ted was shouting. The words he had rehearsed were gone; all he wanted was to smash his fist across Clemming's mouth. Clemming was shouting too.

"Get out o' my way and I'll settle him."

"What's all this?"

It was the policeman who had been on duty outside the door.

There was a silence. Clemming's arms were free, and he shook himself like a dog coming out of water.

"Nothin I can't settle myself," he told the policeman, and a man was telling Ted that he'd better be going. The man was leading him towards the door. People drew back and he found himself out in the raw air of the January day.

A few days later he tried to sell the bureau to a couple who were setting up house, and though he would have taken as little as three pounds there was no deal. Soon the thought of the bureau was like a madness on his mind. In the first flush of easy buying he had written to auctioneers, asking for catalogues to be sent; and now when one arrived it was only a bitter reminder of his ineptitude. At night the thought of it preyed on him, and he tossed and muttered on his bed. His rounds had almost ceased, and he prowled restlessly about the house and holding. And money was getting short. It frightened him one night when he reckoned up and found that in hard cash he had only six pounds in the world.

Then something happened that took his mind even from Clemming. That was on the morning when he found the horse dead in the stable. The knacker who came for it said that he thought it had died of mere age; but he must have been wrong, for Ted put its age at just over twenty, and many a nag was active enough at far more years than that. However, the two bullocks he was fattening for March had to be prematurely sold, and the stout cob he bought on Norwich Hill left him with just one sovereign in the world.

A day or two later Harriet Harefield came round.

"I hoped I should find you in, Edward," she said. "I want you to buy me a really nice sampler. A niece who was staying with us at Christmas took a great liking to the one in the drawing-room, and as she's getting married I thought I'd give her one as my wedding present. Perhaps you'd better see the one at the vicarage and then I can show you just what I want."

He went with her to the vicarage and there she explained that the sampler should be silk, not wool, and that she'd like it to be dated earlier than 1800. He was also to see that it wasn't discoloured or worn. The frame didn't matter so much, though she'd like a nice frame, and the price should be about a pound.

When once more he said that he would do what he could, in some curious way it put a new life in him. He made up his mind that when the moment came he would face Clemming and the ring. That same week a catalogue came from an auctioneer at Tinkersham. On the following Wednesday there was a sale in the town itself, and among the articles listed were three samplers. Two were dated earlier than 1800.

Tinkersham was a good way off and he'd have to go by train, changing at Ouseland. That meant expense, and he hadn't the money. All he could sell was the one sow, and she was about to litter. Three nights later she did litter. Only two were alive; he found the others rolled on and dead beneath the straw, and there might have been others that she had eaten. Mort had always warned him that a sow should have little straw, and he had forgotten and bedded her down far too handsomely.

It seemed to him that Fate was against him, and somehow the symbol of his misfortunes was the bureau. Since he had bought it, nothing had gone right. That brought him back to Clemming, and the old maddening thoughts began a new circling in his brain. On the morning of the sale at Tinkersham, he at last faced something of the truth. Now he knew that he had never really intended to go to the sale. It was not because he lacked money, or that if he bought a sampler it might again not be the kind of thing that Miss Hattie really wanted. Things went far deeper than that.

From the first he had been a fool, and he told himself as much in a sudden surge of self-pity. Clemming had known that the first time he had clapped eyes on him. Miss Hattie had known it when she had seen those shelves of ornaments. Doubtless Uncle Mort had known it, though he had been too kind-hearted to blurt out the truth. And though his mind slurred quickly across that business of the bureau, it was still there. Dr. Soffe had been right. Pigs and horses and cattle —bureaus on four legs, he'd called them—that was what he should have stuck to. Things he knew about and trickery that he could counter. And it wasn't too late. Never again in his life would he so much as set eyes on an antique.

Dolly appeared at her usual time of half-past eight. It was a bitter morning, with more than a threat of snow in the air, and the ground was hard with frost.

"What're you doin today?" Dolly asked him. "Not goin out, are ye?" She laughed. "Might a-knowed that from the muck on them boots o' yours."

He said he'd be in.

"Then you won't want me to cook. Reckon I might do a bit o' tidyin.'"

He had hardly got to the stable when she was shouting to him from the door.

"Ted! Where are ye?"

He was scowling as he showed himself.

"What about that wood you was goin to split? There ain't a mite in the house. Better bring some for the copper."

He made his way to the woodshed, where he had sawn into lengths a bough that a gale had wrenched from an oak. The cold seemed even more bitter, and his breath came like a mist as he swung his arms against his ribs. He found the heavy ax and set the big chopping block in place. Then his eyes fell on the bureau.

He looked at it, staring as if it were something that he had never seen. Then with his brows knitted and his teeth clenched, he moved forward and swung the ax. It crashed and rebounded, for the stout mahogany held. He had a grin like the grin of a madman as he swung the ax till the wood at last splintered. Up to the very rafters the ax would go, and with both hands he would smash it down like a sledge. The top went endways and the small drawers were like matchwood as he panted and swung. Then the top drawer splintered, and he reversed the ax to catch it sideways. All at once he stopped.

He leaned panting on the ax and with the back of his hand wiped the sudden sweat from his forehead. Then he stared at the queer thing he saw. Like white pellets they fell, from above the drawer. He went forward and got on one knee. Hard roundish things they were, wrapped tightly in tissue paper. He rubbed the paper impatiently back with a thumbnail, then stared and held his breath. In his fingers was a golden sovereign!

A moment and a new kind of madness was on him as he gathered the wrapped sovereigns up and scattered the wood in the search for more. Three were still in the little secret drawer, and two others were wedged where the ax had struck them. He searched until he knew he had them all. He closed the shed door, put the ax against it for fear Dolly should come in, and unwrapped each sovereign at the window. Three times he counted them. There were exactly twenty-seven.

A minute or two later he was running up the stairs. At the scurry of him, Dolly looked out of the bedroom.

"Hain't got a minute to spare," he told her. "I got to go out."

He bustled her out of the room; he would have dressed more quickly if he had not been in such haste. He put on the brown suit he had had made by the travelling Ouseland tailor, then was hollering down the stairs:

"Dolly, give them best boots o' mine a bit of a brush up!"

He cleaned the celluloid collar, put on the best ready-made tie, and then realized that he had not washed. He was muttering impatiently as he rinsed hands and face in the little water left in the jug and tried to smarm down his mop of black hair at the wall mirror. Then he was trying on the bowler hat he had bought specially for Mort's funeral.

In the kitchen his fingers were all thumbs as he laced the best boots.

"Fare a rum thing to me, dashin off like this," Dolly told him. "There ain't no one dead, is there?"

He didn't bother to answer.

"And what about my wood? You hain't browt none in."

"There's plenty o' kindlin for the copper," he told her, bringing his best black overcoat from the stair cupboard. Then he was off.

She called after him, "When'll you be back?"

He shouted something she couldn't catch as he went half running along the path. At the road he looked at Mort's big silver watch. Just over two miles to go and less than half an hour in which to do it.

He took the short cut across Church Meadow. On the hard road again, he half walked, half ran; once he almost slipped up on the frosty surface. Old Eli Smith, the roadman, wrapped to the ears at a flint heap, failed to recognize him in his best clothes.

"Morning, Mas' Ted. In a rare hurry, ain't ye?" he said as Ted passed.

"Got to catch the nine-fifteen," Ted told him. Eli held his shovel and watched him till he was round the bend of the lane.

After he had gone a mile, Ted looked at the watch again and

knew that there was no need now for more than a brisk walk. As his long legs covered the ground, his hand went now and again to his pocket to feel the hardness of his purse. Then he would recall the scene in the woodshed, feel the purse again, and know that it was all true. Then a quick surge of some tremendous strength would come, his pace would unconsciously quicken, and his head would be high. Before that walk was ended, a new man had been born. It was not that the miseries of weeks had suddenly sloughed themselves, or that some great burden had fallen Christian-wise from his labouring back. They were only a part of the change, for what had settled on him was a kind of awe at the miracle that had happened, and with it came the realization that the slate had been wiped clean and that he could do with his life what he would. That was what he had dimly known in the woodshed when he had stood at the window with those sovereigns in his hand. In that moment he had been at the crossroads; then he had made his choice. Though he was dimly aware of it, his mind had been made up in that one second of time.

The Ted Burling of two years before had been fooled by self-confidence, checked by circumstance, and embittered by experience. The new man saw, if only vaguely, that from now on life must not be impatience, but watching and listening and a slow learning. Deep within him was a gratitude and a curious humility; and though he could remember Clemming with an even deeper hate, there were no foolish thoughts of a sneering confrontation.

"Thowt you'd bested me, didn't you, when you let me in for that bureau. But that's where you was wrong. I ain't tellin you how, 'cause you wouldn't believe me, but I got more out o' that bureau than you've ever made out o' one in your life."

That thought had come, but it had gone. What he now discovered as part of the patience was that silence had more strength than cheap words. Old Mort had often said that many a man with dung on his boots could buy up no end of the showy ones with their smart britches and polished leggings. That was the real strength—to keep the strength to yourself. Like those sovereigns in his pocket—and he patted the purse again. No one knew they were there, but *he* knew.

When his eye went along the line, he saw that the distant signal was down and that the crossing gates were being shut. But he had plenty of time to get his return ticket, and when the train came in he found a compartment to himself. It was a grand morning, with

the sun lighting the frozen bracken of Rudgham Heath and colour-
ing the twisted stems of the ancient pines, and as he sat by the window he could feel the warmth of the wintry sun against his cheek.
In his heart was a warmth too; and though his eyes might be on the
arable uplands as the train roared towards Ouseland, every now and
again he would smile to himself or nod his head.

The brakes ground and the train stopped at Ouseland station. He
crossed by the footbridge and sat on a seat to wait for his train.

"Mornin, Ted. Hain't sin you for a long time. What ha' ye bin
doin with yourself?"

It was Sam Wrightson.

"Weather hain't been none too good for gettin about," Ted told
him, and moved along the seat to make room.

But the Hareborough and Tinkersham train was coming from the
siding. They found a compartment to themselves and Sam lighted
his pipe.

"Don't smoke, do you, Ted?"

Ted said that his Uncle Mort had never smoked and so he himself had never acquired the habit.

"Maybe just as well," Sam said enigmatically. "You're like me—
goin to the sale, I reckon."

"Yes," Ted said.

"Thinkin o' buyin anything, was ye?"

"Might have a try for a sampler," Ted told him. "A customer o'
mine want one if I think it suit."

"Why don't you let me buy it for you?" Sam said. "I won't
charge ye nothin on the deal. That way you'll be sartin o' gettin it
the right price."

"Reckon I'll bid myself," Ted told him quietly. "Thank you all
the same, Mr. Wrightson."

Sam shot a look at him. It was on the tip of his tongue to say that
some people never learned. But "It's for you to know," was what
he said, and then he began talking about the sale. He knew the house
well, he went on; almost a mile from the station, so they'd have to
look pretty nippy when they got there.

"Fare a lot of good stuff by the catalogue," Ted said.

"Yes," remarked Sam complacently. "Reckon we owt to have a rare
good day."

"Be a lot o' dealers there?"

"Reckon there will. Them Lynn lot'll be there. Don't reckon Shadd will, though. A bit too far for him."

They went through the catalogue together, and Ted learned much. After Hareborough, Sam was minded to try more persuasion, for he had a liking for Ted. At the back of his mind for some time had been the idea of letting the lad do a bit of buying for him: working round villages or going to sales that he could not personally attend. But what could a man do when a young feller showed himself, as he would put it, so sheer pigheaded, and, if it came to that, so bloody ignorant?

But Sam missed his chance. A woman and a boy got into their compartment, and there was no more talk of the sale till Tinkersham was reached. Then they had to hurry to reach the house in time for a quick look round before the sale began. It was a large house in fine grounds, and many people were there. Ted made for the samplers and found them in the drawing room, stacked with some water-colour drawings against a wall. On his catalogue he marked the one he thought the best.

The bell rang and he made his way into the already crowded room. He was not far from the dealers, but somehow that morning they seemed inexplicably remote. He felt a quick hostility, perhaps, at the sight and sound of Clemming, and that was all, for something else caught his eye. What happened then was even more momentous than the discovery of the golden sovereigns, for that was the morning when he first set eyes on Jenny Shadd.

CHAPTER 4

Jenny Shadd

THERE was a slight stirring at the door behind him, and he turned to see the crowd giving way and a man coming through with a lady. It was the short black-bearded man who had bought the marquetry clock; he remembered his name—Mark Shadd, a Yarmouth dealer.

The two brushed him as they passed, and he saw that the lady was little more than a girl. Behind her she left a faint, elusive scent, but he thought no more of her, for his eyes were on the man. Sam had said that Shadd wasn't in the ring, and yet he seemed to have no grudge against the dealers, for he nodded or spoke quietly to this one and that as they made a way through. One or two lifted their hats to the young lady. When a dealer whom he didn't know brought forward a chair and placed it for her, she gave him a little smile of thanks, her teeth showing pearly white. Then she settled herself and looked at her catalogue. Shadd took up his stand with an elbow on the chair itself.

The sale began and Ted set himself to an earnest watching. When an article was held up he would look at his catalogue and try, almost always wrongly, to guess what it would fetch. He noticed, too, that Shadd never spoke, and that his sign to the auctioneer would be an almost imperceptible movement of the catalogue. Ted told himself that in future that must be his way of bidding too. And once Shadd had reached what seemed to be his predetermined limit, it was as if he took no interest in subsequent bids, though now and again he would look to see what person unknown to him had bought the lot, and sometimes he would make a mark in his catalogue.

The lady—he couldn't help thinking of her as that—would make marks in her catalogue too, but she didn't bid. Once she looked up at Shadd and smiled when he had bought a certain lot. Ted guessed then that she must be his daughter. There was little time now before the samplers came up, and though he had tried to school himself to quietness and patience, he could not help feeling a quick excitement. But when the attendant brought the first one round the trestled space, he didn't crane forward, as some people did, to look. That was a lesson he had learned: not to show an undue interest— and the knowledge gave him confidence.

"You've seen the sampler, ladies and gentlemen. How much for it? It's a very good specimen, indeed. What am I bid? Someone start me at a pound."

"Ten shillings," came a woman's voice, but whose voice he didn't know, for his eyes were on the auctioneer. Then he waved his catalogue. There was a thrill as the auctioneer picked up the bid.

"Twelve and six."

"Fifteen shillings."

Now he spotted the bidder: that young lady he had taken for Shadd's daughter.

He moved his catalogue again, this time less blatantly.

"Seventeen and six."

Somehow he caught the young lady's eye, but she seemed to be frowning and shaking her head. He bid again; then she was bidding a pound. That was Miss Hattie's limit—or had it been? The catalogue moved again, and this time he didn't look at her.

"Twenty-five shillings!"

There had been something almost spiteful in that quick bid of hers. Ted shook his head.

"Any more at twenty-five shillings? Any more?

The hammer fell.

"Sold to—"

"Miss Shadd."

"Oh, yes," the auctioneer said, and gave a smile and a little bow. "Sold to Miss Shadd at twenty-five shillings."

It was she who bought the other two samplers: one for fifteen shillings and the third for only five. But the first had been the one he had wanted. Not that he had wanted it that badly—though there was something a trifle depressing in the thought that he'd have to tell Miss Hattie it had fetched more than she'd been prepared to give. It was then that his ear caught the conversation of the two women behind whom he stood. Country women they seemed, and both were middle-aged.

"Fare a rare price, don't it, for old things like that?"

"That it do. I got an old bit o' needlework, or whatever they call it, myself. Used to be my grandmother's. Rare old it is, I know that. People all funny-dressed and so on. Wonder what that'd fetch."

'You ought to put it in some time."

"Don't know," she said. "Sometimes them things don't fare to make nothin."

There was no break for lunch, but the two women left before long and he followed them. Outside the grounds they stood talking for a minute or two and then parted company. He hurried after the one who had claimed to own a sampler. Maybe, as he'd been thinking, he wouldn't go home empty-handed after all.

"Excuse me, ma'am, but might I have a word with you?"

She stopped and had a look at him.

"I just happed to hear you talkin to that friend o' yours at the auction about havin an old sampler. I was biddin for one and didn't get it. Burling's my name. Ted Burling."

"Won't do no harm to have a look," she said; "that is, if I can find it. I don't fare to remember just where 'tis exactly."

At the flint-walled school she turned into a lane and after a few yards came to her cottage.

"You're one o' them dealers, I reckon."

"Not exactly, ma'am," he said. "I shall be one day, though. What I come to the auction for was to buy one o' them samplers for a lady what asked me to."

"Well, come in," she said. "Sit ye down there and I'll have a see."

She climbed the narrow stairs that led up from the tiny living room where he sat. Long years afterwards he could remember that room as if it were still beneath his eye. Above him he could hear her in the bedroom, faintly muttering to herself while she searched. Then at last she came down.

"Here 'tis," she said. "I remember now puttin it in that drawer under them things. Don't know if it'll be any good to ye."

It was just over two feet wide and perhaps fifteen inches deep. His spirits sank as he saw it, for it was nothing like the sampler he had come to buy. It was, in fact, like nothing he had ever seen.

"Tain't no good to ye?" She had seen the disappointment on his face.

He didn't speak for a moment, trying to remember half-forgotten things, and the very intricacy of the pattern was beginning to absorb him. The men and women were dressed in costumes he had seen in his history book at school. All the canvas, as he thought it, was smothered in the design of an ancient house and gardens with people walking about and all the little spaces filled with flowers and animals.

"I reckon it's pretty old," he said.

"Belonged to my grandmother. Where she got it from I don't know, though I reckon it was from where she used to be afore she was married."

"It look real nice in a way," he said. "Make a rare nice picture if it was framed."

"You'll buy it, then?"

"Depend what you ask," he said.

She frowned in thought.

"Owt to be wuth what them others fetched."

He shook a reflective head.

"Don't know as 'tis. If I give ye a sovereign, I reckon I'll be out o' pocket."

"It owt to be wuth that," she said, but he was still shaking his head as he gave her the money. Then she found paper and he rolled it up to avoid creasing it. Years afterwards he would shudder as he thought of those few moments before he had made the deal. There in his hands he had been holding the finest piece of Caroline stump embroidery he was ever to see in his life; yet only by chance had he bought it, and when he left the cottage he had told himself that there was a wasted pound.

At the end of the lane he found himself in the main road again, near the big market square, but he drew back to an opening between two decrepit buildings and looked again at his purchase. He knew that it was old, and something told him that it might be valuable. Or was it like the bureau that looked old and wasn't old at all? He didn't know, and he wondered if Miss Hattie would know, or Dr. Soffe.

As he came back to the main road and turned left, he came face to face with the young lady who had bought the samplers. He checked his stride and he must have gaped, if only because they had nearly collided.

"Oh!" she said, and, "Wasn't it you who were bidding for the sampler?"

"Yes, miss. It was me."

There was a directness about her that was like Miss Hattie's, but she was much younger—maybe not as old as himself.

"You're a dealer, are you?"

"No, miss, but I shall be one day."

"Oh!" she said again. "Then you were buying the sampler for yourself."

"Well, not exactly, miss. A lady I know said she wanted one, so I reckoned I'd try and buy one for her. I've often bowt things at auctions: chairs and so on. Don't reckon, though, as I know much about it—not as yet."

"I should have had that sampler for fifteen shillings," she told him. "It isn't worth more. And you went on bidding just because you didn't know?"

"Reckon that was it, miss." The sheepish smile gave a strange attractiveness to his face, making the gawkishness no longer something with which to be pettishly annoyed.

"What's your name?" she said.

"Burling, miss. Edward Burling, though most people call me Ted. Wickenden is where I live."

She gave a little smile and a nod and was moving on.

"Oh, miss!"

"Yes?" she said, and turned.

"Would you do somethin for me, miss? It's somethin here what I've just bowt."

He was telling her about it as he unrolled the paper, and how, now that he had bought it, he didn't really know what it was worth.

"I reckon you'd know, miss. If you wouldn't mind tellin me."

Her eyes narrowed and her lips went together when she looked at it. Then the eyes went to his face, and he suddenly felt awkward and nervous as she looked at him.

"You want to sell it?"

"All depend," he said.

"You mean, on what you'd be offered for it?"

"Well," he shuffled again, "yes and no, miss."

"Miss Shadd is my name," she told him, and then felt angry some-how at her own abruptness.

"Yes, Miss Shadd."

At that moment she too was at the crossroads. He had already blurted out the price he'd given, and she could have bought that stump-work for two pounds or less. Samplers of the best kind and needlework pictures were the things she'd decided to collect, and in her hands was something of which she could never have dreamed. Its real value she didn't know, but she did know what her father had given for a much smaller piece, and how excited, for him, he had been at the purchase.

"Will you let me show it to my father?" she said. "He's a big dealer and he'll treat you fair, if you really want to sell."

"That's real good of you, miss—Miss Shadd. I was at a sale when he bowt that marquetry clock."

They turned back and she asked him about himself as they walked. Though he was almost a head taller and could have lifted her almost with a hand, he still felt somewhat awkward, but he told her how he'd come to the outskirts of dealing, and about Clemming and the ring. Because she made no comment, he guessed that she too was taking him for a fool.

"Wait here, Mr. Burling," she said when they were almost at the house again. "I'll see if I can fetch my father."

It was some time before she came back with Mark Shadd. Shadd gave him a sharp look.

"My daughter tell me you've got somethin you might sell," he said. "Mind if I have a look?"

From his face Ted gathered nothing. The embroidery was rolled up again and he gave merely a casual nod.

"What do you want for it?"

Ted mumbled that he'd leave that to him. Shadd grunted.

"Might be wuth five pound—and it mightn't."

Standing at her father's elbow, she gave a quick shake of the head and a frown.

"Don't reckon I'll take it," Ted said.

"You let Mr. Shadd take it home," she said, suddenly holding her father's arm. "Then he'll write to you and tell you the most he can give."

"Reckon that'll be all right," Ted said. "Ted Burling, Wickenden, Harford—that'll find me. Everyone know me round there."

"You'll hear from me, then, Mr. Burling," Shadd said, and to Ted's surprise held out his hand. "Better let me give you a receipt, though."

"Thankee, sir, but I don't reckon it matter," Ted told him. "I reckon I can trust you, same as you trust me."

Shadd gave him another look. Jenny gave him a quick smile as the two moved off.

After a minute or two Ted went back to the sale room, but his thoughts kept wandering from the lots that were sold. Now and again he would peer furtively across to where she sat, but her eyes were never his way. In the new and scarcely felt intimacy that had come with that warning smile and frown, there was something that was curiously frightening, if only for the searchingness of the light that it threw upon himself. Twice that morning he had boasted that soon he would be a regular dealer, yet in the clear light of that morning's ignorance he saw the boast as something futile and sham. Still, she had known the value of his purchase because she was Mark Shadd's daughter and, likely as not, had been brought up in the trade. She had never worked as he had, and risked good money and been fooled; the very failures, as he recalled them, would have in themselves the promise of success.

The sale was still on when he left, for his homeward train was at half-past four. Somehow he felt an aversion to Wrightson's company and he hid in the lavatory until the dealer had taken his seat. When the train at last reached Ouseland, he waited till the dealer was at the footbridge before he made a move.

On most nights he would be asleep as soon as his head had warmed the pillow, but that night he was long awake. It was of Jenny Shadd that he thought: the black hair curling over her cheek, the cheeks themselves flushed with the walk in the cold air, but most of all of the quick frown and shake of the head that had made her all at once a part of himself. Against that the miracle of the bureau had a curious unimportance, except that it was something that might give him the chance to see her again. Now, with money in his pocket, he could go to sales and look Clemming and the dealers in the face, for in doing business with a man like Shadd he felt as if he had behind him a man of far more importance than Clemming and his kind. But as he lay waiting for sleep, he frowned uneasily when he thought of Mark Shadd, even if he still could almost feel the shake of the dealer's hand; for against the importance, the natural confidence, and even the very reticences of Shadd he knew what he had known that morning as he had hurried towards the train—the ignorance and even the insignificance of himself.

Thought had not been wholly fallow while he slept, and he woke with a sudden resolve. Books of his own, that was what he needed: books that would tell him about things like that bit of needlework that he had bought. Then, as he sat at his breakfast, he wriggled on the hard seat as he thought of his ignorance again, and how he'd have been almost glad to get back the pound. And now Shadd might be willing to give even more than the five he had offered.

He was still mooning when Dolly arrived. That morning he split the oak logs, chopped a heap of kindling, and shamefacedly put aside what sound wood was left from the ruined bureau. In the afternoon, still fired by his resolve, he drove the eight miles to Ouseland, where he had seen a bookshop. There were two, as it turned out, and neither had what he wanted. The owners doubted if he'd get it nearer than Norwich. So on Friday he went there by train. The morning had brought a disappointment, for there had been no letter from Yarmouth; and when he came to the first shop where enquiries had led him, it looked so big and important that it took a mustering of courage before he walked in.

"Any particular titles have you in mind, sir?" the assistant asked.

"Just books about antiques," Ted told him, not gathering what he meant.

He followed the man through alleys of shelves packed with books.

"Here we are, sir. This is only a selection, of course, but we could get anything else you wanted inside a week."

Their number was bewildering and the prices made him gape; but he was showing no ignorance before the bookseller, though it meant keeping his thoughts to himself and acting on his own ideas. When he left the shop with no less than seven books in the stoutly corded parcel, he was appalled at the money he had spent. There were two illustrated books on furniture, and the two on china had coloured plates. There was one on earthenware and another on clocks.

"What about needlework—samplers and things?" Ted had asked.

The man had riffled through the indexes of various books.

"Here you are, sir: *Modern Antique Collecting*. Two whole chapters on it. Absolutely up-to-date, sir. Only been out two or three months."

Ted had bought it, and then, with his parcel under his long arm, he had looked for antique shops. When he found one, he would stand staring into the window, trying to memorize the kinds of things the dealers sold. Now he knew that his books were not half enough. All the dealers had pictures; most had silver, copper, and glass objects; and some had things to which he couldn't even give a name. Maybe he'd find them in those books, he told himself; and though the parcel seemed heavier and heavier beneath his arms, it somehow gave assurance. More than that: though he was only dimly aware of it, those books were like the first rung of a ladder and the feel of an oak stave under the foot.

That afternoon the homeward train was far too slow and the walk from Harford far too long. It was dark before he reached the house. By the light of the lantern he saw to the sow, racked down the cob for the night, and then hurried back to the kitchen. Even while he was eating the hot meal that Dolly had left in the oven, his eyes were devouring the books. As soon as the meal was over, he made brown paper covers for them. He told himself that he'd have to build a special shelf.

After the fire was stoked, he settled to a reading of the chapters on needlework. What was meant by stump-work he couldn't precisely gather, but there were two drawings of stump-work pictures that were almost the image of the one he'd bought, and they were described as becoming increasingly rare. In one of the furniture books was a picture of three chairs described as Chippendale, and he at once recognized the left-hand one as the very spit of those chairs in the parlour for which Clemming had offered a pound. *Riband-backed* was what they were called, and it took him time to work out for himself that *riband* must have something to do with ribbon. It was long after his usual time when at last he went up to bed.

Though a thin snow had fallen during the night, he was out in the lane after breakfast, watching for Henry Drew, the postman, in his pony cart.

"Only one for you, Ted," Henry called as he neared.

The one was enough, for it bore the Yarmouth postmark. He went into the kitchen and opened it there. When he unfolded the letter the paper was stout and felt good in his fingers, and there was a handsome heading. *M. Shadd & Son* was what it said, and he frowned slightly at the word *Son*. They seemed to deal in everything, according to the heading, but he had only a hazy notion of what it meant by *Valuations Made*. Then he noticed the pin and the cheque which it fastened to the back. He looked at it and couldn't believe his eyes, and then all at once he was on his feet, eyes still staring and mouth still agape.

Mark Shadd had begun the hard way, even if his feet from the first had been in the antique trade. His father had kept a general junk shop, and Mark had left school early to lend a useful hand. Soon he was learning from his father that there was a special value in things that were occasionally picked up, and these would be set aside—under the counter, as they put it nowadays—for the inspection of some favoured and knowledgeable customer. Such things young Mark began to know as antiques, and the extra profit attached to them turned his thoughts to a specialization in that branch of the trade.

Two years after his father's death—he was then twenty-five—he transferred to the shop he was always to have. But it was a modest beginning, and only an enormous aptitude and a flair could have brought him to where he stood in five years' time. Then he married into a good bit of money. His son Gordon was born, and, four years later, a daughter, Jenny. Three years later he lost his wife, and he was never to think of marrying again.

Gordon grew up to be a good-tempered, likeable boy. From his mother, who had been the daughter of an importer of furniture, he may have inherited a passion for working in wood. Mark had sent him to the best school in the town; but schooling was never in Gordon's line, and at fifteen Mark had apprenticed him to a first-class firm of cabinetmakers. When his time was up he took over the repairing side of the business, which by now had so increased that he had three men with him in the carpenter's shop.

Gordon was one of those people who are always at hand and always to be relied upon; and that was how his father came to regard him—a part of the business, as it were, a business that would ultimately be his own. Sometimes, of course, Mark felt a deeper stirring, but with Jenny it was vastly different. She was the apple of Mark's eye, if only because when she was young he had been all her world. She too went to the best school in the town, and her father was something of a bore with his talk of her to his cronies and his boasting of her small triumphs.

At sixteen she left school and took charge of the house, for Mark's old housekeeper had died and they now employed two maids. Then she began insinuating herself into the business of the shop. Mark was delighted, and found her a help with the books. Occasionally he would take her with him to sales, and soon the dealers grew to know her. Before long, with Mark as her teacher, she had a fair smattering of dealer's knowledge. Gordon had made a hobby of collecting fine inlaid ornamental boxes and caddies, and Jenny had a fancy for needlework. Soon the dealers got to know of it, and occasionally one would bring a sampler or picture when he called. That was why there had been no opposition bidding at that Tinkersham sale; and Mark was a formidable enemy, as the ring had learned to their cost.

"You've got a bargain here, my girl," was what he told her as they went back to the auction room. "Reckon he'll take five pound when he come to think it over."

"But, Dad, I don't want it. I want you to sell it."

"Maybe you're wise. Allust take a good profit and then reinvest."

There was some talk about it on the way back that night, and the next day he took it to London; not to a big dealer but to Maple's with whom he often placed articles of fine quality. He asked a stiff price, took much less, but was satisfied nevertheless. Then he did some more business in town, and it was late in the evening before he got back. His meal had been waiting for him, and Jenny brought it in at once.

"What did it make?" she wanted to know.

"Five pound or so," Mark told her.

"Only five pounds!"

Then she knew that he was having one of his jokes.

"Come on, Dad; tell me the truth. What did it make?"

"A fairish bit," Mark said, eyes still twinkling. "What about havin a guess."

She frowned.

"Twenty pounds."

"Forty-five guineas," he told her. "Sixty I asked, but it weren't so bad."

"Dad, you didn't!" She flew across and kissed him.

"None o' that," he told her. "You're like all the women—allust thinkin o' money."

"Dad, that's not true," she told him indignantly, and then knew again that he was laughing.

While he had his meal she told him what had happened during the day, and there was a reprimand. In that rambling house—two houses that Mark had knocked into one when he had bought them—there were only, besides the servants' quarters, the combined living room and office and what Jenny called the drawing room. The rest, except for the minimum of bedrooms, was used for showrooms. Mark, like many other dealers, would now and again buy a piece which specially took his fancy. Some day, as he knew, it would be worth a big sum of money, so into the drawing room it would go as an insurance for hard times. He liked fine things, and was secretly proud of that room where Jenny would always have a fire on a cold Sunday; but sooner or later Mark Shadd the dealer would get the better of Mark Shadd the collector, and away would go the piecrust table or the twin-domed cabinet or the fine old Sheffield candlesticks.

"But you can't just help yourself, Jin," he would say in self-defence. "Don't do to disappoint a good customer. And where'd I be if I kept all the pick myself, same as you fare to want me to?"

Those were his stock arguments, and she would retort that there was no need to let a customer know that there *was* a drawing room. And she'd been specially fond of a cabinet that he'd sold.

"Now, now, Jin," he told her placatingly, as he pushed back his plate. "You leave me alone just once in a while. And what about that bit o' stump-work? You parted with that, didn't you?"

"And that remind me," he went on before she could speak. "You'd better bank that cheque what I give you. What'd you think o' payin that young feller what you bowt it on?"

"I don't know," she said. "I've been thinking."

"Bid him fi' pun ten. He'll take it."

"But, Dad, that wouldn't be fair."

"Fair? Why not? He give only a pound for it, didn't he?"

"Well, it's not that," she said, and to tell the truth she hardly knew what it was. She argued that he was just beginning and that a bit of extra money might make a difference.

"You had to make a start yourself, Dad."

"Not by gettin best part o' five-pound profit out o' one deal, I didn't."

"Besides, he looked so—well, so honest, and it doesn't seem right."

Mark was speechless.

"And besides, he might pick up other things and give us the first offer."

Mark had to shrug his shoulders.

"It's your money, my girl, and if I know you, you'll do as you like when all's said and done." Then he was giving a queer, peering sort of look. " 'Tweren't because that young feller was sort o' good-lookin, was it?"

"You know that's nonsense," she told him indignantly. "Besides, he wasn't good-looking—not really."

The next day she added Mark's cheque to her small banking account and wrote the letter herself. It took her a long time to fix the amount of the cheque she should send. Ten pounds she decided on at first, and then ten pounds as against forty-seven seemed woefully little. When at last she made it out, it was for twenty.

Mark found out. He gave a nod and a wink to the bank manager, for, as both knew, it was Shadd who was behind the account. But he said never a word to Jenny.

CHAPTER 5

Desired Haven

THAT night Ted Burling sat down to compose a letter. He had taken the cheque to Dr. Soffe, who had given him cash for it, and he had bought some special notepaper and envelopes at the post office. But first he read the Yarmouth letter yet again:

DEAR MR. BURLING,

We can offer you twenty pounds for the needlework specimen which you offered us at Tinkersham, and trust this will meet with your satisfaction. Cheque for the amount is attached herewith.

If there is anything whatever of quality which you may have in stock or acquire at any time, we should be glad if you would give us a first offer. Hoping to do business with you in the future,

We are,

Yours faithfully,

M. SHADD & SON

He couldn't help giving another nod of satisfaction before he settled to his own letter. It didn't take long, for he had thought out every word. It wouldn't do, for instance, to let it be thought that he'd been wholly ignorant about things. Because he was thinking of offering Mort's two chairs to Shadd, he had another look at the furniture book and wrote down something in pencil before he dipped his pen in the ink.

DEAR MR. SHADD,

I am quite satisfied with the money and here is the receipt for the stump-work. I have also two chairs which belonged to my uncle who died and he had them from his father. They are Chippendale riband-back and in very good order.

Hoping to hear from you in due course,

Yours respectfully,

E. BURLING

That letter, moulded though it might be on the other, seemed to him to be good; his only worry was that Mark Shadd himself might never see it, but the J. Shadd of the cheque, whom he took for the son.

Three days later another letter reached him. Would Mr. Burling crate the two chairs and send them to the above address by passenger train. Ted crated them. Each crate was a work of art and each chair was swathed in twisted oat straw. The offer that came back was thirty pounds, and the letter was almost apologetic. The chairs were of excellent quality, it said, but Mr. Burling must appreciate the fact that such chairs were really valuable only in sets. At one time there had probably been eight of the chairs, and if Mr. Burling should know the whereabouts of any of the other six—in the possession of other relatives, for instance—Shadd & Son would be keenly interested.

That called for another letter, the composition of which was a much more lengthy and personal affair; but he was enormously disappointed when the answer came, for it merely acknowledged the receipt of his own. By then, however, he had another problem on his mind. The difficulty had arisen when he had taken that second cheque to Dr. Soffe, a cheque that this time bore the name of Mark Shadd.

"Business looking up?" the doctor had asked in that gruff way of his. He had a habit of worming down to the root of things. The tall bearded figure—you can see his very spit in Luke Filde's picture: the slightly hooked nose, the beetling eyebrows, and all the authoritative presence that could hush the noise of village urchins and send their fingers to the peaks of their caps when they saw his trap—all this was too heavily in the scale against Ted's new assumption of reticence. Before he knew it, he was telling Soffe about the bureau. But not about that mad smashing with the ax. The bureau had got a bit banged up, was what he said, and he'd found the money in a secret drawer. Soffe had been so astounded that all he had given was a grunt. Then he did ask whose bureau it had been.

"Don't know, sir," Ted said. "All I know is, I bowt it."

"You bought a bureau."

"Yes, sir."

"What about the sovereigns? Did you buy them too?"

"That was just luck, sir," Ted said, and grinned.

"Good luck for you and bad for someone else."

"Reckon so, sir."

Soffe grunted again. He had a liking for young Burling, and in his next remark there lay a conscious moral purpose.

"It might have been some old woman's, you know. Sold because she needed the money it'd fetch."

The grin left Ted's face. Now he was getting an idea of what the doctor was driving at.

"You mean, sir, I owt to give the money back?"

"Look," said Soffe, and took him by the arm. "I'm a doctor and a busy man, not a parson. You're old enough to think things out for yourself, aren't you?"

"Reckon so, sir," Ted said glumly, and then was being shown out of the door.

When he came to think things out, he couldn't see the other side at which the doctor had hinted. A bureau had been offered for sale and he'd bought it; it was his own money he'd risked. People who sold things should know what they were selling. It was like that piece of stump-work. The woman who'd sold it hadn't known what it was, and was he now to go to her and give her more money because it had turned out to be valuable? It didn't make sense. No one could do business that way. Not that he couldn't see something in the doctor's instancing of some old widow, it might be, who wanted the money; though, if it came to that, he'd wanted the money pretty badly himself. But in spite of himself the thing began to gnaw like an aching tooth, and one night he made up his mind. The next morning, as if resolve should not weaken, he put on his best suit and drove to Diss. A clerk in the auctioneer's office soon identified the bureau. It had been sent in with one or two other things by Colonel Pryne. He seemed surprised that his caller didn't know the name. Ted was told, not quite accurately, that the colonel owned a big insurance company, among other things, and lived at Ladeham Hall. Ted said he had come through Ladeham that morning.

"Then you must have passed it," the clerk said. "It'll be on your right, just along the Kenninghall Road. You'll see a lodge and a drive."

But Ted had no intention whatever of going to Ladeham Hall, for Colonel Pryne certainly could not be in need of money. Why he turned the cob into the drive he hardly knew; perhaps it was because the lodge gate was open; but the farther he drove, the more his own temerity alarmed him. So did the sight of Ladeham Hall.

He drove round the back way to the stables. A groom was washing a handsome wagonette in the paved yard, and it was he who tied Ted's horse to a ring in the wall and pointed to the back door. There was no need to knock, for it was open, and a man wearing a green baize apron was coming out. He looked like a gardener.

"You lookin for someone?" the man said.

"I want to see Colonel Pryne," Ted told him. "It's about a bureau."

The man went back into the kitchen, and Ted heard voices. A maid in pink uniform and white collar and cuffs had a quick look, and it was she at last who told the caller to come in. Ted was to see a Mr. Denny, who proved to be a butler, and it was not till five minutes later that Ted was following him along a passage and out to a spacious hall. He tapped at a door, opened it, and drew back to usher Ted in.

"Mr. Burling, sir."

The room was lofty and seemed crowded with furniture. Two people were sitting by the fire: a young lady who was either sewing or embroidering, and an elderly gentleman who had been reading the newspaper. Both looked round at his entry and the elderly gentleman got up. He was short and erect, and had a military-looking white moustache.

"Mr. Burling, you want to see me about a bureau, I understand."

Ted held his hat firmly against his chest and began to explain.

"But how extraordinary!" the colonel said. "A secret drawer, you say, and sovereigns."

"That's right, sir. Twenty-seven of 'em."

"How extraordinary!" he said again. "What do you think, Marion?"

"It is," she said. "But what has Mr. Burling come for? Doesn't he think he was entitled to the sovereigns?"

"Well, that's how I sorta felt, miss," Ted told her. "Fare to me now as if I bowt that bureau, not the sovereigns."

"That's a very strange thing for you to say, Mr. Burling," the colonel said. "Give me your hat. Come to the fire and take a seat. I gather that you're an antique dealer."

"Only in a small way, sir."

"I see. This is my daughter-in-law, by the way. But to get back to the bureau. I suppose you've never heard Harcourt mention, Marion, where his mother bought it?"

"I've no idea," she said. "Or perhaps I do have the vaguest idea: she bought it in a little shop at Norwich."

The bell cord was pulled for Denny. He remembered the bureau being bought, and that was some eight years ago. The late madame had intended it, if the colonel remembered, for the housekeeper's room, and when the alterations hadn't been made, it had stood on the back landing.

"And hideous it was," the lady named Marion said. As soon as the butler had gone, she gave a little laugh.

"I was wondering something," she told the colonel. "Do you happen to have any of those sovereigns on you, Mr. Burling?"

"Most on 'em, ma'am," said Ted, pulling a hessian bag from his trouser pocket. The sovereigns were emptied on the colonel's newspaper. She examined one; then the colonel tumbled to the idea and began to help.

"That seems conclusive," he said to Ted. "The latest of those sovereigns is 1874, so it certainly looks as if they must have been in the bureau when my late wife bought it."

Ted stared.

"Then what do I have to do now, sir?"

"Do?" Marion laughed. "You don't have to do anything, Mr. Burling, except put them back in your pocket."

"You mean, ma'am, that I'm sort of entitled to 'em?"

"I think so," the colonel said. "I see no means of finding the original owner."

Ted gave a sheepish sort of smile.

"Thank you very much then, sir, and I think I'll be movin along."

Marion held out her hand. "Goodbye, Mr. Burling. I think it was perfectly splendid of you, coming here as you did."

The colonel took his arm and led him across to the French window.

"Excuse me, sir," Ted said, "but my hoss is round at the back."

"You can go this way," the colonel said. "Along the front here, and round to the right. Goodbye, Mr. Burling. You've given me a very considerable pleasure."

He watched till Ted had disappeared round the side of the house. Marion joined him at the window.

"Extraordinary!" he said. "A likable young fellow. But what was he? Just a fool or a really honest man?"

"If he was a fool, he was a nice fool," she said. "I think he was just being honest. He looked honest."

It took more courage than the visit to Ladeham Hall had required for Ted to tell Soffe what had happened. But when he did relate that morning's happenings, he was disappointed because the old doctor paid him no compliments as Colonel Pryne had done.

"What're you doing with all this money?" he asked.

"Holdin on to it, sir," Ted said, and that seemed the end of Soffe's interest.

It was all very well to be the possessor of over seventy pounds, but a living had to be made, and it was to that that he was giving a great deal of thought. Even by the time the small acreage had been sown, he had not made up his mind. Nothing was more certain than the aversion he felt to the old way of life, but that was little help in the finding of a new. Then it came to him that he should specialize in the smaller auctions which the ring found too trivial to attend, and profit by the special knowledge he felt he had acquired from his books. But auctions were rare in the summer, unless one had the means and time to travel over half the county; and that was why, when a catalogue came, he decided, after all, to go to a sale at Windley.

He went by train and walked the mile to the country house where the sale was being held. As he strolled round the various rooms, he suddenly came face to face with Mark Shadd and his daughter. Ted lifted his hat.

"Mornin, Mr. Shadd. And mornin to you, miss."

"Good morning, Mr. Burling," she said, and smiled.

"Buyin anything, young man?" Mark asked him.

"Don't know, sir," Ted said. "Hain't had a chance to look round yet."

"Bowt anything lately?"

"Not as'd be any good to you," Ted told him. "Soon as I do, I'll let you know."

The two moved on. Ted went aimlessly through a room or two

and then found himself going back the way they had gone; but he didn't see them again till the sale had started. Shadd bought several lots but Ted made no bid himself, for book knowledge seemed a scanty reliance now that he had brought it to the ultimate test. The sale went on, with no break for lunch, and as one o'clock neared he was ravenously hungry. He made his way out to the marquee where refreshments were sold and bought two sausage rolls. As he came out of the crowded tent, he collided with Clemming.

"Why don't you look where you're bloody well goin!"

"Why don't you look yourself?" Ted told him. "There's somethin I've been wantin to tell you," he said. "Thowt you was clever about that bureau, didn't you. Well, I made my money on't, and I can prove it."

Clemming gave a little disbelieving laugh and moved on. Ted caught him up and held his arm. Clemming whipped angrily round.

"Somethin else I'll tell you," Ted said. "Some day I'll be as big a man as you are; then you can look out for yourself."

"You?" Clemming said. "A junk dealer, that's what you are, and that's what you allust will be."

Ted's face flared. His fist clenched. Then he dropped his hand and turned away. It was not because of a sudden realization that good intentions had gone awry, but because of something he had seen as he made the step forward towards Clemming.

He turned back. Clemming had gone, and she was now at the main gate. In a moment he was hurrying after her.

"Miss Shadd!"

She turned, and for some reason or other her face flushed.

"Oh, it's you, Mr. Burling."

"I just wanted to explain about me and Clemming. Reckon you thought it was a bit common, him and me standin there like we was."

"I didn't know what you were doing," she said.

They were walking towards the town. She and her father had brought food with them, she said, and now she had come out of the stuffy room in search of fresh air. He told her about Clemming and the bureau.

"What you must do is to know as much as he does," she said. "Then you needn't be afraid of him or the ring."

"I'm not afraid o' no one," he told her belligerently.

"And you ought to have a shop of your own. A little shop, of course, to begin with."

"The very thing I bin thinkin myself," he said.

They were at the twin towers and the abbey ruins, and she was saying that she'd have to hurry back or her father would wonder what on earth had happened. In spite of that there seemed little quickening of pace, and he had time to tell her about the sovereigns, Ladeham Hall, and Colonel Pryne.

"So you see, Miss Shadd, I reckon I've got enough to take a little shop if only I could find one." He moistened his lips. "You don't reckon there'd be a little place at Yarmouth what I could hire cheap?"

"But why should you think of Yarmouth?"

He didn't know. He couldn't even say that he didn't know. Perhaps she said what she did because she had a pity for his floundering.

"I'm sure you're going to do well once you've got a shop. And I think it was wonderful to do what you did about that money in the bureau."

"You really think so, miss?"

The beam went from his face as she said it was the honest thing to do. By then they were at the house again.

"You stay here while I go on," she told him just short of the door.

"And shall I be seein you at any more sales?"

"I don't know," she said. "But I'm nearly always in the shop—at home."

He glanced at her quickly, but her eyes were the other way. When she did look at him, it was his eyes that turned.

"Father'd be glad to show you the shop," she said. "He wouldn't expect you to buy anything, either."

A smile, a curiously hesitant one for her, and she was gone. He watched till she was through the door, and from the doleful shake of his head, the morning, even the last half-hour, might have been nothing but disaster.

The unwitting agent of Fate, or Providence, was to be a worm-eaten tread of a stairway that wound up from Daniel Wrightson's Cambridge antique shop to the crowded storerooms above. Dan's heel went through the tread and he broke his leg. That had been in February.

Ted might have known nothing but for the death of Bina Carman, widow of Mr. Trench's head gardener. Bina's only child, a married daughter, came from London, chose a few things for herself, and decided to put the rest up to auction. Ted put into the auction what he now knew was largely an accumulation of rubbish. It was a small affair that didn't even require the presence of the auctioneer; that of his head clerk was sufficient. Not that it wasn't something of an occasion for Wickenden.

Sam Wrightson was the only dealer there.

"Reckon I shan't be seein much on you soon, Ted," he said. "Not that I see much on ye now."

His father, he said, would do little more than hobble about for the rest of his days, therefore he himself was moving to Cambridge to take charge of things there. Ted's heart gave a sudden leap, and he did not dare to look at Sam as he put the question.

"You'll be givin up the shop, then."

"Sooner I get shut on 't, the better," Sam said. "My missus is at Cambridge now, and I'm sorta hanging on, like."

"Cost a bit for rent and rates, that place o' yours."

"Thirty-five pound all told," Sam said. "That ain't bad, considerin."

"I wouldn't mind it myself, at that," Ted said.

Sam shot him a look. There were times when he liked Ted Burling and there were times when Ted could rile him almost beyond bearing. Though Sam prided himself on his shrewdness and his ability to read men like a book, he would puzzle his wits over Ted and wonder if the artlessness and simplicity were not a subtle show for the concealing of cunning. That he had unsuspected sides to him he knew, if only from that attack on Clemming.

"You don't think o' settin up for yourself?" he said.

"I might," Ted said. "You have to make a start some time."

In the matter of renting Sam's shop, he became something of a sheep in the hands of an expert shearer. There was no question of buying goodwill, though Sam did make the business out to be more than a good living. What he concealed was the fact that not only was a goodly part of that living made through the ring but the Ouseland shop had been a subsidiary of the far more profitable concern at Cambridge. So before Ted was allowed to approach the owner, Sam had arranged to be paid a full half-year's rent due at Michaelmas, and for Ted to take over some of the stock.

It was the very day after Bina Carman's auction that Ted went to Ouseland to inspect the property more closely. As he knew, the shop itself wasn't bad, with its large display window and a central situation in the main street of the little town. More than once he'd driven into the yard and even put his nag in the roomy stable. There was no garden, but the cobbled yard was enormous and there were two good sheds. However, when he looked at the shop in the light of a possible ownership, there was hardly a thing that pleased him; it was the same with the living rooms. Sarah Wrightson, fat and asthmatical, was one of those souls who find a homeliness, if not in dirt, at least in dinginess.

"Cost a bit to have it all smartened up," Ted said.

"That's where you're wrong," Sam told him. "Don't do to have a place like this too smart. People come in them smart places and they don't feel at home. They think you know too much. What you've got to do is to make 'em think they know more'n you. Did you ever run across old Fred Makers what used to have that shop back o' the Angel at Bury? One of the warmest men in the trade, old Fred was. And how'd he make his money? Wouldn't hardly ever allow anyone to do no dustin. Used to leave things sorta layin handy when anyone come in. Might be a fake o' course, but they'd think they'd got some rare old treasure. When they asked him about it, he'd swear blind he didn't know. Might be a bit o' Derby or Chelsea, but he didn't know." Sam chuckled. "You see? Don't do to know too much. Them people what bought a fake couldn't come back to Fred's shop and say, 'That bit o' Chelsea you sold me ain't Chelsea at all,' because Fred had told 'em he didn't know."

The cream had already been skimmed from Sam's stock, and he expected to sell Ted the rest; but Ted had nothing like the price he asked.

"Reckon I'll sorta start in a small way," he told Sam. "Pick up things as I go along."

Sam, balked of a bargain, said he'd have to find a tenant who'd be more amenable, but the bluff was wasted. Had Ted had the money, it might have worked; but there's no argument that can miraculously lengthen a man's purse. Ted finally did buy two oak-cased grandfathers and some oddments, but the two men parted none the best of friends.

It was mid-July when Ted signed the agreement with the landlord. Outside decoration was all the landlord would do, so Ted employed a decorator to strip walls and repaper them, and to whitewash ceilings. The change of name was his own affair too.

"No need to go to all that expense," the decorator said. "What about burnin off just the *Wrightson* and puttin *Burling, late Wrightson?* That 'on't cost you a lot."

It was like selling a young mother a secondhand pram for a first baby. Once the agreement was signed, there was hardly a brick on the place that Ted did not regard with an almost besotted affection. Out Wrightson's name had to come, then, and the decorator at last made a drawing that was approved—a handsome *E. Burling* in green and gold on a brown background, flanked at each side by the word *Antiques*.

Then he fumed and fretted because the landlord was slow in doing his share of the painting of the front. It was not, in fact, till late September that the whole job at last was done. Meanwhile something else had happened: Ted had treated himself to a day at Yarmouth.

CHAPTER 6

End of Beginning

BUT to call that trip a treat, at least in the stages of preparation, was a woeful misnomer. There was the letter which he sat down to write, but which progressed little beyond its opening of *Dear Miss Shadd*. There was the first and almost alarming thought of taking the journey—one of the cheap day trips that ran from Harford all summer and early autumn for less than half a crown. People usually went after harvest, but it was towards the end of July when Ted screwed his courage to the sticking point. Then, too, he was worried about what he should wear. He had begun to study the clothes of those whom he regarded as gentry, and at Ouseland he bought linen fronts and collars to replace his celluloid ones. Though he thought his brown suit good enough, it looked a bit untidy when he dressed on the morning of his trip, and he brushed it more than once before he was satisfied with its appearance.

He was gone before Dolly arrived. When he reached the station, he had time to spare for the eight-fifteen from Harford. Though the train filled rapidly at Norwich, and his compartment was packed, he gave his boots a quick wipe and adjusted the handkerchief in his breast pocket before leaving the carriage at Yarmouth. It was his first visit to the town, and everything was strange and new to him. Following the holiday-makers through the narrow rows to the front of the town, he had his first view of the sea.

The sun was already warm, and he sat for a time on the dry sand, with his back to the sea-wall, watching the bustle of the crowded beach; but all the while his thoughts were elsewhere, and at last he asked the whereabouts of Shadd's shop. When he found it, he surveyed it from a distance across the street. A fine big shop it looked, its vast window a flash and twinkle of colour; and somehow that daunted him anew. But he crossed the street and began a sauntering past, a kind of spying out of the land. Then the shop door opened and a lady came out with Mark Shadd at her heels. So close was he that he heard Mark's thanks and the good-morning. It was too late to turn back then, for Mark had recognized him.

"Mornin, young man. What're you doin in Yarmouth?" Mark said.

"Thowt I'd treat myself to a day off."

"Come in," Mark told him. "And how are things round your way?"

"None so bad," Ted said. "As a matter of fact, Mr. Shadd, I've got a little shop of my own now. Used to be Sam Wrightson's, at Ouseland. Nothin like this, o' course."

"I know it," Shadd said. "Bin in it more'n once." Then he was shaking his head. "I'd hardly a-thowt there'd a-bin a livin in a place like that."

"I reckon I can make a go on't," Ted told him. "You have to make a start some time, y'know, Mr. Shadd."

"True enough, boy; true enough. And how're you off for stock?"

"Can't grumble," Ted said. "I bin out a good few days round where people know me, and picked up a tidy lot. One or two nice little things I've got, Mr. Shadd. Nothin like what you have here, o' course."

"Many a day I've had on the road in my time," Mark said with a reminiscent nod. "I often think I wouldn't mind it now, only things fare to come to me stead o' me havin to go to them. Upstairs was the place I liked to get. That's where you find the real stuff. Reckon there's plenty on it still."

He showed Ted round the room, with a wave of the hand here or a pointing finger there. "Nice bit o' Queen Anne, that. Bowt it cheap," he would say. "Not a bad table. Pity about that veneer. . . . Now that's a nice piece. Right too. Sort o' thing I owt to take upstairs. . . ."

Ted trusted himself to no more than a grunt or nod. Then Mark picked up a porcelain figure, a small figure of two children with flowers in their hands and a lamb lying at their feet.

"What d'ye make o' this?"

Ted moistened his lips as he took it.

"Don't reckon I know, Mr. Shadd—'less it's Chelsea."

"That's what I thowt at fust," Mark said. "But do you know what I now reckon that is? Longton Hall. See how that blue go sort of streaky?"

He called to his foreman to see to the shop and waved Ted up the stairs. Room after room was packed with stock. Tea services and dinner services were laid out on tables, and even the walls were so closely hung that a fly could scarcely settle between the pictures, prints, miniatures, and plates. Ted was in a sweat of apprehension for which there was little need, for there was nothing Mark loved more than to do the talking while he showed off his stock. He did ask one question, however.

"It best me, Mr. Shadd, how you can tell what's new wood. You reckon this bit's new?"

"It's somethin that come to you," Mark said. "You don't have to look. You know. But you want to ask my boy about that. There ain't a better man in England, though I say it, to do with wood."

There were steps on the stairs, and Ted held his breath. But the steps were too heavy. The foreman mentioned a name, and Mark went out to speak to him. It was the foreman who came back.

"Mornin, sir. The guvnor say I'm to take you to see Mr. Gordon."

A covered passageway led from the top storey above the narrow yard to a building beyond. It was wide, and it had a trap door and a pulley block and chains. Ted guessed it was for drawing heavy pieces up from a cart or wagon below.

"That's right, sir," the foreman said. "The guvnor have everything up-to-date. If a piece want repairin, up here it come, and through to where we're goin now."

He opened a door and Ted stepped into the long workshop, with its tang of newly sawn wood. Timber was stacked everywhere, and what looked like old oak rafters and beams lay along the walls. Piled at the end were ruins of chests and tables and chairs. Brass handles and scutcheons hung above one bench like onions on a string, and a glue pot was bubbling on the low fire. Two elderly men were working at carpenters' benches, and an apprentice was on his knees at a job of polishing. Across the room, by the large window, a man was fitting a sideboard drawer. It was for him that the foreman was making.

"The guvnor said I was to bring this gentleman along, Mas' Gordon. He's interested in wood."

It was Ted's first sight of Gordon Shadd, and he liked him from that first moment. It was not because he was in shirt sleeves and wearing a carpenter's apron: it was the friendly way the eyes screwed up as he smiled and held out his hand.

"Burling's my name," Ted said. "Edward Burling. I don't know if you remember, but I sent you a couple of Chippendale chairs."

"I remember. Two very nice chairs. I suppose you never had the luck to run across any of the others?"

He was taller and slimmer than his father, and a dark moustache gave a thinness to his face; but the long fingers that fidgeted with the handle of the screw driver while he was talking were curiously pliant and sinewy. His English was more cultured than Mark's, though every now and again there would be a Norfolk word or phrase.

"I'm just settin up in business for myself," Ted was telling him. "Only in a small way, though."

"You know the old saying," Gordon said, and laughed. "Don't do to gnaw off more'n you can champ."

"I know. No one can't tell me how much I got to learn. Reckon I got to start right at the bottom o' the ladder."

In the next half-hour he learned more than any book had told him. Gordon and the foreman seemed to have time on their hands, and they showed him pieces not yet repaired and others ready for the showrooms. There was one piece of William and Mary walnut that Mark had had for years, perhaps as a kind of monitory finger. That fake, Gordon said, had been made by what he called the famous Sanders brothers of Ipswich, then in their heyday of fakes and reproductions. The foreman cut in with the story of a certain court cupboard, inlaid with mother-of-pearl, and of how the brothers had bought the original from a certain big hall and had sold copies that had deceived the very elect.

"That's right," Gordon said. "The customer'd buy the original, and when it came home it'd be the original far as he could tell. Mind you, Mr. Burling, they choose their customers, Americans, mostly. They're beginning to buy a lot o' stuff over here now."

Re-veneering was being done in the workshop, and marquetry or new carving was being made to match the old in a piece to be repaired. There were pegs for oak work, treated with acid to give a look of age, and jars of beeswax and turpentine for a natural polish.

"What we do isn't faking," Gordon pointed out. "We try to make a damaged piece look like it was before. Nine times out of ten it's pointed out to the customer."

"And then very often they can't tell it," the foreman said. He brought a glass from the pocket of his baize apron. "Have a look at that, Mr. Burling. See if you can tell which is new and which is old."

Ted owned that he was bested. Yet there didn't seem so many wear marks on that strip there, he said.

"You're right," Gordon went on. "You can hammer and dent, but you'll never get the real wear marks. And you can make wormholes, but the wood still won't sound holler when you tap it like this."

There was wood that Gordon showed him—pear, apple, yew, walnut, elm, poplar, holly—lying in corners and being matured. Some of it had been there for twenty years.

"That remind me," he remarked, when at last they came back to the door. "Did you say Wickenden was where you came from, Mr. Burling?"

When Ted said that he'd be there for another month or two before he made the move to Ouseland, Gordon told him that he might be traveling that way soon because an old barn had been pulled down at Kenninghall and he'd as good as bought the timber.

Before leaving, Ted turned to the foreman.

"That glass," he said. "Do you reckon I can buy one like it?"

Gordon said that there was at least one spare one of his own that he didn't want, and that he wouldn't take a penny of payment.

"I'm more'n obliged to you, Mr. Shadd," Ted said. "Real good of you, it's been."

"Next time you're this way, come and see us again," Gordon told him.

Ted followed the foreman down the stairs and out to the yard.

"That'll be your way, sir," the foreman said. "Just round that corner and you're on the front again."

It was only when Ted found himself once more on the front that he felt the quick depression. Every now and again it had been on his tongue to bring in a certain name, and then something would happen to take the chance away. Now the last chance had gone; and suddenly the glow and excitement had gone too, as he had the knowledge of a wasted day. For an hour he walked aimlessly along the front, or watched the paddlers, the photographers, the children on donkeys, and a black-faced man in a gaudy suit who was play-ing a banjo. Suddenly he felt hungry and found a restaurant where he had a meal. Then he wandered aimlessly about again. It was strange that his footsteps should somehow lead him near Shadd's shop. For a long time he stood there, but there was no sign of Jenny Shadd.

He walked along the pier to the far end. People were going into what seemed to be a concert of some sort; for a while he thought of going in himself, then changed his mind. Half-past three found him back at a seat again, almost longing for the time when his train was due to go.

Mark was helping himself to the vegetables that the maid was holding.

"Whuh, who do you think come into the shop this mornin, Jin?" he suddenly said. "That young Burling that sold you that stump-work."

Jenny's cheeks flushed. For the life of her, there was nothing she could say.

"He tell me he've taken that little place of Sam Wrightson's," Mark was telling Gordon. "Reckon he'll hatta scrap pretty hard for a livin there, won't he?"

"He seemed to me the sort who'd get on," Gordon said. "He don't know a lot, but he's like all of us. We all had to make a start. I hope he do get on. A nice young chap he seemed."

She had felt a quick warmth, as if from some maternal instinct, and she simply had to speak.

"Whatever was he doing in Yarmouth, Gordon?"

"He come up for the day," Mark said. "One o' them cheap excur-sions, I reckon. And that remind me . . ."

It was after three o'clock that afternoon when Jenny looked for a moment into the shop and said that she remembered that she had to go out. She made her way along the front. Had she been a minute later, she must have seen Ted as he left the pier. She turned at the far end and began walking back towards Gorleston. Soon after four o'clock she saw him. He was getting up from a seat, standing inde-cisively, as if wondering which way to go. She moved quickly on.

"Miss Shadd!"

"Why, Mr. Burling! Whoever would have thought to see *you*!"

All that day the sun had shone from a cloudless sky, but for him it was only now shining. But it was his own sun, a sun that had emerged from the clouds of misery that had obscured his day. He suddenly felt a tremendous courage.

"I went to the shop this mornin, Miss Shadd, and see your father and your brother; but it was you I really wanted to see."

"Me, Mr. Burling!"

"Yes. I wanted to tell you about a shop I've took at Ouseland. I'm settin up for myself."

They walked and walked, and it was well after five when they neared the shop again. His train left at six. While he sat on a platform seat and waited, he was like a man in a daze. In the morning he had not even known her name. He thought of that last moment when they had stood in the quiet back street.

"When shall I see you again . . . Jenny?" "I don't know," she had said. "But there is a sale at Dereham. I think it's next week." "You'll be there?" "Perhaps." They smiled gently at each other, and then the imminence of separation clouded his face. "Reckon I'll have to be goin. Goodbye then . . . Jenny." "Goodbye, Ted." They looked at each other again. In that moment they were conscious no longer of the street and the houses and even the sounds about them, and there was no one but themselves.

It was he that turned away, and when he looked back she was already out of sight.

That was the queer, remote, spasmodic courtship of Ted Burling. He went to Dereham and he went to a sale at Hunstanton; the latter was half a day's journey. The inevitable moment came when he went once more to Yarmouth. Jenny was waiting for him, and they went to the living room by the back way. Each word had been rehearsed, and yet when he heard Mark's steps his heart began to beat with such violence that he wondered if he were ill.

Mark's eyes opened when he saw the two standing there. As they lingered on Ted, Jenny spoke.

"You know Ted, Father. He wants to speak to you."

Mark's mouth was agape with the *Ted* and the suddenness of it all.

"Jenny and I want to get married, Mr. Shadd, and I thowt I'd speak to you about it so's you shouldn't think there was anything underhand."

"Married!" He glared at Ted from under his bushy eyebrows as if he couldn't believe his ears. The look switched to Jenny.

"You're in on this too?"

"Yes," she said. "I'm going to marry Ted."

"You are?" said Mark with heavy irony. Then a fury blazed in his face. "You get out o' here, my girl. I'll talk to this young man."

"I'm not going, Father," she told him. "Whatever you want to say to Ted you can say in front of me."

"Then get out o' here, both on ye—and you, Jin, you come back when you've more sense. Marryin! How's he goin to keep you? Don't reckon he can more'n half keep himself."

"I can work," Ted told him stoutly. "I'm young, Mr. Shadd, and I'm not afraid o' work. I'd work my fingers to the bone for Jenny."

"We'll get on," Jenny said. "We've got it all worked out."

"You have, have ye?" Mark told her. "Then you can unwork it. I'm not havin it, I tell ye. And you, young man, get out o' here quick, and don't let me see you hangin round here again."

"If that's the way you're going to speak, Father—"

But Mark had gone. Jenny's face was crimson. Ted was licking his lips and shaking a dubious head.

"What're we going to do now, Jenny?"

"What we said we'd do," she told him. "You go now, Ted, and I'll meet you where we arranged. Then we'll see."

Gordon was on his father's side until she talked him round somewhat. But Gordon had a trick of getting at the real heart of things.

"You're really sure about all this, Jin? You think that much of Ted Burling?"

"He's fine and—and good. Any woman'd be proud to marry Ted."

Gordon saw Mark and refused to be brushed aside. Mark might bluster and storm, but Gordon held his ground. However, it wasn't a good report that he brought to Jenny.

"He's set in his mind, Jin. Pure selfishness, that's what it is. You've been here all this time and you're a sort of a fixture. That's why he doesn't want you to go."

Then his eyes were screwing up in that odd way of his.

"I don't reckon it'd be so bad, Jin, if you and Ted were to live here. I think he'd find Ted a job, all right. If you like I'll give him a hint and see how he feels."

"No," she said. "Ted's got his shop and his own business, and that's where we're going to live."

"Have you seen the shop?"

Ted had told her all about it, she said. He thought that over and had an idea.

"Look, Jin. I've got to go to Kenninghall sooner or later, so I'll have a look round and talk things over with Ted. Only you'll have to make up your mind just what you want to do. It's a pretty big step you're taking, you know, and you don't want to make any mistake."

For the next day or two, Jenny almost crept about the house when Mark was in, hoping that he would change his mind. Mark, however, kept himself aloof, and at meals Gordon became a go-between through whom the father and the daughter would say the few words that had to be said. The house had become unbearable when suddenly, on the day before Gordon saw Ted, Mark weakened.

"Let's talk this business over sorta sensible," he told Jenny. "If you're still set on marryin this here young Burling, what about waitin a year or two and seein how he get on? A year or two ain't much to wait. I was best part o' thirty afore I married your mother."

Jenny tried to be reasonable.

"But don't you see, Dad? That was different. You had this shop and you'd got on. Ted's only making a start, and how can he get on so well if he's all alone? That's why I want to get married now."

It was not long before Mark lost his temper again.

"I know you're twenty-one," he told her, "only no one ain't goin to tell me what the law is. And if you talk like that, let me tell you somethin, my girl. Don't come whinin to me for help, 'cause you'll never get it."

"We don't want your help," Jenny flared at him. "Ted and I are going to get on without anyone's help."

On the October day before she left, Mark must have known she was leaving, for she was packing all her belongings and the entire house was upset. The next morning, when she went to find him for a last reconciliatory word, the foreman said he'd gone out. Jenny was crying when she went back to Gordon.

"Don't you fret about Father," Gordon told her. "He's just being pigheaded. He'll come around. You'll see he will."

"But I don't want to make trouble for you."

"I'm my own master," he told her. "You won't make trouble for me. I've stood up to him before, and I reckon I will again."

He took Jenny and the luggage to the station in a hired cab. When Ted met them at Ouseland, the metal of the cob's harness shone like silver and the cart gleamed. Ted had found a man to see to the horse while he was away, and the man's wife had cleaned and polished in the shop and house. Nevertheless, he did not drive straight into the yard.

"What do you think on't, Jenny?" he asked proudly. "Don't look too bad, do it?"

Jenny said that it looked like a fine little shop, and ever so smart; but when she came into the house she gave a little gasp of surprise. Mort's old furniture had been polished and polished, and it looked grand in the spotless parlour. In the kitchen the very saucepans were bright, and the copper pots and pans were like gold. As for the stove, it had been black-leaded and polished till it looked better than new. When Jenny at last came downstairs, she said blushingly that the bedroom was even nicer than the one she'd had at home.

They had to hurry to reach the Register Office in time. Gordon acted as one witness, the register found the other, and everything was over so quickly that Ted could scarcely believe it. Somehow he had thought that he'd feel different, but he didn't, unless it was that he was still nervous. Then the registrar gave Jenny her marriage lines, shook hands with the couple, and wished them well. Gordon kissed Jenny, and Ted would have kissed her too, if they'd been alone.

The woman was at the house when they got back and she had a cold meal ready. But there wasn't much time to catch the London train. It was Gordon who had insisted that there should be a real honeymoon. Jenny would have been happy at Ouseland, beginning a new life in her own new home with Ted.

"I don't like you spending all that money," she told Gordon. "Look at all the expense you've been to already."

"You let me alone, Jin," he had told her with a grin. " 'Tisn't often a sister of mine gets married. And I've got nothing to spend my money on, have I?"

The couple planned to go to a quiet hotel in Victoria Street where Mark always put up when he was in town. What Gordon had had in mind was a hope that Mark might now accept the accomplished fact and make the pretence of a business trip to town some kind of excuse for a reconciliation with Jenny and Ted.

He found them a compartment to themselves in the front of the train. The guard's whistle blew; but Jenny was so nervous and Ted looked so solemn and glum, that Gordon gave a Norfolk farewell to bring something of a smile.

"Well, you'll let us know how ye git on together."

"Yes. We'll write," Jenny said as the train began to move. Gordon's arm came through the open window as he threw an envelope on Jenny's lap.

"Just a little something, Jenny. . . . Goodbye! . . . Good luck!"

They waved till the train was round the bend. Jenny opened the envelope, and at first there seemed to be nothing in it. But there was —a cheque for twenty pounds! Suddenly Jenny's lip puckered, and tears would have come if Ted had not held her close. Then, at the very first stop, two people got in, and they had to sit primly. By the time they drew out of Cambridge, the compartment was full.

It was dark before the train arrived. Though Ted might not have shown it, he was almost frightened by the bustle and noise of the gloomy station. But Jenny was as assured as if she'd been to London a hundred times instead of only twice with Mark. It was she who found a porter; and in less than no time they and the luggage were in a cab and the horse was clattering up the incline towards the street. It seemed ages before they reached the hotel. A porter took their luggage, and at the hotel desk, where the clerk pushed a book under Ted's nose and handed him a pen, Jenny had to whisper in Ted's ear before he knew what to write.

The porter took them up to their room, and when he had gone, there they were—alone. Jenny blushed as her eyes met his.

"Are you happy, Jenny?"

"Oh, Ted!"

He was holding her tight and saying how nice she had looked.

"You looked nice too, Ted."

"Ah!" said Ted, and let out a breath. "You're too good for me, Jenny. I was almost afraid to look at ye when we were in that Register Office. I wish I could do somethin for you, Jenny—just to show."

It was about eight o'clock when he woke, which was more than two hours after his usual time. A faint light was seeping through the blinds, and as he moved he woke Jenny too. A shyness made her snuggle close to him. His arm went round her. After a time she stirred.

"Ted?"

"Yes, Jenny?"

"Ted, you know that day at home when you were sitting on the seat and I came by and we saw each other? The day you first told me about the shop?"

She felt the nod of his head on her hair.

"Well, I did know you'd been in the shop. I was looking for you, just the same as you were for me."

"Were you now, Jenny?" he said, and smiled to himself.

A minute or two went by.

"Jenny?"

"Yes, Ted?"

"Jenny, what was it made you . . . well, sorta think anything about me first?"

She took quite a time to think it out.

"I expect it just happened, Ted. The same as you falling in love with me."

"Yes," he said, but still wasn't satisfied. "But what was it really, Jenny?"

She smiled.

"I don't know, Ted—unless it was that you looked as if you wanted someone to really look after you."

He thought that out and nodded to himself.

"Reckon I did," he said. "And now here's me who's goin to look after you. Long as we live, Jenny, I'm allust goin to look after you."

"Reckon we'll both look after each other," she said, and Ted nodded again.

PART II

Winding Road

CHAPTER 7

Gordon Mortimer

MOST people would have thought it a queer honeymoon, though it was true that Jenny and Ted did see something of the sights. On their first morning they went into Westminster Abbey, then walked all the way along the Strand and Fleet Street and up Ludgate Hill to St. Paul's. Ted had his first ride on a horse bus when they went back to the hotel, and he was all agog to see all there was to see. That afternoon they went to the Zoo.

"What're we goin to do today, Jenny?" he asked the next morning.

"Gordon said we ought to go to the museums," she said. "That's where he always goes when he comes to London."

Ted had not thought of a museum, though he did recall a thing or two from his books. In any event, it was Jenny whom he wanted to please. So they went to the National Gallery, where he had his first sight of fine paintings. That is not to say that he at once despised the daub or two that hung in the parlor, pictures of which Mort had been proud because they were "painted by hand." It took years before he knew a fine picture when he saw it, and he never did acquire an inward assurance that what he liked was really good. That morning, however, he saw paintings that somehow filled him with awe and others—mostly of the Dutch School—whose craftsmanship held him amazed as he pointed out details to Jenny. There was more than much that he did not begin to understand, but the impact had been tremendous. He was unusually quiet as he walked back to the hotel.

That afternoon they went to the Victoria and Albert Museum, and the scanty daylight was all too short.

"What're we doin today, Jenny?" he asked again the next morn-

ing, and she knew by the look on his face what it would be. So they
went to the Museum again, and they were so engrossed that the
morning had gone and they were too late for lunch before they
were aware of it. They found a little restaurant in Kensington and
had their meal there.

That was on Saturday, and on Monday they were back again. Ted
could hardly tear himself from furniture and porcelain, and at every
turn he saw something which he had passed over before.

"Wish I'd brought them books o' mine," he told Jenny; but he
was learning far more than he had ever found in books. Now he
knew Sheraton when he saw it, and Heppelwhite, but it was the
walnut that held him most entranced. All his life he was to have a
love of walnut for the sheer beauty of the wood, and also for a
kind of homeliness that he could never explain but always felt. Jenny
loved everything too. It was she who spoke to an attendant who told
her about the porcelain in the British Museum. There they spent almost a day, but it was the Victoria and Albert to which they returned. Jenny could hardly budge him from the miniatures and
the silver.

Before the week ended, there was a subtle difference in Ted. He
had never been awkward in himself and now he was acquiring a
sober dignity. Perhaps some of it was owing to acclimatization: in
a London which had at first bewildered him he now felt almost as
much at home as he would in Norwich streets. There was the fact,
too, that he was a married man, and of course there was Jenny.

He was proud of Jenny. He loved the play of her nimble fingers
as she did her hair at the bedroom mirror. When the clerk or a
waiter called her *Mrs. Burling*, it never ceased to surprise him; yet
Jenny took it as a matter of course, or as if she'd been married for
years. Above all he admired the deft way she twisted her skirts in
her hand and crossed a street when the traffic eased; but there,
everything about Jenny was wonderful to Ted.

At last the time came to leave. They had written to the woman
who had been left in charge and had told her the time of the train.
On the day before they left, their thoughts turned to home; London
had somehow lost something of its glamour. Their last morning was
spent in the National Gallery and in the afternoon they had a look
at Buckingham Palace; but in their minds was an almost autumnal
quiet and sadness for what had almost gone, and a strange, unspoken

joy, even an urgency, for what lay ahead. When in the train the suburbs of the city were left behind and there was open country again, Ted's eyes were everywhere. Jenny was leaning against him and his arm was round her.

"Reckon it won't be so bad to get home," he suddenly said.

"It'll be lovely," Jenny answered, and he felt her move. "Oh, Ted, I do hope I'll be a good wife to you."

"The best in the world. That's what you are, Jenny. The best in the world."

It took a day or two to settle down. Jenny had to discover all the things she had in the house, and there were new things to be bought for the kitchen. Then, too, Ted had forgotten about curtains, and they had to buy a carpet for the parlour. She was a good housewife. Ted had never known such meals, and now he would be having butchers' meat instead of the endless pork that Dolly had dished up. Then there were his clothes, which she overhauled, and the new things she made him buy, including a dark suit for the shop, across the waistcoat of which he wore Mort's old silver albert. He wasn't even hurt when she rearranged furniture. The pictures had to go and four of her samplers were hung in the parlour instead, and five others in the bedroom. And Ted was told of Mark's maddening habit of parting with things in his own house.

"You needn't worry about me, Jenny," Ted told her, seeing in that despoilment of a home something of a profanation.

The house was Jenny's and Ted did nothing but approve. As for the shop and the business, Jenny was master there too, even if she did contrive to make it seem that it had been he who had first thought of improvements. It was she who suggested the regular advertisement in the *Ouseland and Hareborough Times,* and Ted gave a prideful nod of approval when he saw it first.

> ANTIQUES. Best prices given for old
> furniture, china, clocks, pictures, etc.
> E. Burling, Main Street, Ouseland.

There was a thrill in seeing his name in print, and on the receipt bills and trade cards. And there were a dozen other things she taught him out of the knowledge she had gained from Mark and Gordon. She would never have changed his Norfolk: that was a part of him and something that made him the almost worshipped thing he was, but she did manage to bring a necessary refinement. When a customer came into the shop, Ted would say, "Mornin, ma'am," and, after he had waited a respectful moment: "Is there anything in which you're specially interested, or would you just like to look round?"

Customers were not customers like those of other shops, Jenny said. In other shops people came solely to buy, but they did not always do so in antique shops. There they were often gentry, or people who liked old things, who would often know far more than Ted himself. It was from the customer that a dealer got most of his knowledge, Mark had often told her; and soon Ted acquired the habit of calling attention to one object or another.

"I wonder what you make of this, sir?" he might say, and then he would listen and learn; and even in those days it was the customer who always had to be right.

Then there was the matter of receipts. Ted had been surprised when Jenny had said that to give a mere receipt for, say, a chest of drawers was not enough. A dealer existed on his integrity, even if some, like Clemming, might flourish apparently by sharp practice. That was why a receipt had to be properly made out.

One bow-front chest of drawers, untouched condition and original handles .... £3 10s. 0d.

Or:

One bow-front chest, restored at side. Seven original handles.

Nothing was worse, she said, than for a customer to be dissatisfied or to discover repairs where he'd expected an original piece. Even if candour should spoil an occasional sale, it was the same honesty that in the long run more than paid. As for fakes or reproductions, Mark had hated the very words.

"You're good to me, Ted," Jenny told him one day when she'd been explaining something or other.

"Me!" he said. "Good to *you*, Jenny!"

"Yes, Ted, you are. You never get angry when I say you're wrong about something."

"Whuh, Jenny," he said, and his face was abeam. "Nothin would ever make me riled with you. Why, it don't bear thinkin on. Besides, I wouldn't have knowed nothin if it hadn't been for you."

In the matter of money they had enough, and not much more.

His working capital was about eighty pounds, much of which had come from the sale of the sow and litter and what he had no longer wanted of Mort's old oddments and effects. Jenny's money was not to count. That was one thing on which he insisted with an obstinacy that even her arguments failed to budge. With his own money he opened a banking account. Two pounds a week was what they decided they must make. Now that there was no garden, Jenny would have vegetables to buy, and it was necessary to have hay and oats for the cob and straw for its bedding. Then there were three pounds a year for a little meadow just across from Castle Hill, let alone the main expense of rent and rates, yet in those first weeks the matter of money was not of dominating importance. Then all at once it became something on which their whole lives hinged; that was towards the middle of December.

As one came up the hill from the Bell, there was a greengrocer's shop kept by a Mrs. Martin and her daughter. Then came the Burling shop, and next to it a small general store kept by Ernie Crowe, who was a man of well over fifty and a figure of importance in local politics. His numerous family had grown up except for a boy who was still at school. One of his boys helped in the shop, and the eldest was the local representative of the county paper, the *Eastern Daily Press*. Mrs. Crowe was a stout, even-tempered woman whose life concern was her family, and she was to prove a good neighbour. Of the Martins, Jenny saw comparatively little because a high wall separated their property from the Burling yard, but the wall was low along the boundary on the Crowe side and the two women were soon acquainted. If Ted happened to be out, Bella Crowe would often drop in for a chat.

It was on such a morning that she came round to find Jenny looking pale and queasy. Jenny said that something must have disagreed with her.

"You sure it ain't something else, my dear?"

Jenny didn't understand. Had Gordon married, she might have known more, but her life in the Yarmouth house and shop had brought no enlightenment about sex. It was to be salutary, if just the least bit frightening, to discover that about one vital thing she had been as ignorant as Ted had been about his business.

"Didn't your mother tell you nothing?" Bella was asking. Jenny said she didn't remember her mother, and at once Bella Crowe assumed the role. The symptoms were probed, and there seemed no doubt that Jenny was going to have a baby. Jenny asked about a doctor.

"You don't want no doctor—not yet," Bella told her. "Soon as this here sickness go, you'll feel right as rain. I ought to know after nine of my own."

There was no end of advice, and Bella said she'd drop in more frequently.

It was in bed that night that Jenny gave the news to Ted. Though he had been worried about her pallor and sickness, the news came as an enormous surprise. A dim sense of paternity stirred, and something of pride, and with them an anxiety that he couldn't dismiss. But Jenny reassured him, and herself, and quoted Bella Crowe.

Ted asked: "What'll it be, Jenny? A girl or a boy?"

Jenny said she'd like a boy like Ted and Ted said he wanted a girl who'd be like Jenny. They held each other close, in the dark, like two children who have come to the end of a forest path and see before them an unknown valley.

"It'll fare kinda funny bein a father," Ted said. "Reckon we ought to tell Gordon. Reckon that'll make a difference with your father, too."

He knew that Jenny, though she said little, was always worrying about Mark, and though he would never take the matter up, there was something that hurt him in the embittered way in which she spoke. But it was for Ted that she felt the hurt and the resentment: that Mark, always so understanding in spite of his touchiness of temper, should have been so suddenly blind as not to see the honesty, the goodness, and all that was so fine about Ted.

"Don't matter what Mrs. Crowe say, I reckon you ought to see Dr. Soffe," Ted said.

"But he lives at Larford."

"Reckon he'll come," Ted said, and made up his mind to drive round that way. The first thing in the morning he wrote to Gordon. Early the following week Gordon came to spend a day. Ted met him at the station and they walked to the shop.

"How's Jin?" Gordon asked as soon as they'd shaken hands.

Ted said Jin was fine, but his face was as solemn as if she were already in the pangs of childbirth. Then he asked after Mark and how he had taken the news.

"He didn't say much," Gordon said, "but I reckon he'll come round."

"He didn't send no message?"

"No," Gordon said, "but I had an idea he wanted to."

"You don't think you could sorta pretend somethin to Jenny?"

Gordon said he'd see what he could do. When he got to the house he was surprised, after the gloominess of Ted, to find Jenny just as she'd always been, with a blush or two, perhaps, and, as he thought, a plumpness that showed that married life was not so bad after all.

It had been a morning of frost that turned towards midday into a cold rain. Gordon spent much time with Ted in the shop, and after the meal they talked in the parlour, with Ted's ear alert for the bell. Jenny had never seemed more happy. It was not, as they thought, because Gordon had hinted that Mark might soon be coming round, but because of a blend of innumerable things that she felt but could never have explained: Gordon himself and their childhood, a pride in Ted and the miracle of an imagined child, the cosiness of the little room, and the drowsy warmth of the fire.

"So you think you're getting along all right so far," Gordon was saying.

Ted said that though capital was less, there was more stock; but they weren't well known as yet, and winter wasn't too good a time.

Gordon at twenty-five was a shrewd businessman. Though isolated, as it were, in that repair shop, he had more than a working knowledge of the general trade, and when sales overlapped, he would often be a buyer. Mark had come to rely on his judgment, and though rarely praising him to his face, he would boast of him privately, as he had done that morning to Ted in the Yarmouth shop.

Ted learned much that afternoon, in the intimacy of the cosy room. Those were the days of comparatively few collectors, but the few had discrimination. They were the days when lustre and cottage Staffordshire were beneath the notice of dealers like Mark Shadd; when Georgian gun-metal candlesticks were dear to buy at five shillings and even a now rare Windsor chair with cabriole legs and turned stretchers would have been out of place in a first-class shop. They were the days when a sovereign was money and a thousand pounds meant a fabulous pound a week for life.

"There's no money, not really, in that stuff you have, you know, Ted," Gordon said. "I know half a crown here and five bob there mount up in the course of a week, but that isn't how the money's made. You have to get into the better-class stuff. You turn over half a dozen things, perhaps, and make yourself two quid profit. Suppose you bought one thing. You'd even given as much as fifteen quid for it, and you parted with it for only seventeen. There's the same two quid for only one deal, and with a better class of customer. If you buy for forty quid, you'd get five-pound profit, or ten. By your way of reckoning, that's more than a fortnight's work."

Jenny said that that was all very well but that Ted daren't risk forty pounds, or anything like it, on his own judgment.

"He will do," Gordon said. "It's just a question of experience. He'll have to cast his net wider. Those books are good as they go, but he'll want one on prints and another on miniatures. You know how to date silver, Jenny. That's something you can teach him."

"What about the ring?" Ted said. "Even suppose I knew as much as them, do you reckon they'd let me buy?"

"When you know as much as they do, you're as good as they are," Gordon said. "You see whatever it is and fix a price to show your profit. If they don't go up to it, it's yours. If they go beyond— well, that's their business. And sooner or later they'll get to know you same as they know Mark Shadd. Once they've tried to let you in for something and burnt their own fingers, they'll start to think twice before they try again."

"That's all very well," Jenny said, "but what about now? Ted's going to learn, but you can't do that in a day."

"Go out and look for the stuff," Gordon told her. "There's no end of it there. Cottages and farms and even old barns. The same as that advertisement you've put in the paper. People may write about something they've got; if they bring it in, ask them if they've got anything else."

That brought them to the ethics of buying, and Gordon agreed that it was a tricky business. What one had to do was to sum up the seller and let that seller ask a price. With some sellers, to bid a fair price would only excite cupidity and a deal would be lost, but when a seller got his own price there'd be no cause for complaint.

"Mind you," Gordon said, "it'll never do to look as though you're anxious to buy. Don't exactly crib anything, because that might put the seller's back up, but hang back a bit before you do buy, as though you think the price a bit too high. Then you give it all the same."

There was one way in which Gordon thought he might do the couple a bit of good. Mark had many specialist collectors on his books for whom he would reserve certain items. They collected things which some might think outlandish: old keys, old watches, snuffboxes, and vinaigrettes. Then there were the London dealers who regularly called. Gordon proposed to tell them something like this:

"Look here; you're going through Ouseland. Might pay you to drop off and have a look at a shop my brother-in-law's got there. He might have something in your line. You never know."

Gordon's visit was more than a tonic. But just after Christmas the weather turned bad; snow lay long on the ground, and Ted had only one or two days out in the cart. He went to a sale or two, however, though he bought little, for the prices the ring were prepared to pay went beyond his own, low as his were from a persistent fear to back his judgment. At one sale he saw Mark, but the two avoided each other. Mark made no attempt to speak, and Ted had his own pride. He said nothing of it to Jenny.

At Christmas he had known that Jenny was homesick and still worrying about Mark, for that was when she had bought him the pipe and tobacco jar and he had begun to smoke. Christmas to him had little significance, for in his life with Mort it had merely meant a fowl or a pheasant for the midday meal, and maybe a midnight sound of the carol singers. To Jenny, he guessed, it had been different, and it was she who decorated the house with holly and even put some in the window of the shop.

Spring came late that year, but when it did come, Ted worked as he had never worked in his life. About his industry there lay something of grandeur. Now that Jenny was heavier with her pregnancy, he would be up at earliest dawn, busy with work that would ease her burden in the house. A woman now came on Mondays for the washing; but he would be tidying up the kitchen, lighting the fire, and taking up a cup of tea before he saw to the horse. If he were at home, he found work to do in the house in the chance intervals of attending to the shop. If he were out in the cart, it would be dark, and then dusk, before he was home, and then there would be little jobs in house or shop. When at last he went up to bed, his mind would be busy with the coming day.

Soffe thought the baby would be born on or about the 3rd or 4th of August, but for days before that, Ted never left the house. The town had a maternity scheme to which he had subscribed, and in the last week of July the nurse began a daily call. Bella Crowe would drop in to lend a hand in the house, and, as she afterwards told Jenny, it was Ted who worried her more than herself. Yet it all happened with, for him, a merciful suddenness. There was a sale only two miles away, to which he wanted to go.

"Course you can go," Bella told him. "Nothing ain't going to happen that little time you're away. Do you good to get out for a bit."

And so, against his better judgment, he went. It was August 1, and harvest had just begun. It was a day he would remember all his life. He left the sale early and it was only four o'clock when he started for home. Just after passing Euston he saw field hands cutting oats, and he pulled up the cob for a minute or two to watch the frantic chasing of the rabbits that bolted when the last oasis of oats was cut. The shop was shut and everything appeared normal when he drove into the yard, but when he hastened into the house Bella Crowe was there, hushing him to silence. The nurse was there, she said, and he'd best keep out of the way.

In an agony of apprehension he moved off towards the stable. When he came back, Bella wasn't there. Moistening his lips, he tiptoed to the foot of the stairs. There was a sound, as of a cry of pain, and he winced as if the pain were his own. He listened again, but there was nothing but the low voices of the women, and he tiptoed away and out to the stable again. Before he reached it, there was a patter of feet.

"It's a boy! A beautiful boy, Mr. Burling. You ought to be proud—"

But Ted wasn't proud. His eyes blinked and suddenly he was leaning against the stable door, with his head on his arm, and it was Bella who was tiptoeing away.

Half an hour later he was in the bedroom. His eyes were first for the nurse.

"She's fine, Mr. Burling. As easy a confinement as ever I've had."

Jenny smiled up at him, and the baby lay in the crook of her arm. Queer and tiny it looked, and his cheek brushed its head as he kissed her.

"You all right, Jenny?"

"I'm all right, Ted. It's you I've been worrying about, not me."

She drew back what looked like a shawl, and Ted smiled sheepishly at the face of his son.

"Eight and a half pounds he was," Bella Crowe said. "That's more'n any o' mine were."

Ted nodded to himself. He smiled again at Jenny and Jenny smiled too.

"What're we goin to call him, Jenny?"

Jenny said she hadn't quite decided, and then the nurse told him that he ought to be going, though he might come in for a moment later. Bella went with him down the stairs. It seemed queer to be coming out to the full light of what was still an afternoon.

"Gordon, he ought to be called," Jenny said when he saw her again that evening.

"And what about a second name, Jenny?"

He was thinking that she might like it to be Mark, but when she said that he could choose a second name he knew somehow that it wasn't Mark that she wished.

"Reckon I'd like him called after Uncle Mort," he said.

Jenny seemed to like it, and the baby, she said, took after Ted's side. He had Ted's nose and eyes. Ted maintained that he looked like Jenny—or Gordon. Look at the way he was screwing up his eyes. Out of some miraculously acquired knowledge Jennie said that all babies screwed up their eyes.

CHAPTER 8

The Father

IN less than a fortnight Jenny was up and about again. There was a cradle by the kitchen table, and when the baby was restless at meal times she would rock it gently with her foot, Ted looking approvingly on. It was Jenny who was as yet the revelation of which the small sleeping thing in the cradle was scarcely more than a cause. To him the child was a mystery that stirred him not precisely to love, but to a kind of tenderness and a sense of protection. There was its utter helplessness and fragility. When he held it, with Jenny looking anxiously on, he felt clumsy and awkward; but when Jenny took the baby from him as if she had handled babies all her life, and when she changed a napkin or bathed and powdered, he nodded to himself at the deftness of her, and at the strange beauty of her face as she smiled and talked her baby language or held the small bundle close. Even when he tried to force, as it were, a love which he self-accusingly knew he should have felt, he saw in his mind a child that talked and a boy that would ride with him some day on the cart as he had once ridden with Uncle Mort.

Jenny was feeding the child herself, and when she held it to the breast he shared with her a young shyness. He also shared the anxieties and fears that came from inexperience, for in these first weeks there would be spells of crying or the tiny face would wrinkle in pain. Then Jenny would run anxiously, or even desperately, for Bella Crowe, and he would feel a great relief when it was all nothing, when Bella held the baby in her plump arms and crooned as if it had never been anything else but the healthiest baby that had ever been born. But somehow he would always sidle away when the two women were together, indulging in one of those orgies of adoration, and busy himself somewhere in the shop.

When Jenny was herself again, his desire for work was even greater, and for the first time in his life he felt that he was really learning. On the long nights he would sit with his books while Jenny mended or darned or ironed, and out of all that once ill digested mass of matter there were things that were slowly becoming a part of him. He could even look back and wince at his own ignorance. Take that little matter of silver, for instance.

It had been at a sale near Bury where there were several lots of domestic silver, dated on the catalogue as early Victorian or late Georgian. An elderly lady had been bidding for a set of six teaspoons, and she held her own gaily against the dealers until they dropped out. But Ted felt that there was something curious about that bidding, for the spoons had been sold so cheaply that he had almost taken up the bidding himself. Then the auctioneer spoke.

"Just a moment, madame, before you accept that lot. People often make mistakes, and I hope you're aware that what you've been bidding is for the weight by ounce—not for the actual spoons."

She gave a little, "Oh!" The triumph had gone, and Ted, too, was feeling very much of a fool.

"Better put them up again," the auctioneer said, and this time the spoons were knocked down to a dealer. When Ted came home that night, he was guilty of one of his few pieces of duplicity, for when he told Jenny of the happening he kept back that he himself had been as ignorant as the woman.

There were things, then, that he was beginning to know, and for which he would bid to his predetermined price. They made, as it were, a small bulwark of assurance, and out of that assurance more knowledge was slowly to grow. Take the matter of the two vases that he bought at Eye.

His visual memory was tenacious, and he knew that in London he had seen a pair of vases that were practically the same. There they had been described as Chelsea-Derby. The term had puzzled him, and he had looked it up later in his books. Somehow he was sure about those two vases at Eye. There were the same square bases, the turquoise ground, and the same felicitous design in which one could discern the very strokes of the brush. Even when he outbid the ring and they were knocked down to him at eight pounds, he felt no qualms. It was not that the ring were suddenly fools that he bought them. What he did not know was that their limit had been seven pounds ten and that before the outbidden Ben Harris could catch the eye of Clemming for new orders the hammer suddenly fell.

Some time later Ted saw Clemming and Ben Harris with their heads together. Just as he was leaving the sale room, Harris approached him. Ben was always a deceptively soft-spoken man, even if he had the look of a cattle dealer.

"Them two vases you bowt, Mr. Burling," he said mildly. "Would you be prepared to take a small profit on 'em?"

"I'll take fifteen pounds."

Ben's eyes opened.

"Can't do that, Mr. Burling, but I'll give ye ten."

Ted shook his head. Then as he was in the very act of moving off in the cart, Ben came running up.

"Just a minute, Mr. Burling. About them two vases. What about twelve pound? That'll give you a good profit."

Ted thanked him but said he would rather not sell. Jenny knew the vases were good even before she heard their cost, and she shared his pride in having outsmarted the ring. If she felt a dubiousness about their sale from the shop, she said nothing of that to Ted; but it was to be the matter of their sale that was so surprising.

The two vases had been put in the very centre of the window on a small Queen Anne walnut table that he had bought in a farmhouse at Larford. Within a week of their appearance there had been two enquiries, but the enquirer had boggled at the fifteen guineas he had now made up his mind to ask. The next week, on a lovely October afternoon, he was pottering about in the shop when an open carriage with a pair of chestnuts drew up outside. Two ladies were in it, and one was looking up at the name above the shop and saying something to her companion. The cockaded coachman got down, opened the carriage door, and both ladies moved towards the shop. It was the younger who entered first, and as he gave a tentative clearing of his throat he thought he recognized her.

"Good afternoon, ma'am—"

"It *is* you, Mr. Burling. We drove past and I happened to see the name. I wondered if it might be you. This is the Mr. Burling I was telling you about, Aunt Helena."

The elderly lady gave a little bow.

"I'm pleased to see you again, Mrs. Pryne," Ted said. "I hope you're well, ma'am, and the colonel's well."

"He's very well," she said. "I think he'll be pleased when I tell him I saw you. But you hadn't a shop, had you, when you came to Ladeham?"

He told her how long he'd been at Ouseland. He even managed to mention Jenny and the baby.

"How nice for you!" she said. "I have two boys, but they're both almost grown-up. You'd like to look around the shop, Aunt Helena?"

He showed them around. The furniture was crowded in the little shop, with china on a table or the top of a chest, and he always became nervous when ladies moved about with their heavy skirts. Marion Pryne was as vivacious and animated as she had been on that morning when he had seen her first. The aunt was quiet, almost to taciturnity, but it was she who came back to the two vases.

"So you call them Chelsea-Derby," she said.

"Yes, ma'am. That's how I'm sellin them, under guarantee. There's a pair in the Victoria and Albert Museum in London that you couldn't tell 'em from."

She gave him a quick look at that.

"Fifteen guineas is a lot of money, Mr. Burling."

"Not if you get value for your money, ma'am. You'll live to see the day, ma'am, when them vases'll be worth a deal o' money. I reckon I'll be glad to buy 'em back at far more'n you gave."

"They're perfectly exquisite," Marion said. If her remark had been made with the hope, for Burling's sake, of concluding the deal, it was successful.

"I'll take them," said the aunt.

"Thank you, ma'am. Where'd you like them sent?"

"I'll take them with me. The cheque will be posted."

He found a box and wrapped them elaborately with twisted paper. The ladies were looking around the shop again. Marion Pryne bought for a guinea a pair of early Staffordshire tree-backed cupids which she thought were quaint. Ted packed these also, and stowed the box beneath the heavy fur rug in the carriage.

"I'm staying with my aunt at the moment," Marion Pryne told him, "but some time I must bring my husband. He's a great collector of glass."

The coachman mounted to his seat again and the carriage moved off. Ted watched it till it was out of sight down the hill, then turned to see Ernie Crowe at his elbow.

"Someone who was a bit of an old customer of mine," Ted couldn't help saying with pardonable exaggeration. "Colonel Pryne's daughter-in-law who live at Ladeham Hall."

"That weren't whose carriage she were in," Crowe said. "That was Lady Radnor what live at Ingley. You often see her and Sir Henry drivin through."

Ted went almost soberly to the kitchen. Jenny couldn't help kissing him when she heard of the sale, but her face fell queerly when she knew who the buyer was. But Ted seemed to think that it hadn't mattered if he hadn't addressed her as *my lady*. Not that he wouldn't the next time.

The cheque came, and with it was a short note that merely said, "With Lady Radnor's compliments and thanks." But it was not the money nor the profit that made the event. There was something deeper even than the vindication of his judgment, something that took his thoughts to the desperately cold woodshed and a morning at Ladeham Hall.

At the end of that same October, Jenny had an unexpected visitor. It happened one morning while Ted was out in the Brecklands in the cart. As she went about her work in the kitchen, the baby stirred in the cradle and began to cry. She crooned to it, rocked the cradle, and then gathered it in her arms and soothed it gently to and fro. At the sound of feet on the cobbles of the yard, she turned. Then suddenly she was biting her lip and holding the baby closer in her arms.

"Mornin, Jin. I happed to be this way, so I thought I'd drop in and see how you was."

Mark looked older and he seemed to be unusually untidy. His pointed beard looked untrimmed and there was dandruff on the velvet collar of his overcoat. There was something that hurt her in the humility of his voice, yet she made no move. Her eyes were on his face but she said nothing.

"Reckon I hain't treated you none too well," Mark said, standing irresolutely and somehow forlornly at the door. Still Jenny said not a word. There was a sudden curious softening on Mark's face, and his eyes seemed to wrinkle as Gordon's often did.

"And that's the boy," he said, giving a slow nod and a smile.

Jenny's lip began to pucker, and in a minute Mark was holding both her and the boy.

"Oh, Dad!"

Mark was patting her back. With a hand she dried her eyes.

"Don't take on, Jin. There ain't nothin to cry about."

"But there is," she said, and somehow she couldn't meet Mark's eyes. His finger was on the baby's face. The finger went to the tiny palm, and the small fingers tightened about it.

"He's strong," Mark said. "And the very spit of you, Jin."

But something still lingered. She put the baby in the cradle and wrapped the blanket round him.

"You haven't asked about Ted."

"How *is* Ted?"

"He's well," she said, "but that isn't any thanks to you, Father."

Mark patted her arm.

"Now, Jin, don't you start a-mobbin. I said I was wrong." His eyes went round. "Not a bad little place you got here, Jin."

Her voice softened a little.

"How long're you staying, Dad? You'll stop the night? There's a room I can have all ready."

"Reckon I might have a mite o' victuals if there's enough. Have to be back tonight, though. Reckon I'll catch that five-forty."

Mark spent the day with Jenny, and while she was busy in the kitchen he had a good look at the shop and even the outbuildings. He said he'd hardly have known the place from what it was when he'd called in Wrightson's day. It was a Thursday and early closing day. Jenny had lighted a fire in the parlour, and they sat there in the afternoon. The cradle had been brought in, and when the baby woke, Mark asked to hold it. It was nursing time, but she went up to the bedroom, too shy to let even Mark see her give it the breast.

She told him about Ted, what he had done and what she was sure he'd do.

"Reckon you was right, Jin," he said. "Not that it ain't a bit too early to start talkin yet."

Tea time came, and she laid the things in the parlour, which was heavy with smoke from Mark's pipe. Now he could chuckle when she grumbled at the smoke at mealtimes as she had always done at home. Suddenly Jenny became alert to a sound that Mark had not heard.

"Ted!" she said. "You stay here, Father. I'll be back in a minute."

Ted saw her as soon as he got down from the cart.

"Are you all right, Jenny?"

"Ted," she said, "Dad's here! He came this morning and he's been here all day. We're in the parlour."

She felt him stiffen.

"Ted, don't do anything. Don't say anything. He's sorry, Ted. He really is."

A moment and he kissed her.

"Reckon you know, Jenny. I'll be in in a minute, soon as I've sin to the hoss."

The two men looked at each other when Ted at last came in. Ted's hand went out, but the sight of Mark brought words he hadn't meant to say.

"Glad to see you, Mr. Shadd. Better late than never, so they say, but I'm glad to see you. Reckon Jenny was too."

Mark frowned, but the ice was broken. It was a fine boy they had, Mark said. Gordon might be along to see him any time now.

There was just time for the meal and no more. Ted said he would harness the cob and drive Mark down, but Mark refused to hear of it. When he came downstairs, just before he left, he handed something to Jenny.

"Won't do no harm, I reckon, Jin, if you have this."

It was his cheque for fifty pounds.

"It's good of you, Dad, but I'd rather not."

Mark bridled.

"And why not, pray. You're not all that well off, are ye?"

"I reckon Jenny's right, Mr. Shadd," Ted said. "We're beginning to get on, and it wouldn't be the same if you was to help."

Mark scowled, but the scowl went.

"What about puttin it in the savins bank for the boy? Be a tidy bit by the time he come to want it."

Well, that was different, but then Mark had to be away. Jenny was kissed and then he had to see the baby again, and then Ted and he were off to the station. They took the short cut by Burrell's Works.

"That little walnut table what you've got," Mark said. "Jenny say you're askin seven pound."

"Reckon it's worth that," Ted said.

"Give ye six pun ten and you can put it on the train."

They talked shop till the train drew out.

"Mind you come and see us again," were Ted's last words. Mark reckoned he would, though he couldn't say when.

Winter set in and the Christmas weather was mild. It was a different Christmas that year, for it was a different Jenny who decorated house and shop and made puddings and mince pies. It was a different Ted who ate them. Somehow it was like the end of that honeymoon week in London, for Ouseland had lost what strangeness it had once had and he not only knew but was known. There were the gentry of the town, to whom he would raise his hat, and the fellow tradesmen with whom he would pass the seal of the day or stop for a moment's chat. There were the few friends Jenny had made, let alone the women who would stop to admire the baby when she was out with the pram. And there were, of course, the Crowes, perhaps the best friends they had. Harold, the eldest boy, who was four years older than Ted, would often drop in for a chat. He was acquiring an interest in antiques.

There was also, of course, the reconciliation with Mark, and yet the change in Ted's general outlook on life was owing largely to something within his own four walls. Now there was the child. Baby it still might be, yet it was infinitely more: no longer a swathed and fragile thing that he was almost afraid to touch, but bone of his bone and flesh of his flesh. It was a strong thing that kicked and wriggled in his hands; a plump and dimpled thing that would gurgle and crow when a finger tickled its chin.

"He know me, Jenny!" he told her one day excitedly.

Jenny smiled but admitted far too tentatively that it might be true. Then there was the wonder of the first tooth.

"How long will it be afore he talk?" Ted wanted to know.

Jenny doubted if it would be before a year. Girls were more advanced than boys. Some boys didn't begin to talk till they were almost two. He pulled a bit of a face at that, and in his heart he didn't quite credit it.

When Gordon came, Jenny's eyes bulged at the sight of him.

"Why Gordon, you're growing a beard!"

His grin was a bit sheepish.

"Mark sometimes seems to think I'm not much more than a boy," was his excuse, "so I thought I'd set out to show him."

"It suits you," Jenny said. "Not that I'd like Ted to grow one."

Ted was out, delivering something in the town, but when he returned he laughed at the sight of Gordon, though in the laugh was an enormous affection. But if Gordon was bashful for the moment about his young beard, he was no less shy with the baby.

"Give him to me," Jenny said. "You hold him as though he was going to bite you."

"Maybe he will," Ted said. "What do it feel like, Gordon, to be an uncle?"

"Don't know that it makes a lot of difference," he said. "It isn't like being a father. Jenny and the baby, or so I reckon, sort of make a home. There doesn't seem to be much of a home at Yarmouth, now Jenny's here. I reckon that's what brought Mark round."

"You ought to get married yourself," Jenny told him severely. "It isn't right for anyone to live the same as you do."

"It's not that bad," he said, giving his wry grin. "Somehow I can't see myself sort of domesticated, same as you've got Ted."

"But Ted likes it. Anyone would think this house was nothing but work and the miserables."

"Now, now, now," Gordon told her. "Don't you start a-mobbin, as Mark'd say. I know what you and Ted are like."

When Ted came home after a day in the cart, there would always be the old, "You all right, Jenny?" and only after that would come the baby: a look if he were bathed and asleep, and maybe a few moments to hold him if he were awake. Then as summer drew near there was a new discovery.

"Look, Jenny! He's tryin to stand on his legs! Reckon he'd try to walk if you give him the chance."

"No, Ted. No!" said Jenny, almost frantically, taking the baby herself. Nothing was worse than to let a baby on its legs too soon. Mrs. Crowe said that that was why some children grew up bandy. Ted saw something comical in the idea. Jenny, for once, was not amused.

But Ted never bored either friends or acquaintances with the

achievements of his son, because that son, like Jenny, was something
to be cherished and hoarded. He was too deeply his own. There was
only one story he ever did tell, and that was much later, and to
Gordon. It was a part of that domestication which Gordon had
not failed to notice; and though Gordon roared with laughter at
the end of the tale, Ted's smile still was somewhat sheepish.

On a cold and rainy Sunday morning in April, Ted had just
lighted the fire in the parlour when Jenny came quickly in.

"Hold baby a minute while I warm a clean nappie."

The room was chilly, but soon the baby made a grateful warmth
that seemed to steal deliciously across his knees. He smiled at the
comfort of it, and then suddenly there was on his face something
like horror.

"Jenny! . . . Jenny!"

"What is it?"

"Jenny, you'd better come here quick!"

Jenny came running. But nothing had happened to the baby, and
she couldn't help laughing at the damp disaster. It was a good thing,
she told him, that he'd had on his old working trousers.

As the summer came on and the days lengthened, Ted's domestic
duties were easier, for he could be up at dawn. There was many a
morning when he would have breakfast ready by the time Jenny
was down and still have the day before him. Not that Jenny herself
was a lie-abed; for Ted liked his breakfast at seven, and it would
often be before that that she caught the smell of the frying bacon.
Her day was long too, with housework often interrupted by the
shop. Customers would be leisurely, and it was bad business to give
even a hint that her time was more precious than their own.

Never since their homecoming had there been a cross or too hastily spoken word. Duties had never been defined, and yet house and
shop ran smoothly. The two were somehow dovetailed, and the
scrubbing of a kitchen floor was as important as the finding of a
rare piece or a fortunate sale in the shop. Theirs was an uphill road,
to be faced gladly and together, and now that the baby had come
the road was no less hard. Then suddenly, when summer was wearing on, something happened to cast the first cloud. It was towards
the end of July, and the time was drawing near for the celebration
of a first birthday.

Mark once gave it as his opinion that looking for antiques was something like fishing, a sport he had been fond of in his youth. Ted knew it to be true. There might, for instance, be days when one watched a motionless float. There were days when you caught quite a few small fish, each hardly worth the taking, and then would come the one rare day that paid for the patience of the rest.

It was not that on a certain day Ted caught one of the fishes of his life. It was not again a question of profit, much though the money was needed; it was not that he bought cheaply and sold well enough: things lay far deeper than that. With that July purchase and sale he found himself once more at the crossroads. The matter of the bureau and the lesson that Soffe had taught had somewhat receded, and a new lesson was needed to clinch and bind the moral fabric of a man. After the buying and sale there were six weeks of indecision, with even Jenny wondering what man would emerge. Only when it was over did he know that there had been a crisis.

It came like a tempest out of a clear sky, and it began on a day in mid-July.

CHAPTER 9

The Table

THE Brecklands, too, were becoming for Ted Burling something of a passion. About those wild and silent places there was a grandeur that would often bring a kind of awesomeness, and with it a strange friendliness that somehow made him regard them as long since known and a part of his innermost self. When he turned the cart south towards Bury or east towards the farming lands, there was never the same thrill of anticipation. But to go first north and then due west at the crossroads, that was something to cheer the heart and to give a feeling of home. He would get Jenny to pack him what he called a mite o' victuals and a bottle of cold tea, and he knew the exact spot to which he might arrive by noon: not that group of twisted pines that he had seen on a certain morning, but a deserted gravel pit well beyond Stanford, where the heaths dipped away below him and he could watch the changing colours of bracken and heather and the purple background of plantations far beyond Flintwold.

He had had such a day and had come home through one of the Tofts. He had called to see that Mrs. Chapman again at the cottage by the pond, and had found her out. When he drove on again, it was with a deeper disappointment, for the day itself had been none too good and the cart had only a scanty load. Even the sun had been too sweltering, and in the afternoon it had seemed a certainty that there would be a tempest. But the air had cleared again and he was letting the cob make its own pace.

As he drew near Stanford he remembered a farm he had always meant to visit and somehow never had. That late afternoon there seemed to be time, so he made the slight detour and drove down the dry and rutted track. He put the halter over the bridle, tied the horse to a post, and looked about him. The farm was larger than he had thought. Before him lay the open yard and a choice of ways; but voices were coming from the barn, and he went that way and not to the house.

Two men were working there, restacking some hay at the barn end, and he gave them the seal of the afternoon. One looked as if he might be the farmer himself.

"Don't reckon we've anything much as'd suit ye here," the farmer said. "Might be a thing or two what was her grandfather's my missus might like to sell."

Ted's eyes had roved unconsciously round.

"What's this?" he said.

"That old table? That's what we stack our cornsacks on."

Ted looked at it. It was huge and massive, as it had to be to stand the strain of the piled sacks, and it was amazingly filthy, with dirt that had fallen for years in the faint crackings of the oak, and the dung of generations of hens. Cobwebs hung from beneath its top to its bulbous legs.

"Don't fare much good for anything else," he said, his eye marking the faint signs of carving that ran around the top. A fingernail dislodged some of the grime and dung, and then he drew back and shook his head.

"Tain't much good but it might come in handy for somethin I want. Think you'd like to sell?"

"Reckon I could manage without it. Depend, though, on what you reckon you'll give."

"Can't be buyer and seller too," Ted told him. "What do you reckon's a fair price?"

"A fair price?" He licked his lips. "Don't know. Thirty bob hurt ye?"

Ted shook a wry head.

"A bit too much for me. What about twenty-five?"

The farmer slid down the low stack, came over, and at last compromised on twenty-seven and six. Ted pulled out his hessian bag and handed the money over. The farmer laughed.

"Well, you've bowt it. Now what're you goin to do w' it? You can't git it on that cart o' yours, nor yet two like it."

"Reckon it'd better go on a wagon," Ted said. "You get it to Ouseland and I'll pay ye."

"That's a tidy way. Spoil best part of a day. Reckon that'll cost ye another ten bob."

"Look as though I've made a bit of a fool o' myself," Ted said. "Still, it'll hatta come home. Do you bring it on a wagon and then I'll pay ye the ten bob."

Even then he was far from sure that the farmer might not change his mind, and he offered to lend a hand to load up. A wagon was backed in, but an extra man had to be called in to help. If the top had not been removable, the table would never have been loaded.

Next morning both he and Jenny were listening for the wagon. It came sooner than they thought, for the man had set out at six. Ernie Crowe and Harold were fetched to lend a hand, and at last the table was standing in the yard. The carter was paid and given a shilling for himself.

"What is it, Ted?" Harold said.

"A table, you great gawk," his father told him.

But it was more than a table. Jenny was busy with a brush and Harold and Ted with soap and water. Ernie had had to go, but half an hour later the other three were standing back and looking.

"I don't know what it is, except that it's a table," Harold said. "But it looks good."

"Henry the Eighth, that's what it is," Jenny said, and Ted was rubbing a finger along the carved figures of the date.

Even then, before Ted had spent hours in a further cleaning and polishing, it looked a noble piece. The oak had the natural greyness of age and yet a curious patina, and except for a loose peg where a stretcher joined a leg, it was as perfect as the day a craftsman had looked on it and known himself that it was good. When Ted was at last satisfied with it, nothing would please him but that the table should occupy the whole space of the window. It took four men well over an hour to manœuvre it through and into place. The shop door had to be taken off its hinges, and how they finally managed to get the table through no one knew. But at last it stood in the window, its dated side outwards. Before the day was over, Ted had more than one look at it from the other side of the street. Then Jenny thought it would look even better if the two copper gotches stood on it. Ted at first demurred and then had to agree.

They talked long about price. Ted mentioned sixteen pounds, but Jenny thought he should hold out for twenty. She said it might be better, perhaps, if Gordon would come and have a look at it. Harold might take one of his photos if Gordon couldn't get away. But before anything was decided it was too late.

It was the third week in July, and Ted was in the shop when a middle-aged gentleman walked in. He was tall and clerical-looking, with an aquiline nose and a beard rather like Mark's, trimmed close to the chin. Ted knew him at once for one of the right sort.

"Mr. Burling?"

"Yes, sir. I'm Edward Burling."

"This table, Mr. Burling. What are you asking for it?"

"That table, sir? . . . Twenty pounds."

"I'll take it, Mr. Burling."

It was as sudden as that; so sudden, in fact, that Ted was almost dumbstruck. His mouth gaped rather foolishly before he could say a word of thanks.

"Where do you want it sent to, sir?"

"To this address," he said, producing a card from his case.

The address seemed to be some school at Holt, and the name was Selby.

"It shall be sent, sir. But one thing, sir, I hope you'll agree to. It'll cost a goodish bit to send. I think you might meet me halfway."

"I don't think you need worry about that," Mr. Selby said. "Make the carriage forward to me. Will that meet you?" Without waiting for an answer, he continued: "Just one other thing. I've been breaking my journey to call on a friend in the town and I haven't my cheque-book on me, Mr. Burling. Also, I'm now going to Norway— my usual holiday—and I'd like you to keep the table till I send you instructions. That may be just before I return. I may come personally and give you your cheque and have a further look round."

"That's all right, sir. Everything shall be done as you say. . . . Good day, sir, and much obliged to you."

"I'm obliged to *you*, Mr. Burling," Selby told him.

No sooner had the door closed than Ted was calling to Jenny. Jenny was as pleased as he.

"Almost eighteen-pound profit," he said. "The best deal we ever had. What're you shakin your head for, Jenny?"

Jenny smiled.

"I'm a bit like Father. You know, Ted. The things he used to bring into the drawing room at home because he couldn't bear to part with them."

"Yes," said Ted. "I don't know that in a way I shan't be sorry to see it go."

Had it not been for that inordinate pride, all would have been well. So grand did that table and its copper vessels look in the window that somehow he could not bear to get it out to the shed and wrapped ready for sending. There the table stood. Three days later a London dealer—one sent by Gordon—came in. The buyer for the Oxford Street firm of Montague Grant, he was a young, keen-looking, clean-shaven man. He knew his job well enough to come only at last, and then casually, to the table.

"Not a bad table you've got here, Mr. Burling."

"In collector's condition," Ted said. "I haven't even tightened this here peg."

"Yes, it's quite a nice table. What do you price it at?"

Ted saw no reason why he should lose a free valuation from one who ought to know, and it seemed shrewd to raise the price a little.

"Ought to be worth twenty-five pound?"

The other shrugged his shoulders. He turned his back on the table and resumed the argument on the pair of Adam mirrors. Ted let them go for seven pounds ten.

The very next morning Soffe looked in. A courtesy visit, he said, just to see how Jenny was. He asked after Ted, who was out, and then walked into the shop and straight for the table.

"I couldn't see it too clearly through the window," he said, and his fingers went lovingly over the wood. "A nice table. Where the devil did your husband find it?"

Jenny told him.

"Wouldn't mind having it myself," he said, and saw it in his long dining room. "What's he asking?"

"It's sold, Doctor. Only a few days ago."

"What for?"

"Twenty pounds."

"Twenty pounds!" he glared. "The man's a fool. I'd have given more than that myself."

He had scarcely gone when a telegram arrived. Jenny took it nervously, guessing at once that something had happened to Mark or Gordon. When she read it, it was something she utterly failed to understand.

> Reference table seen our Mr. Williams yesterday.
> Accept price. Notify us time of dispatch.

The reply was prepaid, but she had no idea what to say. What she did send was this:

> Husband away. He will write tonight on return.

That evening she was out in the yard, telegram in hand, when Ted returned. Ted explained and Jenny was the least bit annoyed: not because that table could have been sold for more than it had brought, but because Ted for once had been unbusinesslike. The table should have been taken out of the shop, and then there would never have been all that fuss. Over his meal she told him about Soffe's call and the implied offer, though she made no mention of Soffe's thinking him a fool.

After supper and oddments of household work, Ted wrote a letter to the London firm, and when he wrote a letter it was a letter and not a hasty note. It was unfortunate that he was still at it when Jenny went up to bed. In the morning, when she expressed a wish to see what he had written, she was too late, for the letter had already been posted. That same day the table was got out of the shop and into the main shed, and there it was swathed in sacking till the order should come to send it to Holt.

That was on Saturday. On Tuesday he expected an answering letter, but none came. It was Williams, the buyer, who arrived by the midday train from town. He looked glum when he saw that the table had gone and relieved when Ted told him that it was in the shed.

"According to your letter, Mr. Burling," he said, "you haven't really sold it at all. There wasn't a deposit paid, was there?"

Ted said there wasn't, but the bargain had been implied.

"That isn't a legal sale," Williams said. "There's nothing binding. You're under no obligation to let this customer have the table for a price like twenty pounds. *If* you ever see him again."

"What do you mean, sir?"

"Well, it's a common enough happening. We often get it. A customer comes in and asks for something to be kept, and then we never see him again. He changes his mind or something happens so that he can't find the money. That's why we've had to insist on a token payment before reserving anything."

"That's somethin I hadn't thought of," Ted told him.

"Thirty pounds is our final offer for the table," Williams said. "You'd look a fool, wouldn't you, if you waited for this customer and he never turned up? Even if he does, you'll have lost ten pounds."

Jenny had been listening, and now she came into the shop. She couldn't help overhearing what Mr. Williams had been saying, she said, and there was a question she wanted to raise. If the table was worth thirty pounds, there was no need to think about loss.

"I think we should wait and see if this Mr. Selby does come back. Even if he doesn't, the table will still be worth what you offer."

"No, madam, you're wrong," Williams said. "We're offering a special price because we want it at once for a special customer—an American gentleman. He's leaving almost at once. After that we couldn't bid the same price. We'd have to wait till another customer turned up; and you know, madam, how long that might be."

Jenny said she'd like to talk it over privately and would it be troubling Mr. Williams to ask him to drop in again in a few minutes. Williams was suavity itself.

"I think we should wait," Jenny said. "There's something about that man that I don't trust."

"But, Jenny, it don't matter what people are like so long as their money's good."

"I know that, Ted, but—" She broke off. "What do you really feel about it yourself, Ted?"

"Reckon we'd better wait," he said, but he shook his head nevertheless.

She left him alone to handle Williams on his return. Now the London man made a final offer of thirty-two pounds, saying that if Ted had been frank in the first place he'd never have had that day's loss of time. Something in the slight shortness of temper made Ted a bit short himself, and he was far from sorry when Williams left the shop.

Towards the end of that week another letter came from the firm, with an absolutely final offer of thirty-five pounds. Ted wrote a courteous refusal, but Jenny knew that something had gone against the grain. Though she said nothing at the time, she was worried; and though she was unaware of it, there was a queer withdrawing into herself, a reserve that Ted was soon to notice.

"Aren't you feelin well, Jenny? You seem sorta quiet this last day or two."

Jenny said she was all right.

"Thowt perhaps you was worryin about that table," he said. "I'm a bit worried myself. We're gettin a bit short, you know, and could do with the money. Don't seem right, somehow, to have to wait and then lose all that money on it after all."

"You gave your word, didn't you?"

"Suppose I did," he said, and there once more was that dubious shake of the head.

"Then suppose Mr. Selby comes back, as he said, and found you'd sold the table. Could you look him in the face?"

"It'd have been his fault," he told her doggedly. "It was him who wasn't businesslike. If he'd paid a deposit of only a shillin, it'd have made all the difference."

"You can't buy straightforwardness and honesty with shillings," she told him, but still he seemed not to see what she meant.

The days went by, and there was a difference in the house which brought a sense of grievance. Somewhere he knew that it was he who was wrong, and it was hard to maintain a grievance against Jenny for long.

"Reckon you was right, Jenny," he told her one night.

Jenny smiled. Another moment and she would have kissed him, but in the same breath the admission was spoiled.

"All the same, if that Mr. Selby do turn up, I reckon I ought to tell him what I've been bid. It only fare right he should know."

"And when he does know?"

"Reckon perhaps he might spring a bit more."

That was the first time he had ever seen her angry, and yet an obstinacy kept her from telling him just what was in her mind. When he brought the subject up again the next day, she begged him to let the matter rest. Then it was she who brought it up once more. A stranger came into the shop, and among Ted's comments when he told her what had happened was one that the stranger had been a gentleman.

"Wasn't that Mr. Selby a gentleman?"

Ted said he was, and then wondered why she had left it like that. Once more he slowly puzzled it out and once more he made an admission.

"Reckon it's my business to know who I can trust, Jenny, and who I can't."

"You're right, Ted," she told him quietly. "And there's the other side to it. It isn't only that you look at them, but they look at you. You've got to trust each other. That's the only way to build a business up."

In early September a letter came from Norway, asking for the table to be dispatched. Three days later Selby arrived early one afternoon. It was Jenny who saw him, for Ted was packing something in the shed. She fetched Ted at once and then unashamedly listened.

"The table has been sent?" was almost the first thing Selby asked.

"Yes, sir. By now it ought to be there."

"That's capital," he said. "But perhaps you're wondering, Mr. Burling, why I didn't send you a cheque in the letter I wrote. The truth is I wanted to see you personally. I don't expect you to like what I'm going to say, but I was even a bit worried. It was totally unbusinesslike of me not to have given you at least a small deposit."

"Maybe it was, sir," Ted told him. "All the same, sir, I reckon you're a man o' your word, same as me."

"It's good of you to take it like that, but it would have been my own fault if you'd given me up and sold it to someone else, perhaps for more money."

"To tell you the truth, sir, I thought so more'n once myself. But that was all, sir. You bought the table and it is most likely home by now. All you have to do, sir, if you don't mind my little joke, is to pay for it."

"And that I'm delighted to do," Selby said. He took out his cheque-book and stopped suddenly.

"Twenty pounds was the price?"

"Twenty pounds, sir."

"But didn't you rather suggest that you'd been bid more?"

"I was, sir. Thirty-five pounds."

Selby grunted.

"Well, I shall pay the agreed price of twenty pounds and not a penny more."

"I don't wish you to, sir. A bargain's a bargain."

That was when Jenny came into the shop again.

"Excuse me, Ted, but might I say something to Mr. Selby? Why did you say you were worried about my husband, Mr. Selby?"

"Well, I've just made it plain to him, Mrs. Burling. I was worried because I might have lost the table through my own carelessness. Your husband tells me he could have sold the table for considerably more than my price. I couldn't have blamed him if he had."

"Excuse me again, Ted, and I'm sorry to keep bothering you. But suppose my husband *had* sold the table. What would you have thought of him?"

"Well—" he frowned— "I should have thought him a shrewd businessman who expected his customers to be as businesslike as himself."

"My husband *is* a businessman," Jenny said, and smiled. "But he is an honest man too, Mr. Selby. He doesn't need a cash deposit or a written agreement once he's given his word."

"Yes," he said. "I know that—now."

He wrote the cheque with the pen that Ted gave him and held it for a moment before he handed it over.

"On the face of it, Mr. Burling, you've lost fifteen pounds. That will be made up to you, and more than made up. In future I'd like you to notify me immediately you acquire any furniture of quality— particularly fine old oak. I don't guarantee that I'll always buy, or that friends whom I recommend to come to you will always buy."

He held out the cheque. The hand went out again.

"Good day to you, Mr. Burling, and thank you again." He looked round but Jenny had gone. "And say good day to your wife." The head went sideways and the eyes narrowed. "An honest man deserves a good wife, and you, Mr. Burling, have a good wife."

A wave of the hand and he was at the door before Ted could open it. Ted hurried to the kitchen. Jenny was actually crying.

"Why Jenny, what's the matter?"

"It's nothing. Nothing really," and her head was suddenly buried in his coat.

"But Jenny, what're you cryin for?"

"Just crying," she said, and smiled up at him.

In matters of business he was far from slow-witted, even if the deceptive quietness of his manner might sometimes mislead a customer who himself was too astute. But even in the matter of mere business there were things that were suddenly to strike him as new. It was his inordinate love of, and pride in, that table that had really led him astray, as well as the fact that its finding and re-creation had been wholly his own. Now he could see, though he could find no words perhaps to clothe the thoughts, that a dealer was in some curious way no more than a go-between. What his eyes saw of beauty was not for himself but for the unknown someone who might look into the window or come into the shop and share his liking and feel the same beauty. He himself was no more than a discoverer and interpreter, and the real reward lay in the pleasure of the customer himself.

Behind his hesitancy in sending the table to Selby had lain things he could never bring himself to mention even to Jenny, now that he thought he knew the reason for those unexpected tears. His shame was the deeper for the remembrance of Mort and the realization that no money could have tempted his uncle to break his given word. There was only one thing he did say to Jenny; it was after they had taken stock that October and found they had come through the first year some thirty pounds to the good. After the book had been closed he had reached for his pipe, filled it, and lighted it.

"Reckon it ain't altogether money that matter, Jenny. Reckon it's how you sorta feel . . . sort of inside yourself."

That November he was twenty-four, and what he was then he would always be: a man on whose word a client would rely; a man who could take luck evenly or make mistakes and have no cramping disillusionment; a man whom Ouseland would come to speak of with respect and for whom even the ring—save Clemming—would feel a furtive liking and even an admiration. Ted Burling was, in fact, the man whom Jenny had always known he was, and the man she was sure he would always be.

CHAPTER 10

The Big Deal

JENNY'S first visit home was for the Christmas of 1898. That summer Ted had often urged her to go by one of the day trips, but she had been nervous about leaving the boy: to have taken him with her would have been, as she put it, to inflict him on someone else.

Ted and Jenny were no different from a million other parents who see a uniqueness in their first-born child, but that Gordon Mortimer was precocious even Bella Crowe would not only admit but proclaim. At twelve months he was making his first steps. Ted was never to forget the moment when Jenny held the boy while he himself crouched six feet away in the sunny yard, watching the light in his son's eyes as he tottered forwards till Ted had him safely in his arms. At fifteen months the boy had a vocabulary, though Ted was often hard pressed to find a meaning in the sounds. Jenny, however, always knew exactly what they meant, and Ted sensed something both pitying and patronizing in her smile when she had to translate.

He was a happy child, and Gordon Shadd was not far wrong when he called him a handful of quicksilver. As soon as he could get about by himself, if Jenny's eyes were not on him, he would be away and gone. She was really angry one evening with Ted when she told him what had happened. Almost before she had even missed the boy, she had heard steps and a voice in the yard, and there was Harold Crowe with Gordon in his arms.

"You'd better look after this young fellow, Jenny. Where do you think he was? Right out in the road and going across by himself. Good job I happened to be there."

Jenny had snatched the boy as if he'd come from the very gates of death. When Ted was told, he laughed.

"Reckon he sort of schemed out he'd have a look round for himself."

But he did do something about it, tacking strips on the inside of the kitchen door to make slots and a two-foot high partition. Then, provided other doors were closed and the fireguard was firmly fixed round the stove, Jenny felt happier about being in the house or in the shop. But it was far from long before the partition had to be raised. From upstairs one morning Jenny heard a curious noise and looked out to see the boy picking himself up from the wrong side of the partition and making for the stable where Ted would often take him to pat the horse.

Mark, in his undemonstrative way, was fond enough of the boy, perhaps because he thought he resembled Jenny. In that he showed partiality, for both Ted and Jenny knew that it was his Uncle Gordon whom the boy strongly resembled. Mark had been two or three times to Ouseland, and once he had gone to a preview of a sale near Bury and had stayed for the night. Ted confided in him that the boy was a rare one for his mother.

"That's allust the way," Mark told him. "His grandmother reckoned the same. Boys allust take to their mothers and gals to the fathers. Gordon was a rare one for his mother, but Jenny—she'd leave her mother to come to me."

That was true with one exception, and the exception was Gordon Shadd. On his rare visits it was to him that the boy would always go, and Gordon, as Ted would admiringly say, had a rare knack of keeping him quiet. It was Gordon who made for him a perfectly magnificent railway engine, the body and funnel turned on a lathe and the paint-work finished off in enamel. Behind it was a kind of open tender in which the boy could sit. It was strong, too; and ten years later, when Ted stored it reverently in the workshop, it was as sound as the day it was finished.

Ted and Mark had often met during the year, and though Mark would be affable enough, Ted was conscious of a strange reserve. It was Gordon again who explained it.

"He thinks a lot of you, really, Ted, only he never seems to get over the way you bested him over Jenny. If he'd known what was going on, that might have been different. Mark never likes to be bested."

At previews or sales Mark would always shake hands and ask after Jenny and the boy, but he never seemed to ask Ted himself how he was faring. The two would walk round together and mark their catalogues. If there was something Ted wanted and if Mark had an eye on it too, it was generally Ted who gave way. If it was something not in his line, Mark would suggest a price and say, with something of a flourish, that he wouldn't stand in Ted's way.

"If you want it, do you have it," he would say. "Only don't you go to more'n so-and-so."

But Mark never knew that he was the original on whom Ted had modelled himself: the quick look at something under the glass, the mark in a catalogue, the air almost of indifference when a lot was up, the scarcely perceptible movement of catalogue or head to mark a bid, and the quick look round to mark a buyer when the hammer fell. But the ring knew, and Ted once overheard a remark.

"Course it was Mark," Ben Harris was saying. "Mark taught him all he know."

"And what do he know?" Clemming asked. "Just about enough to get his fingers bit again one o' these days. If Mark weren't behind him, what'd he be?"

It was a measure of Ted himself that, though he could have done it, he gave no sign that he had heard; but he remembered, and he made a resolve. More than once when he had been betrayed into some extravagance of bidding, it had been because of Clemming, though he had drawn back before the ring could lure him too dangerously on. Now he knew that the enmity of Clemming was as deep-seated as his own, yet in his enmity was a sense of proportion and a strange lucidity of thought. Clemming, as he knew, was no hanger-on at sales. Much as he himself had learned, Clemming knew still more. About his very beefiness and the broadness of his accent and his loud blurting laughs there was a touch of the unscrupulous; and though some might say that Clemming dominated the ring, Ted felt rather that it was Clemming who was the ring.

Ted had learned domestic patience, but even he was somewhat harassed by the preparations for the Christmas at Yarmouth. One would have thought, indeed, that Jenny was going for a year instead of for the long week end, and it seemed to him that Jenny was setting no foot in that train until there was no emergency with which she was not prepared to cope. But it did his heart good to see the difference in her when at last they were in the house.

"You're like that nag of ours, Jenny," he said. "Sort of snuffing in the air when he get near home. Go into a regular gallop, he would, if I didn't hold him in."

Jenny had proclaimed that the rest would do her good, but it wasn't long before she was organizing the household. Mark's new and elderly housekeeper was either amenable or sycophantic, however, and there was no friction. Ted's idea of a holiday was to go through shop and workshop, and it was in the workshop that Jenny ran him at last to earth when she wanted him to go with her for a look around the town. That night young Gordon's stocking was hung up for the first time, and his uncle bought a Christmas tree and some decorations. In the morning, however, as soon as the first excitement was over, Ted was going round the shop and showrooms again.

Mark, glad to escape from the women, showed him round, and Ted handled things the Ouseland shop had never seen. Their very multiplicity was bewildering, and yet there were oddments of knowledge that somehow stuck. Battersea enamels, colour prints, glass pictures, Baxter and Le Blond prints, Bartolozzi engravings, pewter, Sheffield plate, snuffboxes, Waterford glass, and a dozen other things would be pointed out by Mark and expatiated on till Ted at last shook his head.

"Fare to me as though it take a lifetime to know what you know, Mr. Shadd."

"That'll come, boy; that'll come," Mark told him. "You know more'n when you started, don't ye? Well, then."

Mark opened the big safe that stood in the office. In it he kept what he called his valuables, though many things in the open shop stood at a price that Ted would have thought long and hard about venturing. There were a few Oriental cups and plates he was keeping for a special customer, and various things he was collecting at what he called a speculation: gold repeater watches and men's diamond rings, seven apostle spoons of which he was trying to acquire the set, and some fine rat-tailed silver. There were a couple of miniatures that he thought were Cosways and which he was talking of taking some time up to London.

Dinnertime came and Ted had his first taste of turkey. After the meal and the generosity of Mark's carving, he was almost comatose; even Jenny went upstairs for a nap. Mark settled down in an easy chair and the half-smoked cigar was soon burning itself out on the ash tray. Gordon gave Ted a nod and they went out and up to the workshop. They were still there at five o'clock when Jenny impatiently called them to tea.

Ted had a passion for learning and Gordon a patience in teaching, and that afternoon Ted heard and saw so much that once more he could only shake his head at the little he still knew. Take the matter of veneers.

Wood, as Gordon proceeded to show, was no dead thing. Till it died from the worm or rot or overdryness, it was still alive and responsive. Take a piece of fine wood. Merely veneer the front, as Ted had thought, and though the wood looked dry and immovable, that veneer, no thicker perhaps than stout paper, would cause it to warp. But put a plain veneer at the back first, then apply the fine veneer, and the pull would be equal.

Take oak panelling, Gordon said, that had been in a certain place for centuries. When it had been put together its life had been allowed for, with just enough give to avoid a warping, and no more.

"You stand in an old panelled room," he said, "and keep quiet, and what'll you hear? Just as if the panelling was muttering to itself. All sorts of little squeaks and groans you can hardly catch unless you happen to be listening. That's the wood sort of adjusting itself to change of temperature and moisture and so on, but it never warps because that was allowed for when it was put together. But take that panelling down and reassemble it or put it up somewhere else, and what'll happen? Nine cases out o' ten it'll warp because it's alive and start absorbing too much moisture from the air or a new wall. And the funny thing is, the harder and more seasoned it is, the more it'll warp."

There was something even more amazing. Gordon rubbed his fingers across the smooth polished top of a mahogany table.

"What'd happen, do you think, if I was to take a fine plane and take the polish off this table top?"

"Reckon you'd never get the same polish on again," Ted said.

"Maybe I wouldn't," Gordon said, "but that isn't the thing. Believe it or not, but that top'd start to warp. It doesn't matter if the wood was two hundred years old, it'd still warp. And why? Because the polish seals the pores. Strip the polish and you open the pores. The wood starts absorbing moisture and then it warps."

Then there was the fallacy of what Ted had called, admiringly, heart of oak. Gordon said there was no such thing. Instead of the heart being the best part of the wood, it was nothing but sap that had to be cut clean out when a tree was sawn. Then there was the question of quartering, which was more or less a cutting across the grain.

Timber cut with the grain was liable to crack. If not naturally dry when finished off, it was case-hardened, as he called it, with a still undried pocket somewhere inside. When that pocket dried, there would be contraction, and the outer case would crack. Quartered wood allowed for even drying and made for a beauty of grain.

"Fare to me," said Ted despondently, "as though I ought to come here as an apprentice, the little I know."

"You don't have to know," Gordon said. "That's for a workman who knows his job. A good workman loves his wood. What he doesn't know by learning, he knows by instinct. Which reminds me. Who does your repairs?"

Ted said that a local man handled the few he had, on Saturday afternoons and the long evenings. Gordon said that it would pay to have a man and a shop of his own.

"We all like stuff in first-class order, but it's the class of customer you have to think of. Some don't mind a bit of repair. Depends how it's done, of course. Slightly damaged stuff comes much cheaper than the other, and you can sell for practically as much as good. Depends again how it's done. All I know is, it'd pay you hand over fist."

Ted said wryly that there were a lot of things he'd like to do. When he felt a bit more secure financially, he might launch out. That was what they were talking about when Jenny called to them from the foot of the stairs.

Before the holiday was over, Gordon had a word with Jenny.

"Ted deserves to get on. Outside you and the boy, he's set on nothing except work."

"It's for us he's working," Jenny said proudly. "And we *are* beginning to get on. Over seventy pounds profit last year and we don't owe a thing."

"Well, you know where to come if you want anything," he told her. "If Mark won't dive into his bag, I know someone who will."

Then Jenny asked him again when he was going to get married. Gordon reckoned he wasn't the marrying sort.

When the morning came for their return, Jenny held her small son up for Mark's kiss.

"Say 'Goodbye, Granddad.' "

"Goodbye, Granddad."

Mark's face beamed.

"Regular man he's gettin." He brought out a handful of change and held up a sovereign and half-crown. "Wonder which he'll have."

For some unknown reason the fingers closed round the sovereign. For a moment Mark looked taken aback, then Gordon laughed and he joined in.

"You won't have to worry about him a-gettin on, Jin. Fare to me as though he know a bit too much already."

The following spring Ted had a stroke of luck, though it was partly due to Harold Crowe. There were few evenings when Harold didn't drop in, for he had as much interest in the business as if it were his own. Jenny liked him too; it was good, she thought, that Ted had someone like Harold for a friend. Harold's hobby was photography, and he plagued his central office with local pictures in which he thought there ought to be an interest. As for Ted and Jenny and, above all, the boy, Jenny had enough snapshots of them all to fill a small album.

"You know that big old house that's up for sale as you go round by Spring Walk, Ted. Do you know what's in it?"

Ted had no idea.

"Some panelling and a rare old staircase. I don't know as much as you, but it looks to me as if it ought to be good."

It was a conspiratorial business, with Harold getting the key and going one way and Ted approaching from another. The house was unoccupied, and once they were inside, with the door locked, there was ample time for examination; but Ted had no need to look at the panelling through his glass. It was modified linen fold that someone had painted a hideous brown, but its condition was almost perfect except for nail holes. The staircase almost took his breath away. The newels and their finials were exquisitely carved, as were the carving and turning of the balusters and the quaint design of foliage and animals that ran along the rails. The wood was unpainted, and beneath its dust and grime it had the patina of age.

The stairway ran up to a second storey, and it was clear that one first-storey room was a later addition fashioned above what had been a gallery. In the downstair room beyond the one from which the staircase led, Ted removed the layers of wallpaper and probed with his pocket knife. There was no more panelling, but above the modern ugly fireplace was a carved chimney beam. At the part they uncovered there seemed to be a shield bearing a coat of arms. Harold stuck the paper back with spittle. Ted was now looking up at the ceiling joists. The plaster of the ceiling was out of place. If it were stripped, he was almost sure that beneath it would be the carved ceiling beams, for when he squinted in a certain way with the light the plaster showed a faint trace of their lines. Had there been anything to stand on, he would have probed again with his knife.

"Think you can take a photo of the panelling and staircase?" he asked Harold.

Harold said it ought to be easy enough when he'd worked out the time exposure according to the next morning's light.

"I must keep out o' this," Ted told him. "Anyone get any idea I'm interested, up might go the price. You find out, Harold, what price the auctioneer think it'll make."

There was the same conspiratorial return to the shop. Jenny was as excited about it as Ted was.

"What about lettin your father know about it, Jenny?"

Jenny's no came like a flash. If Mark once poked a finger in that kind of pie, there'd be nothing but a remarkably small helping for Ted. Even Gordon oughtn't to be consulted.

"What am I to do then, Jenny?"

Decisions of consequence are not always in need of great argument. There was only one thing to do: approach a big dealer. A London dealer, or, better still, why not that firm who had bought the stump-work from Mark?

That was on a Tuesday afternoon. On Thursday morning Ted went to town by the first available train. He took a bus to Tottenham Court Road and at Maple's asked for a Mr. Palmer whose name Jenny had remembered. It was a handsome office into which he was shown, and Palmer himself looked imposing. Ted got straight down to business.

"I reckon you're a busy man, sir, so I won't take up much of your time. There's my trade card. I'm the son-in-law of Mr. Shadd of Yarmouth, who I think you've had some dealings with, though he don't happen to be in on this. What I've come to see you about is some oak panelling and an oak staircase."

"Of what quality, Mr. Burling?"

Ted produced the photographs and mentioned the disfigurement of the paint. He could see that Palmer was interested.

"Just what is your proposition, Mr. Burling? You want us to inspect and make you an offer?"

Ted said it was not so easy as that. What he had thought was that the firm might buy the house and give a fair commission. The house itself was almost derelict, and the auctioneers expected a bid of about £250. The property might go for less, and there it depended on who was bidding. If the firm appeared openly, or if he showed an interest himself, someone might have suspicions and the price would go up. But if it could be bought for the expected price and then stripped, he knew a man who'd put in a new staircase and replaster and make the place even better for occupation than before. That should cost less than £50, and when it was put up for sale again, the house should make somewhere about the same £250. In other words, the panelling and the staircase would have been obtained for under £50.

Palmer gave him a look. Here was a man whose guile was concealed by a studied guilelessness, or was he that rare specimen, a genuinely honest man? He decided to probe.

"You seem to be putting yourself very much in our hands, Mr. Burling."

"That's because I've heard you well spoke of, sir. I reckon a firm like yours ain't far different from a little business like mine. Deal fair and you don't do so bad. Act the other way and it soon get around. Then you might as well put up the shutters."

"Yes," Palmer said. "But why don't you acquire the property yourself through a nominee and then give us the offer of the contents?"

Ted said frankly that he couldn't put the money down. And the fewer people who knew about it, the better.

Palmer did some more thinking. What he'd do was to send a man down in the morning to make a valuation of the panelling and staircase. However, it was not the custom of the firm to handle the matter as Mr. Burling had suggested, but perhaps after the inspection there'd be some way out. In the meantime they were grateful for his confidence and were quite sure that business could be done.

There was a conference that evening in the kitchen. Harold said he'd be prepared to act as nominee for Ted. The auctioneer had already chipped him about his interest in the house and had asked if he were getting married. There'd be no harm in letting his thoughts run on. But Ted didn't like it. It savoured too much of the underhand. What he'd like to do would be to come out into the open at the sale. If afterwards it was known that the property had had a value that only an antique dealer could have suspected, that would never be ascribed to sharp practice. Right-thinking people would know the thing had been handled by a shrewd man who knew his job.

"You're right," Harold said. "There'd be some fine publicity for you, Ted. What do you think, Jenny?"

"I think Ted should buy it," Jenny said. "I've got over eighty pounds."

Ted refused to use her money, but Jenny persisted. Harold said he could put in fifty pounds, so why not form a sort of company. Ted was still loth to agree. What they'd do was to hear the report of the firm's expert, then talk things over again.

It was an elderly man named Green who came down. Harold smuggled him round to the house, and afterwards there was a gathering at the shop. Green admitted that the panelling and staircase were as nice a job as he'd seen for some time. On the small side, maybe, but fine quality and in good order. The paint was a pity, but it would not be too difficult to remove it. What it was worth he regretted he couldn't say. That was a matter between him and the firm. In any case there should be a letter the very next day.

The letter arrived the next afternoon. The offer was £150 for panelling and staircase delivered in good order, and the firm would be grateful for the further offer of anything else that might be uncovered. That evening the offer was accepted and the little company was formed.

All that remained was to acquire the property. The sale was at the

Bell, and no more than half-a-dozen possible buyers were there. Ted bought for £220. A week later the staircase had been temporarily erected in the yard and Harold was taking photographs. For once his paper accepted one, and Ted saw himself in the county paper, hand on a staircase baluster and in the background a special sign that Harold had made: *E. Burling—Antiques*.

The builder got to work. Green came down again to inspect a fine set of carved ceiling beams and a superbly carved armorial chimney beam together with a fireback among the rubble where the open fireplace had been. Forty pounds was the price paid. Those further demolitions added to the builder's account, but it was still under sixty pounds. Then Ted had the small garden smartened up and when the exterior had been painted, the house looked far better than the oldest inhabitant had ever known it. At the September auction it made £240.

It was a cheerful company that held a meeting to dissolve itself. When all expenses had been paid, there was a clear profit of just over £120. Jenny refused to take anything but the return of her investment, so Ted bought her the new cooking stove on which her heart had been set. Harold was equally loth to profit, and Ted had to bludgeon him into taking ten pounds towards the cost of a new camera. But it was the intangible that really mattered: the picture in the paper and the way even Ted could see that local people had for him a new kind of respect. At the very next sale he attended, the auctioneer came up, shook hands, and offered congratulations on what he called a smart piece of business.

Years later Ted tried one day to calculate just what he had gained from the London firm through that one deal. He had to abandon his reckoning, though he knew that his profit had amounted to far more pounds than that first sale had brought shillings. Often too, when he remembered it, he would smile at what had happened between Jenny and Mark.

Mark had seen the picture in his paper and had come hotfoot to Ouseland the very next day, only to find that the staircase was already on the train. At first he stormed, then he was a man with a grievance.

"Never thowt you'd do a thing like that to me, Ted," he said. "All you had to do was drop me a line and I'd a-made you an offer."

"Do you ever drop a line to Ted when you get anything he'd like?" Jenny countered.

"That's different," Mark said. "I can handle the big stuff, where he can't."

"Ted can handle anything," Jenny told him, and added something that Ted was always to remember, even if it made him wriggle uncomfortably at the time.

"As for you, Father, you may be able to pick out a good piece from a bad, but that isn't everything. You didn't pick out Ted. And even now, when he can stand on his own feet, you won't bring yourself to believe it. That's what's wrong with you, Father. You think—"

Mark managed to get between the spate of words.

"Now, Jin, don't you start a-mobbin. Ted and I are good enough friends; aren't we, Ted? And what about that grandson o' mine? I hain't sin him yet."

Jenny knew his way of wheedling, yet she could not resist that mention of the boy. But womanlike, she also could not resist a final word, even if its subtlety passed over Mark's head.

"Mrs. Crowe has him out for a bit, but he'll be back any time now. He's getting more like Ted every day."

CHAPTER 11

Year of Change

IT was 1901 that was to be the year of changes. It was the year when the old Queen died; and for days Ouseland, for all its comparative isolation, had the feeling, in common with the rest of England, of coming to the end of something safe, accepted, and sure, and of standing before the unknown.

Ted took Gordon to the Market Square that cold January morning and held the boy up to see and hear the reading of the proclamation of a king. He himself felt disquiet at what the future might bring. It was true that the war in South Africa seemed to be at an end, but even in Ouseland, and in his own line of business, it had affected sales. Not that he had been at all hard hit. Each year there had been a small profit; and while his stock had increased and its quality gone up, what he called his floating capital was over £200. Local trade never amounted to a great deal, but he had made connections with London firms and even with provincial dealers. Mr. Selby dropped in from time to time, and there were friends of his whom he would send. Then there was Major Pryne, son of the colonel, with whom he had a standing order for glass.

But he was still unsatisfied, if only because he knew that in himself there had also been a change. There had been an enormous increase of knowledge, and with it not only a new assurance but a shrewd competence. Where he had once boggled at a bid of ten pounds and had seen a lot lost, now he would bid his twenty or thirty with never a tremor. He could even—acting on a hint from Gordon Shadd—drop in on other dealers, for even the ring had no animosities or reservations when money was to be made; and then his special flair for fine porcelain would often discern a bargain.

What he wanted he hardly knew, unless it was expressed in terms of real money and a fine shop. Yet even those were only symbols of deeper desires: a wish to handle the best and nothing but the best; to see that best in his shop and to talk of it with discerning customers; to sell it well and to buy more of it; to buy things for Jenny, and, above all, to set aside a good nest egg for the future of the boy. At times his mind would run on and he would see that future and Gordon himself as much a gentleman as some who came into the shop. Maybe he would be a really important dealer with a fine shop in London; or he might want to be a doctor, or a lawyer, or even a high-class auctioneer. But whatever he became, there would be a need for money, and it was always that that came back to his mind.

Gordon himself was on the threshold of change. Babyhood had departed, and now he was a boy who accompanied his father on short walks about the town and prattled and questioned. Harold had taken a photograph of him in the sailor suit he wore on Sundays, and an enlargement of it hung in the parlour. It showed a handsome boy, dark-haired like Ted and Jenny, with her dark eyes and quick alertness. He was tall for his age, and Ted had the idea that he would one day be taller than himself and would reach the six-foot mark. But what the photograph did not wholly show was the happy adventurousness of the boy: the same fearlessness and disregard that had tumbled him that morning over the partition top when he had wanted to see the horse.

Now that school was at hand, Jenny was alarmed at his association with what she called the "rough boys" of the town. Ted refused to see things that way. Compared with his own village school, Ouseland's seemed to him a masterpiece of learning and progress, and the headmaster a man for whom he had a profound respect. And contact with all sorts, as he would tell Jenny, would be good for the boy.

"Nothin like learnin to stand up for yourself," he would tell her, and Jenny would have to admit, if with a difference, that Ted himself had not been harmed by the rough-and-readiness of life with Uncle Mort.

When the time came, Ted said, Gordon could go on to the grammar school like the sons of the leading tradesmen of the town. Even if he failed to get a scholarship, there'd be money to pay his way. Not that he wouldn't stand a chance. Already he could read and write a bit, thanks to Jenny's teaching, and that ought to bring him straightway to the front. Jenny's fears, soothed by Ted's optimistic prophecies, grew gradually less as the day approached; but it was she who took the boy to school on his first morning, fetched him at dinnertime, took him again, and fetched him in the afternoon. Shortly thereafter, a neighbour's son was found to accompany him, then Jenny would become anxious when the boy was late getting home.

"There ain't nothin to worry about," Ted would say. "He'll find his way home when he's hungry. I allust did and so'll he."

That Whitsuntide there was another big change. Old Mr. Brewer, who owned the Burling and Martin properties, died, and his son informed the tenants that he wished to sell. He named his price and gave them the first offer. Ted and Jenny were in a state of perturbation. Were a dealer—even Clemming perhaps—to acquire the property, out they would have to go; and to find another place in the town would be hard if not impossible. With competition business would fall, and a change was a bad thing in any case. And each hated the thought of some new house that could never be quite a home.

Ted went to Yarmouth to see his brother-in-law. Gordon thought the new owner's valuation excessive; but that, as he agreed, could not be helped. Ted said that he and Jenny could find £200, though that might be a dangerous lowering of capital. Gordon refused to commit himself, but a day or two later he brought a friend along to inspect the building.

He did something else that Ted had never thought of: he approached old Mrs. Martin and found that she had no intention to buy. She was, in fact, thinking now of retiring. That opened up new possibilities. Gordon, like his father, could be secretive, and in the matter of the purchase he was also thinking of Ted's surprise. It was more than a surprise. Ted and Jenny were aghast when he came down again a few weeks later.

What he paid for the properties Ted was not to know till years later, when at last the loan was paid off. It was the alterations and additions that took his breath away. The Burling entrance lay along the Crowe property, and what Gordon intended was to pull down the high wall that separated the Burling's property from the Martin's and to throw the two into one whole. The old Martin window might be too small for much display, but the rooms would serve as showrooms, though new windows would have to be let in. Not only that: there would be a new way cut through to make the two houses one, and Jenny could have a larger parlour and Ted an office of his own. But that was by no means all. The stable and twin sheds were of fourteen-inch brick, and Gordon had in mind a long new top storey over both with an outside staircase. The new room would be a repair shop with wide doors to take the largest stuff, and there would be a pulley and block to hoist the heaviest objects from a cart or wagon.

"It's what I've dreamed on myself," Ted said, "but what about rent and rates? Don't you reckon it'll be more'n we can afford just at the moment?"

Gordon said he had it all worked out. All he wanted was a reasonable return on his money, and that would mean no more than an extra five pounds already paid. Then as if to show that there was no question of generosity, he said there'd be a repairing lease and that once everything was in order it would be for Ted to keep it so. What he kept to himself, and what Ted was to discover years later, was that the investment would bring him just over 3 per cent as against the 5 per cent he could have got for his money elsewhere.

"Well, it's good of you, Gordon," Jenny said. "It'll be lovely to have more room in the house, especially now Gordon's beginning to grow up, but . . ." She hesitated.

Gordon asked what was on her mind.

"Well, it's the repair shop. That'll mean a regular man, and he'll have to be paid."

"Gordon and me talked that over once before," Ted said. "He reckon it'll pay hand over fist. Provided, o' course, we get the right sort o' man."

"I don't know as I haven't got him already," Gordon said. "George Warman."

"George Warman!" Jenny stared, then smiled. "What ever does George want to leave for!"

"It's his wife," Gordon said. "She's a Barnham woman and her mother's not so spry as she was. She's been on at George for some time, and he's been telling me he'd like to get something out this way."

"I like George," Jenny said. "He's a dear old man. I remember he used to give me sweets."

"He isn't so old as you'd think. I doubt if he's sixty. And he's a first-class man; been with Mark ever since he started. Knows as much as I do, and more."

"What about pay?"

"Twenty-five shillings for a fifty-five hour week."

Ted stared at the enormity of the sum.

"You'd get a second-rate man for eighteen or twenty," Gordon told him, "and what good'd he be to you? Let you down on some job or other and lose you a customer. George is good. You can trust him. He could even look after the shop if you and Jin happened to be out."

But there was no great hurry about George, he said. Ted could have a word with him any time he happened to be in Yarmouth, or George might come over himself. Other things did want talking about. There would be various pieces of equipment apart from George's own tools, and Ted would have to fix up a bench and a lathe; then there was wood and various materials. The upshot was that Gordon said he'd make out a list. He himself could supply enough timber to start with, and George would know what to do from then on.

"How to thank you, Gordon, I don't know," Ted said, and looked shamefaced, as he always did at the inadequacy of gratitude.

"There's nothing to thank *me* for," Gordon told him.

"But there is," Ted said. "I don't often say a lot—'tain't my way —but I don't want you to think Jenny and I hain't known what you've done for us. If it hadn't bin for you, I reckon we wouldn't a-bin here at all."

Jenny had to shed a tear, and Gordon looked uncomfortable.

"Now, now, Jin," he said, and was Mark to the very life as he fingered that neat black beard of his. "Anyone'd think I was turning you and Ted out o' house and home."

Jenny said she just couldn't help it. Then luckily young Gordon came home from school, and the tears miraculously ceased.

It was not till the end of August that the alterations and additions were finished. Despite all the pride that Jenny felt in what she saw would ultimately emerge, her pride in her home suffered for weeks because of the untidiness that resulted from the reconstruction of the house. She was always complaining to Ted that it was impossible to keep anything clean. Ted took things philosophically, as he always did, and young Gordon was having the adventure of his life. Now he returned home promptly from school; and if Jenny—as she complained to Ted—had not continued to keep a perpetual eye on him, he'd have fallen from ladders or scaffolding and broken a limb or even his neck. Gordon's chief friend was Jack Drew, son of Drew the chemist of King's Street. Jenny thought him a nice enough boy but apt to lead her own son into mischief. Ted had his own ideas. More than once he had delved into the cause of some trouble and had found Gordon the prime mover, and with an aptitude for shifting the blame.

No one, then, was more relieved than Jenny when everything was finished and the last workman had departed. In the house itself there was certainly an enormous difference; there was room to move and breathe, and far more light. All Ted's papers and rubbish, as she had begun to call them, were now in his little office, and not only had Gordon a nicer bedroom of his own but there was also a spare room for Mark or Uncle Gordon. On the outside, however, the property showed little change. Ted had his own ideas of what was fitting, and where sweets had once been seen in the Martin window, there would now be perhaps a single table with china or knickknacks. Above it the almost illegible Martin board had gone, and a small board like that on the main shop announced in similar lettering: *Antiques—E. Burling—Antiques.*

From the yard, however, a tremendous change was visible, for the new upper storey made the old stable and sheds look almost like a barn. As he looked at it, Ted thought that there was something enduring about it, with its neatly pointed brickwork and solid stairway of stout elm. The new tiles were perhaps a bit gaudy, but they would weather with time, and even they could somehow give a feeling of well-being. Sometimes he would stand in the yard and let his eyes run reflectively round, and when he moved on it would always be with a nod or two to himself. Behind his sense of responsibility and his urge for still harder work, he felt the fortifying knowledge that now there could never be dispossession; that he and his were living in what was almost their own house.

Early that September the arrival of George Warman was a new

excitement. Ted had found him a house in Castle Street which was only three minutes from the shop, though Flo, George's wife, would have preferred something along the Bury Road, which would have been a shortening of the walk to Barnham.

George was almost a wisp of a man, five-feet six, perhaps, and bony, with greying sandy hair that barely concealed the baldness of his curiously domed skull. A drooping, untidy moustache—a shrimp net, his mates had called it at Yarmouth—almost hid a dryly humorous mouth, and in his eyes, no matter what he might be doing, there was always a peering kind of look, as if he saw the grain of some unknown piece of wood. His hands were small and knobby, like his frame, and grained deep from the handlings of his trade. His eyes were good, though for close work he would don his spectacles. "Better put on my four eyes," he would say, and then he would pick up a piece of wood and his eyes would wrinkle as he peered. He had the trick, too, of pursing his lips when in thought; then his moustache would rise and waver and fall and rise till it became a fascination for Gordon, whose mother had to reprove him sharply when she caught him at an imitation.

For Jenny, whom he had known all her life, George had deference and a tremendous respect. She would always be *ma'am*, but with Ted it was different, and that was the way that Ted himself preferred it. On his first day in the repair shop it had been *sir*, something on which Mark had insisted. Soon it became *Mas' Burling*, and finally it achieved the ultimate of acceptance and respect with a *Mas' Ted*. Jenny achieved the indirect status of *the missus*.

His manner of speech was slow and calculated, as befitted a man who always had to be making decisions. His dialect had, in intonation at least, a touch of the drawl of Suffolk, and between it and Ted's was as great a difference as between Ted's and Mark's. About Ted's (perhaps because his voice was pleasant in itself) there was almost a grace, something natural and friendly, so that one felt that if Ted had lapsed suddenly into a different English one would have been aware of a different and less likable man. George was natural in his speech too, but besides his Suffolk drawl he used embellishments and words that some had almost forgotten, and he had queer dexterities of circumlocution. To give a plain Yes or No was something that one ceased to expect.

"That chest ready, George?" "Reckon it might be." "Have So-

and-So been?" "Don't fare to've sin him." "Can you lend us a hand, George?" "Reckon I might try." "Ain't that glue hot enough?" "I sin hotter."

And so it would go, till in the early days it got somewhat on Ted's nerves.

"Hain't you ever said Yes or No in your life, George?" he had to ask him one day.

"I'll hatta put my considerin cap on to answer that," George said, and Ted had to laugh.

George was honesty itself, and straightforward with a frankness that some might have taken amiss. On the morning when he arrived with his box of tools, Ted lent a hand to get it up the outside stairs from the wheelbarrow. George unlocked the box, then looked up. "Nothin like makin a proper start," he said. "See them tools, sir? Them's my own and no one else's."

Ted was boss and yet he wasn't, exactly, for in that room George would be boss. No shifting this and that so that he didn't know where to lay a hand on it. If Ted wanted to potter about, then he'd have to erect his own bench.

"That's how I allust worked with *Mas' Gordon* and I reckon that's how you and me's goin to work. Anything else I think on, I'll tell ye."

"Reckon I can shake hands on that," Ted told him. "There's nothin, as you say, like makin a proper start."

Nothing is more facile than to moralize, and few things are harder than to look back and discern from a distance the trifles that perhaps changed a whole way of life. That was why Ted was never to know the importance of George's addiction to peppermint bull's-eyes. George always had handy on the bench, or in a special pocket of his apron, a screwed-up packet containing a sticky mass from which the adhering paper could be moved back only by one who had acquired the art.

"Reckon they do my pipes good," he explained to Ted. "Sort o' keep 'em clear-like."

It was Gordon who discovered the peppermints on his first surreptitious visit to the repair shop. George caught him staring fascinatedly at his moving jaws. Now George was to come to think more of the boy than if he had been his own, but on that morning he regarded his entry with a wary eye.

"Sit ye down there," he said, "and don't you raise a deen. Don't mind you watchin what I'm a-doin on, though."

The boy's fascinated look made George offer a peppermint when he took a fresh one for himself.

"Oh, thank you, Mr. Warman!"

George gave a gratified nod at the thanks and the smile. He never guessed that that was why the boy so often made his way up the stairs. George put it down to an interest in the work itself, and later that was true. Gordon, boylike, would ask questions which George would try to explain. Then one day he was allowed to put his small weight on the end of a piece of wood that was being sawn; after that he would be ready for the sawing before George could say a word. In some way, too, George felt a gratification whenever Gordon laughed at some remark or other that till then he had never thought of as particularly quaint.

"Don't fare to be cuttin," George said one Saturday, referring to the saw. "Reckon I'll hatta tend to th' old sow and pigs."

Gordon stared.

"What old sow and pigs?"

"Ah!" said George, and explained. "See them teeth? Them's what we call th' old sow and pigs."

Gordon laughed and laughed, and at dinner tried it out on his mother.

"Look," Jenny said. "I've told you before and I'll tell you again. I won't have you talking like George or those boys at your school. It isn't sharpen*in*. It's sharpen*ing*."

"But Dad says sharpenin."

"What your father do—" She broke exasperatedly off. "There, you see. You make me talk that way myself. What your father does and what you do are two different things, so let me hear no more about it. And now get on with your dinner."

But Jenny liked the boy to be with George, if only because she at least knew where he was. Gordon had been the same with George, she told Ted. Ted was pleased too. In many ways he was proud of the boy and blind enough to his few faults. He felt a personal gratification that at six his son should be taking an interest in things.

"If he grow up like his Uncle Gordon, you and me won't have no cause to fret," he told Jenny. Even then there was no thought in his mind of what might emerge from the boy's passion for spending his spare time with George. Of his great liking for the repair shop he was to gain some idea later, on one afternoon when he found the boy there. George hadn't seen Ted come in.

"Darn it, no!" George was bellowing. "Didn't I tell ye about the run o' the grain?"

There was the boy, using one of George's precious planes, with George himself keeping an eye on the effort. George looked round almost sheepishly as Ted's shadow crossed the bench.

"Just thowt I'd let him try his hand. You have to make a start some time."

He even apologized for the hacked surface of the wood.

"Reckon I owt to have give him a bit o' deal, not this here woman-grained sort o' stuff."

"Woman-grained?" Ted said.

"Bast! Hain't ye ever heerd o' that?" George said. "Woman-grained. The grain go sort of all ways at once."

"Like a woman's tongue, George."

" 'Tain't only that," George said. " 'Tain't only their tongues."

Then he was grimacing in the direction of the boy and talking about little pitchers having big ears.

Another change, one that was not so much to affect the Burling household, however, was the marriage of Harold Crowe. His wife was what Jenny called a nice, reliable sort of girl. She was the daughter of Henry Macrow, who had the little printing works in Well Street. It was a change in more ways than one for Harold. Henry's health was none too good; he was a widower and Jessie was his only daughter, so Harold resigned from his post with the newspaper and settled down as a printer and binder. He still contrived to find time for his camera work, however, and more than once he was able to do a good turn for Ted.

The couple were married at St. Peter's. Because it was held on a Thursday afternoon, Ted and Jenny could both be at the wedding and at the high tea that followed at the Well Street house. It was some months later when Harold found a good use for his camera.

Ted had received an unusual order from a famous London firm, an order which caused him much thought. The firm was having an exhibition of gate-legged tables, and Ted was commissioned to supply a practically unlimited number. Just where they were to come from he had no immediate idea. It was Harold who found the answer. There should be, he said, a special advertisement both in Suffolk and in Norfolk papers, and posters might be printed and put up in the villages around. One of his hobbies was cycling—he had almost the first bicycle in Ouseland with the new pneumatic tires—and he volunteered to do some bill-sticking himself.

What with the advertising and with purchases from dealers, Ted was almost overrun with tables, and a heterogeneous lot they were. Some had cost as little as five shillings, and never a one more than three pounds, yet when he was to look back some twenty years later he knew that for many of them he would then have almost given the fingers of a hand. Jenny hated the sight and sound of the tables, stacked up as they were in the yard, before the one shed that she used. George had no great liking for them either, with his shop almost full.

Harold took some photographs on a grand summer morning when the whole assortment had been brought to the yard and the vans were ready to take the tables to the train. The picture he thought the best was sent to the paper, and once again Ted saw himself in print. Something of the first thrill might have gone; but both the cutting and the photograph were kept, and once more he was to be grateful for the publicity.

That same autumn Harold's daughter was born. Ted had been secretly amused at the interest Jenny had taken in the event and at the vast fund of knowledge that the birth of her own child had seemed to bring. There was something, however, in Jenny's reactions to the coming of Harold's baby that worried him and made a vague hurt. Had Soffe still been at Harford, he might have ventured to talk the matter over with him.

Jessie brought the new baby round one afternoon in the pram, and to see Jenny crooning and fussing over it sent his thoughts back through the years.

"I wish she was ours," Jenny said, almost to herself, as Jessie waved another goodbye from the turn.

"You can't order them things," Ted told her solemnly, as he'd often told her before. "There was Gordon, sort of turnin up afore we hardly knew it, and now—" He shook his head. "Them things just fare to happen, Jenny. That's the only way I can sort of work it out."

One February night, almost two years later, Jenny suddenly snuggled close to him. Ted was almost asleep.

"Ted? . . . Are you awake?"

"Why, yes, Jenny."

"Ted, I'm going to have a baby!"

He was suddenly wide-awake.

"Whuh, no, Jenny!"

He chuckled to himself with a, "Well I never!"

"Ted, I want it to be a girl. You always wanted a girl."

"Reckon it'll be a girl all right," he said. "Be rare company for Gordon, too. Like you was with his uncle."

She felt his nod and could almost see his smile.

"What will you call her, Jenny?"

Jenny said she didn't know. Maybe, if it was really a girl, she ought to be Bella, after all Bella Crowe had done. But she didn't know. In any case there'd be plenty of time to decide.

"Reckon she'll look like you, though, Jenny. . . . Remember that day in Tinkersham when I showed you that sampler?"

Their voices were quiet in the dark. His arm held her close. It fell away at last when in a silence he dropped suddenly off to sleep.

CHAPTER 12

Catastrophe

WITHIN the range of all but the most important sales, Ted Burling had become a dealer of standing and consequence. The measure of both was the constant apprehension in which he was held by the ring. Often, as when Ted had a known customer and was content to take a meagre profit, the ring would be outbidden. More than once he had bidden to the edge of danger and had dropped out just in time, with the ring left to face a loss. There were times, too, when his specialized knowledge would snatch a bargain out of their fingers, and it might not be till later that they guessed the value of what they had disregarded.

Auctioneers had come to know Ted Burling, as they knew Mark Shadd and others who stood outside the ring. An auctioneer lives on commission, and men like Burling were his friends. It was galling, too, when a client had placed no reserve on an object, to see it make a price that bore little relationship to its known value; but men like Burling at least bid to a reasonable figure and at times beyond what the auctioneer himself had dared to expect. That was why, when Burling and men like him were bidding, the hammer would sometimes fall a shade too quickly. Like most shrewd men of business, the auctioneers had learned that it pays to leave unmuzzled the ox that treads out the corn.

Consider then, at a preview or on the morning of a sale, the anxieties of the ring, with money at stake for each of its members. Mark often told the story of a certain dealer, hostile to the ring, who had been lured to the attic of a Hall during a sale and there locked in till various vital lots were sold. There was another story, about Charlie Pratt of Dereham.

"You remember it in the papers, Jenny, though it was afore Ted

136

was interested. Charlie'd been to a preview, and on his way back he tied up his old nag and went to a pub. A bit of a drinker, Charlie was, and when he come out someone'd cut the belly band. Charlie was all right so long as he leaned forrard, but soon as he leaned backard, up went the sharves and out he went on his napper. Shook him up a bit too, so's he couldn't go to that sale. They put the police on it but they never found nothin out."

Ted knew the story to be true, yet its implications seemed in no way to relate to himself. He was like a man who regards with detachment the mortality of others and sees no reason to take heed to his own end. That the ring regarded him as an enemy he knew well; that it should take its own steps to protect itself was something that had never occurred to him.

But to go back to the ring. It would assemble, then, at a preview or on the morning of a sale, and hold a council of war to make out dispositions. First it had to consider the likely opposition, such as X, Y, and Z.

"X won't be here," one might report. "They tell me he's laid up with a cold."

Someone else might give the news that Y would not be present, either, because of a more important sale near his home. That would leave only Z, and if Z or his representative failed to arrive, the ring could breathe freely and go on with its dispositions: who was to bid for what, and how much.

But the mere presence of Z—especially if Z were someone like Burling, not only outside the ring but definitely hostile—would be a near disaster. Instead of acquiring things at virtually their own prices, the ring would buy little, or else at prices that allowed a very scant margin of profit. Even at the smallest sales where a preliminary scouting or inside knowledge had unearthed perhaps one thing that had real value, the unexpected appearance of a man like Ted Burling could ruin in a moment the hushed schemings of days. At a little sale at Ingley, Ted, having time on his hands, turned up "on spec," as he called it, at a sale so unimportant that the preview was held only an hour before it began. Walter Rape was there.

"Whuh, what're you doin here, Mr. Burling?" he said. "There ain't nothin here you'd give as much as half a crown for."

There had been anxiety mixed with the surprise, however, and the words had rung false. Not only that; Rape tried to hold him in talk, and Ted had only a few minutes to look round before the sale began. Then he knew. It was he who bought—knowing it would be jumped at by Major Pryne—some of the best Waterford glass he had ever handled. As for the rest of the sale, there was nothing in it he would have put in his shop.

In April, the fourth month of Jenny's pregnancy, there was a sale at Mattergate, which is about two miles east of Bury St. Edmunds. Ted's eyes opened when he saw the catalogue, and shortly afterwards he had a letter from Mark. Mark had a heavy chill that was proving hard to shift, and he doubted if he'd be able to come, but he ticked off a few things that he'd like if they were up to description. He left the prices to Ted's own judgment.

What happened was to happen quickly, almost as quickly as the telling. It was a two-day sale with a preview on the one day preceding. Ted was away early and he drove the cob, not only because train connections were poor but because the horse was in far too good fettle and needed the work. He was late in getting away. When he arrived, the ring were there, and with them a dealer or two whom he'd never met. Though he gave no sign, he knew that his appearance had caused some perturbation, for in less than no time heads were together as if some new strategy were being hastily planned.

He had brought food with him and feed for the horse. A groom belonging to the house had offered an empty stall and had shown him a shed for the cart. It was late in the afternoon when he had almost finished his rounds of the rooms. Some of the things he had seen had taken him back to the Victoria and Albert: a green lacquer cabinet on a carved and gilt stand, a cabinet veneered with walnut oyster pieces and inlaid with arabesque marquetry, and a walnut-case grandmother clock with arch dial that even his books had described as very rare.

He was in almost the last of the rooms, examining with his glass a set of prints, when Walter Rape came in.

"How are you, Mr. Burling? Hain't had a chance to see you afore."

"Can't grumble," Ted said. "You keepin pretty well?"

"Not so bad," Rape said, and seemed to shift uneasily. "You comin to the sale tomorrer?"

"I reckon so. Why?"

"Look here, Mr. Burling," Rape said, and there was almost a pleading tone in his voice. "You don't want to come to this sale. You come into my shop at any time and you can have what you like. Anything you like at practically your own price. 'Tain't often you get an offer like that."

"No," Ted said thoughtfully. "I don't reckon it is. All the same, I reckon I'll be here."

Rape failed to move him, and in a minute or two he left. Ted made his slow way through the last rooms and then looked at his watch. It was far later than he'd thought, and he hurried out to get the horse into the shafts. It was a brisk late afternoon and the animal was still lively. As Ted drove through the gates it swerved skittishly, missing a gatepost by a bare inch. It was only a hundred yards farther on that everything happened.

At one moment he was on his seat, leaning back and reining in the horse. The next moment he crashed to the floor of the cart and the cart fell to the ground. His ribs struck the side, the wind was knocked from him, and there was a sharp pain in his ankle as he felt the lash of the cob's heels against the dashboard. That was all he knew.

It was only a minute or two later when he came to himself. Out of the blur and confusion he knew that he was lying on a grass verge and that people were standing round him. He felt pain as he breathed deeply, and when he tried to speak it was as if his lungs were sealed. A man was bending over him.

"How're you feelin now, old friend?"

He caught the words only faintly, as if they came from a distance. Other people were talking about a broken leg and a hospital. He tried to speak, but the pain struck him and his throat felt choked. He moved his left arm and touched his right side, where the pain was.

"Reckon he's bust a rib or two," the man said to the voices, and leaned over again. "You lay quiet, old friend, an we'll soon be gettin you away."

Ted's eyes closed and he lay quiet. If he breathed only gently, there was hardly any pain. Out of the comparative comfort thought stirred like the water that seeps at the slow easing of a sluice. There was Jenny. Jenny and the boy. Jenny would wonder. She'd be frightened—

He tried to speak. Another man bent down to him. This time the words came. He even knew his own voice.

"My wife . . . Don't let her know."

"That's all right," the man said. "Your name's Burling, ain't it? We've got your pocketbook and your things. Some of 'em dropped out when you was pitched out o' the cart."

There was a stirring among the few who still stood round. A wagonette drew alongside.

"Take it easy," the man said, and four or five helpers got their arms slowly under him and raised him from the ground. He groaned at the pain that shot through ribs and shoulder.

"Take it easy," the man said again, "and mind that there leg."

They laid him on the coconut matting of the floor and someone put an overcoat over him. The wagonette moved off. It was rubber-tired and well sprung, and only now and again was there a jolt. All he could see was the cold April sky and the sides of the wagonette, but the loneliness of the sky and the ebbing of the pain set his thoughts stirring again. He wondered if he were being taken to a doctor. After that he'd be able to get home, maybe, and he'd tell Jenny something or other so that she wouldn't be frightened. That made him think of the horse and cart, and he wondered what had happened. He seemed to remember a wheel spinning away just as the seat collapsed, before he fell. Then he worried if the cob were hurt. Perhaps after he'd seen the doctor, he could hire something to take him back to Ouseland.

The wagonette was now in the town, and it drew suddenly in at his right. He saw a tall building rear above him, and there was a Whoa! as the horse drew up.

He lay by himself on a bed in a room lit by gaslight. So great had been his agony when they took off his coat and waistcoat that they had cut away his shirt and vest. There were cushions under his right leg, and the nurse had told him to lie quietly and not to move. He was wondering now what Jenny would think, for the nurse had said she would have to be told. Over a week he would be at that hospital, and maybe more, they had said. All at once his mind was a surge of worry: Jenny and the boy, what would happen at the shop, the sale that would be missed, the commissions that Mark had given, and what had happened to the horse and cart.

It seemed an eternity before someone came again, and then it was the nurse. She smiled at him gravely. The doctor was just coming, she said.

He was a tall, middle-aged, bearded man, and he nodded as he looked down.

"How're you feeling now? Not so bad in yourself?"

"A bit sore, sir," he said, "and it still hurt here when I breathe."

"We'll have a look," the doctor told him. "This may hurt but you've just got to put up with it. Now then, tell me when it hurts."

The cool fingers felt chest and stomach and ribs.

"That's what I want to know," he said when Ted groaned and winced. The fingers pressed and prodded and probed. At last it was over and he was nodding down again.

"You've come out none too badly, considering what happened. We'll have those ribs right in no time. You may be uncomfortable for a few days, but that's nothing. Lucky it wasn't worse."

He had a word or two with the nurse. An attendant came in and lent a hand while the doctor strapped the ribs.

"How's that? Better already?"

"A bit easier, sir, now it's over."

"Right," the doctor said briskly. "Now we'll have another look at that ankle."

He felt far less pain than when they had strapped his ribs, but the doctor seemed to be taking a tremendous time. He tried to raise his head to see what was happening, but the nurse smiled reprovingly and her cool fingers pressed his forehead back. Then at last that was over too. The doctor had another word with the nurse and then went out.

"The doctor will be back in a few minutes," the nurse said. "Would you rather have a cup of tea or hot milk?"

He said he would like the tea, then in the same feeble voice called her back from the door.

"Nurse, what about my wife?"

"She'll have been told by now," she said. "But you can't see anybody yet. It may be a day or two. It depends on what the doctor decides."

She slid the pillows deftly beneath his head and shoulders while he drank the tea. Perhaps there was something else in the cup besides tea, for he began to feel drowsy. If his ribs had not hurt him when he moved, he might have dropped off to sleep. Then the doctor came in again, a different attendant with him.

It was a long half-hour before they left.

"Is my leg broke, doctor?" he had asked.

"Just a comparatively simple fracture," the doctor told him. "You stop asking questions and lie back there and relax."

The splints were in place. He had felt only now and again a twinge and a feeling as of bone against bone. But there was a question that he had to put.

"How long will they keep me here, sir?"

"Can't say," the doctor told him. "You're not out of the wood yet, you know. It'll be a fortnight before we get the plaster on. After that—well, we'll see."

That was a new worry when the room was quiet again, and then the drowsiness came back. He was dozing fitfully when the nurse gently roused him.

"Drink this," she said, "and then you'll feel much better."

She held him while he drank the tepid bitterness from the glass. Five minutes after she had gone he was sleeping like a dead man. When they moved him in the early morning, he thought of it only as part of some disordered dream.

He woke in a small ward of twelve beds, most of which were occupied, and his first sensations were of bright light and a smell like disinfectant. Things came back to him; he tried a movement and still felt pain. Then he saw that his leg hung in a kind of enormous bandage suspended from above the bed, and he wondered how he would sleep when night came again. Then a woman came in—he was to know her as the matron—together with the doctor and a stranger who looked like a doctor too. A nurse joined them and he watched them move slowly round the ward, halting at this bed and that. They came to his own bed, which was in the far corner, by a window.

"Well, Mr. Burling, how are you this morning?" his own doctor said.

"Can't grumble, sir," Ted told him with an attempt at cheerfulness.

He ran an eye over the cradle and said he'd have a look at the shoulder again. He asked about the ribs and the pain, and then had a word or two with the other doctor.

"You're doing well," he said. "You've a fine constitution, Mr. Burling. Your heart's in first-class shape, and that's the main thing."

He tested Ted's heart and lungs again and gave a satisfied nod.

"Nothing to worry about, Mr. Burling. Just lie there and tell yourself you're having a holiday."

"May I ask you somethin, sir?"

"Yes?" he said, and the voice was more abrupt.

"My wife, sir. When'll she be able to come?"

"In a day or two. Don't worry about your wife. She'll be all right."

A nod and he was moving on. Ted's mind was eased, yet he still felt some disquiet. Later that morning he vomited, but without blood. That night he had a draught that tasted less bitter, but his sleep was more restless. His ribs hurt when he moved, and the cradle gave him discomfort. That afternoon he had a visitor. He looked up from his drowsing when the footsteps stopped at his bed.

"Gordon!"

"How are you, Ted?"

"A bit easier than I was. How's Jenny?"

Gordon drew out the chair and sat down before he answered.

"Jenny's all right," he said. "A bit worried when she heard. But she's all right. She'll be along in a day or two. She sent word you were not to worry."

"And the boy?"

"He's all right too." Something else was at his tongue's edge, but he stayed it in time. "Won't be long before you're home again. Everyone reckons you're going on fine. Another fortnight or so and you'll be all Sir Garnet."

The horse was all right, he said, but the cart was pretty badly smashed. From what he could make out, the off wheel must have somehow worked loose.

"But how could it?" Ted said. "I greased them wheels only a day afore. Jenny'll tell you the same."

Gordon said that that was what he had heard. Then he gently hinted that Jenny had been a bit upset, especially seeing how she was. The doctor had reckoned she ought to rest for a bit. Nothing serious, of course; Ted would know how it was. And he was not to fret about young Gordon. Bella Crowe was looking after him and he was thinking it very much of an adventure.

"Jenny'll be along," he said, "only it won't do no good to worry. What matters is you, and she knows it."

There was no need to worry about the shop either, he said. He needed a bit of a holiday himself, so he was putting in a few days at the house. He and George could handle everything between them. Then the nurse came in, saying that it was time for him to go.

That day and the next Ted worried about Jenny. Something told him that Jenny was worse than Gordon had made out. Jenny must be in bed; otherwise she would never have let Bella take the boy. And why should Gordon be there when Jenny and George could run the business?

In the afternoon Ted had a visitor that took his thoughts momentarily from home.

A tall burly man came in with the matron, who smiled and left them together. The stranger drew up a chair beside the bed.

"I'm Superintendent Vane, Mr. Burling. They tell me you and I can have a minute or two to talk about that accident o' yours. Wonder if you could tell me just what happened."

Ted told him, Vane pursing his lips with a trick something like George's, while he listened and nodded.

"I see," he said. "But there's a funny thing, Mr. Burling, or so it seem to us. That nag o' yours slewed round into the ditch not twenty yards from where that wheel come off, but we couldn't find the linchpin. Even if it had worn and got broke, we ought to have found something. What do you say about that?"

Ted said that the linchpin was not six months old and that it had been in place the day before the accident, for he had given the wheels a greasing himself. That was proved by how the cart ran on the way to the preview.

Vane frowned and pursed his lips again.

"Only one answer to that," he said. "Someone took the linchpin out!"

Ted stared. There was something on his face that made Vane stare too.

"You think you know who it was?"

A moment, and Ted was shaking his head.

"Anyone got a grudge against you? Anyone who didn't want you to be at that sale?"

Ted's forehead furrowed but he shook his head again.

"Look, Mr. Burling," Vane said patiently. "You know more about this than you're letting on. It's your duty to speak."

Ted licked his lips. He shook his head again.

"Even if I do, I reckon I can settle it my own way."

"That's no way to talk," Vane told him. "The Law don't stand for anything like that."

But Ted was obstinate and grimly dumb, and at last Vane had to leave him. That evening his thoughts were heavy with misery, anxiety, anger, and his own helplessness. At night the ankle ached with a dull, persistent throb, and his thoughts in the tedious waking hours whirled as madly as on those long-ago nights when he had almost crazed himself with thinking of the bureau and the smart trickery of Clemming. In the morning the nurse frowned after she took his temperature. She had a word with the doctor when he came up.

"Not feeling so well?" the doctor said. He felt Ted's pulse and applied the stethoscope again.

"The leg hurt a bit?"

"It do sort of ache, doctor."

"Well, you have to put up with that for a bit." Something in his patient's look prompted a shrewd question. "Anything worrying you at all?"

"Don't know, sir—'less it's my wife. I can't make out why she haven't come, or writ."

"She'll be along in a day or two," the doctor told him. "But don't worry, man. If you don't cooperate with us, how're we going to get you well? You want that, don't you? So does your wife."

It was a Saturday. In the afternoon he expected Gordon again, but instead a letter arrived. Jenny was almost right again, Gordon said, and she'd almost certainly be there on visiting day, which was Wednesday. The letter contained news about the boy and the business, but it brought more doubt than consolation. So Jenny, as he had thought, had been ill, and Gordon had tried to keep it from him. Maybe there were other things he was keeping back.

That evening he left half his meal. The nurse took his temperature again and seemed surprised that it had gone down. There was another long night in spite of the sleeping tablet; but when the doctor came, Ted simulated cheerfulness. There were patients in the ward who would talk to him and to one another, but when Ted spoke his thoughts were elsewhere. In the afternoon, when there were visitors, it seemed to him that he was the only one who was utterly alone. After tea he asked the nurse for paper and pencil and an envelope, and wrote a long letter to Jenny that eased his mind. That night he slept fairly well, though the ankle still ached and throbbed.

Monday brought nothing, but on Tuesday morning another letter came from Gordon.

I didn't want to upset you about Jenny at the time, but the man who brought the message from the police station blurted out that you'd had a bad accident and had been taken to Bury Hospital, and she fainted with the shock and the doctor had to be fetched in. Gordon happened to be there and was frightened and told George and he fetched Bella Crowe and the doctor.

But Jenny is as good as all right now. The doctor doesn't like the idea of her coming on Wednesday but she says she's coming whatever happens. . . .

P. s. Your letter just arrived. It seems to have done her good. Gordon sends his love and says George is letting him make a bookshelf.

After that he longed for the hours to pass till Wednesday afternoon. He expected Jenny early, by the midday train from Ouseland, but it was almost three when she arrived. He saw her stand at the door, then she saw his waving hand and almost ran across the floor.

"Oh, Ted!"

"Jenny, Jenny."

Something was gathering in his throat. A nurse drew up a chair for her, and Jenny wiped her eyes as she sat down.

"Are you better, Ted?"

"Gettin on fine, Jenny. What about you?"

"I'm all right now, Ted. It was you I was worrying about—not myself."

But she looked far from well. She was thin—thinner than he'd ever known her. The face had a queer pallor and the eyes were dark and heavy.

"Sure you're all right, Jenny?"

"I'm all right, Ted."

She smiled and her hand stroked the unshaven face.

"I think I'd like you in a beard, Ted, after all—when it's grown."

He tried to smile too, but something else was gnawing at his mind.

"Jenny—it didn't—it didn't sort of go and upset everything?"

She looked away, biting her lip, and he knew the answer. As if they were alone in the room, his arm went about her, and the sudden wrench was nothing as he held her close.

"Oh, Jenny."

No other words would come.

"It doesn't matter, Ted—not really. It's you that matters."

She wiped her eyes quickly again. She could even force a smile.

"This is a nice way to cheer you up! Don't look like that, Ted. Everything will be the same again, as soon as you're home."

He thought of that after she had gone. But nothing, he knew, would ever be quite the same. He was glad that he had made out that everything had been an accident and had not worried her with what he now knew. Maybe he would never tell her at all—or at least not till he had got even with Clemming.

He was almost three weeks in the hospital. The ribs were as good as well and, unless he twisted unwarily, he felt never a twinge. The leg was now in plaster, and at first he found it difficult to hobble round with his crutch.

On the midday when the cab brought him from Ouseland station, there was a family reunion to cheer the heart. Jenny and the boy had come to meet him, and at the house were Gordon and George and Bella and Harold Crowe. George even touched his forelock before he lent a hand to help Ted out. Then he cast a dour eye on the crutch and reckoned he could make a better one himself.

Jenny had made a bed in the parlour. There was just a bit of chill in the May air and a fire was burning. Ted eased himself into the grandfather chair and said that it was good to be home. Young Gordon came in with his bookshelves—a miniature affair that would hang in his bedroom and just hold his books.

"Well, son, well!" said Ted admiringly. "And you made this yourself!"

"Yes, Dad. George helped with the polishing, though."

"Polishing's nothing," his uncle said. "Reckon, Ted, we shall have to take this young feller into the firm. Least you can do is buy him a proper apron like George's."

After the meal Ted had a quiet word with Gordon. Gordon owned that he himself had had a private word with the Bury superintendent.

"I think you should let him do something about it, Ted. Whoever was responsible ought to be had up and made to pay."

"What good would it be?" Ted told him. "He'd never find nothin out. And some things, you know, Gordon, can't be paid for in money."

"I don't care what you say," Gordon told him, just a bit heatedly. "They oughtn't to get clear. What about Jenny? What about yourself?"

"You let me handle this my own way." His eyes fell on the other's face. "You and me never had no words yet, Gordon, and, please God, we never shall. I'll find my own way of gettin even with Clemming."

There was to be much the same talk with Mark and much the same outcome. But long before that, on the morning after Gordon left, the doctor called to see Jenny.

She had been looking much more herself since Ted had come home.

After the doctor had seen her, Jenny showed him into the parlour. The two men were left together.

"I've seen you several times, Mr. Burling," the doctor said, "but not professionally."

"I've seen you too, sir," Ted said. "It's Dr. Minns, isn't it?"

Minns said that he'd had a report from the hospital and that he was enquiring about the ribs and the ankle. His opinion was that the plaster might come off in from six to eight weeks and that in a day or two after that Ted should feel fairly spry on his feet again. Then he seemed to be listening for a moment.

"I want a word with you about your wife, Mr. Burling. You know what happened?"

Ted reckoned there'd been a miscarriage.

"Fortunately not too bad a one, but serious enough for all that," Minns said. "What I want to impress on you, Mr. Burling, is this: it'd be extremely ill advised—it might even be dangerous—for your wife to bear another child."

"Not another child!"

"I'm afraid that has to be my advice," Minns said. "I've had your wife under observation, Mr. Burling, and I may tell you I'm rather concerned. It's to do with the lining of the womb—if you understand me. If she were pregnant again, the haemorrhage might return.

"I've spoken to your wife," he went on, "and she accepts the situation. Speaking as man to man, and more frankly than I could with your wife, all this doesn't mean that you have to live like hermits. If either or both of you wish to have a confidential word with me, I can mention simple precautions."

He got to his feet.

"It's been a bit of a shock to you both, but it had to be said. A doctor can't always bring good news, Mr. Burling. All I can hope is that this doesn't prove too bad."

He held out his hand and said he'd be in from time to time. When he had gone, Ted sat like a man in a daze. Not that he had ever thought what that unborn child would be. Had he known Jenny as a girl, he might have pictured a girl of his own as the image of her mother. To look backward was impossible, nor could he look forward and peer into the darkness of time and shape an unknown face. All that he saw and all that gripped him at the heart was Jenny herself: Jenny standing in the yard as Jessie moved off with the pram, her face lighting at the loveliness and the miracle of Jessie's child; Jenny in the hospital, eyes dull with misery and her thin face drawn and pale.

The door opened. She stood there for a minute, eyes searching his face.

"Did he . . . did he say anything to you, Ted?"

On her face was suddenly an infinite pity, and she was across the room and at his feet, with her arms about his knees. A tear ran slowly down his cheek and his arm tightened about her, though he could not speak.

The plaster was at last removed and he began hobbling about again; but his ankle swelled and gave him pain. After some weeks of agony Jenny made him see Minns, and finally it was decided that he should visit a Norwich specialist who would make an examination with the new X rays.

It was Minns who received the report. The fracture of the tibia had been correctly diagnosed at the hospital, but the fracture of the

fibula had not, though it had been present. The use of a wedge for
the inner side of sole and heel was prescribed to correct balance to
a certain extent, though there might always be a slight lameness.

The predictions were to prove correct. The pain disappeared,
though not before a year had passed; and even then, after walking
too much, Ted's ankle would ache, and in rainy weather he felt a
dull rheumatic pain that made him toss restlessly in his bed. A day
or two after he had heard the news from Minns, he spoke of it to
Jenny.

"Clemming ain't goin to get clear with this, Jenny. You never
heard me say a thing yet, did you, that I didn't keep to? Clemming's
goin to suffer if I have to wait till the end o' my days."

"Ted, don't talk like that," she said. "It isn't like you. Besides,
Clemming wouldn't have done it."

"Who was it, then?"

"I don't know. But Clemming wouldn't. It would cost him too
much if it was found out. It was some little man; that's who it was,
Ted. Someone in the ring who thought he'd pick up a pound or two
if you weren't there."

"Even if he was, Clemming was behind him. He's boss o' the ring.
Might have been murder, too. I might a-bin killed for all they
knew."

"No, Ted, no. All they thought was you might get a shock, perhaps; just something to keep you away from the sale. They didn't
know what was going to happen. They didn't see the consequences."

"That ain't no consolation to me, nor to you either," he told her.
"No one ain't goin to do things to you, Jenny, without havin to
pay for it."

She came over and put her arms round him, her cheek against his.

"I know, Ted. But it's over and done with now. Nothing we can
do will ever make it the same. And what's it matter about Clemming? We've got each other, Ted, and we've got Gordon. Doesn't
matter who it was that did it. They'll be punished some day without
us."

Ted said nothing but he nodded. It was not because he agreed
with Jenny, but because he felt and knew.

CHAPTER 13

The Full Man

THE change in Ted Burling was far more subtle than any that had gone before. The experiences of that catastrophic year had been more than enough to ensure a measure of spiritual isolation, for there were some things of which he could speak to no one, and others of which he could scarcely bear to think. There were the long days and the longer nights in the hospital, with their poignant loneliness and the numbing misery of the unknown; there were the pain of the body and the deeper pain of the soul; above all, there had been the irremediable loss and unspoken grief in the eyes of Jenny.

Outwardly there were few signs of spiritual change and maturity, though Jenny noticed his frequent silences and his even greater gentleness with herself and Gordon; but there were physical changes that were noticeable enough. Though his brief beard had been discarded before he left the hospital, he kept the moustache. Since it was untidy, like his hair, Jenny would get him to trim it to the line of the mouth, and she was secretly proud of the dignity and distinction it gave him. Then, with those weeks of idleness in which he could do little more than sit in the shop, he had put on weight; not a portliness but a filling out of his lean frame. With the slight limp his movements were more deliberate, and something of the old bodily tirelessness had gone.

Of the issue between himself and Clemming he never spoke again to Jenny, though she must have known it was always in his mind. That he would sooner or later find his own peculiar and satisfying means to make Clemming pay he had no doubt, even if the means were now uncertain and obscure; but the thought of Clemming was always there. When the ankle irked and ached it was impossible not to remember. There would be the limp and the awkwardness to bring things back, or some chance remark of Jenny's, or even the sight of Jessie's small daughter; but in those early days before the ankle had set, it was the means of evening things with Clemming that fretted him as he sat waiting for a chance customer in the shop.

An antique dealer is a shopkeeper, as is a grocer or draper; what difference there is lies mainly in the nature of his customers, and of these Ted Burling had three main classes. There were the gentry of the town and neighbourhood, people of taste and some discernment, who preferred the antique and mellowed to the modern in furniture or china or silver. There were the collectors whose names he had on his books and who called from time to time or were duly notified when he came into possession of anything that might suit them. Lastly, there were the larger dealers, from London principally, who called or sent their representatives, and found it profitable to buy at provincial prices.

Those, then, were the classes of buyers whom Ted Burling always had to have in mind when making a purchase. Because his capital was limited, he could not afford to keep stock for years or even months, nor could he permit himself a nostalgia or a purely personal liking. It was true that specialized knowledge would at times make him buy with the hope of a sale; and it was part of his business to foresee this future craze or that—for Bartolozzi prints or pewter, for example—and to protect himself against having to buy at the time of such a craze in a market artificially high. But generally his shop and its contents had to be seen through the eyes of his customers, and this it was that limited and cramped an attack on the ring.

Each member of the ring was a replica of himself, for each had his specialized knowledge and his special customer in view. Each, if the ring were challenged, could bid to his own predetermined price; and in opposing him Ted would be on dangerous ground, for something might be knocked down to him for which he had no likely customer himself, and that might mean an increase of stock and a tying up of precious capital. But where the thing bid for had a general value—that, as he saw, could be his chance. There he ran little risk, and by forcing up prices and withdrawing in time he could make the ring pay dear. And out of that baiting—just how he could scarcely at the moment see—might come some false step by Clemming that would give him the grand and clinching chance for a settlement of scores.

At the first sale he attended after his accident, he gave no sign that between himself and the ring there was more than the indifference and disregard which he had cultivated before. His eyes met theirs, and eyes, curious or shifty, met his own; but no word was spoken, even by Walter Rape. From then on, according to plan, he set himself to harry the ring as it had never been harried before. If he made a false step, that, he told himself, was part of the price he was prepared to pay. But whether or not he won a lot, he employed the same studied indifference he had first acquired from Mark. Clemming, he knew, was a blusterer who expected bluster in return; who liked to argue chin to chin; who liked to sneer and intimidate; but something told Ted that open indifference with just a touch of contempt would infuriate Clemming more than vituperation or any mere exchange of words. At that first sale there might have been such an argument.

"Sold to Mr. Burling at seven guineas," the auctioneer said when the hammer fell.

"No, sir, no!" called Clemming. "Seven and a half was bid here."

"Sorry, Mr. Clemming, but I didn't catch your bid. If Mr. Burling agrees, we can start the bidding again."

"Let him have it," Ted said quietly, his eyes still on his catalogue, and the room must have known who was the better man.

Long afterwards he would say that the years immediately following his accident taught him far more of his trade than all those that had gone before. For all his studied aloofness, the relentless duel with Clemming and the ring demanded tremendous concentration. Before a sale he had to be certain of his knowledge; it might have been disastrous to have permitted a more arbitrary approach or a superficiality of judgment. When he looked back, he knew too that he had had his moments of luck, as when the ring had tried to foist something on him and some instinct had made him draw back. He made mistakes, but on the whole they never cost him dear; yet he himself had cost the dealers much. Over those years his presence at sales must have made a difference to them of thousands of pounds.

As for his own business, it might not be spectacular but it was solid and expanding, with enough made to pay his way and something left to put by. In 1910 he was at last able to buy the property from Gordon. It was a fine feeling to plant his feet firmly on something eternally and utterly his own. In the town he was more than ever recognized as a man of standing and probity whose word was his bond. More than once he was approached to take part in borough affairs, and Jenny was secretly piqued because he would never assent.

"It's no use, Jenny," he would tell her. "Politics and all that sort o' thing ain't in my line. Reckon I only vote Conservative 'cause Uncle Mort did. Besides, there ain't a lot o' time. Maybe later on we'll see."

There was another change that that disastrous year had brought. The time had long since gone when Jenny had been the mainstay of both house and shop, and now the handling of the business had become solely his affair. Not that there were never matters about which she would be consulted; but there was now a curious sort of what she called obstinacy about him. It was not obstinacy; it was a clear seeing of the way ahead and the knowledge that that way was best. There were even times when Jenny would feel hurt because his decisions had not included herself, but she could never for long harbour a grievance against Ted. What she did come to have was an innate trust and reliance; and in the matter of young Gordon they were to stand her in good stead.

In one thing, however, she did have her way and Ted had to yield. The cob was sold and a more staid animal was bought.

"Whuh, Jenny," he said, "anyone'd think I wasn't used to hosses, 'stead o' havin grown up with 'em along with Uncle Mort. It wasn't the cob's fault. All he was was a bit frisky. I can handle him and twenty like him; but if you're goin to be frettin and worryin every time I'm out, there'd better be a change."

Then he grinned and Jenny had to laugh.

"So long as you don't make me go round in a dickey cart, reckon I can put up with it. One fule in the business is enough, Jenny, without havin two."

But it was of Gordon that Jenny had been thinking too, for already Ted had been talking of taking him round with him some day in the cart. Gordon was growing, and at nine he was as tall as his mother. He was a fine-looking boy, and everyone found him likable. He had his Uncle Gordon's grin and an even temper, and he was generous to a fault. Jenny often scolded him for giving away his possessions.

Jack Drew was still his chief friend, and Jack had even been admitted by George to the intimacy of the repair shop. Jack was a quiet, well spoken boy, better with his brain than with his hands, and he was quite content to sit and watch or do the menial jobs that Gordon would find for him. Gordon, half a head taller, was a hero to be followed blindly; perhaps it was for that that Jenny came to like the boy so much. Not that Gordon was spoilt. Hers was an unobtrusive discipline that never degenerated into nagging, and it was she whom he feared rather than his father—not that Ted couldn't be stern at times.

There was that occasion of the extra homework. When the time drew near for the scholarship examination, Ted had a word with the headmaster of the town school.

"Gordon's got brains enough if he'd use them," Ted was told. "He ought to be a certainty for a scholarship if he'd only set his mind to it. I think he must have some other interest that takes his mind from his work."

Ted knew well enough what the interest was. Every bit of Gordon's spare time was being spent with George, for he had a passion for woodwork that increased with his years. George claimed that it was a gift and that the boy already knew as much about some things as he did himself. When the boy was ten he made an inlaid workbox for his mother that even his Uncle Gordon genuinely admired; and George would have it that he had had practically no hand in it himself. However, it was now arranged that Gordon was to do special homework, and Ted promised to keep an eye on the boy to see that it was never skimped.

One winter evening, when Gordon seemed to be in rather deep water, he asked, "Mother, may I go and see Jack?"

"I don't see why not," Jenny said. "But you're not to stay unless your homework's done."

He was soon back and at work again. His frown had disappeared and he seemed to be cheerfully copying something into his own book. His father suddenly came over.

"What's this you're doin, son?"

"Just some arithmetic," he said, avoiding his father's eyes.

"But this is Jack's book."

Gordon laboriously and speciously explained that Jack and he helped each other. Jack wasn't too good at English and he himself wasn't good at arithmetic. Ted recognized a glibness. He picked up both books and had a look at them.

"So this ain't your own work at all, son. It's someone else's what you're just copyin down and makin out it's your own."

Gordon's face flushed and Ted ripped the page from the book.

"You know what a fake is, son? You know because George must have told you. It's somethin neither your grandfather nor me would have in his shop. And for why? Because it's a lie and a cheat, same as what you've been doin in that book."

He stood there, grimly looking down.

"Your father's right," Jenny said. "I'm ashamed of you, and so is he."

"Take Jack his book back," Ted said, "and when you get home, work things out for yourself. Tell the master if there's anything you don't understand. Learn to stand on your own feet and never lie your way out. You understand that, son?"

"Yes, Father."

"Then take that book back and never let me nor your mother know such a thing happen again. Better be a fool, son, than a faker and a cheat."

He shook his head after the boy had gone.

"You've never had a hint of this sorta thing happenin before, Jenny?"

"Never, Ted, or I'd have stopped it at once."

"Well, it's a good thing we've stopped it now—if we have. I'd rather the boy never got a scholarship than lie his way into one."

"But all boys are like that sometimes," Jenny said. "When they get older they know better. Gordon'll know better now."

She said no more. Ted was both angry and hurt, and enough had been said. After that, Gordon was at least circumspect enough to arrange any copying elsewhere, and his father could watch his homework with a gratified eye. He also added an incentive to work: the promise of a new bicycle if a scholarship were won.

It was a red-letter day when Gordon first went with him in the cart. It was in early August, and Ted deliberately chose a Breckland route. Of late he had done little hunting in the countryside, though it was something in which he had never ceased to find a pleasure and a thrill. To the boy it was a tremendous adventure, for never before had he spent an entire day in the cart. Jenny had packed a meal for both of them, and at midday they drew up at Ted's old quarry and ate while the horse munched in the nose bag. Then, and while they drove in the cart, the two talked, with Ted now and then pointing out the roof of a distant farm or some rare colour on heath or breck, or telling the boy what would lie beyond a fold of ground or ahead at the end of a rise. There were stories of things he had bought at this place and that, and at the end of the long afternoon he contrived that they should come to the cottage by the pond.

"I allust like to draw in here if I'm this way, son. A rare nice woman live here what give me a cup o' tea and a mite o' cake just afore you was born."

They had tea that afternoon with Mrs. Chapman, just as, in his days with Mort, Ted had been given a drink and a piece of cake at the farmhouses he had called on at their rounds. That night at home, when Gordon had gone up to bed, Jenny saw him smiling once or twice to himself.

"You liked having Gordon with you, Ted?"

"Yes," he said. "It fared like when I was a boy myself."

They had both laughed that evening when Gordon had run into the house to bring his mother out.

"Mother! Come and see what we've bought!"

"So it's *we*, is it?" Jenny said. "And what is it you've bought yourself?"

"Reckon we both sorta bought," Ted told her, and his hand went out to rest on his son's head. "A rare help he was to me, Mother, lookin after the hoss and keepin me awake."

Perhaps that was why he said something else that night when he and Jenny were going to bed.

"What're you smiling at, Ted?"

"About Gordon," he said, "and what he said about *we* buyin the things."

A moment or two later he frowned to himself.

"What do you say, Jenny, to changin that name to Burling & Son, same as your father?"

Jenny smiled but said it was early yet. Gordon might have a craze for woodwork and for being with George, but that didn't mean he would want to come into the business itself. To tell the truth, she felt a vague aversion to changing the name. There were things in which Gordon was more important than Ted, and things in which Ted was more important than Gordon. The name on the shop was more than just a part of Ted and herself: it meant Ted drawing up the cob on the other side of the road on their wedding morning; it meant the pride when they had come back from London; it meant all the things in those early years of which it had been the sure hope and symbol.

After that first day in the country, Gordon became something of a pest, always asking when his father was going somewhere again. Sometimes, in the years that followed, Ted would make such a day an excuse for a holiday, and Jenny was well aware that it was little more than that. Then the time came when the boy was taken to his first sale, when Ted was to hear from his son all the anxieties that he himself had felt in the old days with Mort.

"Why'd you let them have that table, Father?" it would be, or, "I wasn't half glad when you bought that table, Dad," sending Ted back to his own boyhood again. Sometimes at night he would catch himself using Mort's own words: "Better be slippin up them stairs, son." Then Gordon would kiss his cheek and Ted would pat his son's shoulder in the same way that Mort had patted his.

"And mind you say your prayers," Jenny would add, but that was something that Ted himself had never heard from Mort. Jenny had made all that a part of the boy's upbringing. Though there were many things which Gordon would contrive to evade, there was no excuse, however subtle, that would serve to keep him from Sunday school. Now that he was growing up, and Jenny had more leisure, she would almost always take him to evensong at St. Cuthbert's, which was hardly a stone's throw from the house.

When examination day came, Gordon was cheerfully optimistic. Even when it was all over, his view was that he had not done too badly. Jack was his usual diffident self; what worried him were the mistakes he now knew he had made. Ted was optimistic too, so much so that while Gordon was spending the Easter holiday at Yarmouth with his grandfather, the bicycle was bought and hidden, with the connivance of George, in the repair shop.

When the results appeared, seven scholarships were awarded to Ouseland, with Jack Drew at the top of the list and Gordon last but one. Jenny was pleased enough but Ted was disappointed, and so was the headmaster. Gordon had brains enough to have been at the top, he said; what was against him was a too optimistic, happy-go-lucky-approach. George had sometimes said something like it. Once his work was laid out, the boy was first-class; where he was impatient was in laying it out. Planning was irksome.

"Never know'd him spoil much when he was workin at it," George said. "What he don't do is plan. Want to git on too quick, that's his trouble."

But Ted was not niggard of praise to Gordon, and no one could have been prouder than he on that first autumn morning when the boy set out for school wearing his crested cap and the school tie. The pride was not all for the boy. In it was gratitude and a queer humility: gratitude for the ways through which the years had led himself, and humility because those ways had been ordered by something greater than himself. It was good to think that a son of his was going, by his own merit, to a fine old grammar school like Ouseland, to which, in his own first days in the town, the sons of even the gentry had gone. Then there was the headmaster, the Reverend Benjamin Reed, a figure of whom Ted himself stood somewhat in awe, because of his silk hat, fine presence, and the patrician air with which he walked abroad in the town.

Jenny was proud too, though her pride expressed itself in more practical ways. Never was a boy more neatly turned out. Bella Crowe had once hinted that there were social strata in the grammar school, with the boarders coming first and scholarship boys last, and Jenny was determined that her boy should at least be as well dressed as the best. No one's collars were starched more carefully than Gordon's or renewed so often; no cricket flannels were whiter than his. Jenny often corrected his lapses into dialect or reminded him about his manners, though in the latter there was no cause for apprehension, for the boy had a manner that was naturally pleasing.

George, too, had his own peculiar pride. What had worried him was the thought that the boy to whom he had given that first bull's-eye and the boy who had grown up with him in the shop would now become snobbish and that he himself would be looked at somewhat down the nose. George need not have worried, however, for Gordon was the same as he had always been; and though homework might keep him from the repair shop when games at school brought him home late, he was always with George on a Saturday morning, as soon as his few jobs had been hurried through in the house.

There was a new excitement in the repair shop. A man whom George had known and at one time worked with had retired and come to live in the town. A wood carver, a remarkably skilled craftsman, he would now and again be called in to lend a hand with some special repair work. Gordon's chief passion, of course, was thereupon wood carving; it was the one thing at which he exhibited patience. Once, when he was at Yarmouth, he did a small job of reproduction work that made his uncle open his eyes.

As for his school reports, Jenny often thought that they had too much of the reprimand about them. Gordon, they said, could do his work if he set his mind to it. Upon reading this, Jenny would give the boy one of her quiet lectures. Ted, however, was rarely inclined to worry overmuch about Gordon's place in his form.

"Book learnin don't matter all that deal, Mother," he would sometimes say. "Naturally we want him to profit, but I'm not frettin if he ain't allust at the top. What I want to see him grow up to is someone people respect. I've known a good many with brains that I wouldn't trust very far. I wouldn't like a son o' mine to grow up like that."

"People can't all be like you, Ted," she would say, her eyes softening as she thought of the man he had been and the man he had become. "And things have changed. There wasn't even a motorcar when we first came here. People have got to be educated nowadays. Besides, we don't know yet what Gordon wants to be."

Ted still secretly hoped that the boy would want to come into the business; he even thought of the time when he could buy the boy a business of his own. Sometimes, almost furtively, he dreamed of acquiring that fine new shop of Clemming's: the one he sometimes saw in the main shopping street of Norwich, with its handsome twin windows and show display.

Ted had bought, "on spec," as he would say, a little china figure from a woman who had brought it to the shop. She had claimed that it was at least a hundred years old since it had been her grandfather's. Not that Ted placed much reliance on that. People would claim that a grandfather clock was over a hundred years old because it had belonged to some ancestor or other, whereas in the book the maker's name would prove that it was no earlier than mid-Victorian.

But this figure interested him. It was that of a whiskered man wearing a cloak.

"What date do you put this at, Jenny?" he asked her.

Jenny didn't know, though the feel, she said, suggested about 1840. Ted said he had an idea it was earlier.

"May I have a look, Dad?"

Ted smiled as he gave it to the boy. The boy's forehead wrinkled.

"I know who it's meant to be, Dad. It's Lord Dundreary. We had it in our history the other day. Wait a minute, Dad."

He flew upstairs and came down with a book. There was a drawing of a man that was the very spit of the figure. According to what Jenny was reading, the date had to be after 1858.

"Bravo, son," Ted said, and gave the boy a pat on the shoulder. His smile broadened still more. "Reckon you'd better have this for a present. About time you started collectin somethin. Any more I hap to see, I'll pick up for you."

"Coo!" said Gordon, and was off up the stairs again with his treasure. Jenny's eyes met Ted's as she gave one of her self-satisfied sort of smiles. Though she said nothing, she might just as well have pointed out that that was what education did for one.

That summer the Reverend Benjamin Reed retired and Frederick Cole took his place. The new headmaster was something of a collector who a year or two before had been in the shop. In some obscure way the change gave Ted a new hope for the plans he had made for Gordon. Some people said that, after the long and aristocratic reign of Reed, such a change boded ill for the school; and Ted himself sometimes had thoughts similar to those he had had on that cold winter morning when the old Queen had died and the whole country had stood at the threshold of change. But the school was older than change. It was under the new headmaster that Gordon passed his first examination, not brilliantly, as Jack Drew did, but at least he passed. But a new examination was already in view, and he was staying on at school till he was at least sixteen.

Jenny said it made her feel old—that was after she had discovered her first grey hair. Ted laughed at her. Though he, like herself, was much nearer forty than thirty, he had had his first grey hairs after leaving hospital, and now his temples were greying fast.

"Don't matter what you look like," he told her, "though you're as pretty, Mother, as the fust day I clapped eyes on you. 'Tis what you feel like; and you and me hain't got much to grumble about there." He almost added, " 'Cept when this old ankle o' mine play me up o'nights." He kept it back, however, for the memory of that time was still too deep within him, and it might have brought pain to Jenny. Even now, when Jessie and Harold and the girl came round, he would catch a look in Jenny's eye that told him that she too had not forgotten. Besides, there was something else that was worrying Jenny: Mark's health. His heart was none too good, and Gordon wrote that he refused to listen either to the doctor or to him, and that he persisted in his usual way of life. Suddenly, in the summer of 1912, Mark died. He died in harness, collapsing at a sale, and passed away in a matter of moments.

Young Gordon was left with Harold, and Ted and Jenny went to Yarmouth at once. When the will was read, Mark was found to be far better off than even Gordon had suspected. Jenny was left £5,000, young Gordon £1,000 in trust till his twenty-first birthday, and Ted £100 "as a mark of my respect." After a minor bequest or two, Gordon had the rest. He begged Ted to part with his own business and come into partnership with himself. It was Jenny who turned the offer down. It wasn't, as she said, that she and Ted weren't grateful. No one but themselves knew how much they already owed to Gordon, but Ted would never be really happy in a partnership. Ted, chary of hurting Gordon's feelings, knew it for the truth.

Once more he refused to let Jenny's money come into the business. When it was invested, the interest alone seemed a fortune after their frugal life and the slow struggle of the earlier years. Yet Jenny wasn't altogether pleased. It was true that Mark had shown confidence in Ted by making him a trustee with Gordon for the boy, but because of the bequest of £100 it seemed to her that Mark had somehow had the last word over that first coming together of Ted and himself.

"It was you who should have had at least half the money," she told Ted when they were home again. "If father only had £100 of respect for you, and him with all that money, he might as well have left you nothing at all."

Ted stared.

"Whuh, Jenny, such a thing never come into my head. You was

his daughter, wasn't you? and who else should he leave his money to except you and Gordon? Mark and I allust got on well. Reckon it's a mighty fine thing when a man show respect for you in his will."

Jenny shook her head and gave one of her enigmatic smiles. Ted might be right and he might be wrong; but whichever way it was, this time she was the one who felt and knew.

CHAPTER 14

End of an Epoch

THROUGH all those years of waiting, there had been no open clash with Clemming, and then in one year there were two. It was the summer of Mark's death and the year in which Gordon was to leave school.

Clemming himself had somewhat sobered with the years. Now he had more the look of a prosperous businessman than that of a publican or drover. The change, revealed in the less flamboyant clothes that he wore, was perhaps part of a new status that had come with the acquisition of his new shop. Even Ted knew now that Clemming was dealing chiefly in the highest class of merchandise, and that, like himself, he could bid in hundreds where he had once bid in pounds. As for the ring, that had descended to something far more unobtrusive and even furtive. The old days had passed. Auctioneers were wiser and would protect a client by buying in. It was not that there weren't amenable auctioneers and good enough pickings sometimes to be had, but everything was more surreptitious. Men like Clemming became circumspect and kept from outward association with those who had been their cronies.

There was a sale that August at Ouseland. The goods had been removed from the deceased owner's house and had been brought from Barnham to the Oddfellows' Hall. Major and Mrs. Pryne were there, for the catalogue had mentioned some Jacobean glasses with floral decoration and threaded stems. Ted was to buy on commission, a thing he was glad to do, for the Prynes had been good customers. The major had spent many hundreds of pounds on glass, and Marion Pryne on furniture. More than once Ted had kept things for her when he had an assured sale elsewhere: a walnut day bed, for instance; a fine gate-leg table with open-twist legs, and a thirty-hour brass lantern clock with heraldic frets.

The sale was what was known as mixed, and there were two things only that Ted wanted to buy: a late seventeenth century marquetry-top table with ball turning and serpentine stretchers, and a set of eight Chippendale-style chairs. The chairs were not of the very finest quality; they were the sort that one liked inordinately or not at all; but he liked them and he thought he knew where they could be placed.

The table was put up first, and he bought it for sixty guineas, with himself and Clemming the last bidders. Then he lost the glass, for an unknown bidder went beyond the major's limit. Then at last came the chairs. The bidding opened at fifty guineas. It went fairly quickly to a hundred and more slowly to 150. At 200 he and Clemming were the only ones left. The hall was crowded and tense. Such sales as were held there were mostly for the utilitarian; now, however, bids were rising by ten guineas, and it was their own local man who was bidding against a strange dealer.

"Two hundred and eight guineas," came the voice of the auctioneer. "It's with you, Mr. Burling."

Clemming was frowning, catalogue fanning his chin.

"A pretty steep price, isn't it?" Pryne whispered.

Ted shrugged his shoulders. Clemming's bid came.

"Three hundred," Ted said quietly, and the bid was like an echo to Clemming's.

"Three hundred I'm bid. . . . Three hundred guineas. It's with you Mr. Burling. Any more from you, Mr. Clemming?"

There was a moment's hesitation, then Clemming waved a contemptuous hand. He did not laugh, but his tone was the tone of years before.

"Let him have 'em. He've had to buy 'em, haven't he?"

The hammer fell, and the room actually burst into applause. Ted made a note on his catalogue. It was getting near four o'clock and the sale had no more interest for him. There was something else as well. He had been indiscreet enough (so Jenny thought), to mention tea, and the Prynes had been delighted. Jenny had been horrified when Ted had told her and it had required much wheedling to change her mind. The Prynes were real gentry, and real gentry were at home anywhere. Not that Jenny need be ashamed of the parlour, the way she'd arranged it, with her needlework pictures and one or two pieces she'd insisted from time to time on appropriating from the shop. The curtains were in harmony with the wallpaper, and the Rockingham dessert service showed to advantage on Mort's old dresser.

Jenny had to own later that she had enjoyed tea. Gordon came in just before they left, and she was proud of what the major said.

"What a very nice lad that son of yours is, Mrs. Burling."

"And such charming manners," added Marion Pryne.

Before they left, the visitors went round the shop. George had just brought in the marquetry table.

"I think you gave too much for it," Marion Pryne said. "I have one just as nice—I don't know that it isn't nicer—that cost me far less. The next time you're near Ladeham, you must come and see it."

But if Ted looked at all worried, it was not because of the table; it was the chairs that were making him uneasy. His limit had been 250 guineas, and now he had to confess that Clemming for once had lured him on. He had hoped to buy even more cheaply, but at the price he had given he had little expectation of doing more than cut the loss.

No sooner had the Prynes gone than Harold was in. He had been at the sale. The duel with Burling had created excitement, and the reporter in him had scented a news value. Nothing would satisfy him but that Ted should straightaway pose in the yard with the set of chairs. A day or two later the Suffolk paper reproduced the photograph with some letterpress. Ted bought copies and sent them to a likely customer or two. The next day he had a telegram, and in the afternoon a Colonel Hopworth arrived from Ipswich.

"There you are, sir," Ted said. "There's the chairs and you know what I paid. I'm not askin a big profit. Ten guineas will satisfy me, and I reckon all the fuss there's been about it will bring me in far more than that."

The chairs were sold, but it was a lucky escape and he knew it. There had been a certain self-display in the presence of the Prynes, a superficial optimism about his own judgment, and a foolish yielding to those hostilities that only Clemming could provoke. All those things he knew, and none of them, he told himself, should ever happen again.

The business of the table was quite a different matter. Only a few days later he happened to be near Ladeham. This time he went to the front door. Had he been capable of an irony, he must have smiled at the difference in his reception by the same butler he had seen years before.

"Come along into the drawing room and we'll have a look at my table," Marion Pryne said. "This is it, here. Isn't it lovely?"

"Mind if I have a good look at it, ma'am?"

"Of course you may look at it."

He ran his glass over it. He even got down on his knees to look beneath the top, and his fingers moved slowly across the serpentine stretchers. He looked at them through his glass before he got to his feet.

"Well?" she said, and smiled.

"You didn't buy this privately, ma'am?"

"From a dealer," she said. "Major Pryne was with me when I bought it. It cost me forty pounds. We were asked guineas but I got it for pounds."

"You wouldn't like to tell me the name of the dealer?"

"Why not? It was Clemming. But why do you ask?"

"Clemming," he said, moistening his lips with his tongue. "So you bought it from Clemming."

"But I told you so!"

The frown went. A wry smile was in its place.

"If I could write as well as you, ma'am, I'd write a letter for you to Mr. Clemming. But you write it, ma'am, and tell him this. That table's a fake. The top's right, though the marquetry's been heavily repaired. All the rest is made up, probably from the ruins of a William and Mary piece."

"You're sure?"

"Never was surer, ma'am. You write what I advised you to Mr. Clemming. Mention my name and ask for your money back."

That afternoon, when he got home, he went at once to Jenny.

"Jenny, what do you think's happened? I've got Clemming *here*!"

He had jabbed a thumb down on the table. There was a grimness on his face that hurt her, even when she knew what he meant; and for once in her life she feared for his judgment.

"But, Ted, suppose you're wrong!"

"Wrong?" He laughed. "Would I be wrong if someone said that was a mule out there and I said it was a hoss? It's as plain as that."

"But what good will it do you, Ted? I know you ought to protect a customer, but you needn't have asked Mrs. Pryne to bring your name in."

"You let me handle this my own way," he told her. "I've waited a long time, Jenny, and I'm showing Clemming up."

She shook her head as he went out to see to the horse. She knew that there were things she ought to say: about reviving scores that were best forgotten, about opening wounds that had healed. She should try to show him how foolish it was to do so; but there was something about which she could not speak: the difference, the disturbing, almost ugly difference, that had come upon him when he had exulted about Clemming. She dreaded seeing any flaw disfigure the man she knew him to be. At last she shook her head again, knowing it was better to say nothing at all.

That mountain of revenge produced a very emaciated mouse. A few days later a letter came from Major Pryne. It was written from the Norwich offices of the Anglian Insurance Company, of which he had assumed the chairmanship on his father's death.

My Dear Burling,

I ought to have written and thanked you before for the advice you recently gave my wife, but I thought you would like to know the outcome.

I wrote to the dealer in question myself, later saw him and said we had had expert advice about the table, and that it must be taken back unless he wished to court some public unpleasantness.

Well, the table was fetched—we refused to send it—and a cheque has now been received together with a highly specious apology. We are both very grateful to you, you know that, my dear Burling, and if you have not yet parted with your own table, we should be glad to have it. It will be a reminder of our own folly and a pleasant reminder of your very kind self. Our thanks again, and best wishes to your charming wife.

Yours sincerely,
Harcourt Pryne

There was not even the gratification that Clemming had known who had given the expert advice. All he could tell Jenny, after she had read the letter, was that the business must have scared Clemming out of his wits; that Major Pryne, who was a man of wealth and influence, would warn his friends about Clemming—and that that would do Clemming no good.

Gordon had passed his last examination, again with no great brilliancy, it was true, but at least he had passed. Jack Drew had done well and was going to Cambridge, but Gordon was not envious.

The summer term was his last, and Ted and Jenny were always asking what he wanted to do. All that Gordon knew was that he wanted something to do with wood. This vague aspiration demanded a talk with his uncle, who recommended letting the boy employ himself where his liking and his true bent lay. It was he who suggested that his nephew should come to Yarmouth and add to his knowledge by a year or two under his own foreman. There'd be no expense for his parents—not that they were worried about that—for the boy would more than earn his keep and pocket money.

After Gordon went to Yarmouth, the house seemed incredibly lonely. Ted had tried to laugh when Jenny shed a tear on the night that Gordon left.

"Whuh, Jenny, whatever is there to cry about? Anyone'd think the boy had gone for good 'stead o' bein just at Yarmouth. It's sorta like goin home. Besides, he'll be home here from time to time, won't he? And 'tain't as though you can't go and see him yourself. You aren't tied to the house as you was."

Jenny slowly dried her tears, but with Gordon had gone a liveliness, a current of air, a sense of anticipation. Repair shop and house were uncomfortably quiet and curiously stagnant. George seemed to think so too.

"Reckon I'll soon be packin m' old tools in the box," he told Ted one day. "About time I sorta made way for someone a bit younger."

"Whuh, George!" Ted was quite startled. "You can't do a thing like that! Besides, you're a better man than ever you were. I might as well talk about retirin myself. And what about the missus? She couldn't get on without you, George, no more'n I can." He tried to smile. "Reckon you're tryin a joke on me."

George shifted his bull's-eye to the other cheek and put on his considering cap. Maybe he was serious, he said, and maybe he weren't; only things were different now that Gordon had gone.

"He's comin home next Saturday," Ted said. "Reckon he'll be the same as he allust was."

He gave George a pat on the back and left him still shaking a gloomy head. But George got over his loneliness and despondency, whereas Gordon's monthly visits merely served to make his mother miss him more when he had gone. Ted cast about in his mind to see what could be done, and at last he had an idea.

Thereafter, for about a fortnight, he was often out of the shop, and George would be called down to supervise. Jenny could not help noticing it, but he put her off by talking of business in town. Then she began to worry, though pride kept her from more questioning.

Then one afternoon several weeks later, Ted said: "Just slip your hat and coat on, Jenny. I want to show you somethin."

Jenny made ineffective protests but consented to go. They went along Earl's Street, towards the station. Jenny stopped.

"Ted, where are we going? It isn't anything to do with Gordon?"

"Now, now, Mother," Ted told her. " 'Tain't nothin to do with Gordon. Just a little surprise what I've been savin up for you."

Jenny went fearfully on. They passed along the Norwich Road until they came to the big new garage and went round it into the yard. A car stood there, shining in all its newness.

"There you are," said Ted. "What do you think on't, Jenny?"

"It's yours?"

"Ours," he said, and gave the car a smile and a nod.

"Why, it's like that one Gordon said his uncle had!"

"It's better'n that," Ted said pridefully. "His is what they call a Model-T Ford tourer. This here's what they call a town car."

"It's lovely," she said. "But who's to drive it?"

He laughed.

"What d'you reckon I bin doin on this last week or two? Drive it anywhere, I can. Hop in, Jenny, and we'll take it home."

A mechanic appeared from nowhere. Jenny got nervously in, but Ted settled at the wheel as if he were holding the reins of some staid old horse. The car moved miraculously off. Jenny clutched the side as the horn was sounded and they turned into Earl's Street. A hundred yards on and she was even able to smile. Then she thought of something. It was not that she was parsimonious as Mark had sometimes been; it was just that she could never forget those first hard, distant days when even a penny was money and a profit of ten shillings on the shop was almost a fortune.

"Ted, it must have cost a lot of money."

"Two hundred pound."

Her eyes opened wide. Then she said that she thought they could perhaps afford it.

"Course we can afford it. This hoss I'm drivin now don't cost nothin for feed. Look what we'll save. Look how you can get about. Afore you know where you are, you'll be hoppin in it yourself and slippin off to Yarmouth."

But Jenny never learned to drive, and the only driver with whom she felt safe was Ted. Gordon would insist on taking her out when he was home; but he drove, at least for her, much too fast, even recklessly, and the happiest moment would be when she was home again. She liked the comfort and convenience of the car, however, and she liked Ted's pleasure in it. She even felt relieved that he was no longer driving a horse. And Ted said that his ankle was not giving him half the trouble that it formerly had.

Gordon was happy at Yarmouth, and his uncle was delighted with the way he was getting on. He said that when he was of age he should be able to take over everything that he himself had once handled, and that if he showed anything of a liking, he might eventually be brought into partnership.

"Someone'll have to come in for everything when I'm gone," was how he had put it, "and naturally I'd like it to be Gordon."

Jenny would be angry with him, even if dimly gratified, when he spoke like that. Gordon talking as if he were an old man instead of not much more than forty!

"More like fifty."

"Well, fifty then. And what's fifty? Besides, the fault's your own. Years and years ago I used to keep on at you about getting married, and now perhaps you see I was right."

"Mobbin again, Jin," he would tell her with his wry grin. "Reckon if Ted had known what a tongue you had he'd have had nothing to do with you."

"You leave Ted out of this," she would say, only to realize that he was laughing at her.

It wasn't long before young Gordon had a new interest in life, for he had made friends with Wilfred Shefford, son of Thomas Shefford of the Norwich firm from which both Shadd & Son and Ted himself had bought fine woods. Wilfred, who had been at Felsted, was a year older than Gordon. The Sheffords were wealthy people, and Gordon spent a week end from time to time at their fine house just outside the city, along the Dereham Road. Early in 1914 Gordon asked if he might bring Wilfred to Ouseland. Jenny was somewhat flustered by the request.

Gordon had reached six foot. Wilfred was shorter and sturdier, altogether the perfect foil to Gordon; he was quiet, deliberate, and restful to have in the house. His manner was natural and charming, and Jenny liked him from the first. He was appreciative of even the smallest thing, unlike Gordon, who took much for granted or accepted favours sometimes as if they were a kind of homage. A book or a quiet chat would satisfy Wilfred, whereas Gordon was always restless, wanting to be out in the car or scurrying in search of he knew not what.

It made work for Jenny, but it was a week-end she was always to remember. Ted enjoyed it too.

"That Wilfred's what I'd call a real gentleman," he said. "You can allust tell 'em, Jenny. Soon as one step into the shop, you can tell 'em."

"I hope Gordon doesn't go and lose a friend like that," Jenny said. "Not that Wilfred doesn't like Gordon. And don't you think he was—well, impressed by what Gordon knew?"

"Gordon does know," Ted said. "He's my own son, but there's a good many, includin myself, what he could learn about wood."

"All the same," Jenny said with a sigh, "I don't think I could ever bring myself to go to his home as he asked us to. I'd be too flustered and do something I was ashamed of."

"Not you," Ted said. "I reckon you're as much a lady, Jenny, as any of 'em. That was how you was when Major Pryne and his wife come to tea that time; yet you reckoned afterwards how you enjoyed it."

But even when Jenny was in Norwich with Ted, she could never bring herself to visit the Sheffords. Something was about to happen, however, that would change her little world of Ted and Gordon. There were to be anxieties and fears that were soon to take her thoughts from all else but her boy; but that was not till a year later.

When war came, it found Ted more prepared than most. For the first months nothing seemed to happen, except perhaps that the London firms were buying cautiously. Then, slowly, as men realized that this was not a war merely of months, a paralysis began to creep over business, and soon there was little doing in the shop. Ted had no reason for panic, however. What worried him more than the cessation of trade was the inaction that was now forced upon himself. As he told Jenny, if the worse came to the worst they had a roof over their heads and enough to live on till the war was won and things looked up again.

Then Gordon Shadd paid a visit. He had been hit even harder than Ted, with Yarmouth empty of visitors, the town swarming with troops, and the sea-front all barricades and barbed wire. But, like Ted, he had no real financial worries; his worry was that, like Othello, his occupation had gone.

"I've been thinking," he told Ted and Jenny. "What all this business amounts to is this. Are we going to win this war or aren't we?"

"Of course we'll win it," Ted said. "It may take time, but we'll win it, all right."

"Then our course ought to be clear," he said. "I think the same, and this is what we ought to do. Sooner or later it'll be all over. The whole country will be full of money again and people will be buying more than ever. Every penny I can spare I'm going to put into stock. It won't have to pay rent and it can stay there till the time comes. That's when we'll make the money."

Both Ted and Jenny thought there was a lot in what he said.

"I know I'm right," he told them. "You ought to do the same, Ted. Buy at the bottom of the market and buy carefully. Get the good stuff only; fill your rooms and that repair shop of yours. If you find yourself hard up for cash at any time, you can come to me. Mark left plenty, and there's more since he went."

Jenny was asking him anxiously about Gordon. He was all right, his uncle said, and seemed to be worrying little about the war. Quite a lot of his time was being spent with the Sheffords; he liked going over their Works.

"What is it they do exactly?" Ted was asking. "I know they do high-class joinery and that sort of thing, but we never seem to get much out of Gordon."

"Theirs is much more than joinery. They do the panelling and woodwork for big new offices, and renovations for fine old houses. You know the kind of thing: when there's been beetle or dry rot.

When there's an extension to some old Hall or other, they do the panelling and so on in keeping. And they make high-class reproduction furniture."

"What, fakes?"

Gordon laughed.

"No, not fakes. High-class stuff for the big London stores. It's sold as reproduction stuff. People like to have it, and Sheffords make it. That's all it is. You ought to see some of it. Beautiful stuff. Quite as good for some people as the old."

But that was far from shifting Ted's secret contempt for both maker and buyer. What was shifted for Jenny was the worry about Gordon and for some days she was quite cheerful about the house. That was why, in November, the letter was such a shock. She had expected Gordon home but something had always seemed to happen to keep him at Yarmouth or Norwich, and she had even been wondering, thoughtfully and curiously happily, if he had fallen in love with some girl. Then the letter came. It was a morning she was always to remember: a dull, overcast morning with a threat of cold rain. Ted was sitting by the fire, smoking his pipe, when the post came. Jenny heard the rattle of the letter box and went through to the shop.

"Two for you, Ted, and one for me. From Gordon."

She was smiling to herself as she opened it. A moment or two and the smile had gone. She gave a little moan.

"Oh, Ted."

Ted's mouth gaped. Jenny was crying and the letter fluttered to the floor. His arm went round her.

"There, Jenny, there! . . . What is it, Jenny? What's a-matter? 'Tain't nothin serious, is it?"

"Oh, Ted . . . Oh, Ted . . . I knew."

An arm reached down for the letter. His tongue slowly moistened his lips as he read it.

DEAR MOTHER,

This is really for you and Dad, but I thought you'd like to know first. Wilfred and I have enlisted. We couldn't bear it any longer, people looking as if we ought to be in the Army, and in any case we thought we ought to go.

But there's nothing to worry about, Mother. We're both going into the R.E.'s, and no one ever gets killed in the R.E.'s. It'll be what they call

cushy, though we didn't exactly think of that. Besides, we're both putting in for a commission. Wilf's pretty sure of one, and Mr. Shefford
has a lot of influence and thinks it a certainty that I'll be an officer too.
Wait till you see me in uniform!

As soon as I get leave I shall be home, even if it's only for a week end.
Wilf sends his love. His father was very upset at the news but I know
you and Dad will understand how it was. Give Dad my love. Much love
to yourself from

Your loving,
GORDON

PART III

The
Restful
Hill

CHAPTER 15

Waiting

WHEN the spring of 1917 arrived with Gordon still in England, Jenny desperately hoped that the war might be over before he could be sent to France. He was never absent long from her mind. Ouseland was full of troops and just outside the town was an aerodrome. The mere sight of a uniform would set her worrying about her boy. In April a letter came to say he'd be home on embarkation leave. There was only a fortnight, he wrote, and because Wilfred had managed to make the last fortnight of his own leave fit in with Gordon's first, he'd be spending a week with Wilfred at Norwich and the final week at home.

Jenny was hurt about that. A fortnight was nothing; he should have given his parents all his time.

"That's how it allust is, Mother," Ted told her. "Birds have to leave the nest. You can't allust keep 'em under your wing. Gordon's got his own life to live, and what about when he get married? You won't have him then. He might have to live hunderds o' miles away, for all we know."

"If he live to get married," Jenny said.

Ted was angry with her for that. It was unfair to the boy to be so pessimistic, he said; but Jenny replied that he was not Gordon's mother, and Ted could only throw up his hands and give up the argument. He did hope she wouldn't be pulling a long face all the time the boy was home.

Jenny, however, was to surprise him with her cheerfulness. It was hard to be other than cheerful in the presence of Gordon's optimism. He knew that the war would be over pretty soon, he said, and he chanted his old slogan that in any case the R.E.'s never got killed. Jenny was even reconciled to the vast amount of time he spent out of the house, away somewhere in the car, seeing old school

179

friends like Jack Drew, now a schoolmaster at Lynn. There was something to fortify her, too, in the man he'd suddenly become, with his moustache making him look a good five years older. She was proud of him in his uniform, and proud of the way the soldiers saluted him in the streets.

Ted planned a trip for Wednesday afternoon. Because rationing worried Jenny, at times he would take the car to see old friends of his and Mort's, and then he would bring home a slab of bacon and butter and eggs. But this trip was different; it was one that Jenny herself had never made. She looked surprised when the car drew up outside the small cottage.

"Here y'are, son," he said. "Here's where I lived long afore I knew your mother or you was thought on."

They got out and went round to the back door. A stranger was living there who was only too pleased to let Ted see the kitchen where he had spent much of his time. Ted and Gordon even went up to his old bedroom while Jenny and the woman—she had two sons in France—talked as mothers do. It was only half-past three, but she insisted on their having a cup of tea. While they drank it, Ted told them about Mort and himself.

As they came out, Ted pointed to the woodshed.

"That's where that bureau was, Jenny."

"What bureau, Dad?"

"I'll tell you about it later on," Ted said, "but your mother know."

There was the school to which he had gone as a boy; the road, as he told Jenny, was the one he'd scurried along that morning when he'd had to catch the train that would take him to the Tinkersham sale. Soon they were at the level crossing and over the top of Larford Hill, making for the village. As they drove, he told Gordon about the bureau. It was something that he had never thought he would do. He had only intended to give Jenny a change from worries that afternoon, and to show Gordon the cottage he had often told him about when Gordon was a boy.

"Good Heavens!" Gordon said. "Sovereigns, eh? What'd you do with them, Dad?"

"Give 'em back," Ted said, and Gordon's mouth gaped.

Gordon said, with what Ted thought was a certain reluctance, that he guessed it paid to be honest.

" 'Tain't a question o' pay, son," Ted told him. "It's what you have inside yourself. Conscience, I reckon; sorta knowin what's right and what ain't. Soffe knew it but I didn't—not then. That's somethin you've never got to forget. There's only one way in life, son, and it's easy enough to see if your eyes ain't blinded." He nodded and then smiled.

"Sound like preachin a sermon, Mother, and a dry one at that."

"It doesn't do any of us any harm to listen to a sermon," Jenny told him. "Not even Gordon, when it's his own father who's giving it."

They went on to Heathley, past the school and along the Wortley Road, and so at last to Rudgham Heath. They stopped for a time at Ringmere, where the reeds were still grey in the water and the young fronds of the bracken were thrusting through the brown of the old. Jenny gathered some fir cones for the fire and then they went on over the level crossing to the Norwich turnpike. When they got home, she said it had been a lovely afternoon. Gordon had enjoyed it too. For him it had been just a pleasant afternoon; he could not know that one day it was to be far more than that.

He left by the Friday morning train. Jenny said goodbye in the house, for she could not trust herself to go to the station. Just before the train moved off, Ted said words to his son that had been said to himself and Jenny years ago, when Gordon Shadd had lingered by their train that was about to depart for London.

"Goodbye then, son. You'll let us know how you get on."

"Yes, Dad. I'll write whenever I can."

"It's your mother I'm thinkin on. You know how she'll worry."

"I'll cheer her up, Dad. Don't you worry either."

The train was moving. There was a sudden awkwardness, and then Gordon had gone. In a moment he was leaning out and waving, and Ted waved too, till the train was round the bend.

Business was bad that year and worse a year later, when the Germans almost broke through on the Western front. Ted was worried for fear he had invested too heavily. He was afraid that Jenny's money would be lost, for Jenny had not liked Ted's going to her brother and had insisted on his using some of her own money.

But other dealers were far more anxious than himself. One day he went into a shop at Ipswich where the dealer was in despair.

"Anything you like, sir, at your own price. Look—this bureau-bookcase. Thirty-five pounds!"

Two years later the bookcase was to make 120 guineas. In town, prices were the same. Ted bought a three-tier walnut mirror, as exquisite a thing as he'd ever seen. It cost him only forty-five guineas and he thought he'd try his luck with it at Christie's. There it made fifty guineas, but after commission and expenses he'd lost money. At home he was fortunate in that there were still some sales in the shop, if only for the cheaper things. Officers dropped in occasionally, sometimes with their wives; and there were still the discerning collectors whose buying was based on the same confidence that Gordon Shadd had shown.

At the height of the slump Ted had his ideas about Clemming, though he said nothing to Jenny. He had seen little of him for some months, for sales had been almost deserted, and the last thing the smaller dealers wanted to do was to add to an already crippling overhead of stock. One day, when he was in Norwich, he had a long look at Clemming's shop from across the street. Good pieces were in the windows, and the store had an irritating air of solidity, if not prosperity. That afternoon he made it his business to drop in on Major Pryne, bringing some rare glass as an excuse. It was easy to draw the talk round to the slump and to how it had affected the trade.

"I suppose Clemming's weatherin it all right?" Ted asked off-handedly.

"I imagine so," Pryne said. "A man who's got enough capital can ride out almost any storm. By the way, you remember that business of the table? I rather bit off my nose to spite my face. We used to handle his insurance, but—strictly between ourselves—as soon as everything had been smoothed over, he transferred to another concern—the London Authentic, I believe."

That was all the satisfaction Ted got. Truth to tell, together with the quick sense of depression he felt shame for his own furtiveness. He came out into the open.

"You know, sir, if Clemming happed to go wrong, I wouldn't mind havin that place of his myself."

"Really?" The other's eyebrows lifted. "You're not happy at Ouseland?"

"I suppose I am, sir. It's just that there might be more scope."

"What about your wife?"

Ted smiled wryly and doubted if she'd like to change.

"She's a sensible woman," Pryne said. "What would Norwich give you except the chance of making more money? What would the money give you that you haven't got already?" He shook his head. "Sometimes, you know, Burling, I wish I could get back to Ladeham and stay there. There's something about the country that you'll never get in the town. You've got time to think in the country. Things have a different value."

Then he asked about Gordon. Ted said that he was safe so far and that his letters were always cheerful. The major mentioned his own two boys, one in Palestine and the other in France again after recovering from a serious wound. The thought of Clemming seemed suddenly trivial to Ted. His conscience stirred, showing him more clearly the momentary unworthiness that had smirched him.

A week later there was bad news. Ted saw it in the casualty list in his paper, and for a few minutes he was afraid to show it to Jenny. He even dared to hope that it might be someone else of the same name, but he knew that the hope was foolish. Wilfred Shefford had been killed. To Jenny the news was a tremendous shock. She did something which she could never have imagined herself doing: she sat down and wrote a letter to his parents. A day or two later a letter came from Mrs. Shefford, thanking her for her kindness, and mentioning how much Wilfred had thought both of her and of Ted. Gordon had written too, she said:

Whether this dreadful war ends quickly or not, I do hope he'll be preserved to you, for he also is an only son, and we all thought of him as if he were our own.

My husband may write later, but at the moment he is very unwell. The shock, as you can imagine, was very severe, but we trust he will be well again soon.

Again thanking you for your kindness and for all you both meant to Wilfred,

Yours very sincerely,
MARGARET SHEFFORD

Only a week later worse news was to come. A German shell had set off an ammunition dump behind Givenchy, and Gordon had received severe shrapnel wounds. Jenny was almost crazy till the news came that he was in hospital at Étaples and on the way to recovery.

By that time Gordon himself was able to write. It was a not too coherent scrawl that made Jenny think him, in spite of his protestations, far worse than he really was. A fortnight later came the good news that he was in a convalescent home at Richmond, and Jenny and Ted went down to see him there.

He was hobbling around, looking much better than either had hoped. What he kept to himself was that there was still some shrapnel in him and that another operation was planned. He told them that there was some talk of his getting some decoration or other. Finally Ted dragged the information out of him that he had turned out with every available man and had helped to stop a German rush.

"You just don't think about such things, Dad. Before you know where you are, you're down on your belly and blazing away, and then—well, you just haven't time to think."

"And what about this leg o' yours, son? Do you think they'll put it right? Don't want a couple o' cripples in the family, you know."

Gordon said that the doctors had told him that it would be all right. Jenny remarked that she didn't mind if he was a cripple—well, just a little bit of a cripple—now that he was safe. When they left the home she was far more cheerful than Ted could ever have imagined; she was sure in her mind that never again would Gordon have to go to France.

There were two more operations before the medical board gave Gordon his discharge and he was home again, though that was not till the end of the war was in sight. He had been given a Military Cross and he retained his honorary rank of captain. While he waited for new civilian clothes, Jenny regarded with pride the ribbon he wore. There had also been a story in the local paper. Gordon was furious about that.

Ted had been led into the matter by Harold. The news of the M.C. came out just before Gordon came home. Gordon had had no idea why Harold wanted a photograph so badly, and no one was as surprised as he when the photograph and a write-up appeared in the local paper. It was the caption that annoyed him most: LOCAL HERO RETURNS.

"Local hero! What rot!" he said.

"Now, son, you mustn't talk like that in front of your mother."

"Besides, it's true," Jenny said fondly.

"It isn't true, mother. Wilfred was a hero, if it comes to that, and he didn't get anything for it. Besides, it makes you look a fool. What'll the Sheffords think about it?"

The Sheffords thought much of it. Margaret Shefford wrote a long letter, and Jenny was hurt because Gordon seemed to think more of it than of the letter his Uncle Gordon had written. When Gordon alluded, a bit tolerantly, to his uncle as a stick-in-the-mud, she told him a few home truths.

"That remind me, son," Ted said. "What about your uncle's offer? Do you reckon you'll take it?"

Gordon said he didn't know. He'd like to look about a bit before he made up his mind. What he didn't know then was that a week-end in Norwich with the Sheffords was to settle his problem for him.

It was an excited son whom Ted met at the station that Monday night. Hard on the heels of the "Hallo Dad!" came a spate of words. Gordon was still talking when the car drew in at the yard.

Mr. Shefford, it appeared, had decided that his health would no longer permit him to continue his onerous responsibilities at the Works, and he was proposing to retire altogether in a year or two or even before then. It had been his intention to have Wilfred take over; now he hoped, as Wilfred might have hoped, that Gordon would be associated in some way with the business. He proposed that Gordon should enter the Works at once and in his first year should do a certain amount of practical work in each of the departments. After that he could be brought into the office; then, as soon as he had a thorough grasp of things, he could take a managerial appointment. The salary for the period of learning was what Shefford called the nominal one of £500 a year. The salary as managing director he had not yet mentioned, but Gordon guessed it would be £1,000 at least. If it were on a commission basis, it might be much more.

"Look to me like the chance of a lifetime, son," Ted said. "How do you feel about it, Mother?"

Jenny thought it was wonderful. In her heart of hearts she would have preferred his going into partnership with his Uncle Gordon, but pride that people like the Sheffords were thinking so well of her boy offset it. There was also the knowledge that Norwich was even nearer than Yarmouth.

"But aren't you a bit young, dear, for all that responsibility?" Gordon glared and Ted smiled.

"He's two years older, Mother, than when I married you, and you and me set up here. I reckon he'll master it, same as he has most else. But one thing I'd like to say, son. After all, you're my boy and the only one we've got. What I reckon is that me and your uncle ought to go into things with Mr. Shefford. It won't do you no harm, son, and I sorta feel I'd like to know."

Gordon looked down his nose and said that it depended on what they wanted to talk about. Ted saw the chagrin and smiled.

"No fool like an old fool, son. All the same I'd like to know just what a son of mine is lettin himself in for. Nothin underhand, son. Nothin, perhaps, only lookin round the Works. No reason why you shouldn't be there yourself too."

That was different, and Gordon said he'd arrange it. A week later the three met Shefford at Norwich, and a long morning was spent at the Works. Later, Ted talked about it to George in the repair shop.

"Them Works weren't all that big, George, but what you might call slap-up—if you know what I mean. Everything in the right place and all the latest."

"All the new-found-outs."

"That's it. Slap-bang up-to-date. Good buildins, plenty o' room to work, and so on. Sorta smart and workmanlike. And timber? You never saw nothin like it. Timber everywhere. Trees that weren't cut and some that was cut and dryin out in the open. Then there was a big kiln, as they called it, with hot-water pipes and everything a-drying out wood in less weeks than used to take years. Great circular saws goin and band saws and such a deen you couldn't hear yourself speak. Then the joinery shops. Talk about machines!"

"I sin some on 'em."

"Machines?" He clicked his tongue at the staggering remembrance. "Fared regular human, some on 'em. There was one what they called an American Multiple Tenon Cutter, cuttin wood as if it was butter. Morticin machines, planin machines, lathes—never saw the like. A bit of, say, four-by-two goin in one end and comin out all shaped and tenoned and everything, and to the hundredth part of an inch."

"One thing I'll lay ye," George said. "I'll lay ye a farden cake Gordon knew as much about them machines as the next one?"

"Well," said Ted judicially. "I don't know as he didn't. In fact there was some things he fared to know more about than most. But there, I can't remember half the things we was talkin about. Inlays, veneers, carvin o' wood, grainin—and that remind me: somethin might interest you, George. Did you ever hear tell of medullary rays?"

"Can't say as I have."

"Far as I could make out, they're what make the fine grain when timber's quartered. It's a sort o' light what show the grain up."

"Whuh, what the davvul will they think on next!"

"Well, there it is," Ted said. "Only about thirty men workin there all told, and looked to me as if they was doin what used to want three hundred. Grut cranes, there was, pickin up trees like as if they was match-stalks, and saws cuttin 'em into planks almost afore you could wink your eye. Wood goin in rough and comin out smooth as velvet, and shaped and morticed and everything. Regular took your breath away."

"Any woods did they have besides what we've had from 'em?"

"Wood? You never saw anything like it. Baulks of mahogany, George, wide as this and weighin a ton or two. English walnut, Spanish walnut, Quebec pine, as they call it; Austrian oak, Indian laurel—everything you could think on. Holly, teak, ebony, box, laburnum—can't think o' half on 'em."

"Them'd be for inlays," George said, "same as we use 'em for. What is it they make now? Far as I recollect from what Gordon was once tellin me, what they make is chiefly panellin."

"They still do," Ted told him. "Fine fitments; mahogany and walnut stuff and so on. Fitments for ships and all these fine new public buildins. And they do some furniture."

"Furniture?" George was pricking his ears.

"What they call fine reproduction stuff. Reckon some people'd call it fakes, though that ain't what they sell it for. I see a Chippendale suite, as they called it, what they was finishin that might have sucked me in when I was a beginner. Rare good-lookin stuff some of it is. One lacquer cabinet what I saw was a rare nice piece—for them as like it."

"Reckon some of them fellers know their job."

"Old hands at it, George. Regular craftsmen. Do anything, they can. Lacquerin, carvin, fine marquetry—anything."

He let out a breath.

"Reckon I hain't told you half. Soon as Gordon get settled in, I wouldn't wonder but what he have you over yourself so's you can have a good look around. About time you had a holiday, now I come to think on't."

But George hadn't got that mention of furniture out of his head; the way Ted had spoken of it had been very near to treachery.

"Well, you can say what you like and think what you like, Mas' Ted, but far as I'm concerned they can have all their new fangles and machines and a hundredth part of an inch and what not. And even then they can't turn out stuff like this here."

His gnarled old fingers were caressing the wood and delicate inlay of the cabinet at which he'd been working. Ted's eyes softened. He nodded to himself as he watched the fingers slowly move.

"You're right there, George. You never said a truer word. That stuff o' theirs may be all right, but there's somethin—well, somethin sorta crooked about it, if you know what I mean. On the face of it it don't make out it's more'n what it is, and all the same there's a kind o' sneakin look, as much as to say it's just as good as the best."

"Fakes," said George contemptuously. "That's what they are when you get down to it. Don't matter what they call 'em; they're fakes." He shook a reminiscent head. "Remember that fake bit that swindled Mark and how he allust kep it up in the shop? Reckon we owt to've kept that walnut corner cupboard that you was took in over, stead of you a-burnin it."

Ted's nod was sheepish. The corner cupboard was a sore point, especially since it was George who had detected it as a made-up piece.

"Reckon if we'd kep' it," George continued, "Gordon wouldn't have gone a-mixin hisself up with them things what they're makin at them Works."

"I won't subscribe to that," Ted said. "They make honest stuff too, and plenty of it. It take all sorts to make a world, George. Some hatta do this and some hatta do that. I reckon Gordon'll know well enough what he's a-makin."

George still didn't like it. He shifted the conversation to Thomas

Shefford. He'd seen him once only, when he'd come up to the repair shop with Mark.

"Not much taller than me, he wasn't," George said. "A rare gentlemanly-lookin man, far as I remember. Spoke sorta quiet, whereas Mark, he was inclined to do a bit o' bellerin."

Ted had liked Thomas Shefford. He and Gordon Shadd and Gordon had lunched at the house after the morning at the Works. After the meal Shefford had taken the two older men to his study.

"I don't conceal that things have been slack," was one of the things he said. "They've been slack with a lot of people, if it comes to that. We lost a good few men to the war, and in a way we weren't sorry. It enabled us to carry on with the staff that were left. But now that the war's as good as over, we're anticipating a boom. We'll be glad to take every available man back."

"That's been my own idea all along," Gordon Shadd told him. "The country's going to be full of money, Mr. Shefford, especially if we make Germany pay."

"I wouldn't trust the politicians too far," Shefford said wryly, "but in the main I think you're right."

Everything was settled that afternoon. Gordon, Shefford said, was the most promising young man he'd known in all his forty years in the business. He'd go so far as to say he had definite genius. And he had the right manner and considerable tact.

"Well, sir, it's good for his father, and his uncle, to hear you say so," Ted said, "and I only wish his mother was here to hear it as well. She's been the one what brought him up."

"I think you'll both live to be even prouder of him," were Shefford's last words. "As for your wife, my boy told me about her, and I'd regard it as an honour to meet her, Mr. Burling."

But there was something that Ted afterwards knew he had left out, and he made it good to George.

" 'Twasn't only his mother who's entitled to any credit, George. You was one too. If it hadn't been for you, he'd never a-bin takin up the job he's takin up now."

"I don't know for that," George said, but was deeply gratified all the same.

He looked round, and then his fingers closed round a short length of oak.

"Reckon it's like this here piece o' wood. Look at the grain on't.

That's a bit o' wood you can make somethin on. But look at this here. Woman-grained ain't the word for it. Nobody can't make nothin on't. That's how I reckon it was with Gordon. He started off by bein the right sort o' stuff."

"But it was you, George, that did the cuttin out and planin and polishin. Ain't that right?"

George pursed out his moustache. For one moment it looked as if his lips might shape a *Yes*. Then he remarked that some people might say it was right and some that it wasn't.

CHAPTER 16

The Age of Money

THE year after the war, Ted Burling made so much money that at times he would ask himself if it were true. Money was everywhere; for anything saleable a man could ask, and get, almost what he liked. Ouseland, the capital though it might be of Breckland, was an agricultural centre, and even in the war years farming had thrived; but now things were happening that must have made Mort uneasy in his grave. Farmers who had never owned a best pair of breeches to their names had bought their own farms; farms were changing hands at startling prices; and pigs, always an agricultural barometer, were fetching three pounds a-piece, just off the sow. The automobile, which had once been a luxury, now seemed a necessity, and where one had seen wagons and tumbrils there were now lorries. Where one had walked or gone by bicycle, there were now buses. Ouseland even had its cinema.

Ted's best stuff brought fabulous prices, and every dealer was pulling in the money with both hands, some by devious ways. Ted received a catalogue of a sale at a village near Attley; in it were things that in print had more than an attractive look. It was true that there was no preview except on the morning of the sale, and that was something that in itself should have been cause for suspicion. As soon as he arrived at the sale he knew there was something wrong, for no member of the ring was there except Ben Harris and a new man who had opened a shop at Attley. By the time he had looked round, he was an angry man. In the whole of that sale there was nothing that even twenty years ago he'd have had in his shop. There were flagrant fakes and pieces made up, and the so-called Spode dinner service looked still warm from the kiln. It was the sight of it that sent him furiously to the auctioneer.

The auctioneer mumbled that he'd thought Mr. Burling would have known it wasn't his kind of sale. He excused it, too, by saying that that sort of thing was going on everywhere and that his job as an auctioneer was to sell.

"Even your catalogue's crooked," Ted told him angrily. "You don't definitely call a thing antique, but you've put it in heavy type, which is as much as to say it is."

He went raging off to his car, then changed his mind and watched the first hour of the sale. Then he could stand it no longer. The place was packed with bidders and they were giving for rubbish the money that would have bought them the right stuff in his shop. It was crazy and he knew it, but the craze was to continue. It was crazy when he deposited money in the bank and saw his balance; it was crazy when in six months Jenny had her own money back; but through it all he did keep his own sanity. His prices might be stiff but, compared with the prices of others, they were reasonable. The world could not go on being crazy for ever, and his real assets were satisfied customers. Not only that. He stood by those who had stood by him. No tempting offer could make him sell what a valued customer might be likely to want, and it was such a customer who had the first offer.

His shop was busier than he had ever known it. London men were crazy too, and buyers were always coming in; so were old clients whom he had almost forgotten. One day a perfectly strange gentleman came in.

"Mr. Burling?"

"Yes, sir. I'm Edward Burling."

The stranger held out his hand, and Ted liked his smile.

"Glad to meet you, Mr. Burling. I've often heard about you from my father. My name's Selby."

"Selby," Ted said, and the name brought a gratified shake of the head. "So you're Mr. Selby's son. I ought to have knowed it, sir. You've the look of him, now I come to think. And how is your father?"

"He died three years ago. Believe it or not, Mr. Burling, we were talking about you only a day or two before he died."

"He was a fine character, your father," Ted said. "And that table I sold him, sir? You still have it?"

"Yes, and I hope my son'll have it after me." He saw the regretful look. "Even if you covered the top with sovereigns, Mr. Burling, you couldn't buy it."

"It was a grand piece," Ted said. "One of the things I'd like to have in my own house as a sort of reminder."

"Yes," Selby said. "I think I know of what. I've heard my father tell the story a score of times. He always reckoned you, Mr. Burling, to be one of the few really honest men he'd ever met. And he'd speak of your wife, too. I trust, by the way, she's quite well?"

Ted called to Jenny. She snatched off her apron, patted her hair, and came in. She was as pleased as Ted to meet the son of Mr. Selby.

"I was telling your husband, Mrs. Burling, how my father used to quote him to everybody as an honest man."

"Wait a minute, sir," Ted said. "Only last week my wife here made me buy a new hat, and I don't want it to get too small for this here head o' mine. There ain't none of us what are really honest. I'll tell you somethin, somethin I've never even told my wife. It do you good sometimes to have a look at yourself and know you ain't the same as some people paint you."

It was just before the war, he said, and the vicar of a certain parish was raising funds to repair the church roof. He had asked Ted to inspect a table that was in the vestry, venturing to think it might be worth ten pounds.

"It took your breath away, sir. A kind of bright brown paint all over it, but underneath as fine a piece of Chippendale as ever I saw. Carvin that Grinlin' Gibbons hisself couldn't have bettered. I said ten pounds was a lot o' money—you know how us dealers do—then I give it to him. When I got it home and my man had it cleaned, I got a bit worried. It began to keep me awake o' nights. I don't say I was thinkin o' hell-fire or anything quite as bad as that, but all the same it's a master funny business to go robbin a church, which is what it really was.

"I sort of wobbled up and down. One time I'd say it was a proper bargain, then I'd think the opposite. The upshot was that when I sold it, I kept five pound for commission and give this here vicar an extra forty or so pound. Even then I couldn't sometimes help wonderin if I'd been a fool. So you see, sir, it don't do to talk about a man bein honest—not till you know."

Selby laughed.

"But you've proved my case! You *were* honest. You were honest because you simply had to be."

"I don't think my husband's told it in the right way," Jenny said. "What you and I call honesty, Mr. Selby, he prefers to call his conscience."

Ted protested but the other two laughed him out of it. Then Selby asked if he might look round the shop.

Gordon had received the money he was entitled to under the terms of his grandfather's will. Ted had never spoken to him about money, but he had an idea that Gordon was pretty well "britched," as they say, what with his Army pay and gratuity and various other items. There was also his civilian pay of £500 a year; and though he had taken very nice rooms in Norwich, his rent and keep could hardly amount to half.

At first Gordon was immersed in work; it was two months before he came home, and that was on a Saturday afternoon. He had written to say that they need not meet him at the station because he was bringing his own car.

"I had an idea he'd be investin in a car," Ted told Jenny. "All these young fellers nowadays seem to be crazy on a car."

Jenny said that it might be necessary in his work because his rooms were over two miles from the Works. Besides, she continued, anyone of Gordon's importance ought to have his own car. Though Ted had to agree that she was probably right, neither was quite prepared for the car in which he appeared. It was an A. C. two-seater sports that had cost him 500 guineas.

"Rare smart car you've got there, son," Ted said admiringly, and called to Jenny that Gordon had arrived.

"Absolutely the latest thing," Gordon said. "Did over seventy easily across Rudgham Heath. Held the road steady as a rock."

"Hadn't better tell your mother that," Ted said dryly.

Gordon kissed his mother and began showing her the car.

"Whatever did it cost!"

"Not as much as you'd think," he told her. "A bit different from the old Lizzie, eh, Dad?"

"If she stand you in as good stead as the Ford's stood me, you won't have no cause to grumble," Ted said, feeling a bit hurt at the deprecation of an old friend.

Over his tea Gordon gave them his news. Obviously he liked the work, and Jenny had noticed at once how well he looked. For a month, he said, he'd been working in the timber yard, wearing dungarees just like any of the men. He got on well with them, he said.

"You've got to talk in their own language, Mother. That's what you've got to do."

"I hope that doesn't include swearing," Jenny said severely.

Gordon laughed.

"I don't know about that, Mother. What I meant was you don't have to swank. When you're working alongside men, you've got to be one of them."

"That sound to me the right way, son," Ted told him.

After the timber yard he'd gone to the sawmill and the drying sheds. In a day or two he was going to Lynn. Baltic timber was coming in again, and he had to learn to inspect, grade, and sort cargoes and, as he put it, all that sort of thing. He might be a month at Lynn.

It was only after he had given all his own news that he thought to ask about business in the shop. Ted said that he couldn't grumble. Business had been pretty good. That made Gordon remember George. He was nursing a nasty cold, Ted told him, suggesting that Gordon might do worse than slip round to see him. After that they went into the shop.

"Same old smell, Dad," Gordon said, and at once there was the old argument, Gordon always claiming there was something musty in it, a charge that Ted would indignantly repudiate. It was honest bees-wax and turpentine; it was the smell of any good antique shop. Jenny insisted that there was also a faint scent of potpourri, and Gordon always laughed at her about that.

He pottered about the house for a few minutes and then put his automobile in the shed, which Ted had cleared. He spent quite some time on the car, wiping off the dust of the journey and polishing it. Ted took no hand, but he thought of his own care of the Ford in the days when it too had been shining and spotless, and he laughed about it to Jenny, who saw that it did him good to have Gordon home. But Gordon didn't stay long.

"What about coming down to the Bell for a drink, Dad? I thought I might meet some of the chaps there."

Jenny looked horrified. Ted frowned at her for silence.

"Don't reckon I will, son. They'd be readin the Riot Act if any-one see me in a pub."

Jenny clicked her tongue when he had gone.

"Now, Mother," Ted told her, "you've got to remember that things ain't what they was in our young time. All these young fel-lers have been through somethin. They're sorta used to excitement and they've got to work it out o' their systems. They'll settle down soon as they've got it worked out."

Jenny didn't know what the world was coming to. The young people even spoke a language she didn't understand.

"As for all that craving for excitement, as you call it, it isn't healthy, Ted, and you can say what you like. The sooner Gordon gets married and settles down with children of his own, the better for everyone, if you ask me."

Ted tried to laugh at her, and almost achieved an epigram.

"That's a master funny thing about you women, you know, Mother. Almost before you're married yourselves you're thinkin about grandchildren."

"And what's nicer than grandchildren?" Jenny demanded. Her eyes softened at the thought of it. Ted grinned to himself and changed the argument, but it might have been better if he had not.

"Do you know, Jenny, I don't know as I was right—not goin down to the Bell."

"You, Ted? Whatever would people think!"

"Well, Jenny, you and me feel Gordon sorta slippin away. No use denyin it. It's somethin that's got to be faced. Fare to me, then, what we've got to do ourselves ain't sorta keepin to ourselves and watchin them go their own way. We've got to go with 'em, far as we can. Let 'em see we ain't such old fogies as they think. Sorta show an interest in the things they're interested in." He broke off almost exasperatedly. "If I'd had your education I'd tell you what I mean. All I know is I sorta feel it myself."

Jenny said tartly that if he meant doing some of the things at which she wouldn't even allow herself to hint, then she by no means agreed; but she was to think about it nevertheless. Gordon came in, all apologies, at well after nine o'clock, and found supper waiting. To Ted's surprise there was no scolding; Jenny actually asked Gor-don if he'd enjoyed himself. That night in bed she admitted that in some ways Ted had been right.

"But that doesn't free us from our duties as his parents," she had to add. "Gordon may be a grown man and have an important job and men under him, but that won't stop me speaking my mind when my conscience tells me."

"You're right there," Ted said, "so long as you don't do it too often and too brown." Then he gave a little chuckle. "Fare to be two of us in the family now with a conscience, Mother."

Jenny was not amused. It was the way Ted's arm went round her and tickled her that made her smile.

Soon after breakfast the next morning, Gordon was off to Bury to see some old school friends. He said he'd be back to lunch.

"Why can't he say dinner?" Jenny asked in exasperation. "It's always been dinner here, and it's going to be dinner."

"Don't matter much what you call it," Ted told her. "It's what's on the table that count."

Gordon was late getting home, and how Jenny kept back the reprimand she didn't know; when she said how pleased she would be if Gordon would go with her to church that evening, there was another surprise.

"Why, I've got to be off before tea!" Gordon said. "I've got to be on the job in the morning, first thing. I must have a bit of time to settle down tonight."

He went, and it was a cool cheek that Jenny turned as he kissed her goodbye; it hurt her even more when he failed to notice the coolness.

"Now, Mother, what on earth are you cryin for?" Ted anxiously asked her.

Jenny hurried back to the house. When the tears were wiped away, her face was grim.

"I never thought I'd be glad to see his back, but I am. If that's the way he's treating his parents, I'd rather he didn't come again."

Ted kept quiet. Jenny was in one of her moods, as he'd put it, and experience had taught him the virtue of silence. At teatime she remembered something else.

"Ted, do you know what Gordon didn't do?"

Ted said dryly that there were plenty of things he hadn't done.

"He didn't go to see George."

Ted's face fell.

"Disgraceful of him, I think," Jenny said, "and after all George thinks of him. For goodness' sake, Ted, don't let George know he's been home without seeing him. It'd break his heart."

But the time for that was gone. The next morning Flo Warman came round to say that George was worse and that the doctor said he had pneumonia. Ted went round at once but there was nothing he could do, for George was in a high fever and didn't even recognize him. Jenny called in the afternoon, the nurse telling her confidentially that there was little hope.

Ted called in a local man and the two made George's coffin themselves of good seasoned oak. George was eighty-two when he died; even Ted was surprised when he heard it, for he had somehow come to think of George as the man he had been when he had first come to the shop. A new man was found easily enough, for the money was good—three pounds a week as against George's first twenty-five shillings—but for Ted the repair shop would never be the place it had been. The new man was about forty; he was quiet, competent, and respectful, but he wasn't George. George, as Ted told Jenny, hadn't been made to a templet or mould; George was George and that was all you could say about it. But he was even more. His very absence poignantly brought into focus the years that had gone. Though his own life had been unpunctuated by change and stir, George, with his sure rejection of the trivial and the insincere, had been the epitome of a lifetime of honest labor.

Meanwhile business continued to be fantastically good. Ted's stock was getting lower than he liked to see it go, but he knew of no means of replacement except at grossly inflated prices. When the new man had been initiated into the running of the shop, Ted tried a day or two in the country, but he found that even there the old times had irrevocably gone.

Antique dealing was not what it had been. East Anglia had been alive to the trade long before the rest of England was conscious of it, with Norwich and Ipswich as the main centres. For years the villages had been combed; now even the less informed had an idea of values, and with the rise in prices they increased their demands proportionately. When Ted found something in which he was interested, the mere show of interest was enough to bring a preposterous demand. At a small farmhouse at Pentwold, well out in the Brecklands, just before the war, he had purchased many items from old Ike Norton, leaving some things unbought that small dealers might have jumped at. When, on one of his recent visits round the countryside, he called on Ike again, it was more as a matter of courtesy than anything else.

"Reckon you owt to buy this here chest o' drawers," Ike told him, and he actually seemed anxious to sell. "You could a-had it afore."

The craze now was for oak, and the chest Ike offered was chestnut, of recent make, and in none too good order at that. Three of its original handles were missing and the polish was patchy, yet Ike was asking five pounds for it where he'd once have taken less than one. That was how things were, with fingers crooked to rake in money that had lost its old value. The original collectors had largely disappeared, now that the supply of rare antiques was dwindling. Even the owners of junk shops were alive to the value of what could once have been picked up for pence. Now collectors were far more shrewd; and now the era of newspaper advertising began. Notices were inserted, such as: *Private collector wishes to buy* . . . or *Top prices paid. No dealers.* That sort of thing drew away private buying from the dealers and helped to make windfalls a thing of the past.

It was in 1920 that Gordon Shadd had a talk with Ted and Jenny one week end. Gordon was looking older, the spit of Mark when Ted had first met him, but possessing an acumen and range of knowledge that even Mark had never acquired. Yet he was as likable as he'd always been. Where Mark had stuck obstinately to the guidance of what he had called his instinct, Gordon went deeper. He talked with people, and he read.

"This ain't going to last for ever," he said, speaking of the boom. "What we've got to do is go slow and not worry a lot about stock. The time's coming, mark my words, when the bottom's going to fall out of things. Cling on to your money. You'll want it then. That's when you'll be able to buy things for nothing, the same as in the war."

"Yes, but what about sellin?" Ted wanted to know.

Gordon explained. The old background and values had gone. This was a new world—a fact that had to be recognized. From now on trade would be largely what one might call the utilitarian-antique; one would have to rely, in fact, on the class of customer who bought for a home the things which he knew were "usable." As for the better-class stuff, that would be dear to buy and dear to sell; but there'd be a new kind of customer—the Americans. England would be full of them, and every one would be a potential buyer. Ted would have to make himself conversant with the branch of the trade involving shipping, customs, and so on—and it might pay to be at once on the lookout for what one called Americana.

Jenny said that they'd had an American customer or two, and that Ted had found them easy to deal with. She was speaking as if Gordon were rearing mountains where there were not even mole-hills.

"That doesn't signify, Jin," he told her in one of Mark's old phrases. "Do you know what I'm going to do? Advertise in some of the American papers. You can't sit at home and hope for trade; you've got to study their market. Take walnut, for instance. No trouble to sell good walnut here, but for America—no. The dry heat in their houses makes veneer peel. They'll buy mahogany and oak but not walnut. Don't force it on them unless you want a dissatisfied customer. I've had one experience of that."

Ted couldn't help shaking his head. Strange, he said, but the older you got, the more you found you had to learn. There'd been times when he'd thought he really knew his job, and inside-out at that. Now he reckoned he knew little more than the beginning.

Gordon had seen very little of his nephew, and his parents had seen little of him too. Even his letters were irregular, though he had promised to write at least once a week.

All that they knew was that he was happier than ever in his work and that Shefford continued to be pleased with him. The time had already gone when he should have been getting an insight into the workings of the office, but he had asked to stay on for an additional period in the joinery and assembly shops. As for his week ends at home, they were now so rare that Jenny had almost become inured to not seeing him. Then came a letter from her brother that made her wonder.

"Ted, you know how I said it was funny when that letter came with a Lynn postmark in it when Gordon was supposed to be hard at work in Norwich?"

"Yes?" Ted said. "What about it, Jenny?"

"Read this," she said, giving him the letter from Yarmouth.

Ted raised his eyebrows. Gordon Shadd said he'd happened to be in Lynn the Saturday before, in Yelmer's shop, when who should go by but Gordon, with a very good-looking girl. Yelmer hadn't known who she was, but Gordon had run into the couple later, by chance. There had been some highly suspicious blushes on the part of the nephew, and the girl had been introduced as a Miss Hughson. They had refused his offer of tea because they were going to the cinema.

I always was a bit of a Nosey Parker, Jin, as you know, so I had a look in the telephone directory. There was only one Hughson and that was some people at Hawby. So I had a word with someone I knew and it was that Miss Hughson that Gordon was with. They're people with money from what I could make out, who came to Hawby just before the war. They live in that house on the right as you come in from Sandringham—a Georgian house that looks like a Hall, though it's only a private house really. Ted will know where it is.

"If there's anything serious in it, I think it's wrong of Gordon not to let us know," Jenny said.

"Reckon you'd better keep out o' this, Mother," Ted told her. "Either there's something in it or there ain't; if there is, you'll hear about it all in good time."

"That's all very well," she said, "but where is Hawby, Ted?"

"Just north o' King's Lynn. Not a bad little place."

"The wedding'd be there," she said, and when Ted began laughing she was almost annoyed with him. She was remarkably diplomatic, however, in the letter she wrote. All she said was that Gordon's uncle had said he had seen him in Lynn.

It was enough to produce an answer, though a tantalizingly vague one. Ted wrote that he'd made some friends in Lynn when he was working there and that he had kept the acquaintanceship up. That was a shallow foundation for Ted and Jenny to build either fears or hopes on, but in less than a month they received a letter announcing the engagement. The following week Jenny and Ted met the couple in Norwich, where they all had lunch at the Maid's Head.

Clarice Hughson—Clarrie was her pet name—was two years older than Gordon: a tall, slim girl who was as good-looking as Gordon

Shadd had hinted, but with a restlessness and modernity that made Jenny curiously uneasy. Towards Ted she seemed almost patronizing, and when she spoke of Gordon and herself the *we* was barely a courtesy for the obvious *I*.

Clarice smoked and drank and used make-up, and when they got home that night Ted was hard put to it to make a defence.

"I don't care what you say; I know she's not the right girl for Gordon," Jenny said. "Look at the supercilious way she spoke when I mentioned cooking. How will Gordon be able to afford a maid? And that house she was talking of taking. And that nonsense about it not being necessary to wait. They've got to wait, Ted, till Gordon's in his proper job and earning more money. As for that mother of hers, I didn't like the sound of her at all."

"Now, Jenny, you can't judge like that," Ted said. "For all you know she may be a real nice woman. So may Clarrie. You just hain't got used to her yet." And at Jenny's little snort: "What you and me's got to realize is that Gordon and her are gettin married—not us. It's what they think of each other that count."

Though Jenny had nothing but forebodings, she did have to admit that Mrs. Hughson's letter wasn't other than nice, even if the notepaper was too stylish. When Ted kept a tactful silence, he was accused of a shameful lack of interest in the future of his own son, and soon he found himself wishing that Gordon would hurry up and get married and allow a return to something of normality for himself. As it happened, he did not have to wait for long.

CHAPTER 17

The Coming Change

THE parents met in January of 1921, which was six weeks before the wedding, and again Norwich was chosen as the halfway house. The Burlings drove in early, for Jenny had decided that she must have some new clothes and Ted had promised her a fur coat. He said that he wanted Jenny to look as smart as the next one at the wedding and that it was about time they dipped into the old hessian bag.

It was to be a long time before Jenny was to have more than an inkling of the manœuvres that lay behind the wedding, not to say the intricate economics of the Hughson family. Edgar Hughson, who had inherited a sound drapery business from his father, had built it up to a thriving suburban store, and in 1912 he had sold out to a large multiple firm and retired to Hawby, the home of his father. There had been a family of five girls and two boys, with Clarice the youngest. Because her schooling had corresponded with the most affluent period in the family career, she had had an expensive education. Each of his children had cost Edgar Hughson a considerable sum, which at the time he had not grudged; for when he retired with four of his daughters married, he apparently still had sufficient to lead, in Hawby, at least, a full and comfortable life.

Having successfully married off four girls, Agnes Hughson was determined to find for Clarice the perfect husband, though it had been her interference that had ruined more than one of her youngest daughter's chances of marriage. Unfortunately, when Clarice did become engaged, her fiancé was killed in the very last month of the war.

Agnes Hughson, the daughter of a Streatham doctor, was irked by the comparative dullness of her Norfolk village, yet found that it was not easy to win a footing in that superior social circle to which she considered herself amply entitled to belong. The war, therefore, was a godsend to one as determinedly aggressive as she. In less than no time she played a leading part in the wartime activities both of Hawby and of Lynn, and in addition roused Edgar to perform his share.

When the war ended with Clarice still unmarried, her single state was merely an annoyance when compared with the Hughson's financial reverses. They had suffered far more than Hawby was allowed to suspect. Certain members of the family had been hard hit and had had to receive help. Hughson himself had been hard hit too. Thanks in no small degree to the prompting of his wife, he had made foreign investments that had yielded a high interest with apparently little risk. Now, however, two of the larger investments represented a total loss. It was not that the Hughsons had become beggars or even embarrassed; it was merely that money had to be handled carefully and luxuries renounced. There was, in fact, just enough and no more: a fact that, on the part of Agnes Hughson, demanded considerable camouflage and deft control in the now more than ever necessary finding of a husband for Clarice.

In Gordon Burling she knew she had found the man. It was not so much that Clarice professed to be in love with him as the result of her own guarded enquiries. Yelmer, for instance, whose antique shop she had formerly patronized, had told her that Ted Burling was reckoned one of the warmest men in the trade; it was also from him that she heard about Burling's wife, who was said to have come in for a pretty penny on Mark Shadd's death. Then there was Mrs. Burling's brother, reputed to be one of the most substantial men in Yarmouth; and, as he was unmarried, doubtless Gordon would ultimately get his money. All that, perhaps, was the reason for the letter which Jenny had thought so nice, for the special notepaper on which it had been written, and for the Norwich meeting of the parents which Agnes herself had suggested.

Ted liked Edgar Hughson. He was genuine, made little pretence, and, like Ted himself, was quiet-spoken. He was well over sixty, tall, and just a bit stooped. He had mousy greying hair and moustache, and his slightly adenoidal voice had just a trace of a London accent. His wife was tall—a fact which put Jenny at an immediate disadvantage—and heavy-bosomed, with a voice that had something of a boom. It was she who took charge of affairs in the lounge of the Royal and told Edgar to see about drinks. While Ted was chatting to Edgar, Mrs. Hughson's loud voice was an inescapable background, yet she somehow contrived to hear most of the talk of the men.

No sooner were they seated for lunch than she was telling Ted that she had heard that he had a very thriving little business.

"I don't know as I'd say that, Mrs. Hughson," said the cautious Ted.

"But you must call me Agnes and my husband Edgar. As I was telling Jenny, it seems so foolish being stiff and polite and all that, now we're going to be almost relations."

Jenny waited until she was driving home with Ted before voicing her opinions.

"I tell you I don't like her, Ted. I agree with you about him, but there's something about her that I just don't like."

Ted admitted that she might be just a bit bossy.

"I'd call her bossy," Jenny said snappily. "She's got Clarice under her thumb and that's where she'll have Gordon. Before they know where they are she'll be running that house. And do you know what she actually hinted? That we should buy the house as a kind of wedding present!"

"Now, now, Jenny; she couldn't a-thought that."

"You don't know her as I do," Jenny said with a click of the tongue. "I'll tell you this, Ted, while it's on my mind. If that girl's going to live the way her mother expects her to, then they'll have to pay for it. I believe in young couples living within their means. We had to, Ted, and it didn't do us any harm."

"Reckon you're right there, Jenny," he said. "I'll have a word with Gordon on the quiet."

"That house is too big, for one thing. And how're they going to pay for a cook-general like Mrs. Hughson was talking about?"

"You let me handle this, Jenny," he told her placatingly. "All the same, they ought to manage. A thousand a year's what Gordon'll be gettin."

"And it isn't worth much more than half what it was before the war. One other thing, Ted: I knew I'd have to go to the wedding, but I wasn't looking forward to it; you know that. Now I wouldn't keep away for anything. I'm going to be there and I'm going to keep my eyes open."

Jenny was there, and Ted was very proud of her. Her fur coat had cost him just over £100, but when Jenny was wearing it, it seemed to be worth infinitely more. It was easily the grandest affair that he had attended in his life, though he felt self-conscious and awkward in his new clothes. Jenny, however, took everything in her stride. It was she who planned everything: going by train over-night instead of in the old Ford, having a room at the Lynn hotel, and even the wedding presents. Her own had been a cheque—Ted never knew for how much—and one of her best samplers; Ted gave the couple a fine old draw-leaf table and a chiming bracket clock.

The Sheffords were there, driving from Norwich in their big Daimler. Most of the Hughson family seemed to be present; and what with the Norwich and Lynn friends of Gordon and Clarice, together with Hawby friends, the little church was full. There was a long wait while the organist played "Jesu, Joy of Man's Desiring" an incredible number of times; even Jenny felt uneasy and thought that something had gone wrong. At last the procession moved down the aisle and Gordon and his best man slipped in from the vestry. Jenny didn't really see him till it was all over and he and Clarice were moving back along the aisle. It was hard to keep back a tear when she saw how fine her boy looked—as much a gentleman as anyone there. She tried desperately to catch his eye, but Gordon seemed a bit nervous and kept his eyes straight ahead.

Jenny, Ted, and Gordon Shadd walked back to the Grange, as the Hughsons had renamed it. It was a large Georgian house with showy gardens, but Ted was to regard its contents with a very mixed eye. On the way they overtook the Sheffords, and Margaret Shefford said that she and Jenny must have a long talk together. Jenny was glad enough to squeeze into a comparatively lonely corner when they got back to the house, for the whole place seemed to her to be in a deafening uproar. A Lynn firm was doing the catering; and what with waiters, the innumerable guests, and the queue that was passing by the married couple, she could hardly hear herself or Margaret Shefford speak. After an inspection of the wed-ding presents, she and Ted were bustled out to the lawn for photo-graphs of Gordon and his wife with their parents and then a further one that included the best man and the four bridesmaids. Jenny was a bit annoyed with Ted when she discovered too late that the carnation in his buttonhole had been broken off, but she'd been proud enough of him at the formal toasts.

"I didn't come here intendin to make a speech," Ted said. "As a matter o' fact, if I'd a-known I was expected to make one, I reckon I'd a-stayed back there in the church. All I'll say is that if my son and his wife are as happy as I've been myself in my married life, then there won't be no need for me to wish them well. And I reckon that's about all."

Then Jenny was buffeted about by people moving here and there. Separated from Ted, with strangers coming up and introducing themselves, it was not till the couple were ready to go away that she found him again, and her brother with him.

"Goodbye, my dear," she said as she kissed Gordon. "Have a good time and mind you be sure and write. Goodbye, Clarice, and mind you look after each other."

She had almost said, "Look after *him*," but before she could begin worrying about that there was a mad scurry to the door and off the couple drove in Gordon's two-seater, amid shouts, laughter, and confetti.

An hour later Jenny was saying to Ted, as she loosened her shoes in the hotel bedroom, that she was glad it was all over. Gordon Shadd had come with them in the hired car and was staying on for a real cup of tea. In spite of what Jenny had said to Ted, she felt a certain gratification at the elegance of the wedding, viewed, as it now was, in something of retrospect. Ted seemed pleased too, at the way everything had gone; only Gordon seemed to show a lack of enthusiasm, or so she thought.

"Don't reckon weddings are much in my line," Gordon said; "more designed for women. Don't you think so, Ted?"

"It's only right that Clarice should have something to look back on," Jenny told them. "It's the most important day in her life."

Ted said it didn't need a lot of show to remind a woman of her wedding. What about his and Jenny's own?

Jenny did not know why her brother was a bit critical of the wedding, or why he should have said that the money spent on it might have stood the young couple in good stead—a statement with which the usually frugal Jenny was wholly in disagreement. The previous December, however, Gordon had come to Yarmouth to see his uncle, stating his real business with some difficulty.

"I don't like going to Father, Uncle, and I was wondering if you could lend me a few pounds."

He instanced the tremendous expenses that setting up house would involve but painted his own prospects far less dismally. In a couple of years, at the most, the money could be paid back.

"Depend how much you want," his uncle said. "What do you think you can do with?"

"About £500."

There was a stare; but a budget was being produced, and finally the cheque was handed over. Nevertheless Gordon Shadd was shocked, and that was why he had insisted on a formal receipt, even from his own nephew. That, too, was why his wedding present had been the (for him) almost niggardly one of a cheque for twenty-five pounds.

There was a last pleasant echo of the wedding. On the way home by train there was a short wait at Tinkersham. Ted suggested that Jenny and he should take a later train, allowing them to have, for old time's sake, as it were, a look round the town. After lunch at the George, they retraced the steps of that far-off day when they had first met. Ted even called at the cottage where he had bought the piece of stump-work, but the woman was long since dead and no one even remembered her name. They walked to the very corner where they had once almost collided, but Jenny suddenly drew back again, her handkerchief to her eyes.

After the couple came back from a fortnight's honeymoon in London, Jenny was loth to call on them at Norwich till she was invited, though she heard that Agnes Hughson had been there. Now that she and Ted were really alone, she seemed to be settling happily down, even leading something of the life of a lady, with a woman coming in most mornings to help with the house.

Ted was as busy as ever in the shop, for the boom showed few signs of abating. It was not, in fact, till the following year that he began to discern a change; in a letter Gordon Shadd had mentioned the same thing. The slump, however, was to be far more slow in appearing than the boom had been. Gordon reported that at the Works there was more than could be handled, that orders, in fact, had to be turned away. He wrote that he had tried to impress on Mr. Shefford the need for expansion, but it was clear from his letters that Shefford was the same kind of stick-in-the-mud that his Uncle Gordon had been, for Shefford's face was resolutely set against expansion and change other than the introduction of such new machinery as would reduce costs.

A telephone had been installed in Ted's home soon after the war, and Jenny often rang the Norwich house. It surprised her how often she found no one at home, or was answered by Susan the maid.

"I can't make it out," she said to Ted. "Why do they have to go gadding about so much of a night?"

"They're young people and they've got friends," he told her. "They'll settle down, Jenny, if you give 'em time."

It was not till the middle of June that she had what amounted to a formal invitation to visit the young couple. She was very relieved, for she had announced to Ted that she had no intention of going till she knew she was wanted, though that, as Ted knew, was largely resentment and jealousy of Agnes Hughson. She went fairly early, by train, so as to have a full day, and she had to admit to Ted that she had been agreeably surprised. But while she could appreciate the insincerity that had marked her own conduct during the day, she had been unaware of the degree of calculation that had gone to the reception she received from Clarice, and even from Gordon.

It needed no astuteness on the part of Clarice to form an estimate of her mother-in-law. That her standards of judgment had been both biased and superficial did not necessarily invalidate the broad results of the analysis on which Clarice's conduct was based: Jenny was rigidly old-fashioned, which was why certain aspects of the new ménage needed deft explanation and others concealment; she doted on Gordon, and therefore the accent must be on Gordon rather than on herself; Jenny was domesticated and probably house-proud; Jenny had no particular liking for the cinema and had never gone to a dance in her life; Jenny was careful with money; Jenny was as besotted about her husband as if they'd been married months instead of nearly thirty years.

All this was why Clarice herself answered Jenny's ring at the door, wearing a rather too pretty apron.

"Darling, how lovely to see you at last! The time went so quickly that I was perfectly horrified when I heard the bell and guessed it was you. . . . Take your things off in our room. The bathroom's just through there. Soon as I've finished just a tiny-weeny job I'm doing in the kitchen, I'll be back."

Jenny admired the handsomeness of the bedroom and even pretended an admiration of the twin beds. It was only to Ted that she gave it as her opinion that twin beds were almost indecent. Clarice was wearing little make-up that day, and it was by an over-sight that the dressing table was piled with an array of powders, creams, scents, and general frippery that made it look, as Jenny was again to tell Ted, more like a counter in a chemist's shop.

Jenny even concealed her dislike of Clarice's alluding to Ted as *Mr. Burling*, rather than *Father*, though she was somewhat placated by the way in which she spoke of him.

"I do admire Mr. Burling. He's so handsome and distinguished-looking. You must be very proud of him, really. Gordon's always singing his praises—almost as much as your own."

There was quite a nice garden at the back, and the two women walked round it. Darling Gordon, Clarice said, was so dreadfully busy that he had no time for it, so they had a man twice a week; she herself, of course, did what she could. It was dreadful, in a way, about Gordon. When you were in business, you had to make all sorts of contacts, and often, of an evening, when Clarice herself would much rather have been at home, she had to accompany Gordon.

"It's my duty to go," she said. "I think a woman can make quite a lot of difference, don't you? There's all sorts of ways in which we can help."

To Susan's vast surprise, Clarice helped bring lunch to the dining room. Gordon came bustling in, but Clarice had met him at the door.

"Just a minute, darling. . . . Yes, she's here. And I forgot about the garden. I had to tell her I did a lot myself. . . . Yes, I told her that."

Gordon kissed his mother affectionately and gave and heard the news. Clarice helped to bring in the second course.

"Don't you think Clarice is looking well, Mother?" Gordon asked.

"Very well, my dear, and so are you. Just a bit tired, though."

Gordon pooh-poohed it. There was plenty of work, but he was taking it in his stride.

"I didn't offer your mother a drink, darling," Clarice said as she came in with the salad bowl. "I knew she'd prefer water."

Clarice preferred water too, she said, but she couldn't repress a longing glance at the cocktail cabinet that had been artistically draped to resemble a miniature sideboard. It had been removed for that purpose from the lounge, as they called the drawing room. They returned to the lounge after the meal, and Clarice brought in coffee. It was still short of two o'clock when Gordon said he would have to be getting back to the Works.

"Oh, my dear, no!" Jenny said. "Must you go back? I was counting on you spending a whole afternoon with us. It's so long since I really saw you."

Gordon had more than enough explanations, but he said he would meet his mother and Clarice at the Royal at half-past four for tea. Jenny was going back by the five-forty and that would be on the way.

"Do you like going to the cinema or not?" Clarice asked when she came back from seeing Gordon off. "It's just as you like, darling. All we want to do is what you want to do yourself."

Jenny said that the pictures always gave her a headache, and Clarice was sympathetic. She and Gordon had very little time for the cinema, she said, though they did like to go when there was anything especially good.

"Now you must tell me all about Ouseland," she went on, as she produced some knitting. "Gordon has told me such a lot about it and already I'm looking forward to seeing it—when Gordon isn't so dreadfully busy."

When Clarice and Gordon got back to the house that evening, Clarice at once rang up her mother.

"Hallo, darling . . . Oh, yes, she's just gone. We saw her off at the station . . . Darling, it was simply agony! You've no idea. Wondering if one had said the right thing . . . Oh, splendidly. I think it was a mistake, though, to have tea at the Royal. Much better to have had it here. So much more domesticated . . . But of course she did! When she kissed me goodbye she was simply oozing with affection . . . Yes, Gordon's all right. Still bearing up . . ."

"What's that about Gordon?"

"Just telling Mother about today," she said. "What your mother thought of me, and so on."

"Mother's all right," Gordon said tolerantly. "Anyone can get round Mother."

As for Jenny, it was true that her generous heart had really felt a warmth when she had kissed her daughter-in-law goodbye at the station. Except for one or two things which could not help jarring on one whose life had had the natural simplicities of her own, she had found little to criticize and gratifyingly much to admire. She could even tell Ted that she had been unjust in many ways to Clarice, who seemed to be proving an excellent wife.

"I think it does me good to get about a bit too," she said. "Not that I should dream of going without being asked."

Ted didn't see for why, as he put it. Just as this was Gordon's home, so his home ought to be his parents' home, if Jenny knew what he meant. It was Jenny who said that things were different from what they were, and Ted was far from disposed to argue the point. Jenny's own peace of mind was what mattered most, if only because that meant peace of mind for himself.

The year moved unworriedly on, with Jenny, and sometimes Ted himself, ringing Gordon and Clarice. At last the time came when one had to think about Christmas, but Jenny had left it till too late. The couple had already arranged to spend Christmas at Hawby.

"Oh, Gordon, how could you!" Jenny said into the telephone. "You ought to have known we'd be expecting you both here."

"Sorry, Mother, but you know how it is. Next year definitely, though."

She was hurt, though Ted told her she had no cause. Even after the reconciliation with Mark, he said, they had rarely spent a Christmas at Yarmouth.

"It isn't the same," Jenny answered. "We had Gordon and this was Gordon's home." Then she gave a sigh. "I wonder when they'll begin having a family."

Gordon Shadd came for Christmas, and on Boxing Day they went to Harold's for tea and the evening. Harold's business had thrived and his family had increased to four, with the youngest boy now at the grammar school. It was the kind of evening that Jenny loved. After tea Harold's eldest girl, now almost a young woman, played the piano and they all sang carols, and when the younger children had gone to bed their elders sat round the fire talking of old times. When they got home, Jenny said it was as nice an evening as she'd ever known.

Yet that night in bed, when he himself was usually asleep, he heard her sobbing quietly to herself. Tears were always near the surface with Jenny, and his arm would have moved towards her had he not known that; but he lay there with a steady breathing that simulated sleep, thinking that another Christmas had gone, and of Christmases that had been and some that might have been. Jenny was quiet again now, and it was her silence, at last, that sent him off to sleep.

CHAPTER 18

Marriage Progress

THE following Easter, Clarice could no longer evade a visit to Ouseland. Because of the preparations that Jenny made and the way that Ted was harried, as he put it, from pillar to post, one would have thought it was the Royal Family who were coming for a week end.

Gordon and Clarice arrived on Good Friday morning and left early on Monday afternoon, but Clarice was to find it all less boring than she had feared. Jenny made a great fuss over her, for one thing, and refused to let her soil her hands in spite of Clarice's calculated insistence. And there was nothing with which Gordon's wife did not appear to be thrilled, from the bedroom where Gordon had been born to that of his parents, where Jenny actually apologized for the double bed. She won Ted's heart by an apparent enthralment in what he told her as he took her round the showrooms and by telling him how many people had admired the wedding present of the table and clock. She even thought the old Ford delightfully quaint, praising the way Ted handled it when the four were taken for a ride round Breckland on Saturday afternoon.

Because of Gordon's deft management, it was not necessary to stay in the house all the time, and on Saturday night they had a lovely hour or two at the Bell. On Sunday morning she insisted on lending Jenny a hand, and in the evening, if only to kill time, she accompanied Gordon and his mother to church. Before she knew it, what had been thought an ordeal was virtually over. The last slow morning *was* rather like waiting in a train that refused to move off, but at last it was afternoon, bags were packed, goodbyes were said, and there she was in the car again, giving a final wave at the market turn.

"Well, it wasn't so bad as I'd thought," Jenny said, and there wasn't even a tear for the going of Gordon. "Not that I want them to come every week."

Clarice's addition to that rider of relief was vastly different. Now that the visit had been paid, there was the happy feeling, as after a trying time with the dentist, that there was no need for it to recur for a very long time—so long, in fact, that it might be dismissed from the mind. At some time or other, of course, Jenny would have to have another invitation to come to Norwich, but that, too, was now a matter of no imminence.

"Wasn't half bad being home again," was what Gordon said. "Not that I could ever live in Ouseland. What's wrong with that place is that it wants waking up. All very well for Father and Mother, of course. They've never been used to anything else."

That Easter had made Jenny curiously happy, even if Clarice was showing no signs of pregnancy. Had she been her own daughter she would have spoken about it, but as it was she had said nothing, even to Gordon. There was much that she could have said, and often did say to herself when she was alone in the house: about children making a home, and what a dreadful loneliness it must be for those who in middle and old age had not been blessed with children. When she said something of the sort to Ted, he gave his usual slow nod or two and reckoned that he agreed. When, in the early autumn, Jenny spent another day in Norwich, it was actually he who asked if there were any signs. Jenny said that there were none, that she had ventured on a private word with Clarice, and that Clarice had talked about consulting a doctor. It would have shocked her inexpressibly if she had heard Clarice laughing about it later to Gordon.

But soon Jenny had things other than unborn grandchildren to worry about. It was Ted who was slowly becoming her principal concern.

In the momentary exultation of having got the better in some deal, Mort once remarked to Ted that only fools never made mistakes. That was a puzzling paradox to the boy till Mort added the explanation that real fools went on making the same mistakes to which they'd never admit, whereas a wise man never made the same mistake twice.

Ted Burling was to make a mistake, and if it was not exactly a mistake that had been made before, it was at least sufficiently reprehensible in being a variant. There were several reasons that were excusably contributory, especially in that spring of 1923, when the slump was plain enough to be seen.

Though there was no longer need for the sustained industry of his earlier days, it irked Ted to think that life might become, as it had once been during the war, an inactivity that was both monotonous and unprofitable. It was not that the justification both of risks and of forecasts had given him delusions of grandeur; it was rather that it had made him seem quite as good a man as he was. When others about him had been almost in Queer Street, he had had no qualms; when money had been made, he had made it—and far more honestly than some. It was constantly being thrust upon him that he knew his job better than most.

There was the Bury dealer who had bought Walter Rape's business when the latter died. Ted went into his shop and found a man of a different type from Rape; he was a Londoner by the sound of him, and he appeared to know his job. There was nothing in the shop that Ted wanted to buy till the dealer opened his safe and produced two majolica dishes.

"What do you make of these, Mr. Burling?"

"They *look* like majolica," Ted told him warily, and, "you're wondering if they're right."

"I think they're right enough. What I haven't had time to do is work out the value."

"What're you askin?"

"A protective price," he said. "A hundred guineas the pair."

"I'll take them," Ted said, and pulled out his cheque book. That same week he sent the Italian majolica dishes to Christie's and was gratified at the cheque he received.

There was another instance that same year. This time it was the young buyer from a London firm who came into Ted's own shop, full of importance and knowledge. As Ted showed him round, he proved critical: one object was far too late, another too rococo. It was the first time Ted had heard the word, and it puzzled him till he looked it up. The criticisms went on with a wave of the hand here and a shrug of the shoulders there, and even the imperturbable Ted found his customer's arrogance hard to stomach. As they came

"Now, Mother, 'tain't no good talkin like that. 'Tain't a question of what caused it. What we have to think on is what we've got to do. And, if you ask me, this business o' Gordon and Clarrie's just as important as the money itself."

"What *can* we do?" Jenny asked. "What do you think, Gordon?"

"About them? I don't know. It's a funny business to start interfering between husband and wife. He isn't a boy. He's getting on for thirty and she's two years older. Start to interfere and before you know where you are, you've made things worse. And maybe I've been exaggerating things a bit. I don't think I have but I can't be sure."

Ted and Jenny talked it over after Gordon left on Sunday evening. He had said that Hughson was very far from being a wealthy man; that in his usual careful way he had made enquiry and that the Hughsons were cutting expenses down. Where once they had had a cook and two maids, they now had a cook-general; and where a man and a boy had been employed in the gardens, now they had only a part-time man. And, of course, Jenny remembered little things she had noticed and heard at Norwich. Her questions worried Ted, who was even less well informed than she. At last Jenny made up her mind: she was going to have a word with both Gordon and Clarice. It took more than Ted's arguments to dissuade her: in fact there had to be a rare assertion of authority.

"Then I'll do it my own way," she said, but the way she chose was the worst she could have taken. She cashed some of her War Savings Certificates and sent Gordon a cheque for £100. Ted was shown the relevant passage in the letter that accompanied it.

I am sending you the cheque because I know that things are not always easy in these expensive times, but I do hope that if at any time you find yourself at all in difficulties, you will let me and your father know. You know how we've both always hated the disgrace of debts, not that you and Clarice should ever run into debt. Your father and I had not much more than this cheque between us when we were married, and we always managed. I know that things are different now, but it's the same principle. Principles never change, and I want to be always proud of you as I am of your father.

When Ted told Jenny that it was a fine letter, and scolded her gently for referring to him, he had no idea of the time and thought that had gone to its writing. Jenny hoped for great things from it, and she was relieved and gratified at the letter that came in return.

Money's always handy, Mother, and it was grand of you sending us that cheque. Not that there was anything to worry about. Things are always a bit difficult when you first start off, but I've got other irons in the fire besides my job, and in a year or two I wouldn't be surprised if we're pretty well off.

Jenny sent a copy of that to her brother, who gave his wry smile at her implied reprimand. Ted, however, saw a new cause for worry in his son's letter. One evening, when Jenny was at a concert with Jessie Crowe, he rang Gordon up and happened to find him in. He heard noise and tumult at the other end of the wire, as if Gordon were having some kind of party. At last Gordon had to ask him to hold on while he closed the door.

"Something's been worryin me, son: what you said in that letter to your mother about havin irons in the fire outside your job at the Works. What sort of irons, son?"

"All sorts, Father," Gordon said with a little laugh. "You put somebody in touch with someone else and collect a commission on the deal, or you put someone in the way of making money. That's why we have some people in tonight. Something I've got in mind where there's a bit to be made out of it. I can't explain over the telephone. It's all very confidential. Besides, you wouldn't understand."

"And what about Mr. Shefford? Does he know about it?"

"Why should he?" Gordon asked tersely. "He only has my working time and he's more than satisfied with what I do for him. My leisure time's my own. Even you ought to know that, Father."

"All right, son; all right," Ted told him just as tersely. "I just thought I'd like to know. No fool like an old fool, as I've told you afore. You're well, are you, son? And Clarrie?"

Gordon said they were both fine, and Ted gave a fairly satisfied nod as he replaced the receiver. Gordon snapped the receiver on and hurried back to the cocktail party. The cheque he had received from Jenny had paid off two urgent instalments due on Clarice's car, and very little had been left over. Not that Gordon was worrying. In a year or two he really believed that he would not have a debt in the world.

Some days later Ted had a telephone call from Edgar Hughson. After asking about the Burlings, he said he would be in Norwich on Friday; if Ted should happen to be there, he would be glad to see him at the Royal at half-past twelve. Agnes, he added, was in London but would be returning on Saturday. There was even a hint that he and Ted could kick up their as yet not too aged heels.

Ted made it his business to go. He liked Edgar Hughson; he enjoyed seeing him again, and he enjoyed the lunch that his host insisted on paying for. That afternoon Edgar was like a rabbit that had escaped miraculously from the hutch and was frolicking on the lawn, knowing that at any time fingers might descend to have him by the ears and into the hutch again.

"You know, Ted," he said in his quiet, almost inaudible voice, "I think Aggie's been wrong in seeing such a lot of our young people. They're old enough not to want interference. Aggie's got big ideas about Clarrie—too big, if you ask me."

Ted said that Jenny had never interfered or tried to put ideas in Gordon's head.

"Aggie always liked to cut a bit of a dash," Edgar went on. "I can't stand it myself. I'm all for a quiet life. Had too much rushing about in my time. If you ask me, Ted, it's the same with Clarrie and Gordon. About time they stopped going here and everywhere and started having a family and settling down."

"Just my idea and Jenny's. And all this rushin about, as you called it, must cost money. If you ask me, Edgar, they're not findin it any too easy to live within Gordon's means."

"Aggie was hinting the same thing some weeks back," Edgar said. "I had to tell her it was as much as we could do to look after ourselves. And that reminds me, Ted. I think it was real good of you to buy Clarrie that car."

His eyes were on his plate or he must have seen the gape and the start. There was nothing Ted could say, and Edgar took the silence for modesty.

"Real good of you, Ted, and Clarrie appreciates it, as I know. But there, everything's all right now, financially, I mean. According to Gordon, they're doing fine."

Ted decided to say nothing to Jenny, but as soon as he was in the house she asked questions and he changed his mind.

"Well!" Jenny said. "Making out that you bought that car!" She clicked an angry tongue. "Ted, I don't care what you say; I'm going to see her and Gordon and speak my mind."

"Now, Jenny, just you think it over. They're gettin on. Edgar said so and Gordon said so, so why go stirrin up trouble? She've got the car and it's bein paid for, so why not let it rest? Mind you, I hate lies as much as you do, Jenny, but callin her a liar to her face —which is what you'd have to do—might make an enemy of her for life. And Gordon as well. He's bound to stick up for her."

So Jenny changed her mind again. But neither, she said, would get another penny of her money. If there were children, that might be different.

"I don't see as I'm entitled to do anything either," Ted said. "What little I've got is for you, Jenny. Anything happen to me, there'll allust be enough for you. Not much more, though, as things are. Gordon'll have to stand on his own feet the same as you and me did. Soon as he learn to do that, then we might see."

CHAPTER 19

Veneer

WHEN stock was taken that year, Ted found himself, by his own standards, a well-to-do man; had he decided to retire, there would have been ample for Jenny and himself for the rest of their days. Not that at still under fifty he had any intention of retiring: nothing, in fact, was more distant from his thoughts. But his prosperity gave him a comfortable feeling that would make him recall Mort's remark about farmers with dunged boots and torn breeches who could have bought up the flashier ones. He and Jenny were not parsimonious: theirs was what might be called a middle course, denying themselves nothing that they really needed and always prepared to subscribe to the charitable needs of the town. Take the old Ford, for instance. Some might have run her for many years more, but even Jenny agreed that the car was just a bit shabby, so they bought the newest model. Harold, who had just acquired the latest Morris, laughed at Ted for his conservatism; but the old Ford had been such a friend that to have bought anything else but another would have been a kind of treachery.

The time was very near, however, when Ted was to begin looking at his money in a vastly different way. That was in the following February, when he received a letter from Major Pryne one morning. It was headed *Private and Strictly Confidential*, and Ted's eyes opened at that:

My Dear Burling,

Mrs. Pryne and I were delighted with the glass and thought your price most reasonable. It may be my own last purchase, for I've been thinking—between ourselves—of presenting the collection to the city, and I gather that they'll be glad to accept.

Some time ago you asked me about the financial position of a certain individual, and I told you what I then knew. The information I have now is somewhat different, and if you happen to be in Norwich at any time I might be able to tell you more. Certain business, by the way, that was transferred to another concern has now come back to us.

Geoffrey tells me he has been to see you, so you probably know he hopes to collect Nelsoniana. I told him he was starting twenty years too late, but you can't teach these young fellows anything.

Best wishes to your wife. I saw your son the other night at some function or other. They tell me he is doing remarkably well.

Many thanks again,

Yours sincerely,
HARCOURT PRYNE

Geoffrey was Colonel Pryne, the major's eldest son, who had left the Service after losing an arm in the last months of the war. It had done Ted's heart good to see him.

"I knew your grandfather, sir, one of the finest gentlemen I ever met in my life; and your father and mother have been customers of mine ever since I set up here."

He heard all about the Nelsoniana and the major's deprecations. Anyone would have thought that Ted was a boy again from the way he laughed and from what he said.

"Now, sir, if you like to come sort of *in co.*, you and me are goin to make your father open his eyes. There's still plenty of what you want knockin about, and I'll find it for you. I've got a couple of pretty good Nelson mugs here now what I was savin up for a certain collector. And don't you worry about prices, sir. You and me's just goin to show your father that the young uns know as much as the old uns."

But it was a vastly different man who read the letter. He would have liked to show it to Jenny, but the mention of Clemming, rather than the request for secrecy, made him keep it to himself. It was Clemming who for the next day or two was uppermost in his mind. If he was in Queer Street, which was what the letter implied, then he might jump at an offer. Not that that offer would be made direct. Clemming would never know who had bought his business till the contract was signed.

That was the moment he could hug to himself.

"Yes, Mr. Clemming. I'm the one who've bought your business. The one you reckoned was nothin but a junk dealer. The one what

told you years ago that he was goin to be a bigger man than yourself. And somethin else, Mr. Clemming. Do you remember well over
thirty year ago comin to a little village called Wickenden where
there was a boy what sold you a little Chelsea figure? Do you remember . . ."

Jenny heard him one morning talking to himself in the shop.

"Why, Ted, I thought there was someone in the shop."

"Just talkin to myself," he said a bit sheepishly, and she gave him
a shrewd look.

The best part of his money, he thought, might be needed to buy
out Clemming, and he busied himself with figures: what the Ouseland place and business would fetch, the differing values of stock.
By chance he happened to buy in town two fine pieces of Venetian
glass. That was on a Wednesday, and he knew that Major Pryne
was always in Norwich on Thursdays.

He drove in and parked the car by the market. His way to the
offices of the insurance company took him past Clemming's shop,
where he halted on the other side of the road and had a good look
at the windows. The first cursory glance showed little that was different from what he had seen a score of times before. He felt a brief
disappointment, for somehow he had expected a change. What
change he hardly knew, unless it was that Clemming was making
merely a show of depleted and inferior stock. Then his eye caught
something in one of the windows. In a moment he was crossing the
street and staring in the window, not caring if Clemming himself
were in the shop.

He had been right. In the window were the two finest early
Georgian commodes he had ever seen; the sheer beauty of them and
the magnificence of the craftsmanship made him nod with apprecia-
tion as he stood there oblivious of people moving by. Around each
ran a plinth with unconventional inlay, and below were three
drawers with carved rope-pattern borders. At the corners were
lions' masks carved with foliage and ending in paw feet; it was
metalwork that had a quality that he had rarely seen. In fact he saw
in those twin pieces a mellowness and a uniqueness that made him
peer and frown as he tried to assess their value. Five thousand? . . .
Eight thousand? . . . It depended on who wanted them badly
enough and what he was prepared to pay. Even at Christie's they

should be a sensation. If Clemming sent them there, he'd doubtless place a big reserve; though if he had sense he'd try to get in touch with some important collector.

At last he moved on. Then suddenly he realized the implication of what he had seen; the knowledge struck him like a blow and made him halt momentarily in his tracks. How could a man be in Queer Street when he owned a small fortune in those two commodes? Then as he moved on again he was smiling relievedly to himself. They were not Clemming's property; they simply could not be. They were something he was selling on commission. Yet they could hardly be that. Why expose to a chance buyer in a place as comparatively small as Norwich? London was the place to show them. Clemming never had been a fool, and it was a million to one that he knew their value.

His thoughts were still busy as he entered the building. He had five minutes to wait before he was shown into the major's room. His secretary was just leaving, and Ted got a smile and a wave of the hand.

"Miss Arnold, you might send us in some coffee, will you? And see that I'm not disturbed for at least a quarter of an hour?"

His long legs pushed back the chair from the desk.

"Nice to see you again, Mr. Burling. What've you got there? Something for me?"

"Just a little present, sir, to wind up the collection, so to speak." He unwrapped the glasses and stood them on the desk.

"Lovely. Perfectly lovely. But I'm going to pay for them."

There was a friendly argument and the major had to give way. He mentioned Geoffrey, and Ted had a good laugh to himself. When the coffee was sent in, the major looked into the corridor and then closed the door again. He poured the cups for Ted and himself before he spoke.

"That private business we were discussing once. I don't think there's a man outside this building that I'd tell what I'm going to tell you now. That's a reminder, and perhaps a compliment."

"You can rely on me, sir," Ted told him.

It was the duty of the company, the major said, to be informed about the affairs of clients who carried heavy liabilities. In the case of a man like *our friend*, as the major alluded to him, such enquiries were always necessary, and he instanced that tricky business of the marquetry table. His information now was that their friend was short of money. For one thing, he was carrying a notably smaller stock. For another, he had always been a sporting and betting man, and his fingers had been badly burned in a skating-rink project which had failed after the investment of very considerable funds.

That was all. Ted asked if he might have a little say, and mentioned the commodes.

"We know all about them," the major said. "Our man had to see them for insurance purposes, and I don't mind telling you they're insured for a very considerable sum."

"Then they're his, sir."

"Oh, yes, they're his. I know the Hall where he bought them privately. Strictly between ourselves, he gave £1,000 for the pair."

Ted stared.

"I know," the major said. "The seller was hard up and he was a fool. Our friend stands to make a remarkably substantial profit."

"Tell me somethin, sir. Why's he got them in his shop?"

The major smiled.

"If you had them, wouldn't you like to show them in your shop?"

"Reckon I would, sir. But what about sellin? Has he found a buyer do you happen to know?"

"I know even that," the major said. "He has a buyer who hasn't yet inspected but who's absolutely certain to buy. That's why he's had them so long. The buyer's abroad now but he's due back almost at once."

Ted gave a ruminative grunt and asked how then could their friend be in Queer Street.

"I didn't say he was," the major reminded him. "I told you the information we had about him. The real point is this. Even if our friend makes, say, £6,000 profit, one swallow doesn't make a summer. He has big overheads and probably considerable liabilities; £6,000 isn't going to transform the situation entirely. But tell me something, as man to man. Were you still thinking of buying his business?"

"Well, sir, I have been thinkin and I haven't."

"Take my advice, my friend. I call you that because you *are* an old friend. This is neither the time to buy nor sell. This is the time to sit quiet and watch. Such times come in cycles—you should know that. Stick to what you know is safe. If you really must change, then choose a more suitable moment. It will come. But you've got to wait."

Ted called at two antique shops in the city, but somehow his heart was not in business. He walked slowly by Clemming's window again and knew that the commodes were better even than he had first thought. He wandered on, passing the windows of a house agent. He wondered if he should go in and ask for tentative enquiries to be made as to whether Clemming would accept an offer, and what the offer should be. He was moving on again when suddenly he began to feel hungry. A certain innate frugality and the pull of old custom made him choose a pub, where he had a hot meal. Then he went to the Works for a word with Gordon but was told that he was in London on business. From Gordon's office he rang the house, but no one was in. He thought that that was strange, because he knew that Susan had Wednesday afternoon off; at any other day she would rarely be away after two o'clock.

There seemed nothing else to keep him in the city, so he started for home. At Windley he called at Fred Morgan's shop and bought a Georgian tallboy in none too good order. It was at his usual tea time when he reached home. Something was wrong with him, as Jenny always knew when he omitted his, "You all right, Jenny?"

"You saw Gordon?" she asked at once.

He told her what had happened, and she said that it was too bad that Gordon had not called to say he would be in London. As for there being no one in the house, a maid's half-day off was something that was always liable to be changed. Then he told her what Major Pryne had said about meeting Gordon, allowing her to think that it had been said that morning and not in the letter. Jenny was pleased.

"All the same, Jenny," he said, "I reckon we ought to be a bit nearer than here. I don't mean you're to go interferin like Agnes Hughson, but Norwich is a pretty good way away. You never know what's really happenin. Look at today: makin sure I'd be seein Gordon and him in London all the time."

He might pride himself on his ability to keep a secret, as he had done that morning to Major Pryne, but there was rarely a secret he could keep from Jenny. More than that: in all the uphill journey together that had been their married life, his only secrets had been the ones, like the purchase of the original Ford, that had been intended to be a happy surprise. There had been a kind of boyishness both about them and about himself. But this, she knew, was far different. It was something he had harboured for years, something that for the last few weeks had so gnawed in his mind that he had talked to himself in the shop and tossed restlessly in his bed. It was like veneer on a fine piece of wood that needed nothing but the beauty of its own natural grain; a veneer that had somehow curled and peeled and was all the more ugly because one could see beneath it what it had cheapened and disfigured. She felt sure that it was that old business of Clemming, a foolish ambition that could sacrifice old friendships and tear up old roots. She had had such thoughts before, but they had passed; now they returned. But only when she was sure could she begin to fight, and fight she would.

"You mean you're still set on going to Norwich?"

"Well, not exactly set," he said, and fidgeted for a moment uneasily on his seat. "Perhaps I'd better tell you, Jenny. It's somethin I happed to hear about Clemming."

It did him good to make a comparatively clean breast of things as he told her confidentially that the time looked near when Clemming might be bought out. He mentioned the commodes and what a grand feeling it might be to see things as fine in that window; things that were his own in a shop that was his own.

She needed time. A new and decisive phase had arrived, and her own weapons were far from ready.

"It's something that's got to be thought about, Ted. A wife's place may be with her husband, but that isn't everything. You know what I think about Norwich. I'm going to think it over; but you'll have to give me plenty of time."

"No hurry, Jenny." His face had lighted up. "No hurry at all. Reckon you'll come to look at it my way, though."

There it was: *my* way, not *our* way. But she needed no time to be certain of what she would do when the moment came. Even if nothing should happen to change his facile optimism, she had no fear for the future. Somehow she had always contrived to bring him to her way of thinking—*their* way, as it had always proved. Now that the issue was at last clear, she too felt easier in her mind. But something did happen, and it came like a thunderbolt out of a blue sky.

It was Sunday morning when Gordon unexpectedly rang.

"That you, Mother? I thought I'd just drop in for lunch if you didn't mind."

"My dear, as if we should mind! We'll love to see you. Are you coming alone or will Clarice be with you?"

"Alone," he said, just a bit abruptly. "You know I'll have to go again almost at once."

"That doesn't matter, dear," she told him, and then he had hung up before she could say another word.

"Must be something peculiar," Ted said, "to bring him all that way just for an hour or two. Wonder what it is."

Jenny said that he was probably at a loose end or that perhaps there was some matter of business he wanted to discuss. If there'd been anything wrong, he'd have mentioned it. Ted said that she was probably right, but he was on the lookout for Gordon's car and came down from the repair shop as soon as it drew into the yard.

"Glad to see you, son. How are you? All right?"

"I'm all right, Father."

But he avoided his father's eyes, and there was even a querulousness in his tone as he got out of the car.

"Clarice all right?"

"Clarice?" His lip curled. "She's left me, Dad. Gone back to her mother."

"Left you!" He stared. "You can't mean it, son. . . . Reckon, though, we'd better go and have a word with your mother."

As soon as she kissed him, Jenny knew that there was something wrong. She looked at Ted and he frowned. Gordon flopped wearily into a kitchen chair.

"Just been telling Dad, Mother. Clarice's left me. Gone to Hawby and says she's not coming back."

"Gordon!"

It was a shock. Ted moved across to where she stood.

Gordon's lip curled again.

"Nothing to be shocked about, Mother. It was the way she did it that upset me. Between you and me I'm glad to be shut of her. It's been bad the last few months."

"Son, you're upsettin your mother. You mustn't talk like that."

"I can talk how I like about my own wife, can't I? You want the truth, don't you?" His hand was slowly brushing his forehead and his face looked unbearably tired.

Gordon's version was that life had been nothing but quarrels and rows. When he had tried to check her extravagance, she had flown into mad rages; she'd even accused him of lying to her about his family.

"I didn't lie, Dad. I said you were well enough off and no more. You know I never applied to you for money, even when things were a bit tight. It was she who did the lying—making out her father had plenty of money and she could have anything she liked. That was before we were married, of course. It was a different tale later, when she had to keep coming to me for money."

He had gone to London on the firm's business and had come back only the previous day to find that she had gone, taking the car with her and every thing she could possibly consider her own. She had left a curt note saying that she had no intention of coming back and that it would be up to him to arrange a divorce.

"My dear, it would be dreadful," Jenny said. "However could she think of such a thing! The disgrace of it."

"No disgrace in that," he said. "I'll be glad to be finished with her." His eyes were blinking again. "Mother, you've no idea what it's been like."

Suddenly his arms were on the table and he was sobbing his heart out. Ted shook his head and moved self-consciously away. Jenny's arms went round her son.

"There, my dear . . . there."

Before he left, the rest of the tale was told. On Saturday afternoon he had at once rung Hawby. Agnes Hughson was at the other end of the line, and one could imagine her listening grim-lipped to his questions.

"I wonder you're not ashamed to be talking at all," she had said, "after the scandalous way you treated Clarice. She's not coming back, and the sooner you realize it, the better. If you've any decency left, you'll arrange for a divorce."

Then she had hung up, but he wasn't prepared to leave things like that. He had gone to Hawby, and it was from there that he had telephoned after seeing Edgar Hughson. Of Agnes Hughson or Clarice there'd been never a sign, though he had had a good idea that Agnes had been listening while he was having his few words with her husband. For one thing, Edgar had been unexpectedly belligerent.

"I asked him about the car, Father, telling him that it wasn't paid for and that it wasn't hers, but he reckoned that was for me to worry about. He reminded me how I'd said I'd bought it for her with your money."

It was on the tip of Ted's tongue to say something about liars having good memories, but he kept the words back.

"Let's get down to the root o' this, son," was what he said. "Marriages don't break up if there ain't good cause. You reckon it was her extravagance."

"So it was, Father."

"And you, son, you weren't extravagant yourself?"

"Well, that's different. Mine wasn't what you call extravagance. I have to spend a good deal the firm never takes account of. But that wasn't it. Everything was beginning to go all right. I didn't tell her because she'd have wanted to spend the money in advance, but I've got £500 owing to me, Dad. That would have put us on our feet. And there might be more to come."

"One of those deals you were tellin me about?"

"That's it, Dad. Nothing at all to do with the firm."

Jenny cut across to what was most in her heart—what Gordon himself was going to do. If he was sure that he could never live with Clarice again, what was going to become of his home?

"I'll get some unfurnished rooms, put the best of my stuff there, and sell what I don't want. There're plenty of places in Norwich where I can have my meals if I don't want to have a housekeeper."

"What about our wedding presents?"

The draw-table and the clock were all right, he said, but Clarice had taken the sampler, saying it had really been given to her. A flush of colour showed in Jenny's cheek.

"I'll tell you something now, Gordon, and for your own good. Clarice never was any good to you, not from the very beginning. I hate the thought of divorce—"

"That's because you're sort of old-fashioned, Mother. You can't expect two people nowadays to go on being tied to each other like that. Besides, I'm practically sure there's another man. There must be."

It was the blow to his own vanity that made him say that; it had always been easy for Gordon to temporize and to play on Jenny's weak points. But she hadn't finished yet.

"That might be different," she admitted, "though what your father thinks I don't know. But you've been to blame too. If ever you should get married again, I hope it will be somebody sensible; and I hope that you have children and make a real home. No one can have a real home without children, and now you've found it out too late."

Even in the tragedy of his son's unfortunate marriage Ted Burling saw at least something that justified himself.

"Now you see I was right, Jenny. If you and me was in Norwich we wouldn't have to worry about Gordon. He might even come and live with us till he see how everything get on."

It was a weapon against which she had no defence, and there was nothing she could say; but for some days, as she watched him, she was aware of his complacency and his triumph. There had never been depth or splendour in his vision of their future, but it was she who discerned the tawdriness and the transparency of his self-deception. Then one evening she was ready to speak. They were in the parlour; Jenny was knitting in her chair by the fire and Ted was reading a trade magazine.

"Ted," she suddenly said, "about this going to Norwich. Let's leave out Gordon and look at it with just our two selves."

It was strange that she should use the same arguments that had once been used by Major Pryne.

"Just what do you expect to get out of it, Ted?"

"You want us to get on in the world, don't you, Jenny? You don't want me to stay a little man all my days?"

"You're not a little man, Ted, and you know it. You may live in a small town, but you have a reputation that many a big man hasn't got."

"That isn't it. Here we haven't the scope."

"Scope for what?"

"Well, for gettin on. To get in the really big trade."

"Listen to me, Ted," she said patiently. "We *have* got on. If anyone'd have told us years ago how we'd have got on, we'd never have believed it. We've got enough so that we never need worry again whatever happens. Suppose you do go to Norwich and have scope, as you call it. Suppose you do make more money. What will you do with it? Do you want to change our whole way of life?"

"Of course not, Jenny. You haven't got it right."

"Then if we're not going to change our way of life, then why worry about making more money? We've more than enough for ourselves, and to leave one day to Gordon. And still you're set on going to Norwich."

She checked him as he was about to speak.

"Let me finish what I have to say. If it isn't the money, what's Norwich going to give you? You never were one for importance, Ted, and I wouldn't like you to change all that now. So why do you want to sacrifice everything?"

"Sacrifice?"

"Yes, sacrifice what we've taken all our lives to make. Good friends like the Crowes and heaps of others who stood by us when we weren't what you think we are now. And there's the reputation you have in the town. Even ourselves, and everything this house has meant to us. Where we came to after we were married. Where Gordon was born." She shook her head, and it was an effort to keep back the tears. "You ought to know, Ted, what it is that you're sacrificing."

Her logic disturbed him or he would never have spoken as he did.

"Look, Jenny, will you let me have my own way for once? All these years I haven't gone far wrong yet, have I? Haven't I got enough sense now to judge what's good for us both?"

Her lips clamped suddenly together, and two red spots came to her cheeks. There were mistakes she could have instanced, the folly of his own arguments, the way he was brushing her inconsequently aside.

"Very well, Ted," she said. "But I'm warning you that I still haven't made up my mind."

"No hurry about that," he remarked, and the very assumption was a new hurt. "I hain't heard any more yet about Clemming."

"Why Clemming?" she said. "You're still not harbouring that old grievance?"

"Grievance?" He almost glared. "You call this leg o' mine just a grievance? Or what happened to you?" He shook his head. "The trouble with you, Jenny, is you forget things too easy."

"No, Ted," she told him quietly. "The trouble is that I remember too well."

He was sure, however, that he could bring her round, and even out of that night's talk there emerged for him a new certainty.

When he was in his own shop he would see himself in Clemming's store; and when he looked out of his windows and failed to see the busy traffic of Norwich streets, he would be almost surprised. To him the acquisition of the shop would be the culmination of a lifetime's work and patient waiting. The foot that had once been cautiously set on the first rung of a ladder was now firmly at the top.

But again something happened. It was incredible. It was so malicious and personal an interposition of Fate that even when it stared at him from his newspaper he refused at first to credit it. It was with a scowl that he showed the paper to Jenny.

"What d'you think o' that, Jenny! You wait all these years and now look what've gone and happened."

She took the paper and her tongue moistened her lips as she read. Clemming's shop had been practically gutted by fire on the previous evening. There was a picture of firemen playing their hoses on what looked like little more than a surge of smoke and a gap in a blackened wall where there had once been a window.

CHAPTER 20

Whirligig of Time

FOR the next few days Ted Burling was a frustrated man. One would have thought that he had been deliberately singled out from the myriads of humanity to prove the devious and grossly partial workings of Fate, that he had lost a limb, or that some irremediable disaster had come upon him, instead of the single frustration of a lifetime otherwise successful. Something of the sort had happened once before, he remembered. For years he had meant to have a quiet word with Walter Rape to get him to talk about that business of the linchpin; then, almost on the very day that he had decided to see the man, he had heard that he was dead. But that was a petty thing compared with the loss of Clemming's shop at the very moment when it had appeared to be falling into his hands.

That a new shop would certainly be built where the old had stood was little consolation. It might not even be an antique shop and, even if it were, he could not visualize it or bring himself so ardently to covet it. Then there was Clemming himself. At his age he would probably now retire, which would remove him from Ted's reach, and the final laugh would be Clemming's. Jenny, capable now of a mild duplicity, revealed an understanding she had not previously shown; it was partly that that reconciled Ted to an aggrieved acceptance of what he had no power to change.

As soon as Gordon had found a small flat, Jenny had helped to sort out his furniture and had seen him properly settled in. Unknown to him or Ted she had had a long talk with Margaret Shefford, who had heard Gordon's own version of the affair and now was glad to hear that Jenny's views coincided with her own. She, too, she said, had never liked the Hughsons or what she had heard of them, and both she and her husband were happy that Gordon was so quickly recovering from what might have been a tragic experience.

Jenny was bitter about the Hughsons. It was not only the business of her sampler. Without the knowledge of Gordon or Ted she had written a letter to Agnes Hughson and had received a reply almost as curt as the words that had been spoken to Gordon on the telephone on that Saturday afternoon. It was that that determined Jenny to involve herself once more in her son's affairs. She even had a week end at Yarmouth.

Gordon Shadd took no credit for having been right. On the Monday morning before she left, he decided to tell her about the loan, though first he had her promise that no word should be said to Ted.

"But he'll pay you back, Gordon," she told him. "He's got a lot of money owing to him, but he'll pay you. I'm sure he will. If he doesn't, then I'll pay you myself. His father's already paid the balance on that car of Clarice's, so as to avoid trouble."

"I'm not worrying about the money," he told her. "Five hundred pounds will neither make me nor break me. What I'm sorry about is letting him have the money and not telling you and Ted." He gave his wry grin. "Gordon's got a very convincing manner. All the same, if he hadn't had that cheque of mine to play about with, things might have been very different."

Jenny said that he had nothing for which to reproach himself. The fault lay in Gordon himself, and in her and Ted for not having kept a closer eye on things.

"I was wrong," she said. "Something always told me he would have done far better to have settled down here with you. If only I'd have persuaded him more, I think he might have done it. Even now I wish he was here."

She had told him about Ted, and though he had been on her side he had also shown an understanding of Ted's point of view.

"I'm different," he said. "The only interest I have seems to be making money. I don't mean it's the only thing I think about; it's just that I can't help making it in the way of business. We don't want Ted to get like that, Jin. Why don't you make him take an interest in the town? Put up for the council, or whatever they have there. It'd do him good. It'd take him out of himself."

"Ted's set in his ways," she said. "It's become business with him, first and last; but he's a bit more like himself than he was a few days ago. I'm fairly sure now we'll hear no more about Clemming."

"I hope you're right," he told her. "Years ago he had his two chances: to go after Clemming or let the whole thing drop. It doesn't do a man good to take things into his own hands, the same as Ted did. Sooner or later you always find you're wrong."

Towards the end of March, Major Pryne called Ted one afternoon on the telephone.

"I wonder, Burling, whether it would inconvenience you too much to see me here tomorrow morning?"

"I don't think so, sir. What time?"

"Eleven o'clock, if you can do it."

Ted said that he'd be there, and both he and Jenny guessed that his help was being sought concerning the gift to the museum of the collection of glass. Ted caught the early train and, on his way to Major Pryne, stopped for a minute or two to look at what had once been Clemming's shop. All that was left was a huge crater where the basement rooms had been, with baulks of timber shoring up the blackened walls of the buildings at each side. It was hard to visualize the shop that had once been there, and he gave a wry shake of the head as he moved on.

There was quite a long wait before he was taken to the major's room. The major was not alone. Three other men were with him: Quadling, the firm's assessor whom he had met once before, and two strangers, one of whom, a tall, burly man, gave him a look of shrewd appraisal. Pryne mentioned no names.

"Gentlemen, this is Mr. Edward Burling. I've known him a good many years, as I've told you, and we can rely implicitly on his discretion."

There were handshakes all round. Ted was waved to a seat.

"To come straight to the point, Mr. Burling, this is a question of the Clemming fire. You know the procedure, I take it, in the matter of a fire?"

"Well, sir, I do and I don't. I know what have to be done if I have a fire, which, thank God, I haven't."

"It's very simple," Pryne said. "As soon as we're notified, we send our assessor to assess the damage and the value of any salvage. When that's done and if everything's in order, then we pay accordingly. On the other hand, if from our point of view everything is not in order—to be blunt, if we have a suspicion that the fire wasn't all it was supposed to be—then we refuse to pay. That leaves the onus on the insured person to sue us for the money; whereupon the company," he nodded towards the burly man, "communicates with the police. Is that clear?"

"Clear enough, sir. But just one question. What do you mean by 'suspicion'? Something that show that fire didn't start itself?"

"I think you've got it exactly," Pryne told him. "Even the fire authorities who were called to the scene of the fire might have noticed something suspicious and themselves have communicated with the police. But let's assume that the police *are* taking an interest in that fire. There was a certain amount of salvage, thanks to very prompt action, and naturally it's been most carefully scrutinized. At my special request you have been called in to add your opinion to those of two other experts about one very definite matter. I refer to the two Georgian commodes. You and I had some talk about them from a personal point of view. You knew they were right."

"Of course they were right, sir."

"Why are you so sure, Mr. Burling?" the burly man asked.

"Why, sir? Because I can't afford to make mistakes. They were as right, sir, as this chair I'm sittin on is Heppelwhite. I've never examined them, sir, but I'd give Major Pryne 150 guineas for the set."

There was a laugh. Pryne said that Mr. Burling had been right. Those commodes were what they were supposed to be, and they were in that shop window on the very evening of the fire.

He got to his feet.

"Now, Mr. Burling, this is what we want you to do for us. We'd like your opinion on these various pieces of wood. Just look at them and tell us what you think. I have a glass here."

"I'll use my own, sir, if you don't mind," Ted said, and followed the major across to the side table. On it lay a score of pieces of wood: two, badly charred, were about eight inches long and some were little more than fragments or splinters.

He took a good ten minutes examining each by the clear light of the window, and another five minutes to sort the pieces into three sets. He gave a nod, blinked his eyes a bit, and put his glass back into his breast pocket.

"Well, Mr. Burling?"

"This lot here, sir, come from those commodes. The others didn't."

Eyes met and there were nods.

"But what beat me, gentlemen, are that these bits from the commodes aren't right."

"You'd swear to that in a court of law?"

"Why not, sir? They're not right. I don't know how it come about but they aren't. That piece there, the one with the bit of cotton tied round it, is what you might call practically new."

"Why are you so sure?" asked the burly man again.

"Why, sir?" He smiled. "The same way I know these chairs aren't wrong. You bring me a duck, sir, and you say it's a hen. I say it ain't a hen; it's a duck. When you know, it's as simple as that. It's my job. My livin depend on it."

"Well, that's all, Mr. Burling," Pryne said. "We're most grateful to you, and we know you'll keep it implicitly to yourself. If anything develops further and we should need your help, we'll let you know."

There were more handshakes and Ted made his way down the stairs and out to the street. He went into a shop where he had once been with Gordon and had a cup of coffee and a biscuit. Amid the hubbub of the crowded room he began to think. One thing was obvious: something was fishy about that fire. Clemming *had* been in Queer Street, and he had set fire to his premises to profit somehow by the insurance. Those commodes had been involved, but how was still a mystery. According to Major Pryne they had been in the shop at the time of the fire, and yet no trace of them had been found. Or had it? Had charred fragments been found and had it been unnecessary for himself to see them? The pieces he had examined had come from what were probably two similar commodes which were, frankly, fakes. Then why four commodes? Why have fakes with the genuine stuff? Surely Clemming hadn't thought to collect insurance on the fakes as well?

It was too confusing and, at the moment, he knew too little. But one thing he did know: in the near future Clemming was likely to be in the dock. By the time he reached home he was full of the news.

"Jenny, somethin's happened! Don't ever breathe a word or you might land me in jail myself."

"Ted! What is it? What have you been doing?"

He laughed.

" 'Tain't me, Jenny. It's Clemming. Remember that fire of his? Well, it look as though he started it himself."

"Ted, you can't mean it!"

He told her what had happened that morning and that he was practically sure that the burly man was connected with the police. It certainly looked as if Clemming were going to be in the dock, and as if he himself would have to give evidence against him.

"But, Jenny, what're you lookin so upset about?"

"It's horrible," she said. "A man to end up his days like that. And what about his wife, if she's still alive. What'll *she* think?"

His lip curled, and for a moment she almost hated him.

"Haven't I told you all along? He never was nothin but a cheap swindler. Look at how he did me out o' that Chelsea figure when I was nothin more'n a boy. Look at that bureau. All his life he's been swindlin people and makin money the crooked way. Now he've just gone a bit too far. Thought he was clever, but he wasn't. And look where it's goin to land him."

She let out a slow breath.

"What about you and me, Ted? Haven't we ever done anything wrong? I know I have. I've done things I don't like to think about. And so have you, Ted, if you'll only stop condemning other people and look at yourself."

"Me, Jenny!"

"Yes, you," she said. "Look at what you told that young Mr. Selby that day. Suppose that vicar had found out what that table was really worth and brought a case against you. What would you have looked like then?"

"But he didn't! You've got it all wrong. I give him what it was worth."

"Afterwards, you did. But you didn't look at it that way all the time. You said yourself that it was touch and go whether or not you made a big profit for yourself."

"But I didn't," he told her exasperatedly.

"The sin was there," she said. "It was a sin to think about it, Ted, and you can't deny it. I know you did right in the end, and I was proud of you for it; but that doesn't give you the right to claim you never did a wrong thing in your life and to condemn even a man like Clemming."

"You fair best me, Jenny. Sometimes I can't understand you at all. . . ."

But Jenny had gone, and he dismally shook his head as he went back to the yard to garage the car.

Jenny was unnaturally quiet that night; it was a symptom that always made him uneasy. With someone like Agnes Hughson, he flattered himself, he could have coped; but Jenny's silences, or her quiet, almost patient way of speaking, and that set kind of look on her face when she had a grievance were things with which he had never been able to come to grips. But he could not bear to have anything come between them; and in the dark of the bedroom that night he felt that he had to say something, even if it was little more than a shallow covering of the thoughts that lay hidden beneath.

"Don't reckon you and me, Jenny, are going to fall out over anyone like Clemming. It look like bein all over and done with now. Reckon we'll never have to think about him again."

He expected a grateful response, but all that Jenny said was that she'd be glad never to hear his name again.

"Something else I wish you'd do, Ted. Don't go and give evidence if it ever comes to that. Surely there're plenty of other people they can call in?"

"I don't know," he said. "You wouldn't have me shirk my duty, Jenny. Besides, if you get called in by the Law, you can't get out of it. Not that I should state anything but the facts. All I'll be asked is about that wood. Come to think on it, 'twouldn't do to let it be known what I think of Clemming."

She had winced at his complacency, his hypocrisy, but that was how they left it.

Each morning, now, Ted would listen for the fall of the newspaper through the shop letter box, fetching it hurriedly and as hurriedly glancing through it for news of Clemming. Jenny could see the disappointment on his face when he found nothing there. Then one morning Major Pryne rang up again. Ted was somewhere in the back and she took the call herself.

"Mrs. Burling, is it?"

"Yes, Major Pryne."

"How are you, Mrs. Burling? It seems a long while since I saw you last."

"I'm very well, thank you, Major Pryne. I hope you and Mrs. Pryne are well too. But were you wanting to speak to my husband?"

"If it's no trouble—yes."

She found Ted in the garage. His face lighted up and he hardly seemed to limp at all as he hurried into the house.

"Burling speaking, sir."

"Morning, Burling. I'd very much like to see you tomorrow if you can manage it."

"I've nothin else on, sir."

"Fine! Then meet me in the lounge of the Royal at twelve-thirty. You can manage that?"

"I'll be there, sir," he said, and hung up.

"The major want me to meet him in Norwich tomorrow," he told Jenny. "Reckon somethin have turned up."

He was exulting so in his own thoughts that he failed to notice her face. He was actually humming a tune to himself as he went on into the shop, and all that day he acted as if he had heard good news. Then the telephone went again after the evening meal. It was the major once more.

"Oh, Burling, I've been thinking about things and I wonder if you could bring your wife with you tomorrow."

"I'll ask her, sir."

He cupped the receiver. Jenny shook her head. He frowned but she shook her head again. Then reluctantly she consented.

"Yes, sir, she'll be glad to come."

"But not at the Royal," the major said. "We'll have an informal meal, just the three of us, in my office. Will that suit you? . . . At twelve-thirty, then. Goodbye."

That change somehow cheered Jenny, for now she knew that the invitation was only a friendly one and had nothing whatever to do with Clemming. But she said nothing of that to Ted. In the morning she took quite a time in making herself presentable, wearing her fur coat because she knew it suited her. Even Ted noticed how smart she looked.

"Darn, Jenny, you don't look hardly a day older than when I first clapped eyes on you. How you do it I don't know. Reckon it must be the way I treat you."

She smiled because he expected her to smile, and on the long drive she was almost herself, though just a bit nervous, as she always was of what she called company. At Norwich she did a little shopping and met Ted at the Insurance Building as arranged. When they stepped into the major's office there was a pleasant surprise, for Marion Pryne was there.

Jenny quite enjoyed the lunch. The Prynes were the easiest people in the world with whom to feel at home, in spite of the qualms she had felt on the journey, but what most put her at ease was that there was no mention of Clemming. Mrs. Pryne talked about her sons and their wives and her grandchildren, and the major laughed heartily as he accused Ted of taking a hand in the collecting of Nelsoniana. Jenny blushed once or twice to find herself talking far too much.

Mrs. Pryne looked at her watch and said that she must fly. Jenny said that she and Ted would have to be going too.

"No hurry," the major said. "We'll go back to my room for a bit and have coffee there."

Marion Pryne surprised Jenny by suddenly bending down and kissing her on the cheek.

"Goodbye, my dear. It's been so nice seeing you. . . . Goodbye, Mr. Burling. I hope we shall see you both again soon."

They went through to the office. Coffee was there on a tray.

"White, Mrs. Burling, or black? . . . Sugar? . . . I know your husband's tastes already."

He was smiling as he handed them their cups.

"Light your pipe, Burling, if you've got it with you . . . A cigarette, Mrs. Burling?"

Jenny said she didn't smoke. The major lighted a cigarette for himself. His voice changed curiously when he next spoke.

"I want to talk to you two good friends of mine. I hope you both believe that both myself and Mrs. Pryne really regard you as friends!"

"That's kind of you, sir," Ted said.

"It's the truth," he said quietly. "That's why I had to resort to a kind of subterfuge to get you both here today. I want to talk to you. I want to talk about Clemming's fire. Clemming, you see, was arrested this morning. In spite of that," Pryne went on, "I'm asking you both to regard what I'm going to say as confidential. I think you'll see it's to your own interests to keep it so. But about that fire.

"Both we and the fire people had suspicions from the first and we refused to pay. Clemming found a lawyer, we had some correspondence, and finally we were threatened with an action. It was up to us to lay our cards on the table and compare notes with the police."

He took a paper from his wallet and glanced at it.

"This is the sequence of events, and before I forget it, Mr. Burling, there'll be no need for you to give evidence. We have enough for a conviction without it. But to get back to events. Clemming was undoubtedly badly pressed for money. Then he had the good fortune to acquire those commodes which would bring a handsome profit. But it wasn't enough, as we know now, to get him really on his feet. That was why he decided to have a fire.

"What he did was to have two sufficiently good reproductions made, and that was why, on the pretence of having a buyer abroad, he had to keep them for a considerable time. When the reproductions were made, he was ready to act. It didn't matter if a close examination would show the reproductions to be purely reproductions. A man like you, Mr. Burling, probably wouldn't have been deceived at twenty yards away, but that wasn't the point. I don't know if you remember, but it was a dark, stormy February afternoon. Those commodes were taken out of the window, or so we think, at the very last moment and the others put in their place. The light was bad by then and no one would notice the change.

"We know now what happened to the original commodes. They were packed up and taken by lorry to Liverpool to a shipping agent. The New York police are holding them. Whether Clemming had a buyer in New York or was going to offer them there we don't yet know; in any case he thought to make double their value after we'd paid up. The shipping agent, I should say, wasn't any sort of an accomplice. He was perfectly innocent of what was going on. After all, a man in Liverpool isn't interested, even if he reads in his paper—a very unlikely thing—about a fire as far away as Norwich. I don't think a single paper, outside the county ones, so much as mentioned it."

"One thing I've been meaning to ask you, sir," Ted said. "What about the metalwork on the fakes?"

"It didn't matter about the quality of that, so long as it looked a bit like the original," Pryne said. "Clemming knew the fire would melt it out of all recognition, which it did. It was the wood that gave him away. The fire was started in a workshop room underneath the showroom where the commodes were. What he didn't allow for was the fact that that was the first place on which the firemen would start playing their hoses. Then the ceiling collapsed above and what came down helped to save some of the wood from being burnt entirely. Not much, but enough."

"What do you think Clemming will get, sir?"

"I don't know. We mustn't allow ourselves to anticipate the law. But he's well on in years and that might be a mitigation. You never know. Also, it might depend on whether he pleads guilty or not guilty."

There was a sudden silence. Ted was shaking his head. Jenny's eyes were on Pryne's face with a curious intensity.

"Was that all you had to tell us?"

"No," he said slowly. "Unfortunately it was not. I'd hoped you might have guessed by now what it is my duty to tell you. It was about those fake commodes. You know who made them?"

Jenny knew. When the older woman had kissed her, the kiss had not been a casual sentiment or even a moment of affectionate impulse. There had been something far deeper than that.

"Yes," she said. "I think I know who made them. It was my boy."

CHAPTER 21

Evening

JENNY had dried her tears. She was ready, she said, to see Gordon.

"You're sure?" Pryne asked her. "It's been a great shock to you, Mrs. Burling, and I don't want you to be distressed any more. Your husband and I can see him alone."

Jenny insisted. What she wanted to know was the absolute worst, and at once.

"I'd rather you did the talking to begin with," Pryne told Ted. "I'll hold a watching brief. It'll be better that way."

When Gordon came in his eyes were on his mother, but she made no move.

"Come in, son. . . . Sit down here. Your mother and me want you to tell us about this trouble you've been gettin yourself into."

He sat down nervously. His face had a pallor, and against it the hollows were darker beneath his eyes.

"I've done nothing wrong, Father. All I—"

"Let's leave out wrong and right too," Ted told him. "Just tell us what you did do, son. We'll know whether it was right or wrong."

"Well, I made those reproduction commodes. Clemming asked me to, and I made them. As far as I was concerned, that's all there was to it."

"How did Clemming know you?"

"Know me?" He looked surprised. "He didn't know me except from what I did. That exhibition we had in London came on here. He knew the kind of stuff we turned out. Everybody did."

"Go on, son."

"There's nothing else to say," he said, looking almost defiantly round. "He showed me the original commodes and wanted to know if I could make two like them. I said of course I could, except the metal work; he'd have to arrange that for himself. I said I *could* do it, but I'd want more time. He wanted the whole thing done in a month."

"Just a minute, son. You haven't told us why you made 'em. You knew you was makin fakes."

"But they weren't fakes. He told me he wanted them for a special customer who'd know just what they were. Reproductions, that's what they were. The price he suggested was £100 each, and I told him I wouldn't look at it. As I said, he was going to get highly specialized work. I wanted £250 for each, and that was what we finally agreed on. He paid me fifty pounds down—in cash."

"Don't think I'm doubtin your word, not at this stage, son; but wasn't that a lot o' money? Clemming had to have his own profit on top of that, and he wouldn't be satisfied with less than £100 or £200. Are you tellin me that anyone short of a fool would pay over £300 apiece for reproduction commodes?"

"They were more than reproductions when I'd finished with them," Gordon told him with just a flush of annoyance. "They were works of art, the antiques of the future."

"I've heard that once afore, son," Ted said dryly, annoyed at a vanity so ingenuous. "But where'd you make these works of art, or whatever you call 'em?"

"They were made in my own time," Gordon told him with what he intended to be dignity. "They were made in the shops, except the assembling, and that was done in Clemming's workshop. He wanted it done that way. And it was handier. Some of the trickiest work was done by two of my best men, and I paid them out of my own pocket. It took us about a month and we only got the job done just before the fire."

"You saw Clemming after the fire?"

"Of course I did. He told me that my stuff had been burnt with the originals before he could get it sent away."

"You believed him?"

"Why shouldn't I believe him?"

"He paid you up for the job?"

"Well, no; he didn't. He said the fire had hit him pretty hard and he'd pay the very moment he collected from the insurance people. I didn't even know where he was insured. That shows how little I knew about the whole thing."

"Well, I think that's all I've got to ask, sir," Ted told Pryne. "I don't know if there's anything you want to ask this young man yourself?"

"I'm afraid there is," he said, and got to his feet. "Mr. Burling, you don't seem to realize the seriousness of the position in which you're likely to find yourself. Let's look at this from a different angle, the angle of the prosecuting counsel if you find yourself in the dock alongside Clemming."

"But they can't do that! I've done nothing."

"Who says so?"

"I say so, sir. I'll swear it in court."

"Will Clemming swear it? Why shouldn't he implicate you? Why shouldn't he bring you down with himself? You can prove nothing. Where are your witnesses? It's only your word against his. And, whatever happens, it'll be a dirty business, Mr. Burling."

Jenny gave a little moan and her handkerchief was at her eyes again.

"Burling, take your wife out," Pryne said sharply. "I won't allow her to be distressed about all this."

"I'm all right," Jenny said. "Let me stay here. I want to know. I must know."

Pryne let out a breath. A grim look was on his face as he turned to Gordon again.

"Let's take the making of these so-called 'reproductions,'" he said. "If everything was honest and above board, why didn't Clemming approach your firm? Why didn't you tell him that when he first approached you? That's one of the specialized jobs of Shefford & Son, isn't it? Why did you do that job yourself, and in what must seem a very furtive way?"

"Well, I didn't see it like that then . . . and I needed the money."

"Wouldn't that be a pretty damaging admission for counsel to draw from you? Do you realize the impression it would make? Then there's the actual wood. Did you pay for it?"

"The wood wasn't worth five pounds."

"Answer my question," Pryne told him sharply. "Did you pay for it?"

"I *can* pay for it."

Pryne shrugged his shoulders, then threw out his hands.

"That's all. You still refuse to see how you stand. Don't blame any of us here if you're charged with being an accessory before the fact."

He moved away.

"May I say something?"

"Why, yes, Mrs. Burling. You've every right to say anything you wish."

"Gordon," she said. "Don't lie to us. The time has gone for that. Tell us the truth. Did you really know what you were doing?"

"I didn't, Mother. I swear I didn't. You don't know how plausible Clemming was about it all. I couldn't help believing him."

She shook her head as if she still could not believe it.

"Then if Major Pryne doesn't want you any more, you must go straight to Mr. Shefford and tell him the whole thing."

"That's right, son. Go straightaway, and mind you keep nothin back."

"Well, if you want me to," he said, moistening his lips. "It may mean losing my job."

"Your job!" Ted said. "What's a job compared with some other things? Remember that day, son, when we had that ride round by Wickenden and what I was tellin you about that bureau? A pretty dry sermon, as I told your mother, but it wouldn't have done you no harm, son, to have taken in what I said."

He turned to Major Pryne.

"I reckon that's all, sir."

"And Gordon ought to come straight home," Jenny said. "Tomorrow's a Saturday and he can come in any case."

"That's right," Ted said. "Whatever happen, son, you're to be home tomorrow afternoon."

Gordon went out and Pryne closed the door after him. He said that it had been a trying afternoon but that things had to be faced. If Mrs. Burling would have a cup of tea, he'd see to it at once.

"Afore you do that, sir, let me ask you one question," Ted said. "I see the position my son stand in. What it look like to me is he's in Clemming's hands. If Clemming like to swear that Gordon was in with him, then Gordon can't disprove it, whether it's right or not."

"I'm afraid that's so. It's something that's got to be faced. And—I hate to say it—your son won't be a very good witness in his own defence."

"No, sir," Ted said, avoiding Jenny's eyes.

"But there's one ray of comfort," Pryne went on. "If you'd antagonized Clemming yourself, he might want to get back at you through your son. And there we've had a remarkably lucky escape. You remember that made-up marquetry table? how you suggested to my wife that she should quote you as the expert opinion? Well, I didn't do it. It wasn't more at the time than a kind of business reluctance to mention actual names, but I didn't do it. If I had done it, there'd have been something to be badly afraid of now."

"Yes," Ted said slowly.

"You and Mrs. Burling are not to worry," Pryne said. "I'm going to do all I can, but if Clemming turns nasty, then I'm helpless. Whatever else you don't face, you must face that. And now I'll say no more. You and Mrs. Burling are to have some tea. I insist on it. My wife should be back and she'll join us."

That night in the parlour, when the fire glowed and the curtains were drawn, the house was a kind of refuge from which the outside world had been shut. Norwich and the agony of the afternoon seemed remote. Each spoke quietly, as if words themselves were of no consequence when compared with thoughts. There was a strange gentleness, as if each knew the thoughts of the other and the need of a comfort that lay beyond mere words. Jenny was knitting. As she said, she had to be doing something with her hands. Ted was looking at his morning paper, which he'd had no time to read, and long minutes would pass before he turned to another page.

He was afraid. Not for the impact of things on himself or even on Jenny. Whatever had happened in the past, they had faced it together: that was how he saw the unspoken thing in the comparative safety of the room and in a light that was not the hard cold light of day. The fear, urgent and imminent, was somehow for his own life as he had lived it, seen in the light of Pryne's unconsciously ironic words: "If you'd antagonized Clemming yourself, he might want to get back at you through your son." But Major Pryne hadn't known; no one had known, not even Jenny, that most of his life had been a deliberate antagonizing of Clemming. In his time he had cost Clemming hundreds, if not thousands, of pounds, and now things had moved Clemming's way. Clemming had his chance of a final settlement, and in his heart of hearts Ted had no doubt of the course Clemming would take. Clemming and Gordon in the dock together, and the root of everything would be himself. Gordon in jail . . .

"Reckon I'd better try Yarmouth again," he suddenly said, getting to his feet. He went gently from the room and came as gently back. Jenny was still at her knitting.

"He'll be here in the mornin," he said. "The twelve o'clock train, he reckoned. I didn't tell him nothin, 'cept that he ought to get hold of Gordon and bring him down at the same time."

"It'll be nice to have Gordon here," she said, meaning her brother. "Now I'll be going up to bed, Ted. I feel all washed out."

"Mind you take two of them tablets what Mrs. Pryne give you," he told her. "She reckoned they'd do you no harm and make you sleep."

An hour later he went up the stairs in his stocking feet, as Mort had always done. Jenny was sound asleep and made no stir when he bent over her. He quietly made his way down the stairs again. There seemed ample fuel for the fire. He stoked it again and drew the settee round for a bed. But it was a wretched night. He tossed and turned, and when he had slept for a few minutes he would wake again and look at his watch. Towards dawn, however, he slept more heavily, and it was after six o'clock when he woke.

He arose in a world in which he was suddenly tremendously alone. Once more it was as if the house had need of silence, and he moved with incredible quiet as he relighted the parlour fire. Then he lighted the kitchen fire and boiled the kettle for his shaving water. His unshaven face looked haggard and drawn, and his hand was shaking queerly. It took him a long time to shave because of his fear that the razor might slip. Then a queer thing happened. He found himself in the yard; and he knew that his thoughts had been so much in the past that he had gone out, as if it were years ago, to see the cob. But there was no smile on his face as he came back. With the same slow earnestness he made himself a cup of tea and took one up for Jenny. She was still sleeping, but he thought it best to rouse her.

"A cup o' tea for you, Jenny. I'll boil an egg and make you some toast. Reckon you'd better put on a dressin gown and slip down and have breakfast. The fire's lit."

She came down. He had never felt less like breakfast, but he ate to keep her company. That morning he pottered about in the shop and went up to the repair room; but the memory of George seemed to haunt him there, so he went back to the shop again. Soon after eleven Jenny brought him a cup of coffee. She set it on the table beside him, then suddenly bent her head and kissed him.

"Whuh, Jenny!"

But she had gone, and something was in his throat. He stifled it back and slowly drank his coffee. He pottered about again, then went to the garage to smarten up the car. A quarter of an hour before the train was due he was at the station. That morning he had been afraid to look at his paper, but now he bought another one and looked through it in the privacy of the car. There was no word in it about Clemming.

When Gordon and his uncle came off the train, Shadd gave no sign that anything was amiss, though he must have heard everything on the way down from Norwich. But he lingered behind with Ted when the car drew into the yard.

"A nasty business this, Ted. How's Jin taking it?"

"She don't say nothin. If she'd only say somethin, I'd know more what to do. She's keepin everything to herself."

"We'll have a quiet talk," Shadd told him. "This is a case where money might talk too; if so, we're going to spend it."

The talk was in the parlour that afternoon, and Jenny insisted on being there. Everything was gone over again. Shadd was patient and sympathetic, trying to understand both points of view.

"I don't like it," he said. "I don't like saying it in front of you, Jenny, but Clemming's got us all in the hollow of his hand. I don't know if I'd be allowed to see him, and even if I did I don't like the idea of trying to buy him off. It doesn't seem right, somehow, to square one dirty bit of work off with another."

"You're not to do it," Jenny told him, almost angrily. "I won't stand for it and Ted won't either. Gordon's done wrong—"

"I haven't really, Mother."

"That's enough from you, son," Ted told him. "You let your mother have her say. She know what's wrong better than you've fared to do."

Jenny had no more to say except that she'd never forgive her brother if he tried to bribe Clemming. Ted thought of something he'd been meaning to ask.

"Yesterday afternoon, when we were with Major Pryne, you told us, son, as how you'd wanted Clemming's money. Just how did that come about?"

Gordon was voluble in excuses. There'd been the expenses of setting up house, Clarice's extravagance, the money he'd had to spend himself, and the position it had been necessary to keep up.

"I don't need to keep any position up, as you call it," Ted told him. "Neither do your uncle, and he could buy up twenty such as you and not even know it. Funny how you look back and see things, like I was doin this mornin. Even when you was a boy it was never you that was wrong. Not that that matter now. What we want to know is how you stand with regard to money."

It took some extracting. He owned to the debt to his uncle, though that would have been cancelled he said, when Clemming paid. He had also borrowed £200 from a moneylender.

"You're goin to sell that smart car o' yours," Ted told him. "If that don't make enough to square things up, then I'll square them myself. Now tell us again what happened atween you and Mr. Shefford."

"Well, I think I can smooth things over. He was pretty annoyed, of course, till I explained."

"You told him the truth?"

"Of course I told him the truth."

"No need to get riled, son. There have been times, you know, when you've come as near to tellin lies as make no difference. But what do you think about Mr. Shefford, Mother?"

"Gordon's got to leave," she said. "That'll make things look better, if it doesn't do anything else. And he'll never be able to hold up his head again in Norwich, whatever happens."

"I don't see it, Mother."

" 'Tain't what you see, son," Ted told him with a grim quietness. "You've been seein things your own way long enough. You're leavin Norwich as soon as you've faced up to whatever you've got to face. Whether your uncle'll take you on I don't know."

"Of course I'll take him on," Shadd said, fingering his greying beard. "He could have come to me before. He'll have to start near the bottom and learn the business, but he's young yet. The time'll come when he looks back on all this and knows things happened perhaps for the best."

"That's settled," Jenny said decisively. "You'll give in your resignation to Mr. Shefford, and I hope you'll have the grace to thank him for all he's done for you."

Shadd had said that he had to be away by the evening train, and Gordon left with him. The oppressive silence had lifted from the house, as if their voices still lingered, but Jenny said little except what a comfort it was to have someone like her brother.

"Reckon it might be the makin of Gordon, him goin to Yarmouth," Ted said. "It'll take him right out of himself. It may be a bit of a comedown at first, but he'll get over that. Reckon we shall live to be proud of him yet."

He had almost added, "Like that time he come home after gettin the medal." But that brought disturbing, even frightening thoughts. It was like Lucifer—so high and a fall so low. People would remember the homecoming, the piece in the paper, and Harold's photograph. Tongues would wag, the finger of scorn would level, and the knowing ones would say that they had always known.

That night in bed he reached out and drew Jenny to him.

"I've been thinkin, Jenny. If the worst was to happen to Gordon, I reckon we could face it here after all. We might even know who was our friends and who wasn't."

"The Crowes will stick to us, and to Gordon too," she said. "So will most people, if I know them. Friends are real friends when you live in a little place like Ouseland, Ted. You get to know them just as you know yourself. It isn't like those so-called 'friends' that Gordon and Clarice had in Norwich. And if you come to think of it, Ted, they're not our friends because of anything we've ever done for *them*. It's they who've always done things for *us*. Look what Harold has done for you. Look at me, before Gordon was born, and what Bella did."

"Reckon you're right," he said. "If this business hap to turn out right after all, Jenny, reckon we might try doin something for them for a change."

"Not because of that, Ted," she told him. "We'll do it because we want to do it. Because we ought to have done it before."

On Sunday morning the house was silent again, with Jenny working in the kitchen and Ted in the parlour. Within the confines of that room his fears were very near again. Once more he went over the years of his business life, trying to visualize each clash with Clemming. He put himself in Clemming's place and faced the question of what he would do if he were Clemming. There was only one answer and he knew it. Even the knowledge that the circumstances could never have been the same made no essential difference; the artificiality ceased to be artificial in the damning presence of undoubted fact. Had there been the chance of himself bringing Clemming down, he would have taken it, and have felt a personal triumph in his ruin. When he realized that, even the hypocrisies that he had hugged to himself came into the light: the pride he had taken in his own honesty, and the Pharisaical drawing away of his skirts from a man like Clemming. And now his own son might be shown up as no better than Clemming. Even if he was not proved an accessory in the matter of the fire, he had been a trickster and a liar and as good as a thief.

Jenny went to church that evening and for the first time in years she asked if he were going too.

"Don't reckon I will," he told her, adding with a touch of bitterness, "Reckon the roof'd fall in or somethin if I was to go after all these years."

When she had gone he sat by the fire thinking of Gordon's boyhood, of how Jenny had made him go to Sunday school and of the way in which she had brought him up. He felt that it was in himself that the fault must lie. As George had said, the grain had once been straight; how, then, had it become distorted and unworkable?

When Jenny came back from church, she found the house empty. It worried her and she hurried round to Jessie, thinking that Ted might be there. When she got back to the house, he was just hanging up his overcoat. The house had been stuffy, he said, and he had gone out for a walk.

"Look, Ted," she said. "I know you can't help worrying and neither can I, but let's worry as little as we can. Major Pryne is doing all he can; he told us so."

"I've been thinkin too, Jenny," he said. "What if I was to see Clemming somehow, and sort of apologize for what him and me have been. Do you reckon he might drop anything then agin Gordon?"

"No, Ted. Anything'd be better than that. It's as bad as what

Gordon was talking about when he was here, and worse. I'd rather have you as you've been these last weeks than that. It'd be a kind of trickery. Even if you did apologize, as you call it, your heart wouldn't be in it."

"But it would, Jenny."

"It wouldn't, Ted. If nothing of this had happened, it might have been; but not now. But let's not talk about it. I'll get the supper and we'll go to bed early and try to get a better night."

His hand gripped her arm. The grip was so tight that it hurt, but she gave no sign.

"Jenny, you're better than ever I was. If it hadn't been for you, where would I a-been?"

She smiled.

"I'm not so good as you think I've been. And what about what you've done for me?"

"Nothin, Jenny—nothin."

"Whatever it was, it was more than enough," she told him. "And now let me take these clothes off or we'll never get any supper."

That night, just as she was dropping off to sleep, he said another strange thing.

"Jenny, I reckon you were right about Norwich. When I think on't now and what happened Friday afternoon, it fare as though I could never face goin there again."

Monday morning came, and with it another week to be faced. There would be more weeks, perhaps, before anything was known, and Jenny wondered how she could face them. Then there was Ted. At breakfast that morning he looked wretched and ill, and during the night he had twisted and turned and even muttered in his brief periods of sleep. It was for him that she was worried most, for Gordon was little more than a dull ache in her heart.

She heard the telephone bell that afternoon, but Ted was there first. In a moment she had guessed that it was Major Pryne.

"Yes, sir?" Ted was saying; then he was listening, and suddenly his face lit up. "You have, sir?"

The face fell again. He was nodding as he listened.

"Thank you, sir. We'll be here."

"That was the major," he said. "He think he's got better news for us. He's at Ladeham and he's comin on here."

Their eyes met but nothing was said. Jenny hurried upstairs to make herself tidy, and Ted went back into the shop. The sound of his feet pacing might keep him from hearing the coming of the car, so he drew up a chair facing the window and waited there. It was an overcast afternoon in early April. Normally he would have switched on the light, but now he preferred to sit in the gloom. Half an hour went by, then another, and it was drawing near six o'clock when at last a dark shape drew up outside the window and the major got out of his car. As soon as the doorbell tinkled, Jenny was in the shop.

"There you both are," Pryne said as Jenny switched on the light. "As I told you, Burling, I think I've got better news for you. In fact, I think it's the best. I hear on the most reliable authority that Clemming's going to plead guilty."

There was a blankness on their faces that showed no realization of the implications.

"You don't see what that means? It means that there'll be only a formal calling of witnesses, as it were, to establish the case. I doubt if it will be necessary for your boy to give any evidence at all."

"And what about Clemming, sir?"

"You mean in relation to your boy? Well, I have some reasonably good news about that too. Clemming has made a statement in which he doesn't attempt to incriminate your boy in any way. In fact it practically verifies your boy's own account. That, by the way, is most highly confidential. Clemming referred to you in it, if that interests you. A very rambling statement, I may say."

"You say he referred to *me*, sir?"

"I copied it down. I have it here somewhere. . . . I'll read you what he says: 'I hadn't met him before till he came into my shop.' That's your boy he's talking about. 'I knew his father, of course. Him and me have been in the same line of business and he never did me any good, though I hold no grudge against him for that. I knew his mother too, a nice little woman who used to be a daughter of Mark Shadd who was also in the same line of business.'

"That's all," Pryne said, putting the note away again. "I thought you might be relieved that Clemming has no intention of doing that which we all feared. Your boy won't come into the matter at all. I can only say I hope he's had his lesson."

Jenny was suddenly gone. Ted shook his head.

"How I'm to thank you, sir, I don't know. . . . God bless you, sir."

Something in his throat was too much for him. He felt the grasp of the major's hand on his shoulder as he turned away, then there was the sound of the bell and the closing of the door.

After a minute or two he made his way to the kitchen. It was empty. He looked in the parlour and it was empty too. He listened and seemed to hear a faint sound upstairs. Another shake of his head and he was making his way out to the dusk of the yard. The repair shop was lighted up; then he remembered that the man was working late at that tallboy he had bought at Windley. He moved on in the dusk to the still open garage and leaned there with his head against the cool of the car. Now that relief had come, it was almost too much for him; he could hardly believe that it was true. Yet in his own heart there was still an ache, in spite of the way things had turned out. There was Gordon: he wondered what he would make of himself at Yarmouth; and in the depth of his mind he knew that all the truth had not yet been told, that trying times would lie ahead. Above him, in the repair shop, he heard the noise of feet, and that made him think of George again. He was glad, somehow, that George had had no part in those heartbroken days. Then he thought of something that George had once said. They had been in the repair shop one cold afternoon; he could remember how snug it had been, with the stove going and the glue pot merrily bubbling on it. George had just advanced his theory that people were like wood— straight-grained, showy-grained, twin-grained, cross-grained, and even woman-grained.

"Take the missus, now," he had said. "She's what I call a rare nice bit o' grain, what you can make somethin on."

"What d'you call me then, George?" he had asked.

"You, Mas' Ted? Reckon you're a tidy workable sorta grain. The straightish sort."

"And what about yourself?"

"Me? Reckon I'm a bit o' tough old ellum. Ain't so bad when you get down to it but take a bit o' workin."

George had been right, he told himself, and the thought brought a fresh poignancy for all that had gone. But what of Gordon? What grain had he been? Showy-grained, maybe, or, please God, twin-grained: the sort one could cut through with a saw, discarding the showy and doing a good job with the rest. Maybe the flashy and unreliable had been cut out now and there was something left on which to work.

That brought him to Clemming. What of his grain? Maybe there the tree had been wrong from the start. Or there'd been too quick and scamped a drying, like that wood Gordon Shadd had shown him at Yarmouth, with a hard case, but flawed, cracked and warped because of the unhardened core within. Then he shifted his thoughts to the relationship between Clemming and himself. Strangely, he felt no shattering of self-esteem because Clemming had taken almost with indifference the enmities and baitings of those years. To him Ted Burling had been simply another hostility, one, perhaps, among many, merely a part of the rough-and-tumble of business. And now, even to himself, those hostilities seemed curiously detached and remote. He was aware of how fortunate it was that he had not been mentioned in connection with the marquetry table; of how his own pride of deed and tongue might so have angered Clemming that he could neither forget nor forgive. With that, slowly, almost imperceptibly, his deep pity and compassion were stirred; he could feel almost a warmth for the man; and he wondered if there were anything that he could do for him.

At last he straightened himself and closed and locked the garage doors. He looked up at the sky. It was stormy, but a star or two shone in the heaviness of cloud. Slowly he made his way back to the house, as if his ankle were giving him pain. There was a movement at the kitchen door and then beyond the step. Jenny was there, framed darkly against the light from the window.

"You all right, Jenny?"

"I'm all right, Ted," she told him, and smiled.

His arm went quickly about her shoulders. It was almost as if he had come home late after a day in the Brecklands, coiled the traces, and sent the cob to the stable. He smiled gently to himself at the thought, and then they went together through the door.